I0550251

THE LOST SOULS

Also by Matthew Wilkinson:

LINOLEUM

Copyright © 2013 Matthew Wilkinson
www.Matt-Wilkinson.com
@AuthorWilkinson

All rights reserved.

ISBN: 0615834035
ISBN-13: 978-0615834030

For Carissa

I

Prisons aren't particularly nice places at the best of times, especially those that cater primarily to extremely violent or clinically insane people. The cell walls have scratch marks all over them from where the inmates have tried to claw their way through the brick with their fingernails, the doors are dented from incessant kicking or head butting, and the stone floors have little messages etched into them, like 'tonight I die'.

The particular prison we were in was deep inside Kentucky and, thankfully, had been closed decades ago. The whole place had been shut down after an exceptionally high death rate had been uncovered over years of mismanagement and neglect; during its one hundred years of use, over ten thousand inmates had ended up dead. Built in 1880, it had been used to lock away anybody that seemed a bit odd and, because of a lack of understanding of mental illnesses, the poor souls who ended up here rarely got out, and were quite often treated as though they were Beelzebub's second cousin.

By the time 1980 rolled around, medical science had vastly improved and human rights had suddenly become a hot topic. A local newspaper article on conditions inside the facility had caused an uproar that ended up going nationwide. Shortly thereafter, St. Joseph's was quickly emptied and the doors locked for good.

We'd just unlocked them.

It was just after seven in the evening and, accompanied by a local guy who for some reason had a key to this hellhole, we were allowed inside. The whole place stank of decay and I dread to think what else; it was obvious that once the final patient had been evicted and the doors bolted up, nobody had come back. Ever.

The man bade us farewell and then locked us inside; that was the hook for our TV show, *The Lost Souls*. The leader of our three man party was called Brad and the best way to describe him is the human incarnation of Scrappy Doo. Boundless energy, full of spectacularly bad ideas, and totally oblivious to the fact that he acts like a total dickhead for most of the time.

The role of Scooby Doo was filled by Kurt, who was a good looking skinny guy; the perfect televisual juxtaposition to Brad being good looking and buff. Kurt would always be the one on the receiving end of Scrappy Doo's terrible ideas and had this amazing ability to never, ever realize just how bad the idea was until he was locked in a closet full of rats, or buried in a coffin or something.

And then there's me, which if I take the analogy to it's final conclusion, makes me Shaggy. My name is Todd, and I'm the video and audio technician that the other two clowns need in order to try and catch their ghosts. I'm the reluctant one that tags along, protesting about something or other in the vain hope that Scrappy will see some sense.

It never works.

I fished one of the many video recorders out of my backpack and switched it on. The light was fading, but there was just enough to get an intro monologue. After that, everything else would be done via night vision camera so the rest of the footage would have that eerie green glow to it to emphasize just how scary our daft job was.

"So," hissed Brad in an overly-dramatic whisper, "here we are. Locked inside this place. Ten thousand people died here. *Ten thousand*!"

He paused for dramatic effect and then gave a little shake of his head. "I can just feel the spirits all around me. We're gonna get some serious evidence tonight guys. This is gonna be epic!"

Then his whisper became slightly quieter and more serious. "But guys, and this is important, we've got to really watch each other's backs tonight, yeah? With this many ghosts and spirits that have unfinished business, they could come at us at any moment. Stay on your toes, guys, okay?"

I swung the camera to get Kurt's face in the shot, and he solemnly nodded his head. Brad and Kurt gave each other a fist-bump, and then I had to give the same over-serious acknowledgement of the imminent danger we were in, followed by a fist-bump with Scooby and Scrappy.

I couldn't believe that anybody took this nonsense seriously, but our show had huge ratings figures, which was why I continued to take part in these daft 'lock-ins', as the show called them. The other thing that I could never quite get my head around was the fact that Brad and Kurt actually believed everything they were saying. They truly thought they were surrounded by spirits that were about to leap into action at any moment.

Brad signed off from his monologue in an even quieter overly-loud whisper. "Here we go. Let's hope we make it out of this one."

I gave a night vision camera each to Brad and Kurt, and we headed deeper into the prison. It was dank, moldy, and in total ruin. Noticeboards were hanging off walls as we made our way through the office complex; cups of unfinished coffee had become petrie dishes and now grew little gardens of bacteria, and papers were scattered everywhere. It looked more like the place had been evacuated rather than simply closed down.

I looked at some of the bits of paper on the noticeboards. One was a list of recently deceased people, dated 1979. I pointed it out to Scrappy Doo and we got filming again.

"Oh man," he hissed in his pantomime whisper, "Guys, guys! Come and look at this!"

He beckoned us over as if he'd just uncovered the sheet of paper and pointed excitedly at it. "Look! Probably the last inmates to die in here! They *must* have unfinished business with this place. This is wild, dude! *Wild*!"

I filmed a close-up of the paper and made a mental note of a couple of the names and how they died; I had a feeling this would come in handy later on.

Both of them would have blundered through these rooms without seeing any of the TV gold that was around us; they just wanted to get to the scary parts of the building so they could whisper more urgently at the tops of their voices. However, being the good team member that I am, I called out to Kurt and pointed at a desk for him to go and examine. I just knew he'd be able to make something out of absolutely nothing, as usual.

I turned the camera on and followed his progress.

"Woah!" he blurted in a loud hiss. "Guys! Look at—"

He paused as something caught his eye; I knew something would. He urgently began scrabbling through papers on the desk and pulled some close to his face.

"Dude! Fuck!" — I always had lots of bleeping to do in the post production suite — "Oh my god! Listen to this! *Psycho analysis for Jacob Landon: November 23rd, 1979. Parole: no. Release: no. Straitjacket: all times.*"

Brad had gone too long without speaking, so he butted in. "Dude! That must be, like, a patient's sanity analysis or something. And a straitjacket the whole time? No way!"

I desperately wanted to compliment him on his amazing powers of deduction, but remained silent and continued filming. Apparently this was what the American public enjoyed watching, and it made me a lot of money, so I let Scooby and Scrappy solve the mystery.

"Oh my god!" blurted Kurt, grabbing another piece of paper. "Here's another one! But get this!"

"What, what?" urged Brad, almost hopping from foot to foot with excitement.

"*Mental evaluation: Extremely dangerous. Solitary confinement, straitjacket always.*"

"Woah," gasped Brad solemnly, "they really liked their straitjackets in this place."

"But get this," Kurt continued, almost breathless, "The patient's name was *Isabella Peyton.*"

I zoomed in on Brad as the cogs turned. "Wait... *Isabella*? A woman? So this place had men *and* women here?"

Of course, had either of them read the research papers on this place that they'd been given, they'd know that there was a male and female wing, but it didn't matter. This astonishing discovery would make for great TV.

Kurt turned the page on the woman's file. "Dude! Fuck! Oh my god! Oh *god*!"

He thrust the page to Brad; it was always good TV to have the star of the show make the earth-shattering discoveries.

He read for a few seconds, and then looked right into the camera and took a deep breath. "There's an update to her file. She died shortly after the psycho analysis. Cause of death?" He paused and breathed heavily a few times. "She ruptured her own spine while trying to escape from her straitjacket."

I swung the camera to Kurt. He looked at me and shook his head slowly. "Woah. They killed her with a straitjacket?"

This was amazing stuff; some smart editing and I knew I'd have a captivating opening to this episode.

We continued through and into the female wing of the prison. The light had really gone now, and it was tough to see where we were going. Quite why we could use night-vision cameras, but not also use night-vision goggles so we could see what was going on was beyond me; I guess having three guys bumbling around in the dark, tripping over stuff that everyone at home can see clearly adds to the drama.

5

Brad turned to the camera and whispered, "One of these cells here housed Isabella. And that was where she died."

Now, don't get me wrong, just because I don't believe in ghosts or spirits or any of that, doesn't mean this place wasn't creeping me out, because it was. It was horrible. The thought of people having to spend their days in these tiny concrete cells and sometimes end up dying in them sent a shiver down my spine. It was a foul, abhorrent place that made me question how anybody could build or run an institution like this and still be able to sleep at night.

"Hey Todd," hissed Kurt, "did you get footage of Isabella's file?"

Of course I had. I knew full well what was about to happen.

"Yeah," I hissed back, "let me pull it up."

Kurt was now filming me rewinding the footage until I got to the file. "You want her cell number?"

"Oh dude! This is terrifying. Yeah, what was it?"

I peered at the brightly lit screen. "38B. So the B means the second floor, because we're on floor A."

We clanked our way up the metal steps to the next, equally horrific level, and Brad tracked down cell 38.

"This is where it happened," he said quietly.

I looked into the tiny, bare, concrete cell. A woman had spasmed so hard in here that she'd snapped her own spine. What a gruesome thought.

"Are you sure you wanna go in there?" asked Scooby, his voice almost trembling.

"We have to," replied Scrappy bravely. "It's what we came to do. We have to gather our evidence."

So, I began setting up our 'evidence gathering kit', which consisted of a night-vision camera on a tripod in the corner of the cell to capture any sightings of a spirit that might pop in for a chat, and also a digital recorder to record what it said. By the time I'd finished, Brad reappeared and, from somewhere, had found a straitjacket.

"Kurt, I think you'll make a connection to Isabella if you put this on when you're searching for her."

Anybody else would have told Brad that he was a lunatic and there was no way they were going to sit in a stinking cell in an unwashed straitjacket, but not Kurt.

"Dude! Of course! She won't be able to resist!"

The darkness hid the roll of my eyes. Kurt obediently allowed Brad to strap him into the straitjacket and we locked him into the tiny cell.

"Stay safe, dude," said Brad unhelpfully.

We retreated to the offices where, earlier, I'd set up a whole bunch of monitors, laptops, and speakers. Glowing back at me was the green form of Kurt sitting on the small bed in the cell. He looked around uncertainly, and I just knew he'd finally had the moment of clarity regarding Scrappy Doo's hair-brained scheme.

"Okay dude," said Brad into his radio, "we're in position. Let's do this."

Kurt cleared his throat and said, "Isabella? Isabella? I need to talk to you."

He waited for a response, and got none. This, however, was not unusual.

"Isabella, why are you still here?"

Another pause.

"Do you have unfinished business?"

I slid my hand into my pocket and pressed a button on a small device that I always carried with me. I'd just emitted a short, high frequency burst of static that was inaudible to the human ear, but would almost certainly be picked up in some form on the recorder.

After another pause, Kurt asked, "Why are you scared of me?"

I pressed the button twice this time.

Kurt continued asking daft questions to an empty cell for another twenty minutes and then completely freaked out when he thought the ghost of Isabella had just begun climbing the stairs. A loud clank had convinced him of this and he immediately got on the radio that we'd wedged into his hand inside the straitjacket.

"Dude! Fuck dude! Holy crap! Come and get me! I'm done, man! I'm done! She's coming to get me! Get me out of here!"

"On our way," replied Brad in the calmest voice he could muster.

We went and rescued a properly terrified Kurt from the cell and took off his straitjacket. Back in the office he described what had happened.

"Man! I was, like, asking her questions and then I suddenly became super cold, and heard her begin to climb the stairs. Thank god you guys reached me in time!"

Of course, this happened to us on almost every lock-in in a building that had much in the way of metal in it. As the night-time temperature drops, the metal contracts and occasionally makes a creak or a groan. But, to Kurt, locked up in the stinking cell in almost total darkness, it was a footstep of a previously completely silent ghost, and that made for far better TV.

With a trembling hand, he played back the recording of his 'interrogation'. Naturally, the sensitivity on the microphone was turned up to max, which meant that the slightest noise, no matter how meaningless, was amplified. After Kurt's question of whether she had unfinished business, Brad almost exploded with joy as he convinced the world that the faint burst of static he'd just heard was Isabella saying 'yes'.

Kurt's next question was why was Isabella scared of him. This time, the two bursts of faint white noise were translated into 'straitjacket' by Brad, who then almost orbited the room.

"Oh my god! Of course!! I mean, there's absolutely no explanation for that voice, so it was clearly Isabella communicating with you. And of course she's scared of you, dude, you're in a straitjacket! *The very thing that killed her!*"

"That's totally crazy, bro! Oh my god, what if that was *the* straitjacket?"

"Oh, man! You mean the spirit of Isabella guided me to pick up the *exact straitjacket* that she died in? That is wild, dude!"

"What other explanation can there be?"

Brad paced a few times, his face screwed up in concentration. "None. That has to be what happened. There's no other explanation. That is some serious evidence right there."

Because I didn't want to overdo it with the spirit replying to them, they got nothing more from the recording, but they were happy as clams.

Then we moved onto the video footage; nothing special for the majority of the time he was in there, but immediately after Kurt had heard Isabella coming up the stairs Brad leapt at the monitor, nearly knocking it over as he jabbed at the screen.

"Dude! Look! There she was!"

I rewound it and replayed it. I had a hard time seeing anything, and then saw what Brad was seeing. A tiny speck of dust had clearly been disturbed when Kurt freaked out, and the night-vision was amplifying the light reflection off it to give what seemed to be a small glowing light that fluttered around for half a second and then faded out.

Kurt gasped. "Oh. My. God! Something had been right behind me the whole time! D'you think it was her?"

Scrappy pursed his lips. "Maybe. But who was coming up the stairs for you?"

"Oh, dude. That was a close one. Multiple spirits converging on me."

"We had your back, bro."

After everyone had calmed down and recovered from the 'interaction' with Isabella, there was lots of fist-bumping, and we discussed where to head for next.

"How about the morgue?" I suggested, trying to hide a grin.

II

The moment we stumbled our way into the morgue, in pitch blackness, I just knew this episode was going to be our best ever.

I shone my flashlight around the room and quickly realized the place was even more grim than the cell blocks. We'd become kind of numb to the dank, decaying smell in the other parts of the facility, but this room took it to a whole new level. It was deep inside the bowels of the prison, had little in the way of ventilation, and there was an added metallic tang to the air that really topped off the putrid stench.

There were a couple of old steel gurneys in one corner of the room, one of which listed at an odd angle thanks to it having a wheel missing; on it was a tray with some old surgical implements. I walked over and shone my flashlight onto the rusting, gruesome-looking tools and noticed some dark spots on the blade of the scalpel. Upon closer inspection with the flashlight, they turned out to be mold, but through the NV camera, it could only be one thing.

"Brad! Kurt!" I hissed dramatically. "Take a look at this!"

Brad shot over to me from where he'd been inspecting the broken wheel. "What have you... Woah! Dude! That is gnarly! Surgical tools? Still in here? Why?"

I held my camera's view-screen up to Brad's face, all the while recording, and let him look at the scalpel close up. "What's that on the blade?" I whispered, in what I hoped sounded like disbelief.

An audible gasp from Brad. "That's… It's… that has to be… It is! It's blood!"

"But surely they'd have cleaned the implements before closing the place?" I asked, goading Brad into the one conclusion he was sure to come to.

I swung the camera from the scalpel and got a close-up of Brad's face. He had his knuckle on his chin, and was clearly deep in thought.

"There can only be one explanation," he declared solemnly. "One of the spirits in here must still be operating on something."

"Or some*one*," added Kurt quietly.

"Dude! Serious evidence. Right there."

I had to get them off this subject before it got too ridiculous even for our viewers, so I paused the recording and panned my flashlight around the room before letting out a theatrical gasp. This is guaranteed to get both of their attention from whatever it is they are currently 'investigating'. They turned and looked where my flashlight beam had landed, and then moved so fast that I almost didn't have time to get the camera rolling again.

"Guys, look at this," said Brad loudly, forgetting his dramatic whispering. This new discovery was now his.

"Oh fuck!" yelped Kurt.

We were now all huddled around four metal doors that were in a two-by-two formation, set into the back wall of the morgue. At one time, I'm sure they would have been gleaming and spotless, but now they were tainted and dull, which just added to the gloriousness of the footage.

"The ice-boxes," declared Brad.

"Fuck," said Kurt again.

This was too good of an opportunity to miss, so I planted the seed that I would edit out later. "Think how many bodies found this to be their final resting place. I wonder if the spirits return here each night?"

A light-bulb went off in Scrappy Doo's head. "Dude! Of *course*! Talk about unfinished business! They probably return here every night, looking for their physical bodies."

A little over five minutes later, poor Scooby was lying on one of the cold, metal trays that you pull out of the body freezer, and I was putting the finishing touches to an NV camera and digital voice recorder inside the small space so we could record every fabulous minute of Scrappy's daft idea that he was, as usual, inflicting on somebody else.

"Okay," I said, gratefully sliding my upper body out of the adjacent space for a dead body. "We're all set. Kurt, don't forget that we won't be watching the monitors this time. Brad wants to explore the rooms beyond here, so make sure you ask the questions with the walkie-talkie open, okay?"

Kurt nodded enthusiastically. As usual, it wouldn't be until he was irrevocably involved in the plan that he would suddenly realize how incredibly stupid it was. In this case, we were about to lock him into the ice-box where corpses used to be kept. Admittedly, the freezers were no longer plugged in, but it was still a horribly stinking, claustrophobic place to be locked into.

Brad slammed the metal door shut with a huge clang, and put the latch on; there was now no way out for Kurt.

He got on the radio. "Kurt, dude, is everything cool?"

"Yeah, man. I'm all set. If there are spirits returning here, I'm gonna find them."

I quickly moved my hand into my pocket once more and hit the button three times. I wasn't sure how well that would come out, but it was worth a shot. Anything that Scrappy and Scooby couldn't turn into a word would be edited out anyway.

"Okay, dude. We'll be back in thirty minutes, yeah?"

"Stay safe, guys," said the man locked inside a freezer for dead bodies.

Scrappy patted me on the shoulder and whispered loudly, "let's go."

He charged off through a door we'd never been through before and, within several minutes in the darkness, had got us totally lost. At that very moment of realization, the radio crackled into life.

"Errr, guys?"

"How's it going, dude?"

"I'm not so sure this is such a good idea."

"How so, man?"

"I think the spirits that visit this place are pissed at me, dude."

"You mean pissed just at your presence?"

"Yeah," Scooby was sounding quite nervous.

"What makes you think that?"

A pause. "One of them just tried to open the fucking door, dude."

"Holy crap! Okay, we're coming to get you out."

"Hurry, man! Fuck!"

I butted into the conversation to make sure he was as freaked out as possible. "We'll be there as soon as we can, but it might take a little while because we're... err... lost."

Another pause as this sank in. "You're lost? Fucking *lost*? Guys! Get me the fuck out of here! *Hurry!*"

Brad thought for a few seconds and then got back on the radio. "I guess the spirits led us down a strange path and made us lost." He looked up slightly at the ceiling before finishing with, "nice ambush, guys."

Kurt exploded in terror. "Dude! A fucking *ambush*? What are they gonna do to me? *Help me!*"

He was freaking out more than I was expecting; it must have been terrifying locked in that little box, so I tried to calm him down a little. I didn't want him having a heart attack, or something like that. "Kurt, ask the spirits some questions, let them know you're not there to hurt them. But leave the comms open."

"Okay," he replied in a trembling whisper, "errr, spirit? What... uhhh... what's your name?"

While Brad was trying to figure out where the hell we were, I pressed the button in my pocket twice.

Brad crashed his way through the wrong door, trying blindly to find his way back to the morgue, and I followed, filming everything in wondrous night-vision wobbliness for added dramatic effect.

Kurt pressed on, his voice trembling. "Spirit... I'm not here to hurt you."

I considered pressing the button again, but didn't want to overdo it.

The radio burst into life once more. "Shit! Fuck! Guys! The spirit tried to open the door again! Get me the fuck out of here!"

I desperately wanted to ask him why a spirit would bother trying to open the door when it could move through walls, but that wouldn't make for good TV. A terrified guy locked in a freezer that was freaking out about ghosts, however, would.

I got back on the radio. "Kurt, keep focused. Ask the spirit some more questions."

Brad barged his way down random corridors, stumbling over lumps of plaster that had fallen from the decrepit walls, all the while making confident predictions about that fact that *this* time he just *knew* he was going the right way.

He wasn't.

Kurt resumed his conversation with what he thought was his new roommate. "Spirit, I know you died in here. How did you die?"

It took me a few seconds to think about the answer, and then I pressed the button six times. I also knew we needed to get back to poor old Scooby and that this little prank had gone on long enough. Brad would have over-confidently bumbled his way around the rest of the county before finally getting back to Kurt, but I have a fairly good sense of direction and had never really lost track of where we were. I let Brad stumble through one more doorway before I let out a revelation.

"Brad! I *recognize* this room."

"Huh? You do? It all looks the same to me."

And, of course, that was because he was charging along using only his flashlight. I, on the other hand, was allowing the lovely night vision of my camera to show me each room in glorious green clarity.

"Yeah, I know where we are. Take that door on the left."

So he did.

"Now that corridor on the right."

Off we lurched, Brad stumbling and tripping in his desperate attempt to free our intrepid team member from the clutches of an evil spirit trying to open his freezer door.

At the end of the corridor, I barked another order. "Right again."

I resumed recording on the camera as we entered the room and pointed it at Brad. Even he couldn't fail to notice the large sign that read 'Morgue' over the door at the far end.

He scanned his flashlight around the room and caught the sign. With a whoop, he got on the radio. "Dude, we're here! I've found you! Hold tight."

There was no reply from Kurt.

Brad clattered through the door to the morgue, and headed straight for the ice-box that Kurt was locked into. He fumbled with the latch for a few seconds and then threw the door open, sending it crashing against the steel wall behind. He reached in and dragged the tray out of the freezer. Kurt was lying on it, his eyes the size of saucers and his breath coming in short, sharp gasps.

"Holy fuck!" exclaimed Brad. "He's been possessed by the spirit! Shit!"

What had actually happened was that Kurt had worked himself up into a frenzy and was now hyperventilating, which meant he was sucking in a higher quantity of oxygen than the amount of carbon dioxide that he was exhaling. This leads to an imbalance in the lungs and will eventually make you pass out so your body can get itself together again, and he wasn't far away from that.

Whilst Brad was leaping around, convincing himself that a spirit was inside Kurt, I needed to do something useful. I'd had some basic medical training and knew that ideally I needed a paper bag, but I didn't have one, so I had to improvise. I cupped my hands over Kurt's panicked mouth and started talking calmly to him.

"Kurt! Kurt! Breathe slower, man. Breathe."

I got a terrified response. "Spir... *gasp*... it... *gasp*... ins... *gasp*... ide me."

"Shut up! Just breathe slowly."

I was annoyed that I'd let it go this far. Locking a guy that believes in ghosts into the freezer box of a morgue inside a mental prison in the dead of night, whilst simultaneously winding him up about the whole thing to get some good footage was not something I look back on and am proud of. Of course, Brad wasn't helping.

"Shit!" he yelled, "See what I mean? Kurt knows it too. How does the spirit feel, dude? In fact, spirit can you speak via Kurt?"

I wanted to point out that the only reason Kurt thought he was possessed was because Brad had brought it up, but I was too busy trying to stop Kurt from getting brain damage.

Gradually, as my tightly cupped hands made Kurt breathe back in the critical carbon dioxide that his was body was missing, his rate of breathing began to slow and, a few minutes later, he was back to normal. I collapsed back onto the cold floor and took some deep breaths myself.

Brad suddenly burst into life. "Fuck! My camera wasn't recording! I must have forgotten to hit the button. Was yours?"

I wanted to punch him in the face, but kept as calm as I could. "Of course not! I was trying to save his fucking life!"

"Oh yeah, man. Good job on that. You got rid of the spirit! How did you do that, dude?"

I was fuming at his utter idiocy, but I thought about my bank account and how much it would be swelling after this episode aired. "Let's get a recap of all that," I suggested through gritted teeth.

I found the camera on the floor where I'd tossed it after seeing the state of Kurt, and switched it back on. It still worked. I pointed it at Brad.

"You ready?"

"Yeah, dude. Wow. What an incident."

"Okay, you're on in three, two, one... go."

Brad looked earnestly into the NV camera, and I could see on the viewer that his pupils were enormous and reflecting amplified light into the lens of the night vision equipment. "Well, that was the most conclusive evidence we've ever had that there are spirits living amongst us."

He gestured down to Kurt on his tray. I panned down and zoomed in on Kurt's heavily breathing face; he wasn't in the mood to say anything, so I returned the camera to Brad.

"While some of the spirits in this place had led us and got us hopelessly lost in the maze of corridors and tunnels, the others actually attacked Kurt. I'm not kidding! There can be no other explanation for what happened! Here's what went down, guys: we left Kurt in the morgue, all ready to communicate with the spirits. I felt the need, no a *compulsion* to explore deeper into the building with Todd, and this must have come from some of the lost souls in this place, meaning to distract us from their main plan."

He looked down at the floor and shook his head slightly. Then he looked slowly back up at the camera. "And it worked. They distracted us enough to get lost. We got lost! Can you believe that? And while we were lost, they set upon Kurt, and one of them possessed him. Can you believe that? Kurt has just been possessed!"

Kurt let out a groan from below and I zoomed down to him. When Brad realized he wasn't center stage any more, he leaned down and tried to sound like he cared.

"How did it feel, dude?"

Kurt looked up at him. "Was I really possessed?"

Brad nodded solemnly. "You were, my friend. There's no other explanation for what happened."

"Fuck."

"Somehow Todd exorcised you. And with his bare hands!"

That last sentence was definitely going to be edited out.

III

Back in the dank office area, we huddled around the monitors. The first thing that Brad wanted to get to the bottom of was the spirit trying to open the door.

We watched the green footage of Scooby lying on the tray. After a few minutes, there was a loud clanking noise that caused him to freak out slightly before he lay very still again. Another clank came a few minutes later, and that was when he got on the radio to us.

"See what I mean?" gasped Kurt at the noises. "The spirits were trying to get at me, man!"

"Undoubtedly," whispered Brad seriously. "Oh man, that is amazing. That was a close one. It's a good job they weren't able to operate the latch."

As usual, the clanking noises were metal cooling down and contracting, but this was yet more brilliant footage that I wasn't about to let logic or common sense get in the way of.

"Let's see if you got answers to your questions, dude!"

I replayed the digital recording that, naturally, had the mic volume turned up to max, and we huddled round and listened in silence. After our clattering sounds of preparation ended, the huge clang of the door closing could be heard.

Then Kurt made his radio transmission that ended with, "If there are spirits returning here, I'm gonna find them."

Three hisses of static can be heard, seemingly in reply. In Scrappy's head, I knew this would be three words, and he didn't disappoint.

"Dude! The spirit spoke to you! Todd, replay that!"

"Oh man," said Kurt, "I didn't even ask a question! It was communicating *to* me!"

I replayed the hisses of static over and over, and finally Brad understood what the spirit had said.

"Oh god," he said urgently. "Did you guys hear that?"

"I can't quite make out the last word. The first word sounds like 'you'."

Brad erupted with enthusiasm, "that's exactly what I got, dude! But I understand the last word too. This is serious shit, guys. Oh, sorry Todd, this is so serious that it shouldn't have a bleep in it. Edit that bit out and use this: I understand all three words, guys, and this is serious."

I replayed the 'spirit' talking to Kurt once more and Brad closed his eyes and silently mouthed something. "I've definitely got it," he announced. "Play it once more and I'll say the words over the top of it. But Kurt, dude, be ready for a shock."

Kurt's eye's went wide. "What, man? What did the spirit say?"

I replayed the recording and, bang on cue, Brad spoke over the top of the three bursts of white noise. "You… will… die."

Kurt leapt back and crashed into a table, sending papers and pens scattering everywhere. "Fucking fuck, dude! Holy shit! Fuck! I'm gonna die? What the hell?!"

Brad replied in his most sincere whisper. "Man, that was seriously close. I hope you guys at home understand the risks we're taking investigating this stuff for you. Wow, but talk about evidence! There it is. Right there."

"What about my questions?" gasped Kurt.

I replayed the first one that he'd asked, and Kurt's slightly crackly voice filled the room. "What... uhhh... what's your name?"

Two whispers of white noise was his response and Brad jumped for joy. "The spirit answered you, dude! Incredible! Play that again, let's figure out what its name is."

I played it over and over, and even Scrappy Doo was having a hard time figuring out a name. He threw out all sorts of bone-headed stripper-name suggestions, like Sta-cey, Brit-ney, and Court-ney, and then I played my trump card. The one I'd been saving up since the moment we walked into the office several hours ago.

In my hand I had the list of the final people who died in the place, and I made a big thing about running my finger down the names before making my amazing discovery.

"Arthur!" I announced. "Ar-thur."

Brad span around and looked at me with an open mouth. "That's *it*! Arthur! His name is Arthur. How did he die?"

I suppressed an extremely smug grin and then replied. "He died... oh my *god*! You've nailed it again, Brad! He died on the *operating table*!"

"I knew it!" exploded Brad. "Arthur died on the operating table, cut open by those very scalpels and instruments that we saw down there."

"Oh *fuck*!" screamed Kurt. "He was trying to operate on *me*!"

"There's no other explanation, dude. Oh my god that was close." Brad thought for a moment. "Wait, you asked him how he died, didn't you?"

"Errr, I think so, yeah. I was kinda freaked out at that point though."

I found the part in the recording where, I hoped, my *pièce de la résistance* would play out. Kurt asked the spirit how he died, and six bursts of static was the reply.

Brad screwed his face up for a few seconds. "Replay that, Todd."

I did so, over and over, and then Kurt got it.

"Oh fucking fucking fuck! Did you hear that? It *was* Arthur!"

"I'm not quite getting the whole thing," replied Brad.

Kurt found a chair and sat down with a heavy thump. "Play that again, Todd, and I'll clarify what he said."

I did so, and Kurt took a deep breath before speaking over the top of the meaningless static. "Op — er — at — ing — ta — ble."

It took a few seconds for Brad to put the syllables together, but once he did he went almost apoplectic. "Oh my *god* dude! That absolutely confirms it! Arthur! The guy who died on the operating table in... in..."

"1979," I added.

"Yeah, in 1979, is *still here*! And his spirit is looking for closure. There can be no other explanation. The evidence speaks for itself." He turned and looked right into the camera. "There you go, guys. Absolute, concrete proof that a spirit, a lost soul if you will, is still in this place, crying for help. And we tried to help. We really did, but I guess Arthur is looking for something else. I mean, there can be no other explanation for the clear voice of Arthur that we heard. He said his name, and how he died."

"And he told me I would die," added Kurt shakily.

"Yeah, that too," continued Brad. "So now we know for sure. This place is full of spirits, but I guess that's no surprise. I mean, over *ten thousand* people died in here. And Arthur was just one of them."

Brad tried to fist-bump Kurt, but he wasn't really in the mood, so I gave Brad a fist-bump instead. I panned out so Brad was standing sort of heroically over the slumped figure of Kurt in the chair.

"I think that wraps this up, guys. Conclusive evidence. Our work here is done."

I turned off the camera, and looked down at Kurt. "Are you okay?"

His eyes were darting around all over the place. "Huh? Am I...? No! Of course I'm not okay. I've just been fucking *possessed* man!

Would *you* be okay? I'm freaked out, dude. I need to get out of here."

Scrappy let out a huge sigh. "Oh, man. Really? We have so many more rooms to explore."

"Dude, you are not, I repeat, *not* locking me up in any more freakin' cells or coffins tonight. Got it?"

Brad looked genuinely shocked. "Woah! Okay, dude! Chill, okay?"

Kurt pulled himself up into a sitting position and glared at Brad. "Chill? Fucking chill? I nearly got operated on by a bunch of fucking *ghosts* dude! Don't tell me to chill! Where the hell were you?"

"Dude, the spirits got us lost, and—"

"Lost? Freakin' *lost*? It's a rectangular building, dude! How do you get lost in a rectangle?"

"The spirits kept making us take wrong turns and go round in circles," replied Brad, slightly miffed. "But eventually, I figured it out and fought back, man. Then I came and got you. You should be grateful."

Kurt rubbed his head, and calmed down a little. "Yeah, man, yeah. You're right. Thanks dude. I'd have been toast without you."

I gave a little cough. "So, are we done here then?"

"Fuck yeah," spat Kurt. "I need to get away from these crazy spirits, dude! And that Arthur guy? He's nuts."

"Brad?" I asked.

"Yeah. Kurt's in a bad way, and I think we've unintentionally disturbed a whole lot of lost souls tonight." Brad looked at the ceiling and ended his sentence, "sorry guys. And Arthur especially. Isabella, too."

I fished into my backpack and pulled out a bright yellow walkie-talkie. Obviously, we weren't really alone in any of the places that we were locked into; we had a crew in a truck parked outside waiting for us to get bored and come out.

I hit the transmit button. "Guys. You copy, over?"

There was about a ten second pause, which was normal; most of the crew would be asleep at this point. Then I got a crackle on the radio, followed by a slightly groggy voice. "Errr, huh? Yeah, Cool. Copy. Over."

"I think we're done in here tonight, guys."

Another crackle and a different voice. "Hey Todd, it's Duff. You guys need an exfil?"

Duff was in charge of our mobile unit, and was ex-Special Forces.

"No, man, no. It's cool. Kurt had a bit of an episode, but we can make it out on our own."

"Only just," mumbled Brad from the other side of the room.

A slightly over-excited voice came back on the radio. "Episode? Do we need to come in and get you guys? I can blow the wall adjacent to the—"

"*No!* No, Duff, it's all cool. Okay? We'll be heading back to the entry point in about ten minutes. Can you be there to unlock it for us?"

He sounded almost deflated that there was no emergency that needed fixing. "Umm, sure. Just unlock it?"

"Yeah."

"Okay. Roger that. We'll be at the extraction point exactly ten minutes from now."

"Duff?"

"Copy."

"We might be fifteen minutes. Or twenty. Or more."

A pause. "Oh, okay. I guess we'll wait for you guys, then."

"That would be great."

"Roger that. Out!"

We rarely spent the entire night in any of the places we ended up in, and usually for a reason similar to this one: Scrappy Doo putting Scooby Doo in a situation that was close to making him go insane in the quest for his 'evidence', helped along with my little spirit-talking-back trickery. They fell for it every time.

I packed all of the kit away while Brad was trying to get Kurt to explain what it felt like to be possessed, and we headed out of the office and back the way we came. Duff was there, as promised, standing vigilantly on guard.

"Coast is clear," announced Duff as if expecting an army of ghosts to be chasing us out of the building.

"Kurt got possessed," said Scrappy, excitedly.

"Sounds gnarly, man."

"And then he almost got operated on by a ghost called Arthur," continued Brad as he clambered into the van. It was like listening to the ramblings of a six-year old that had just watched *Goosebumps*, and I wasn't sure if Duff actually believed any of it or not.

"Are you sure you guys don't need me in there with you as backup in future?" said Duff, reinforcing the point by patting the pistol holster on his belt.

Brad shook his head. "No, dude, we don't want to scare the spirits. If we go in packing heat, that'll just freak them out. We'll look like we're aggressors, and we don't want that."

Quite how you go about shooting a ghost wasn't clarified, but Kurt then agreed that we wouldn't want to be making the spirits angry as they were scary enough as it was.

Once settled in my seat, I put my head back and closed my eyes.

IV

The following morning after not nearly enough sleep, we trooped back over to the prison, and filmed the dramatic moment of us emerging, blinking, into the daylight. As usual, despite the fact that we'd all only had about four hours sleep, Scrappy was bouncing off the walls with excitement.

The same local that had locked us in, was there to unlock us, and he clearly thought we were all stark raving mad.

"Fun, was it?" he asked us in a tone that made it clear he didn't think it would have been.

"It was *awesome*, dude," blurted Brad.

"I got possessed," added Kurt, now considerably sprightlier than he'd been at the end of the previous night.

"Did you," said the local as he locked up the prison once more.

"Yeah, and he was almost operated on. By a *ghost*! We have all the evidence. It's irrefutable. There can be no other explanation."

The local guy looked in my direction for some semblance of sanity and I gave him a little shrug in return. He left us to it.

Now the real work began for me; following these two intrepid adventurers around with a camera was the easy bit. Now I had to turn the idiotic footage into something that grabs the casual viewer's attention and makes them watch the whole show. Because this trip was a slightly extended one and we had another 'investigation' to make in a few days time, we weren't bothering to trek all the way back to the west coast. The TV network, of course, still needed a fully edited episode.

So, while Duff drove Scooby and Scrappy around to see some sights, I hopped into a cab and was whisked to a local TV station, where we'd rented one of their editing suites. Most editing suites in TV stations around the world are pretty much identical, so the moment I walked in, I knew exactly where everything was and felt at home. I uploaded the hours and hours of footage from all of the various cameras we'd used, and got to work.

The most critical part of a daft show like ours is the first thirty seconds of footage. On American television, once the previous show ends there is no commercial break or any gap whatsoever; it moves immediately to the teaser for the next show. This is a stroke of genius because by the time the viewer has realized the previous show is over and has spent a few seconds searching for the remote to change the channel to something less ludicrous, they're already sucked in to the next episode, as long as the teaser is good enough.

After about thirty minutes, I had my teaser, and it was absolutely killer: The first thing you see is the grainy, green night vision footage of Kurt being locked into the ice box. Then it cut to a shot of him inside, totally trapped, before cutting to Brad getting us lost. Then I overlaid subtitles of Kurt's panicked radio transmission about the spirits trying to get him, and followed that by a snippet of the wobbly footage I took of Brad crashing his way desperately through dark corridors trying to find out where he was.

It was fifteen seconds of pure televisual gold, but I wasn't done. I ended the thirty second teaser with Kurt in the straight jacket, locked into the cell and freaking out. Once again, subtitles were overlaid just to add to the dramatic effect, and then I finished the whole thing off with Brad's revelation about what the spirits had been saying. Of course, I didn't actually give away what they'd said, I just used the footage of Brad preparing Kurt for a shock, and the subsequent reaction to it.

I had a lot of bleeping to do, but the end result was amazing. Nobody would be able to watch that teaser and not want to know what happened to the three ghost-chasing clowns.

I spent the rest of the day finishing the episode, and writing the lines our gravelly-voiced narrator would need to record from the booth in LA. I'd overlay those tomorrow, along with some dramatic snippets of music, and then the whole thing would be complete.

Of course, I also did a bit of sneaky enhancing of various portions of the footage. The 'ghost' that was behind Kurt in the cell, for example, became far more prominent in the final footage thanks to some Photoshop trickery, and the 'voices' that Brad and Kurt translated became just a little bit crisper and, thanks to some pitch and phase-shifting of the audio, ever so slightly closer to the syllables that they were convinced they heard.

The following day, after I'd added all of the voice-overs and music, I watched the entire show from start to finish. An hour-long TV show in America is actually only forty minutes once you remove the commercial breaks, and I was overjoyed with the result. I'd always managed to make the final edit entertaining, but none of the previous shows came close to this one.

That evening, I met Scooby and Scrappy for dinner and told them how amazing the episode was.

"I knew it, dude," said Brad. "From the moment we walked in, I just *knew* those spirits were gonna come at us."

"I can't believe I was possessed."

"Yeah, man, that was incredible. Lucky for you that Todd managed to get that spirit out of you. Who knows what could have happened otherwise?"

Brad and Kurt raised their glasses of Bud Light and tapped them together solemnly, and then Kurt turned to me. "Dude, thanks for saving my life."

He raised his glass, and I lifted my glass of Merlot. "Any time, man. It's what I'm here for."

"So," said Scrappy excitedly, "where are we going next?"

This happened on every assignment, despite the fact that we all got given the same information packet: I was the only one that bothered to read it.

"Virgina," I replied. "We're going to have dinner with some ghosts!"

"Wow, dude, awesome," said Brad.

I continued. "There's a building that was built in the 1700s near Portsmouth, a sort of executive mansion that was home to a British guy called John Roberts that headed up a tobacco company. He made use of a lot of slaves and was, apparently, an evil sonofabitch."

"And this place is haunted?" asked Kurt.

"Apparently so. It's said that this British dude was really big on everything being absolutely perfect, and that was never truer than for when his slaves were serving him food or drinks. Spilling something would earn the slave a beating from Roberts himself."

"Woah, gnarly, dude!"

"Well, the really bad part is that the severity of the beating would depend on how drunk Roberts was when the spillage occurred. Apparently there were several instances where he ended up beating the slave to death."

Kurt and Brad blinked back at me, a slightly shocked look on their face.

"Fuck," said Kurt.

"And then, on one famous occasion, his food arrived cold. Firstly he beat the slave to death, pistol whipping her repeatedly onto her head. He then loaded that same Flintlock pistol, went downstairs to the kitchen and executed the woman that was doing the cooking. Point blank. Shot her in the head. Right in front of the stove."

"Oh my god," gasped Brad. "That's serious shit, dude."

"So is the place abandoned?"

"No, it was lived in by various wealthy families over the centuries, and is now a museum. Apparently it played a part in the civil war. But here's the interesting thing…"

Brad and Kurt were rapt with breathless attention.

"Once Roberts left, all the future occupying families complained of the same thing: clumsiness from their servers and maids. Apparently food would be regularly spilt, dishes would be broken, servants would trip and fall all over the place. Stuff like that."

Brad thought for a moment, and then came to the conclusion I knew he would. "It's the spirits, dude. I'll bet they're pissed that they got murdered by that British guy, and they want others to suffer like they did. So what do they do? They go round tripping up staff, knocking things over, all in the hope that these other servants will get beaten too."

"Makes total sense to me," agreed Kurt. "Did these other servants get murdered?"

"No. None of the other occupants were as maniacal as John Roberts."

"So that's why the spirits are still doing it," declared Brad. "They keep on trying and trying but they're not getting the result they want."

"And," added Kurt, "they must be doubly angry that there aren't any servants there now to mess with. How long's it been a museum?"

"Since the 1950s."

"Woah," breathed Brad. "Decades of servant-less torture."

"Man, they must be *really* pissed," said Kurt after a sip of beer.

Brad put his glass down with a solemn thud and looked at us with an expression that was equally so. "They need our help guys. Those tortured souls need us to communicate with them."

If I was a tortured spirit, the last thing I'd want to be doing was hearing from Scooby and Scrappy, but I kept quiet.

Just to amp up the tension ahead of the 'investigation', I said, "do you think we're ready for this? It sounds dangerous, guys."

"Absolutely," said Brad on Kurt's behalf, "but we're gonna need to be careful, and I think I've got just the thing to help us avoid being ambushed like in that prison."

I tried not to let my excitement show. I just knew that he'd somehow found some sort of weird ghost-hunting equipment store and bought himself a new gadget.

"What is it?"

"I found a place in town, and I came across *this*!"

He rummaged in his bag and produced a plastic case, about twice the size of a regular walkie-talkie. It had a couple of *Fisher-Price* type knobs on it, and had clearly been hand made by someone who didn't really have an eye for detail. There were blobs of congealed glue lining the edge of where the two halves of the box had been stuck together, and badly cut into the face of what must be the front of the thing was the only concession to any type of readout: an old, analog decibel meter with the needle that moves in a semi-circular fashion. It looked like it had been ripped out of a mixing desk from the seventies. The three buttons had hand-made labels under them: On, Off, and Reset.

"Isn't it awesome?" asked Scrappy excitedly. If there was one thing he loved more than looking for ghosts, it was the crazy gadgets he found to help look for them.

"Oh, man," said Kurt. "That's incredible. What is it?"

"This," said Brad proudly, "scans the ether for the voices of spirits and lets us hear them. You know how our digital recorder only gets audio in the room? Well, this little baby covers all the frequencies that we can't hear. It's got a patent pending too."

"Woah, dude! That *is* awesome! They'll never be able to sneak up on us ever again!"

I was just contemplating how much cash this idiot had parted with, when Brad piped up. "And it only cost me twenty-five hundred bucks!"

"In our line of work," said Kurt dramatically, "that is a bargain."

"That was how I saw it, dude."

I had to know more. "So, err, Brad, how exactly does this thing work?"

"Oh man, it's amazing. Every five seconds, it scans all of the frequencies that we can't hear. You know, the ones the spirits typically use to communicate."

"Uh huh. And then what?"

"Well, it lets us hear them talk, dude!"

"Every frequency?"

"Yeah."

"Once every five seconds?"

"Yep!"

"Wow," I said, trying to sound enthusiastic, "that *is* amazing. And for only twenty-five hundred bucks."

"I know, right?!"

I desperately wanted to let Brad know what a moron he was, but this could turn out to be something truly amazing. Basically, this device would play a small burst from every radio frequency, and cycle through them over a five second period, before starting again. It was the modern day equivalent of those old radios that had a tuning knob: as you move the dial, you get all sorts of weird and wonderful sounds as it burps, hisses, and bleeps its way through the frequencies, picking up tiny snapshots of each broadcast or, more than likely, static. I could have got some bits from Radio Shack and made one for less than ten bucks.

What we'd hear, I assumed, would be a snippet of a word from a DJ, a song, perhaps a taxi driver nearby, and a whole lot of static at different pitches and frequencies in-between. The end result would be a meaningless mess to anybody other than Scooby and Scrappy who would, I was sure, find an amazing message hidden in one of the transmissions.

I couldn't wait.

V

Two days later, we were being shown around the executive mansion in Virginia by one of the local experts that was well versed in the stories regarding the property. We'd arrived early that afternoon, set up our equipment, and recorded our opening segments and segues that I would weave into the footage later.

As the guide showed us round the place, I was the only one with a camera so Scrappy and Scooby could really ham it up for the viewers. I'd insisted on touring the bedrooms first, because nothing really happened up there and, despite much prodding from Brad, the guide couldn't really come up with much in the way of ghost stories.

Then we moved downstairs, though the grand hallway, and into the executive dining room.

"Oh... my... god!" gasped Brad. "This is where it happened, right?"

The guide beamed; she was in her early forties, made up to the nines with bigger hair than you can imagine, and she clearly had a thing for our intrepid leader. "It certainly is! I'm impressed, Brad, that you know so much about what went on here!"

Brad flashed her one of his trademarked grins that made most people want to punch him in the face. "Oh yeah, I mean, this is what I do. I need to know about this stuff."

She giggled and blushed slightly. "So, you probably know th—"

"I do," interrupted Brad knowledgeably.

Another giggle. "Well, in this very room, John Roberts was having dinner…"

Barbara then regaled the story of what went on that fateful evening before taking us to the kitchen, which turned out to be in the basement. Kurt immediately went up to the stove and began running his hands along it with his eyes closed.

"Oh man," he said, "she's here alright. I can just feel her tortured soul all around us. Y'know what? Since I got possessed, I've definitely felt a stronger connection to the spirits around us."

"He was possessed," Brad told Barbara rather pointlessly.

"Oh my god," she exclaimed. "It's a miracle you're still alive."

"Todd here managed to get the spirit out of him just in time. You can see it all in our next show."

Barbara giggled excitedly. "I think it's just *amazing* that you guys can communicate with the spirits. I watch every single episode and I just *know* that these souls, these spirits exist, despite some people saying they don't. And now we're blessed with you guys who actually gather evidence to prove they exist. It's amazing. Not that your conclusive evidence seems to persuade those elite, snobby, so called *scientists*. I mean, what more proof do they need?"

"Yeah, well," said Brad, "they're locked up in their labs with their test tubes and clipboards, while we're out in the field actually doing real stuff. Gathering *real* evidence."

"Oooh," shrilled Barb, "you guys are so brave! I can't believe you risk your lives every episode just to try and help these lost souls."

"It's what we do," declared Brad heroically.

I couldn't stand any more, so I went back to the truck to get my backpack ready. As I got near, Duff walked over.

"Hey, dude!"

"Hi Duff. You guys all set out here?"

"Yessir. Look, Todd, I've been thinking. Are you guys *sure* you don't want me in there with you? I can be in the next room, out of sight. And I'll be carrying. And ready."

"No, I don't think Brad and Kurt want to risk upsetting the spirits any more than we already do."

"But you'd never know I was there."

I hated myself for the next words that came out of my mouth. "The spirits would."

He thought about that for a few moments, and then nodded at me in a way that didn't give an indication as to whether he thought I was a halfwit or not. "If you get into the slightest bit of trouble, you holler, y'hear?"

"Will do Duff. We really appreciate it."

Satisfied that he'd done his hero bit, he walked back to his bag of guns. I finished loading up my backpack with the NV cameras, recorders and monitors, and put Brad's nonsense-gatherer on top. I was just zipping everything up when Scooby and Scrappy came bounding over.

"Oh, *dude!*" blurted Brad.

"That place is full of spirits, man! I can just feel them all around me."

"So are you guys excited about this one?"

"Oh yeah, man," said Brad, almost hopping from foot to foot. "That crazy Brit apparently murdered eleven slaves."

"And that was just the *confirmed* murders," added Kurt. "I felt a whole lot more than eleven sprits in there, guys. And they were pissed! I feel such a connection to them now."

"We're gonna have to watch our backs tonight, guys," I said, just to amp them up even more.

"It's a good job I've got my new device. No more sneaking up on us this time."

I pulled out a camera and started recording, pointing it at Brad. "Wanna give some final thoughts before we head in there?"

Of course he did. "Well, guys, this is it. We're about to go into the executive mansion where this crazy British guy had a liking for beating people to death. Kurt's felt some serious activity, which I did too. There are definitely some lost souls in there that need our help."

I panned to Kurt. "Yeah, after being possessed, I feel so close to them. I can just *sense* them, and there's a lot of them in the dining room. I guess that's where most of the beatings happened. The cook is seriously angry, too, stuck down there in the kitchen."

"We're gonna need to be extra careful tonight, guys."

I piped up from behind the camera, "the sun is starting to set. Time to get to work."

After numerous high-fives and fist-bumps, we headed over to where Barbara was waiting to lock us into the mansion. Waiting with her were three members of one of the best restaurants in Virginia: two waiters and a waitress. The plan was that we would be based in the executive dining room, where Kurt could 'feel' all of the activity, and these three would bring us food that they had plated in the kitchen downstairs. The food would arrive at regularly spaced intervals from various take-out places nearby.

One of our producers suggested to Brad that we should test whether the house still made waiters clumsy or not. Brad thought this was a great idea, and Kurt was happy because it meant he wasn't going to be locked into anything for a change. The producer found the best restaurant within a hundred mile radius, and agreed to pay them a big chunk of cash *and* heavily promote their restaurant during the show. He'd somehow magicked up these three in less than twenty-four hours.

I pointed the camera at Brad again, and he began his monologue. "So here's the deal, guys. Barbara is going to lock us into this haunted executive mansion. These three guys are gonna be serving us a five-course meal over the space of three hours, and we're gonna see whether the spirits try and mess with them. I made a call to a friend of mine at *Big Eagle*, one of the best restaurants in Virginia, and he agreed to let me borrow some of his best waiters, and here they are: Cory, Mike, and Whitney. Thanks for doing this, guys. We'll make sure you're safe, don't worry."

We went inside, and into the dining room. It was now dusk, but there was still enough light to see fairly well, and the three servers set the impressive oak dining table for the three of us. Brad would sit at the head of the table, with Kurt and me on either side of him.

I got to work rigging up NV cameras at various angles and locations around the dining room, the large hallway outside, at the top and bottom of the stairs, and also in the kitchen. The one concession that we'd made to our we-only-do-things-in-the-dark hook, was that the kitchen was allowed to have its lights on. It was well away from us in the basement, so we'd get no light pollution, and the three of them needed to have some sort of chance of actually getting the food on the plates instead of all over the floor.

By the time darkness had fully fallen, we were all set. There was a sliver of moon that night, so the dining room and hallway weren't completely pitch black, but it was still darker than you'd like if you were ferrying plates around.

There was a knock on the door. The first course had arrived.

I'd set up the various monitors so we could watch what was going on in the other rooms, and we saw Cory go and get the food from the front door and take it down into the basement. His passage down the stone steps was fairly slow, as you would expect from someone navigating them in the dark with armfuls of bags.

"I think it's time to see if they're talking about us," said Brad reaching for his device.

I'd taken it apart and rewired it slightly so the output would go not only to the speaker on the device, but into a digital recorder as well. Brad turned it on, and it sounded exactly as I thought it would: lots of tiny bursts of static at differing frequencies, as well as the odd chirp and bleep of a voice or music. It was complete mush.

"Woah, they're agitated, dude," said Kurt. "I told you."

"I just knew they would be, man."

I watched the monitor in the kitchen and saw our first course being plated, which was to be appetizers from a nearby Chinese restaurant. Everything got put on the plates, and they loaded up their arms with everything we'd need and headed out of the brightly-lit kitchen.

The human eye is an amazing thing. After five minutes of sitting in the dark, it will adjust as best it can and use the receptors around the iris to pick up as much ambient light as possible; the pupils are pretty much useless in these conditions so the eye switches into the best-night-vision-it-can-offer mode. Now that we'd been sitting in the dark dining room for close to thirty minutes with a faint amount of moonlight, we could see reasonably well, but the wait staff had just walked from a brightly lit room into darkness, so their natural night vision hadn't had time to kick in.

From the scrambled mush of noise coming from the SED — the Spirit Eavesdropping Device — suddenly a word was audible, and it couldn't have been better. Kurt leapt to his feet in shock, while Brad nearly went into orbit. It was only short, but it was perfect.

"Holy shit!" yelled Kurt. "Did you hear that? Should we warn them?"

"No, dude, this is a scientific experiment, remember? We have to let events happen."

The word from the SED had been, or at least sounded exactly like 'trip'. My guess was that it had come from an advert for a travel company, or perhaps a taxi nearby, but Scooby and Scrappy took it to mean that the spirits wanted the waiters to trip over, and they were going to make them do so.

We watched the slow progress of Whitney, Cory, and Mike as they climbed the stairs. Whitney and Cory made it up the stairs without incident but, amazingly, on the very last step, Mike tripped and fell forwards, sending his plates of food smashing to the floor. Brad and Kurt were beside themselves with amazement.

"*Dude!* Oh my god!" blurted Brad with a squeak.

"Fucking hell, man! They really tripped him!"

"And we heard that they were going to do it,"

"That SED is incredible," said Kurt. "Without that there might have been some doubt as to whether it was just an accident or whether the spirits did it deliberately."

"Evidence, dude. Right there."

Now, it must be borne in mind that these poor waiters were virtually blind, and loaded up with plates, whilst simultaneously climbing up a stone staircase made in the 1700s. It's a miracle that *any* of them made it up on their first attempt. But, they had also been chosen for another reason: they completely believed in ghosts and spirits. To add to the physical conditions they had to contend with, they were genuinely nervous about the spirits they thought were around them that night.

Mike went back down to the kitchen to clean himself up, while Whitney and Cory carefully made their way, in the darkness, to us in the dining room. Of course, what the viewers at home would be seeing was the green NV footage, so they'd quickly forget that they were watching people trying to serve a table in almost total darkness.

The burbling and beeping from the SED suddenly produced the word 'fall', and Brad gasped.

"Did you guys hear that? They're gonna do it again!"

"We need to warn them, dude," said Kurt urgently. "They might get hurt."

"No way, guy. Science, remember? This is sort of like Schubert's Dog."

"Oh yeah," said Kurt. "Sorry, man. I just know what these spirits are capable of."

I couldn't hold back any longer. "*Who's* dog?"

Brad looked over at me. "You know, the guy who put his dog in a box to see if it was dead or not? Classic scientific experiment. Just like what we're doing."

I let out a little sigh. "Brad, are you talking about Schrödinger's Cat?"

"Who?"

"Schrödinger, the physicist? The Quantum notion of a cat in a sealed box being in two states at the same time — dead and alive — until the box is opened?"

"I thought it was a dog."

"No, it's a cat. And it isn't real. It's a theoretical experiment."

Brad thought about this. "So he didn't really put his cat in an airtight box?"

"No, Brad, he didn't."

"Good. Because that would have made him an asshole."

Kurt butted in. "Look, guys, we need to warn them that they're in—"

And at that moment Cory had his fall as he came into the dining room. Plates crashed to the floor and smashed into pieces, and Kurt freaked out.

"Guys," he hissed in a very loud whisper, "this is getting out of hand! The spirits have done this twice now! *And* they've told us in advance!"

"They're taunting us," said Brad in a hushed but serious voice.

Of course, the fact that I'd deliberately laid lots of cables unnecessarily across the doorway to the dining room without bothering to tape them down wasn't helping the poor waiters in the dark. The word 'fall' from the SED was, I assumed, either from an advert for something to do with an upcoming sale in the Fall, or perhaps an ambulance-chasing law firm looking for people who'd had a fall at work.

Either way, only Whitney remained standing as she came into the room. She had four plates, one in each hand and one balanced on each arm, and she was visibly trembling with fear.

"Are they in here too?" she gasped, her voice close to tears.

"We think so," said Brad quietly. "But don't worry Whitney, we won't let them hurt you. I promise."

"Umm, okay. Because I'm... err... kinda scared right now."

"It's perfectly natural. Not many people get to be this close to the spirits, so it takes some getting used to. Just ask Kurt."

Before Kurt had time to reply, there was a huge bang from upstairs followed by an equally loud crashing and tinkling sound. It was totally unexpected, and I was caught completely by surprise.

"What the fuck was that?" I blurted.

"I dunno," said Scrappy, grabbing his NV camera, "but we need to go and find out."

The three of us left poor Whitney in the dining room to serve our food, alone and in the dark, while we made our way upstairs to find out who was up there. I thought back to Duff asking me if we needed him in here with us and suddenly regretted not taking him up on the offer.

As we reached the end of the flight of stairs, Brad turned to us. "Kurt, I think you should enter each room first, and I'll follow with the NV camera, describing everything that goes on. Cool?"

As usual, Kurt nodded enthusiastically and took first place in the stack. Brad was in the middle, and I was bringing up the rear.

I must confess to being a little nervous at this point.

VI

Duff would have been unimpressed with Brad's Method of Entry, or MOE in Special Forces speak. It basically involved getting Kurt revved up outside every closed door with lots of urgent whispering, persuading him to turn the handle, and then Brad shoving Kurt into the room, sending the door crashing into the wall. Kurt would then stand there in the middle of the room, looking for spirits or something, while Brad would film the back of him with an NV camera, giving a monologue about how dangerous this all was.

We went into every bedroom, and nothing had been disturbed. I knew I'd heard a proper, real-world crash, and not some imagined spirit noise. Someone, or something, had made a noise up here, and we were supposed to be the only people in the house.

The only room left was in front of us now, and it had to have been where the noise had come from. Once again, Kurt was heroically shoved into it by Brad, and it turned out to be the only bathroom on this floor. The moment I looked inside, I saw what had caused the noise: a heavy-framed mirror had fallen off the wall and smashed to pieces on the floor.

Brad leapt over to the largest remaining bits of it. "Dude! The spirits are *pissed*! They're throwing bits of furniture around! This is wild!"

Kurt looked around him in awe. "This is our first proper physical interaction with them. Holy crap!"

"Oh *man*," said Brad, almost beside himself with excitement, "we need to be seriously careful, guys. In fact, we need to get back down to Whitney and the dudes. This could have been a distraction designed to leave those three alone for the ghosts to possess! And they're not used to experiencing what we do." A sudden, terrible realization crept across Brad's face and he snapped his head up to look at Kurt. "Oh, no! It *was* a distraction! We need to move. *Now!*"

There was a mad scramble by Scooby and Scrappy to get back to the dining room. Of course, we'd been using flashlights and turning lights on in all the rooms we searched, so our night vision was shot. The pair of them ended up tumbling down the last few stairs and landing in a heap on the floor in the hall of mansion.

I was still in the bathroom as I heard them pick themselves up and clatter their way, in total darkness, somewhere-or-other.

I wanted to check something while I was in the room where the noise had happened. I couldn't help noticing that the large window in the bathroom was open, and it was right by the toilet. I peered into the toilet bowl and saw substantial skid-marks, and knew exactly what had happened and guessed that Brad was, unwittingly, the culprit for the mirror falling. I made my way carefully, by way of NV camera view-finder, back downstairs.

When I got there, Kurt and Brad were busy helping Whitney pick up the larger pieces of the plates that she'd dropped when the two of them had gone barreling into the dining room and collided with her. She was utterly terrified, and Brad wasn't helping.

"And Kurt got possessed in the last place we were in a few days ago," he finished saying as I walked into the room.

"He *did*?" she gasped.

"Oh, yeah. And almost got operated on by some ghost dude called Arthur who was pissed off because he'd died on the operating tab—"

I cut Brad off. "Hey guys. What happened?"

Brad was standing with the single piece of plate that he'd picked up, while Kurt was scrabbling around on the floor getting the rest of them. "We got tripped, dude. By those angry spirits! Kurt and I were trying to get back to poor Whitney here as quick as we could, and the spirits tried to stop us."

"But," added Kurt, "we managed to get to our feet and make it into the room just as the spirits pushed all the plates out of Whitney's hands. It was a close call, dude."

Brad turned to roughly where he thought Whitney was in the dark room. "Did you feel them? Could you feel the spirits inside you?"

Whitney swallowed loudly. "I... I did. My whole body shivered. Then I tingled all over. It must have been a ghost passing through me."

"Or trying to possess you," added Kurt.

"There it is, guys. More evidence. Right there. There's no other explanation."

Eventually, all of the larger pieces of broken crockery were picked up, and Whitney headed down to the kitchen, almost in tears.

Brad sat down with a heavy thump. "That was so close, dude."

I sat down at the table, and couldn't help noticing that the room now smelled of Chinese food, none of which had made it to the table.

"They really *are* messing with the staff," said Kurt.

"Yeah, well, they've been left alone for *decades*, remember? They're probably letting out all of their pent-up frustrations on these poor guys."

"I wonder," said Kurt thoughtfully, "if these spirits will let any food make it to our table tonight?"

Brad thought for a moment, and then said vaguely, "Oh, they will. But I'll put money on there being something wrong with it."

I could see on the monitor that Whitney was now sobbing uncontrollably on a chair in the corner of the kitchen, and Cory was trying to comfort her. There was a loud knock on the front door, signifying course number two had arrived, which Mike was sent to go and fetch. Just like Cory, he took the armfuls of bags and made his was slowly down the narrow stone steps. He got to the bottom without incident aided, no doubt, from the light spilling from the kitchen that he was heading towards.

"I guess the spirits are going to let them put the food on the plates before they mess with them," hissed Brad conspiratorially.

"It looks that way," whispered Kurt.

While we watched the monitors show the progress in the kitchen, our night vision had pretty much kicked back in and once again we could see fairly well in the low-lit room.

Brad piped up in his exaggerated whisper, "You know, guys? I can't believe that dude tripped over in here. I mean, it's not *that* dark."

"He didn't trip, dude," replied Kurt solemnly, "he was pushed."

"He must have been. No other explanation for this, so we have yet more evidence. On camera. Right there," Brad paused for dramatic effect. "Pushed. By ghosts."

Quite why they were insisting on speaking in whispers was beyond me. Even if spirits existed and were roaming the house with iPods in their ears, they'd hardly be oblivious to our arrival, bearing in mind the previous fifteen minutes of blundering around upstairs, crashing through doors and turning on lights.

There was a little pause, and then Brad said, "what's the next course, dude?"

"Soup," I replied. "French onion soup, to be precise."

This was a stroke of genius by our producer. I couldn't think of a more difficult dish to carry up narrow steps, in the dark, whilst simultaneously avoiding all of the cables I'd left everywhere.

We could see on the monitor that the soup was now in bowls, and lovely-looking chunks of freshly-baked baguette were loaded onto plates. I rather hoped that this course *would* make it to our table. Whitney had been consoled, although I could tell from her heaving shoulders that she was still sobbing, and it took the guys another five minutes to persuade her to actually leave the kitchen, which she finally did, reluctantly carrying her bowl of soup and plate of bread. The order this time was Mike, Cory, and then Whitney, who was spilling soup with every sob and heave of her shoulders.

"Look!" hissed Brad, "the spirits must be toying with her. Do you see that? They're not tripping her, just messing with her bowl of soup."

"Oh man," added Kurt, "these lost souls are being kinda mean."

"Yeah, well, dude, they've got a lot to be mad about. If someone murdered me for forgetting the salt, I'd be pissed as hell."

Mike and Cory made it up the stairs without incident, but Whitney was taking every step agonizingly slowly, the increasing darkness clearly unnerving her. Suddenly, something made her spin around with a gasp, which in turn made her right foot slip off the narrow step, allowing gravity to take over and do its thing. The bowl and plate smashed on the stairs, while Whitney tumbled down the few steps that she'd managed to climb, and landed in a heap on the cold, stone floor. Soup and bread had gone everywhere, and poor Whitney was now a sprawled bundle of arms and legs, sobbing once more. I felt really bad for her, but this was making for absolutely amazing TV.

"Oh my *god*!" gasped Kurt. "They threw her down the stairs!"

"With no warning either," said Brad solemnly. "I wonder if they've wised up to our SED?"

I leaned over and switched it back on. "Brad, you turned it off when we went upstairs."

"I did?"

"You did."

"Oh, okay. Well, at least they haven't figured out our new device."

"Yet," added Kurt.

The dining room was filled, once again, with the beeps, crackles, and farts of the rapidly changing channels. Suddenly, for a brief, brief moment, something that sounded quite like a snippet of laughter came from the SED. It might not have been, of course, it could have been the middle of a word, or a noise from an advert, and, had we heard this at a different time it probably would have been meaningless, but that didn't matter. The timing couldn't have been better.

Brad shook his head and looked down. "Oh man. They're laughing at her."

"Fuck," gasped Kurt. "Poor Whitney."

Mike and Cory, not wanting to risk going back down the stairs in the darkness with full bowls of soup, called out to Whitney that they'd be back to help her as soon as they'd dropped off the soup. They made steady progress across the hall, and Cory warned Mike about the cables across the doorway; I'd edit that out later.

They made it into the room and slowly approached the table, before setting two bowls of soup and two plates of bread down very nearly in front of us. Brad let out a whoop.

"Way to go, guys! You made it! Could you feel the spirits trying to mess with you?"

"Err," said Mike, "I think they were focusing on Whitney, because it was a pretty easy walk for me. I mean, I had to be careful in the dark and all, but other than that, it was okay."

"I guess," said Kurt knowingly, "that they all ganged up on Whitney. They're more powerful if they work as a team on one person."

"Oh, okay," said Cory nervously. "I wonder if they're going to take turns with us."

"Very possibly," said Brad seriously. "Very possibly."

"Err, okay then," said Mike. "Um, enjoy your food."

They turned and made their way out of the room, leaving us to our soup. We moved the bowls so they were in-between the three of us, and Brad took a sip.

"Uuggghhh!" he blurted, and spat his mouthful of soup back into the bowl. "It's cold!"

I dipped my little finger into the soup and he was right; it was stone cold. And, of course, this made total sense to me: first of all it had the journey from the restaurant. Then it had to wait at the front door to be collected and slowly taken down the stairs in darkness. Then they spent a while finding the bowls to plate it, and after all that they had to comfort Whitney for a while before she'd leave the kitchen. And, after *that*, they had to move at a snail's pace bringing it to us because the place was so dark.

Of course it was going to be cold. In fact, if we got any even remotely warm food that evening it was going to be a miracle.

"You were right, Brad," said Kurt. "The spirits messed with the food and chilled it."

"I knew it. The only reason the spirits let us have this soup is because they'd ruined it."

"Oh man, these guys are smart."

The SED had offered nothing this time, other than meaningless bleeps and blips, which was fine. I couldn't believe the luck we'd had with it in such a short space of time, so if that was all it contributed to this episode, I'd be happy.

We sat, listening to mush and smelling cold onion soup for about ten minutes before Cory came to take our dishes away, which he expected to be empty. We saw him leave the kitchen, and the SED let out the word 'two' before reverting to meaningless noise again.

"What do you think they're saying?" asked Kurt. "Two? Two what?"

Of course, it could have been 'to' or 'too' as well, but that wouldn't have been nearly as interesting an interpretation.

"Well," said Brad, his forehead furrowed in concentration, "it's not the number of people coming to get the food because this time it's just Cory. Maybe it's the number of ghosts that are in here with us?"

"No way, dude," replied Kurt. "I feel *way* more than two. I don't know for sure, but the number eleven keeps popping into my head, so I think that's how many we're facing right now."

"Woah, dude. Are you sure? Eleven? That's a lot of spirits to have around us at once."

Kurt closed his eyes, and whispered his reply. "I can feel them, man."

"Well, what can 'two' mean, then? I mean, they have no idea that we're listening in, so they're speaking freely, so this must be relevant to something. We need to find out what, guys. This could be important."

Cory carefully made his way into the dining room, stepping almost comedically over the cables across the doorway and asked us how the food was.

"Cold, dude," replied Brad.

"No way! It was hot when we plated it. I think."

Kurt gave a little chuckle. "Yeah, but the spirits are messing with us, man. They chilled it, and allowed you guys to serve it to our table."

"Wow, that *is* amazing," said Cory as he picked up the bowls and plates, "so they turned it into Gazpacho?"

"Worse," said Brad extremely seriously. "They turned it into cold soup."

I couldn't help myself. "So, Cory; Kurt and Brad just heard the spirits say the number two. Does that mean anything to you? Is it significant in any way?"

Cory screwed up his face and thought for a few moments. "Two... two... No, not really. I mean, there's three of you, and three of us, and—"

Brad suddenly blurted out, "not downstairs there isn't! You've been separated, and now there's only two of you downstairs. *Two*!"

"Oh, fuck!" gasped Kurt.

"Wha... what d'you mean?"

"Dude! The spirits have done it again! *Man*, these guys are smart. They've divided and conquered, and now there's only two of you down there in the kitchen where the cook was murdered. I guess she's about to get her revenge."

"She's *what*?! Oh, holy crap!"

Cory turned with his armful of plates, and moved as fast as he could out of the room to try and get back to his comrades. Of course, his panic meant that he'd completely forgotten about the cables across the doorway and therefore went tumbling into the hall, smashing all of his bowls and plates as he fell, coating the stone floor with soup.

He scrambled his way back to his feet, and lurched towards the narrow stone staircase that was also covered in the soup that Whitney had dropped. Five steps from the bottom, he slipped and bounced his way to the hard floor beneath him. We watched in amazement on the monitor as Cory rolled around in pain for about thirty seconds, and then hauled himself to his feet and limped back into the kitchen.

"I think I understand now," said Kurt. "'Two' means they were gonna trip Cory over twice on his way back to the kitchen."

"I was thinking differently, dude," replied Brad. "Remember who tripped coming into this room with the Chinese food?"

"Cory," breathed Kurt.

"Exactly. Two. They tripped him in the same place two times."

"And," I added, "there are two of them left stranded downstairs. Cory goes to try and rescue them, and what happens to him?"

"They tripped him," declared Kurt.

"Exactly," said Brad. "There can be no other explanation. The spirits are messing with us, and giving us riddles to solve. We need to pay close attention to the SED for more of their pranks. 'Two' equalled two of them in the kitchen, two times that Cory tripped in the same place, and two times that he was knocked over in that one trip."

"And," added Kurt thoughtfully, "we only got two portions of food."

"Oh, *dude*! I hadn't thought of that!"

"They've really been playing us, man. We need to put a stop to this, right now. We need to help these lost souls."

Brad looked thoughtful for a few moments, and then looked at the camera I was pointing at him. "You're right, dude. This needs to stop. Now."

VII

For once, Brad and Kurt were right, and it did stop.

What would never be known to viewers at home was the reason it stopped: Whitney was on the verge of a nervous breakdown, and Cory was in a huge amount of pain that, we discovered later, was because he'd fractured his forearm when he fell down the stairs. Mike was now convinced that the ghosts had been picking them off one by one and, him being the only one of them left, meant he was next. It was Mike that brought the being-served-by-waiters-in-the-dark idea to a crashing halt.

Brad, Kurt, and I were sitting in the dining room, staring intently at the monitors. We'd watched Cory stagger into the kitchen and sit down on a chair. Mike had been comforting an utterly terrified Whitney when he noticed Cory. They had a conversation that we wouldn't be able to hear until we were back in the truck and listened to their feeds that they didn't know about, and then suddenly Mike completely freaked out and ran screaming from the kitchen. He lurched up the stairs at great speed in the dark, his night vision once again ruined, and slipped on the soup that Whitney had dropped. He crashed forward face-first onto the stairs, and slid down a few steps before scrabbling his way back to his feet and continuing his screaming journey of terror.

Kurt breathed, "dude, what the fuck?"

"I think he's been possessed," whispered Brad.

We watched as poor Mike made it to the top of the staircase and ran across the hall, straight onto a puddle of soup that Cory had left behind. His feet flew forwards from under him, and he hit the stone floor hard on his back, his head bouncing off it as he landed.

"Ow," said Brad, unhelpfully.

Mike lay still for a few seconds, and I started to get worried, but then he slowly crawled back to his feet and limped his way to the front door, which was locked. He hammered on it and screamed for someone to let him out.

"Oh, man," said Kurt. "That guy is definitely possessed."

"No other explanation, dude."

I watched the monitor as Mike banged away helplessly on the thick wooden front door, and I didn't need to hear a mic feed to listen to him. His terrified yells were filling the dining room.

"Let me *out*! For god's sake, someone open this door! *HELP!*"

When, after about thirty seconds, he hadn't calmed down, I knew I needed to take action. I reached into my bag for the yellow walkie-talkie and contacted Duff.

"Send Barbara to unlock the door," I told him. "The three wait staff are coming out, and two of them probably will need some help."

"And the third?" asked Duff excitedly, clearly wondering if we'd finally had a fatality at the hands of the spirits. Bearing in mind what happened with the stone stairs, he wasn't that far off the mark.

"Oh, he's waiting right by the door. You won't be able to miss him."

"Copy. Do you guys need an exfil?"

I wished. "No, we're going to do some more investigating, but you can cancel the rest of the food orders."

"Copy that. The staff will be evacuated sixty seconds from now."

"Thanks Duff. Oh, and watch out for the soup on the floor and the stairs."

His reply was a little out of breath and I could tell that he was sprinting towards the front door, in true Special Forces style. "Soup, over?"

"Yeah, soup over everything. The stone floor will be slippery, so just be careful, okay?"

"Roger that."

Duff arrived exactly sixty seconds later, as promised, and he unlocked the door. For whatever reason, he'd failed to hear Mike's screaming and, the moment Duff pushed the door open a fraction, Mike yanked it back and stormed his way to freedom. Unfortunately for Mike, Duff's training took over and, after a swift punch to the face, the waiter was wrestled to the ground and swiftly trussed up with Plasticuffs. Fearless as ever, Duff then braved the soup-covered floor and extracted Cory and Whitney, leading them sobbing from the executive mansion, past the writhing and screaming body of Mike.

I was watching all of this commotion on the monitor open-mouthed, and I was sad that it would never get to see the light of day, because it was pure gold. Duff locked the door, leading the injured and terrified back to the parking lot, and I turned my thoughts to how we were going to get enough footage to fill this episode. Our main hook had now left.

"That was gnarly, dude," said Kurt. "Poor guy. I can't believe he got possessed!"

"It's a shame Todd wasn't able to help him, like he did you."

"He couldn't interfere, man. Science, remember?"

"Yeah, dude, you're right. It just hurts me, y'know?"

"I know man. I know."

I piped up, an idea occurring to me. "Hey guys, hand me the flashlight. I need to go and check something out."

"Okay, dude," said Brad, "we'll keep our ears peeled with the SED and let you know if the spirits are about to try anything."

Inwardly, I groaned. "Thanks, guys."

I shone my powerful flashlight beam around me in the hallway, and carefully avoided the soup. I navigated my way down into the kitchen, grabbed some paper towels, and mopped up the soup from the stairs. Then I started poking around in the wooden cabinets in the kitchen, of which there were many. None of the literature had mentioned what I was looking for, but bearing in mind the time period when the mansion was built, I was really hoping there would be one.

Drawers were of no interest to me, so I continued opening the larger of the cupboards when a crackle came through my radio. It was Brad.

"The spirits just said 'now'."

I grabbed it from my belt and replied. "When did they say that?"

"About two minutes ago. We thought you should know."

I couldn't shake my head at their stupidity because they were watching me, so I replied as calmly as I could. "Thanks guys."

"We've got your back, bro."

A few cupboard doors later, and I found it. I wanted to do a little dance, but kept my cool. After turning off all of the kitchen lights, I headed back up the stairs and found an almost hidden door in the wall in the hallway. It hadn't been opened for a long time and was a little stiff, but the hinges quickly remembered what their job was and it swung open revealing the other part of what I needed. I was now sure we could finish this episode.

I made my way back to the dining room, turned off my flashlight, and sat down to allow my night vision to kick back in. They were both looking at me expectantly.

"I've found a dumb waiter," I said.

There was a pause, and then Brad said, "I thought they all just left."

I rolled my eyes. "No, dude, a dumb waiter. You know, the little elevator thing that really old houses had when the kitchen was on a different floor to the dining room? It's operated manually by rope and pulleys."

"Oh wow! Why weren't we using that to serve our food?"

This was one of the few logical questions I'd ever heard Brad ask. And, of course, the answer that I wasn't going to tell him was that it wouldn't have made for good TV. Soup delivery, in the dark, up and down a dangerous stone staircase did.

"None of the experts seemed to know about it," I said.

"Perhaps it's broken," said Kurt.

"Let's find out," I urged.

"What's the point?"

"Well, think about it. All inhabitants of this house have complained of their food arriving cold. The logical way, as Brad said, to bring food up from the kitchen is—"

"Is with the elevator," Brad finished for me, slightly incredulous. A light bulb was about to go off in his head.

"Right," I said, "which means—"

"Oh my *god*! Which means that there must be a spirit that is trapped *inside the elevator thing*!"

"The dumb waiter."

"Probably."

It was time to get the NV camera rolling again. A seed had been sown in Scrappy's head, and it was about to play out.

"Guys," said Brad urgently as the camera rolled, "follow me. I've got an idea!"

A little under ten minutes later, Kurt was scrambling his way into the small dumb waiter, and Brad was waiting nearby with a bowl of very hot water.

"Oh man," said Kurt excitedly. "This is gonna be awesome!"

"Okay, guys," whispered a green-colored Brad into the camera lens, "here's the plan. Kurt here is going to make some journeys up and down from the hall to the kitchen with this bowl of hot water, and we're going to see how long the bowl of water takes to cool down. If it happens too quickly, then we'll know there's a lost soul trapped inside the elevator deliberately cooling any food or drink inside, with the hope of causing the wait staff to be murdered. Because we do things scientifically, we've set up what's known as a control experiment in the kitchen, which is another bowl of hot water, and we'll compare the temperatures as the experiment goes on to know whether the water in the elevator is cooling faster." He looked at Kurt. "You ready, dude?"

"Oh yeah, man. Let's do this!"

"Okay, dip your finger in the water."

"But it's hot, dude. We know it's hot. It's just been boiled."

"But the guys at home need to make sure it's still hot. And we do, too. What if we'd accidentally picked up the wrong bowl, or something?"

Kurt thought about this. "Yeah, I guess you're right dude."

He looked at the camera and then stuck his finger into the steaming bowl of water before pulling it out again quickly. "Aggh! Fuck! Shit! That is fucking hot! Owwww!"

"Okay, good," said Brad to the camera. "We're all set."

As usual, I'd fitted the dumb waiter with an NV camera and audio recording device. And, as usual, I'd had a helping hand in the proceedings; the 'control' water in the kitchen was considerably hotter than the water that Kurt had. It was also a slightly bigger bowl with more water in it, so it would cool slower as well.

Brad closed the door, and Kurt was now locked inside the dumb waiter. Scrappy then gave the rope an almighty heave, and Scooby went lurching upwards towards the hallway. The sudden movement caused some of his bowl of water to spill, which landed on Kurt and we heard an assortment of muffled swear words through the wall.

A few more tugs on the rope and Kurt was at hallway level. I hit the walkie talkie button. "Kurt, how is everything?"

"Other than the third degree burns, man, great."

"You got burnt?"

"Yeah, I got fucking burnt! Every time you pull that rope, the water spills, dude! And it's hot!"

"Okay, I'll tell Brad to be more careful on the way down."

"Good."

"How's the water temperature?"

There was a pause and then a shriek of pain. "Still hot, dude."

"Okay, let us know when you're ready to come back down."

I'd insisted on not allowing Scooby out of the dumb waiter, and instead have us send him up and down in the tiny, pitch black space for as long as he could stand it. I didn't bother to remind Brad to take it easy on the rope, and Kurt's downward journey was almost free fall. He screamed as he felt himself plummet in the darkness, and then let out a yelp of pain as Brad yanked him to a stop near the bottom. More hot water had splashed everywhere.

A muffled shout came from behind the door. "Dude! Fuck, dude! Take it easy, man!"

"What did he say?" asked Brad.

"He wants you to go a bit easier on the rope. Apparently all the jerking about is spilling the water on him."

"Oh! Sorry, dude! I'll pull more gently from now on."

"Good," was the muffled response.

Scrappy then remembered what the scientific experiment was all about. "Is the water still hot, dude?"

"Of course it's still hot, bro!"

"Have you tested it?"

"You just spilled most of it over me, man! Trust me, it's still hot!"

Brad thought for a moment. "Perhaps it's been chilled while we've been talking. You'd better test it again. Science, remember?"

A muffled yelp was clearly audible. "Still hot, dude."

Scrappy turned to me. "I wonder why the spirit hasn't chilled the water yet?"

I shrugged my shoulders. "Maybe it knows we're doing an experiment and Kurt isn't actually delivering the water to anybody?"

Brad snapped his fingers. "Of *course*! That makes total sense!" He turned to the wooden door. "Kurt! Change of plan, dude."

"What?"

"I said, 'change of plan'."

"Dude! I heard what you said! What's the change of plan?"

"Oh! Sorry, bro. Anyway, I've just realized that the spirit isn't doing anything because it knows you're doing a test and not trying to deliver that bowl to anybody. Todd's gonna go and wait upstairs in the dining room for his 'soup', while he listens to the SED. Then I'll send you up, come and get you out, and you can take it to him. I think that will make the spirit interested."

"Okay, man. Sounds good."

I headed up the stairs and sat at the dining table, where I radioed Brad. "All set."

"Okay, dude, let's bait this spirit!"

I could only assume that one of the things Brad believed about spirits is that they're all deaf, because he usually announced his grand plan very loudly before embarking upon it.

I watched on the monitor as Brad gripped the rope and, slowly this time, began to pull. I got on the radio to Kurt. "Is that better, dude?"

"Yeah, man. Awesome. Nice and steady this time. No spills."

Brad pulled a few times, and then his actions changed slightly. He was still sort of pulling, but in shorter tugs. Eventually he stopped, and my radio crackled.

"It's stuck, dude."

"The dumb waiter?"

"No, man, the elevator."

"How the hell did it get stuck?" asked Kurt, butting in.

"I dunno, dude, but it's stuck."

"Well," said Kurt, slightly alarmed, "get it unstuck, bro!"

I left the dining room and headed back down to Brad and, when I got there, he was yanking furiously at the rope. I hadn't anticipated this wonderful turn of events, but I suspected that the ancient and unused pulley had seized up through lack of use and, most importantly, lack of oil for decades.

Brad got on the radio to Kurt. "I think the spirit has jammed the elevator."

"*What?* Why?"

"Not sure, dude. Is the water any colder?"

There was a pause while Kurt dipped his finger in it before getting back on the radio. "Oh my *god* dude! It *is*! It's still warm, but I can leave my finger in it. It's like bath water now."

"Hold on," said Brad, dashing over to the control. He dipped his finger in and let out a strangled scream. "Aggh! Dude! The control is still super hot!"

He relayed this information to Kurt, who then freaked out. "Oh shit, man! The spirit's in here with me! I can feel it! Guys, get me *out* of here!"

"Talk to it. Find out what it wants."

"It's pissed, dude. I can feel it. Errr, spirit? What... errr... why are you doing this?"

We all waited in silence. I didn't use my spirit voice gizmo this time because I didn't want to overdo it for the people at home. If the spirits became too chatty, people would figure out what was going on. I was hoping that the SED would have picked something up that I could use in the final edit. If it hadn't, then Scrappy was sure to declare that the spirit was being silently malevolent; it worked either way.

Kurt tried again. "Uhh, spirit? I'm not really a waiter. I'm just here to help you, so you can release the elevator now, okay? We're not here to hurt you."

Brad hit the radio. "Good, dude, good! Keep trying to communicate with it!"

Scrappy gave one final yank of the rope, and nothing happened, so he let go of it. "Todd, what are we gonna do, man?"

There was an ominous creak from somewhere behind the wooden door.

"What was that?" I asked.

The radio crackled. "Guys, did you hear that? Was that you?"

Brad thrust his walkie-talkie to his mouth. "No, dude. Not us. Any word from the spirit?"

There was another, longer and drawn-out groan from something behind the wall, and Kurt let the noise subside before answering a little shakily. "Errr, not that I'm aware of, man. I've asked them some questions ab…*aaaaaaahhhhhhhhhhhhhhhhhhhh!*"

The next sound we heard was the dumb waiter crashing to the floor of the elevator shaft.

VIII

Dust blasted from around the edges of the wooden panel that concealed the dumb waiter, and the noise of splintering, smashing wood echoed in a muffled fashion all around us.

Both Brad and I staggered backwards, partly from the shock and partly from the rush of air that assaulted us that, you have to remember, was all happening in the dark.

"What the hell, dude?" gasped Brad. "What was that? A spirit rushing us maybe?"

"Brad! Just shut the fuck up for a minute," I hissed as I scrambled around on the floor for the walkie-talkie that I'd dropped.

"But, dude, it could have been—"

"I said, shut *up*. Help me find my radio. No, better yet, give me yours."

Brad did so, and I hit the button. "Kurt! Kurt! Can you hear me?"

I heard nothing in reply, and there was no sound of movement from behind the wooden panelling. I was getting worried, but Brad hadn't seemed to make the connection between the noise we'd just heard and what had actually happened.

"Brad," I yelled, "the door. Open it."

"Got it, dude," he said and headed towards the stairs.

"Where are you going?"

"To open the front door."

"No, for Christ's sake, the door to the dumb waiter! Open it!"

"The what?"

I rolled my eyes in the darkness. "The elevator, Brad. Open the door. *Now!*"

"Oh! Oh, yeah! Sure thing."

He grabbed the hidden recess behind the panel and gave a tug. "It's stuck, dude."

"Pull harder."

He gave it another heave. "It's still stuck."

I got back on the radio. "Kurt! Kurt! Speak to me, man."

Nothing.

"Brad, we have to get that door open."

"Do you think he's been possessed again?"

Exasperated, I shoved Brad out of the way and began wrenching at the wooden door. It seemed that the hinges had become a little deranged during the impact of the fall and were no longer true, so the door didn't want to open easily. I yanked on the door as hard as I could, and eventually it began to move. A few seconds later and the door was open, revealing a whole lot of dust, a mangled and broken elevator, and Kurt lying in the middle of the wreckage.

I stuck my head inside. "Kurt! Dude! Can you hear me?"

There was a cough and some of the broken wood began to move.

Brad stuck his head in the opening too. "Woah, dude! What happened?"

"The cable must have snapped. Help me get this crap off him."

The pair of us carefully moved old planks of wood off Kurt, who was beginning to stir. He blinked a few times and rubbed some dust out of his eyes. "Fuck."

"Thank god you're okay, dude," I said, utterly relieved. Having, once again, been the architect of this little scheme, I could never have lived with myself if something had happened to Scooby.

"Did you feel any spirits in there, man?" asked Brad with spectacularly terrible timing.

"Spirits...? Dude, I just fell down a fucking elevator shaft."

"Oh yeah, sorry bro. Are you okay?"

"No. Every bit of me hurts."

We slowly helped him out of the pile of debris, and he stood in the kitchen coughing for a while. I looked inside again and saw what had caused the failure of the elevator: the pulley had been ripped from the wooden mounting at the top of the shaft. Either the wood had been rotten, or Kurt was heavier than the elevator was intended to cope with. I showed Brad.

"Oh, dude. The spirits must have been working on loosening that the whole time Kurt was going up and down. And we thought they weren't bothering with us. Man, they're smart."

I reached in and pulled the bowl out of the wreckage. Amazingly, not only was it still in one piece, but it still had a small amount of water in it.

Brad stuck his finger in. "*Guys*! It's stone cold! Oh my god! Let me check the control."

He crashed his way over to the bowl of water on the side and stuck his finger in. "Still warm guys. It's still warm!" He looked right into one of the static-mounted NV cameras. "Evidence. Right there. Not only did the spirits try and kill Kurt by loosening the pulley, but they also took the time to cool the water in his bowl, just to show us how powerful the paranormal can be. *Man*, that was close."

"Tell me about it," spluttered Kurt with a wince.

Of course, another reason there was a difference in water temperature was because there was virtually nothing left in Kurt's bowl, so it had cooled quicker than the control, which had been hotter to begin with.

"Okay," said Brad, turning back to us, "what are we investigating next?"

"Dude," gasped Kurt, "I'm in pain, man. I think I need to see a doctor."

"Are you sure it's not just the spirits making you think that you're in pain?"

I butted in. "He just fell about fifteen feet in a wooden box. I'm pretty sure that's gotta hurt."

"Yeah, good point, dude. Okay, record this."

I switched on my portable NV camera, and pointed it at Brad. "Okay, go."

"Well, guys, this is a first for us. We have no choice but to end our lock-in early. This has never happened before, but all this crazy paranormal activity has injured Kurt, and we need to get him checked out to make sure he's okay." He gave a sigh, which led to a dramatic pause. "These are the risks we take investigating this stuff for you. But, dangerous as it is, it's worth it to uncover the truth about the other world, and we do this in the name of *real* science. Okay guys, this is Brad, Kurt, and Todd signing off." Another dramatic pause. "Let's just hope the spirits allow us out of here in one piece."

Kurt, who was limping quite badly, was helped up the stairs by Brad, while I gathered up all of our cameras and recorders. I'd given Duff the heads-up, and he was waiting at the front door; his military background came in handy, thanks to part of his training being paramedic skills. He gave Kurt the once-over, establishing that there was nothing seriously wrong; just soreness and bruising.

"You'll be fine. A little sore tomorrow, but nothing's broken."

"I'm sore right now."

"Well, expect it to be worse tomorrow. How the hell did you fall down an elevator shaft?"

Brad interrupted. "The spirits, man! They loosened the pulley mounting that was holding the cable while Kurt was inside the elevator!"

"This house has an elevator?"

"It's one of those little ones for moving food between floors."

"Ah. Why was Kurt in it?"

"Science, dude."

I left the three of them to it and finished loading the rest of the kit from the dining room into my backpack before joining them outside in the SUV.

"Aww, man," said Brad. "We didn't get to review any of the recordings we made. Wanna do it when we get back to the hotel?"

It was well past one a.m., and I felt exhausted. "Let's take a look tomorrow morning. I think we could all do with some rest."

Brad reluctantly agreed thanks to some soft moaning from Kurt and, the next morning, we reconvened in my room to review what had been recorded. Scooby was very stiff and every time he moved he let out a yelp of pain.

The green, grainy footage of increasingly terrified wait staff slipping and tumbling had come out really well, and even the random noises emitted from the SED were remarkably close to what Scooby and Scrappy had declared them to be. The conversations recorded in the kitchen between the three waiters also provided some interesting soundbites; initially, they were full of bravado about not caring they were surrounded by spirits, and they then went through the full spectrum of emotions to the point of nervous breakdown at the end.

While Scooby had been locked in the elevator, the SED had been recording, but it was tricky to match up exactly what sound came when because there's no timestamp on the audio. However, it did make some sounds, and I was more than happy to fudge the timeline a little bit for dramatic effect.

"There, dude!" Blurted Brad. "Did you guys hear that?"

Kurt and I shook our heads, and so I rewound it and played it again.

"I couldn't quite make it out," said Kurt.

"It said 'wheel', dude!"

"So?"

"What does a pulley consist of? A *wheel*!"

71

"Oh, fuck!" gasped Kurt. "They were discussing how best to make me fall!"

"Absolutely dude. There's no other explanation!"

This was a bit of a stretch, even for our viewers, but it would do. Later in the recording, roughly around the time that Kurt had his fall, there was another burst of noise from the device, and this was more of a hiss. I played it over and over for Scooby and Scrappy, until Brad declared he knew what the word was.

"The spirit said 'die', dude!"

"When was that said?" asked Kurt, turning to me.

I had absolutely no idea. "Approximately just before you fell."

Brad lurched from his chair and paced anxiously around the room. "Oh, man. Oh, *man!* That was so close, dude."

"It was closer than close," whispered Kurt. "They dropped me down an elevator shaft, man! These crazy spirits didn't just want to mess with my head, they wanted to fucking *kill* me, dude! *Physically* kill me."

"We could always go back for another lock-in tonight?" suggested Scrappy hopefully.

"No way, dude. No fucking way. I am never going back to that place ever again."

This was helpful for me, because it saved me having to explain to Brad that our producer had received a call from the manager of the trust that owns the property. Apparently the call was short and unpleasant, and could we please never go within a hundred feet of the place ever again or they'd have us arrested. The dumb waiter had been the oldest known device in North America, and we'd destroyed it; to say we were unpopular was an understatement.

"Kurt's right," I said. "We proved what we came to prove."

Brad nodded and looked at me. "Yeah, you're right. We conclusively proved that there are a bunch of angry lost souls roaming around in that place, just like the myths said. Our work here is done."

"I wonder how they knew?" said Kurt quietly to nobody, a thousand-yard stare in his eyes.

"Knew what, bro?"

"Knew to choose me. Knew that I was the weak one. Easy to possess. The last place proved that. But how did these guys know to pick on me?"

Brad paced some more. "They can't have known, dude. They must have just got lucky."

Kurt shook his head slowly and looked down, wincing as he did so. "No, man. The moment we started moving around that place, I could feel them all swirling around me. I didn't think much of it at the time, but now I'm convinced that they knew I was the one. I was the one they could get to. They came after me."

Despite my knowledge that this was utter nonsense, it was clear to me that Kurt believed this deeply and was shaken by it. "Kurt, man, it was just bad luck. You were locked into the wrong dumb waiter at the wrong time. That's all."

Kurt got slowly to his feet and hobbled toward the hotel room door. "I need to get some more rest," he said vacantly. "I feel drained."

"Are you sure you're okay?" I asked his retreating figure.

At the door, he opened it and paused. He half-turned his head and looked down at the floor over his right shoulder. "You guys need to prepare yourselves for the reality of what's going on. I'm not going to make it out of one of our lock-ins alive, and that moment isn't far away. I just know it."

And with that, he shuffled into the corridor and let the door close behind him.

There was a pause, and neither Brad or I said anything for nearly a minute. Part of me was hoping that Kurt was going to burst back through the door and tell us that he was just kidding, but he didn't.

Finally, Brad spoke. "Fuck, bro. Kurt's being targeted by the spirits. He is, like, totally freaked out."

This reminded me of something. "Speaking of freaking out, I wonder what it was that spooked Mike so much that he went nuts and tried to escape?"

"Oh yeah, dude! I'd forgotten about that. Can you pull up the audio in the kitchen?"

I switched files and started playing the relevant mic feed back to us. I whizzed through a couple of hours of idle chatter and silence. And then, finally, I reached the point where Whitney could clearly be heard, sobbing hysterically with Mike trying to comfort her. Suddenly, in the background, there's a thumping sound accompanied with some yelps; this was Cory falling down the stairs. Mike suddenly shushes Whitney to silence.

"What was that?" he said, clearly scared.

Whitney gave a huge sniff. "What was what?"

"Shhhhhh! Just listen."

There was silence and heavy breathing for about twenty more seconds, and then Mike speaks again. "Cory! Are you okay?"

I remembered from the footage that Cory walked over and spoke to Mike. He sounded shaken beyond belief and was out of breath from the fall. "The ghosts. They spoke to me."

This was when we'd seen Mike become visibly agitated at what Cory was saying but, at the time, we didn't have the audio feed.

"Spoke to you?" gasped Mike. "What did they say?"

Cory gulped down some air. "After I fell, I went into an almost trance-like state, and I think part of my soul was up there with the spirits. Perhaps they thought they'd achieved the first one and they were speaking too freely."

I could only assume that Cory's trance-like state was mild concussion from his fall, and his hearing and thought processes had probably been all out of whack for a little while, just like when you hit your head hard.

"First one?" asked Mike, terror evident in his voice. "First one of what? And what did they say?"

There was a slightly crackly pause in the audio, and then Cory continued. "They said 'two to die'. I think they thought they'd managed to kill me. I was supposed to be the first to die, and they were preparing to move on to their next victim."

Two was the last word we'd spoken to Cory, and so this had clearly been ricocheting around his brain in various forms: two and to. His fear and imagination had provided the final word: die.

The audio then allowed us to hear a terrified scream, and things being knocked over as Mike made his failed break for freedom. I stopped the audio playback.

Brad looked at me. "Fuck, dude. They wanted to kill Cory *and* Kurt tonight."

Tonight's episode was going to turn out far better than I'd been expecting.

IX

"Do you think it'll happen, bro?" Brad asked me as we sat at the bar in our hotel, waiting for Kurt.

"What," I replied after swallowing my sip of Grey Goose and tonic, "you mean will he actually show up for dinner, or will he die during a lock-in?"

It was the evening of the same day of Kurt's epic prediction of his own death, and we'd all spent the day doing our own thing which, for me at least, involved going through as much of the footage as I could and jotting down time codes of the parts I wanted to use for the final edit of the episode. We were flying back to LA the next day, so I didn't have to borrow an editing suite this time; I'd simply wait until we were home to work my magic.

Brad had missed my dark humor entirely. "Die during a lock-in, dude. We've come pretty close the last few times. We need to figure out how to improve our safety precautions."

As far as I could tell, we didn't have any safety precautions to improve. "What do you have in mind?"

He paused for thought, and the lady behind the bar delivered him another Bud Light. "I dunno, man. Perhaps have Duff in there with us. He's really keen on that."

"I know."

"Yeah, well maybe he could help us out?"

I looked at Brad and tried to appear like I was thinking deeply. "How, though, dude? If Duff had been with us last night, the elevator would still have fallen."

"Not if he'd been monitoring the pulley at the top of the shaft."

"Listen, man, the only reason we know we should have been keeping an eye on the pulley is because we now know that it had a catastrophic failure. Up to that point, if you'd asked me how the spirits would drop the dumb waiter, I'd have said they'll cut the rope."

"Kurt isn't a waiter, bro."

"Drop the elevator."

"Oh! You think they were going to cut the rope as well?"

Thankfully, at that moment, Kurt appeared next to us. "Hey guys."

"Dude! How're you feeling, man?"

"I hurt, bro. And half of my body is, like, black and blue."

He rolled up his sleeve and showed us a bruise the size of a grapefruit on his upper forearm.

"Ouch," said Brad unhelpfully, and looked at me. "Was the footage we got worth it?"

I nodded, and swallowed a mouthful of drink. "It was, guys. The recordings definitely back up your theories, no doubt about it."

Of course, what I wanted to say was watching a bunch of idiots stumbling around in the dark and falling down elevator shafts was going to make for an absolutely hilariously entertaining episode, but I didn't.

We were shown to our table, which took Kurt a while to hobble to, and Brad continued. "See, man? It might be dangerous, but we *have* to do this. The people have a right to know about the paranormal activities that go on around us *every day*."

Kurt seemed to be in a less sombre mood than that morning. "Yeah, I know dude. The results we get are amazing. I'm not gonna quit, bro, I just have to accept the truth of what's gonna happen. And I have."

"Todd's gonna improve our safety precautions, don't worry man."

Kurt shook his head. "No way, dude. We've been as successful as we have because the spirits feel safe interacting with us. If we have Duff letting rip with an AK every two seconds, they're gonna get scared and we won't get the evidence we need."

Brad's eyes widened slightly, and he looked from Kurt to me and then back again. "Are you sure, man? They tried to *kill* you, dude!"

Kurt stared directly at Brad. "It's a risk I'm willing to take. Every trap needs bait, and I'm prepared to be it. This is for science, remember?"

Brad let out a long breath of air and then raised his glass of beer, wiggling it in Kurt's direction. Kurt, because nobody had bothered to order him anything, raised an empty water glass and chinked it against Brad's beer.

"I think," said Brad incredulously, "that you are the bravest person I've ever met. You have my total respect, dude, and I thank you."

I chinked my glass against theirs. "To science," I managed to somehow say without falling off my chair laughing.

Once we'd all ordered, and the wine was flowing, Kurt brought the conversation back to a subject he'd touched on earlier. "I'm telling you guys, these spirits communicate with each other somehow. They knew, just *knew* to pick on me. How?"

"I think it was a coincidence, bro."

"Perhaps they use gmail," I said with a chuckle. "Ghost mail."

Kurt shot a look at me. "I'm serious, dude. Those crazy spirits targeted me."

Brad suddenly had an epiphany. "Maybe Kurt's right! Maybe they do have some way of passing messages to each other. I think we should make this a focal point of our next investigation."

This was going to be interesting. "What do you have in mind?"

"I'm not sure yet, but I'll think of something."

I had a funny feeling that this would result in the use of some half-baked piece of hobbyist technology, and I couldn't wait to find out what. Whenever Scrappy had a new invention, it always made for good TV, just as the SED had proved the night before, and I just knew that whatever ghost-busting device he uncovered wouldn't disappoint.

"It should involve multiple locations," said Kurt thoughtfully.

"We can't split up, man."

"No, no. I was thinking of using two teams. We'd be at the primary location, and use a secondary team somewhere else. Somewhere far away."

"Like the next state, you mean?"

"No, dude. Another *country*."

Kurt said the word 'country' like he was suggesting we go to another planet. This was going to be a logistical nightmare for the person organizing this, which of course was going to be me, but it would certainly be a first. After the mind-blowing success of the first season of our show, a rival TV network recently started with its own version called *Ghoulish Vacations* and was, quite frankly, crap. Their team of three morons focused on hotels and hostels that were allegedly haunted, but what they were missing was an equivalent of me; someone who knew it was all nonsense and actively cheated to get some ghostly action. I'd always assumed that it was glaringly obvious to everyone other than Scooby and Scrappy that there was some funny business going on, but this seemed not to be the case; people really believed that we were recording ghosts.

Of course, Brad's take on why *Ghoulish Vacations* very rarely even got a creaky floorboard, let alone a spirit 'talking' to them, was because they didn't have the psychic prowess that he and Kurt had, and also the *GV* crew didn't have gadgets as awesome as ours.

Poor as the show was, it was still competition, which meant I always had to be on top of my game, and doing two simultaneous lock-ins in two separate countries would certainly set our show even further apart from *GV*.

"I like it," declared Brad in a voice that suggested this idea would shortly become his.

I thought about possible venues for this, and then a thought struck me. "Churches!" I blurted. "Let's find the oldest haunted church in America, and we'll have our lock-in there. The second team can be somewhere in Europe. Their churches are centuries old."

"How about Spain?" suggested Kurt, surprisingly intelligently. "Remember the Spanish Inquisition? Think of the spirit activity in the churches there."

"I saw that on Monty Python," said Brad. "I didn't get it."

"Thousands of people were murdered in the name of religion. I read a book about it. It was a crazy time. If you weren't what the Catholic Monarchs considered a devout Catholic, you'd end up in front of the Spanish Inquisition."

I was genuinely impressed; I had no idea that Kurt had any interest in history, other than what he'd been doing the day before. Mind you, I could hardly consider myself any sort of historical expert, and I didn't know that much about the Spanish Inquisition. "And then what happened?"

"Oh, dude. That was a place you didn't want to end up. There were all manner of things they called heresy that they'd look for: Witchcraft, Blasphemy, Bigamy, and Sodomy."

Brad spat his mouthful of wine across the table as he chuckled to himself.

Kurt continued undeterred. "And that was amongst any manner of other 'crimes' you could be randomly accused of. But, once they got their hands on you, whether their accusations were true or not, you'd end up in front of the Inquisition."

Brad had suddenly become serious again. "How did they find their victims?"

Kurt took a sip of wine, clearly troubled by his knowledge of this. "The Inquisition would travel from city to city, staying for three to four weeks. During this time, the city folk were encouraged to come forth and repent their sins."

Brad's eyes went wide. "That sounds like a stupid thing to do."

"Yeah," continued Kurt, "it was, but lots of people did it because their fear of being involuntarily discovered made them. And that was far worse. If you came forward under your own steam, you had a good chance of the church reconciling with you, on the condition that you denounced others in your city."

"Oh, dude, that is gnarly. But how did these people know if other people in their town were witches or whatever?"

Kurt looked at Brad and screwed his face up slightly. "They made it up, bro. They got off the hook by accusing some other dude of something they most likely hadn't done."

"*Super* gnarly."

"And so," I asked, "when the accused finally got in front of the Inquisition. Then what?"

Kurt took a deep breath. "Well, typically, you were detained for about two years. Then they'd try to get the facts for the upcoming trial by torturing you."

"Woah," blurted Brad. "Tortured? How?"

"Well, bro, they liked to hang people from the ceiling by their wrists."

Brad put his hands above his head, his wrists together. "Dangling, like this? Doesn't sound too bad."

"No, dude. Put your wrists behind your back."

Brad did so.

"Now imagine being suspended from the ceiling by your wrists."

I felt physically sick at the thought, and Brad went pale.

"Yeah," said Kurt looking at us both. "Exactly. Guess what else they used to like doing?"

Brad and I shrugged, still shaken at the thought of the brutality of this time period.

"Water boarding."

Brad looked shocked. "I thought George Bush invented that."

"No dude. It has an old Spanish name that I'm probably going to pronounce wrong: *interrogatorio mejorado del agua*. And this was in the fourteen hundreds, bro! George Bush just took credit for it."

I needed to get off the subject of torture. I said, "okay, and after they'd got their 'information', what then?"

"Then they'd have the trial. At that point, you're pretty much fucked, dude. You might be penanced, which meant you'd end up on a huge galleon boat rowing an oar until one day you died of exhaustion. If you were reconciled, you'd probably be flogged, thrown in jail for the rest of your life, and have all of your property taken away."

"Fucking hell, dude," breathed Brad. "those options don't sound great to me."

"There was one more," said Kurt solemnly. "*Relaxation.*"

Brad let out a sigh of relief. "Well, bro, that sounds more like it. That's the option I'd take. You made it sound like these Spanish dudes were, like, barbarians or something."

Kurt looked at Brad. "Relaxation means you were freed from the church's grasp."

"Like I said, that's what I'd choose."

"Because," continued Kurt, "the church didn't kill."

"And that's a good thing, bro."

"You were 'relaxed' to a secular group that would then burn you alive at the stake. In public."

"They'd *what*? That isn't very fucking relaxing, dude."

"You could always repent."

"Would that mean I wouldn't be burned alive?"

"Yeah."

"Then I'll repent. Seems pretty simple: relax and repent."

"So now you'll be shown mercy."

"Good."

"By being garroted."

"*What?*"

"You'd be garroted to death. Slowly, of course. And then burnt at the stake, probably still half-alive. That was the merciful way the Inquisition killed people."

My head was spinning and I called for the check. I was horrified by the little history lesson I'd just heard, but also intrigued by what this could mean for our show. At the very least I saw a two hour special; just documenting everything that Kurt had told us could fill most of that, and we needed to fit the antics of the intrepid adventurers in as well.

One thing I knew for sure that was this upcoming episode, if we could pull it off, might be the best supernatural reality show ever recorded. Weaving the horrors of the Spanish Inquisition with the two of them bumbling around in full, green, night vision glory would be the perfect intermingling of the unthinkable and the absurd.

I also knew that in order to achieve this, the primary team, in other words us, needed to be the ones in Spain.

X

It was such a relief to be back home again. We'd been on the road shooting the previous couple of episodes for nearly two weeks and I was worn out. Scooby and Scrappy don't have a mean bone between them, but being in their company for protracted periods of time was mentally exhausting. On top of this, shepherding them through somewhere as evidently complex as an airport was like being in charge of a couple of five year olds on roller skates in a toy store.

Brad still hadn't seemed to grasp the concept of what the metal detector did and, therefore, ended up having to go back through about six times gradually removing large chunks of metal from his person. Kurt got bored easily and, while we sat waiting at our gate, would invariably wander off somewhere and very nearly miss the flight.

Every single time.

Because this always delayed our flight while people tried to find him, I wanted to avoid this on our return trip home, so after he'd been absent from the gate for about ten minutes, I went to look for him. When I finally found him and dragged him back to the gate, Scrappy was missing. I made Kurt promise to stay put and went to find Brad. Upon returning to the gate with him, Kurt was now gone again. I repeated this hilarious sequence of events until I suddenly realized that the name being called over the PA system was mine, and could I please show up to the gate because my flight was about to leave.

I sprinted to the gate and got on board, only to find both Scooby and Scrappy innocently sitting in their seats. I sank, panting and sweating profusely, into the leather seat across the aisle from them and tried to catch my breath.

Kurt leaned over. "Dude, you nearly made our flight late. Where were you?"

I managed to refrain from punching him, but only because I didn't want to be thrown off the flight.

So, it was with much relief that I dropped my bags inside my apartment, fetched a beer from the fridge, and gratefully slumped onto my couch to watch some TV. We'd left Virginia at lunchtime, had a layover in DC that allowed for more *Spongebob*-style airport antics, and after my cab ride from LAX to Venice it was now just after eight p.m. pacific time; I was worn out. I flicked through some channels on the TV, trying to find something that would hold my interest. The vast majority of shows were some sort of reality TV and, because I made shows like that for a living, I couldn't bear to watch them. I knew that the editing was done to make much more out of a situation than it actually was, cutting to looks of shock or offense that happened at totally different times, and so any attempt at suspense or drama was lost on me. If it was some sort of reality cooking competition show, I could usually tell the order that the contestants would be kicked off, just from watching the way their introduction reels, played at the very beginning of the show, had been edited.

I was halfway down my second beer when suddenly there was a commotion near the front door of my apartment. I looked at the clock glowing at me from my DVR, and it was 9:24 p.m.; too late for anybody to be cleaning or doing maintenance where I lived.

By some stroke of good fortune, I'd stumbled into this ghost-hunting gig, which had become extremely popular and ended up paying me very well, so I was able to afford a very swanky two bedroom apartment in the well-to-do canal area of Venice, California. Each floor of the apartment complex had just two spacious apartments, with the front door of each leading to a communal corridor that led to the elevator. The front doors had been staggered in location so that if both were open, you couldn't see straight into the other apartment; a nice touch that paying a bit extra gets you.

The noises I was hearing were heavy breathing, hushed tones, and thumping footfalls. This was surprising to me because the apartment opposite was empty, and had been for months. I could only assume that the footsteps were heading in my direction, and I wasn't expecting any company, so the hairs on the back of my neck suddenly stood up on end, and I felt a chill run down my spine. Had Scooby and Scrappy been filming me, this would definitely have been a paranormal encounter in their expert opinion.

Duff had given all three of us many lectures on the importance of security now that we were, as he put it, famous celebrities. Scooby and Scrappy had lapped it up and taken it all very seriously, promising to always take different routes everywhere and to always look behind them to see if they were being followed, which of course they always forgot to do. I hardly considered us celebrities, despite the fact that we were on TV. The way I saw it, we were three clowns that clattered around old buildings making fools of ourselves on camera. The way most of our rapidly growing American audience saw us, however, was three heroes putting their lives on the line to rescue lost souls and communicate with spirits, and this never ceased to amaze me.

Our internet forum now had hundreds of thousands of members who actively participated vigorously and dissected every episode, pointing out possible ghostly voices or sightings that we'd missed during our 'investigations', or over-confidently confirming the 'words' that Brad or Kurt had heard spoken. Not a single post ever questioned what we did or suggested that it was all just made-up nonsense; each and every one of them truly believed in what we had on offer, and they loved it. So did our network.

For the first few episodes we'd been finding our feet, so the ghostly 'evidence' that we discovered was pretty thin on the ground and, frankly, the first few nights we spent locked in dank, dark, stinking places were pretty tedious and miserable. On our fourth lock-in, I brought the small device I'd made, just for fun, to try and spruce things up a little for us; my intention had been to scare Kurt and Brad and have a good old laugh at them. The parts had cost me just a few bucks at Radio Shack, and I'd been able to fit them neatly into a little plastic case about half the size of a deck of cards that had a single, slightly recessed button on it.

It was that episode, when it aired, that saw our viewing figures jump to nearly ten times that of the previous ones. Social media went wild over the 'clearly audible' spirit voices that my little white-noise generating gizmo had produced, and the re-runs attracted even more viewers once word got out. The show suddenly went viral on the internet, and it became a massive hit with every god-fearing, ghost-hunting, spirit-chasing idiot in America. And, it turns out, there are a *lot* of them, so I decided not to mention to anybody that the 'voices' everyone had heard had been created and then embellished by me. Brad and Kurt's explanation for why we were suddenly hearing the spirits talk was that we were now trusted in the paranormal afterlife because the ghosts had spent the first few episodes getting to know us. This, amazingly, seemed to make sense to everyone, and saw us suddenly rise immediately to the top of the alarmingly large pile of people that spend their time hunting ghosts. We became revered amongst the paranormal-chasing community, and I made sure from that moment on to never disappointed them.

I'd made my little box of tricks as a joke, but it had turned out to be incredibly lucrative not just for me, but for the network, and everybody involved in the show, so I saw it as a good thing and continued using it. Part of me knew it was wrong to deceive people like this, but at the same time I couldn't help thinking that these people were wanting to be deceived; they desperately wanted 'proof' that spirits and ghosts existed so they would feel better about the unavoidable end of their lives. It wouldn't be them simply not being alive any more, and instead they'd be floating spirits offering random words to reality TV stars like us, which in their eyes is far better than just being dead.

After the noises in the corridor had gone on for a little while, I gently put my beer down and, as quietly as I could manage, made my way towards the front door. Perhaps Duff had been right and there was a mob of fans waiting to jump me, or perhaps some criminal gang thought I had a safe full of cash hidden behind a picture frame and they were going to storm my apartment and—

Get a grip!

I stopped and tried to calm myself down, which was when I realized that my hands were shaking. I was also suddenly aware of the fact that I didn't have my cell phone with me, because it was on my coffee table. I was four feet from the front door, so should I creep back and get it, or just plough on regardless?

And then, as suddenly as they'd started, the noises in the corridor stopped.

This freaked me out even more. Perhaps they'd heard me approaching and were now all silently pressed against the walls either side of my front door, just waiting to pounce the moment I opened it. I stood motionless for several seconds, not really knowing what to do, and also feeling a bit stupid. I couldn't help feeling that I'd allowed too many Hollywood movies to interfere with my common sense, but at the same time I felt vulnerable and naked; the apartment opposite was empty, and I had no cell phone.

I listened for the slightest creak, whisper, or breath for about thirty seconds, but heard nothing. I took another tentative step towards the door, and still there was no sound of any kind from the other side of it. Two more cautious and very slow steps and I was at the front door; the eerie silence, which had simply been silence up to this point in my life, continued. I peered through the peephole and saw the wall opposite, as well as the nice little antique oak table with an expensive flower display on it.

I waited what seemed like a lifetime, and no other suspicious sounds were heard, so I finally plucked up the courage to open the door a little.

Nothing.

I opened it further and stuck my head through the gap. I peered to the left and right into the corridor.

Still nothing.

Then I looked down and saw something made of cloth on my doorstep. This was odd, and clearly a trap, my brain confidently informed me. I had no idea what it was but, naturally, I was intrigued and wanted to find out. I opened my door fully and looked each way down the corridor; it was deserted. I looked down at the pile of cloth again; it was slightly off-white, and made of a heavy fabric, but I couldn't make out what type of garment it was. After another glance all around me, I reached down and picked it up.

I was surprised at how heavy it was, and then held it out in front of me. With a yelp of surprise, I threw it back down on the floor and lurched backwards in shock, knocking over a small table that held a little dish with keys and coins in it. Things crashed everywhere around me, and the porcelain dish smashed to pieces on my wooden floor. The cacophony of noise seemed deafening, but my brain was trying to process something far more alarming, and I didn't quite know what to make of it.

I took some deep breaths and tried to steady my shaking hands before I picked up the garment again, held it out in front of me, and stared at it. It was still what it had been the first time I'd picked it up.

It was a straitjacket.

Not only was it a straitjacket, but it was a straitjacket with a name tag sewn onto the left breast. The name tag said 'Isabella'.

It was a joke, I assured myself. It had to be. This had absolutely no connection to our lock-in at the mental prison; there was no way it could have. Ghosts and spirits do not exist, I told myself firmly, and they certainly don't go around leaving bits of clothing on people's front doorsteps.

A joke, then. By Kurt and Brad? No, they didn't have the wit to pull something like this off and, besides, I doubted they'd even remember who Isabella was. I knew it wouldn't be Duff because, aside from not having a sense of humor, he also didn't watch our shows, so he'd have no idea who Isabella was in the first place. I doubted our over-worked and stressed producer would have the time or inclination to pull something like this, so who could it have been?

"Oh, hello!" said a voice that seemed to come from all around me.

Startled, I span around in about six different directions before I saw a woman standing in the hallway behind me. I had no idea where she'd come from, and I hadn't heard footsteps. I stood still, hands trembling, and just stared at her.

"I'm Isabella," she said, which made me let out a loud gasp and drop the straitjacket. Her smile changed to a look of mild concern as I clutched my chest and began to perspire. "Are you okay?"

"Um... I... errr. No. I mean, yes. Hello."

"Sorry I startled you. Are you sure you're okay?"

I tried to get a grip. I told myself sternly that I was absolutely not talking to the ghost that had died decades ago in that prison. "Errr, yes. Isabella, you say?"

"Yes. Isabella. And that's my straitjacket."

This pushed me over the edge, and I totally freaked out. I leapt backwards and crashed painfully into my doorframe; when I'd spun around looking for the voice, I'd lost all track of which direction my body was facing.

I blurted out, "I'm sorry! I'm sorry! I didn't mean to touch it! Isabella, you can take it back. I wasn't trying to do anything to it. I'm sorry!"

She screwed her face up a little. "Woah, it's okay. I must have dropped it when I was moving that last load of boxes into the apartment. I've just rented the place, so now you have a neighbor."

I swallowed hard. "With a straitjacket."

She gave a little chuckle. "Oh, is that what's upsetting you? Don't worry, it's just for a bachelorette party that I'm going to in a couple of weeks. I haven't been institutionalized or anything! Yet, ha ha."

I tried to laugh with relief, but it sounded more like I was being strangled. "Ah. Ha ha. A party? I see. Ha ha. Well, it was nice meeting you. Bye!"

And with that, I darted back into my apartment and closed the door, locking it immediately behind me.

I heard Isabella's voice from the other side of my door. "Nice to meet you. I'm sure we'll be seeing much more of each other. In fact, I know we will. Sleep well!"

I crunched my way over the remains of the porcelain dish that I had been quite fond of, and threw myself down onto the sofa. My whole body was trembling. What did she mean when she said she knew we'd be seeing more of each other? Was that her letting me know she was going to haunt me?

There are no such things as ghosts or spirits!

I told myself over and over that this was just one of life's eerily bizarre coincidences. There are lots of people named Isabella, so that was coincidence number one, and she was going to a party that involved everyone having a straitjacket. Perhaps that was a common thing with bachelorette parties; coincidence number two. Said straitjacket happened to land outside my door after I'd been in a mental prison, trying to communicate with an inmate called Isabella who'd died in a straitjacket; coincidence number three. Had this happened a year ago, it would have had absolutely no meaning for me at all, and Isabella and I would probably be having a glass of wine right now as she unpacked her stuff.

Without realizing it, I'd curled up on my sofa in the fetal position and was trying to rock back and forth without falling off it. The entire time, as flashbacks to Isabella's cell, the straitjacket, and the encounter I'd just had crashed around inside my mind, I tried to keep thinking the same word over and over: *coincidence*.

It wasn't working.

I dragged myself back to my front door and peered through the spy hole again. I couldn't see anything. I was still shaking, so I went and poured myself a large glass of scotch, and paced around my living room as I tried to make sense of what had just happened.

Coincidence.

Bizarre, yes, but a coincidence nevertheless. The mother of all coincidences. As Brad would say, there can be no other explanation.

I paced around for another half hour, then tried to take my mind off what had just happened with some TV. That didn't work. I tried reading the paper, which also didn't work. I picked up the book I was halfway through and spent twenty minutes reading and re-reading the same sentence over and over, none of it sinking in. My brain was elsewhere, and nothing was holding my interest.

I went to bed.

XI

"Fak me, you look like crap," said Tom when I walked into our production office the following morning. Tom was our producer; tall, gangly, operated at about a million miles per hour, and hailed from the east-end of London. I sometimes had absolutely no idea what he was talking about when he went off into a rant in Cockney rhyming slang, but I liked him a lot, and he was absolutely awesome to work with.

I'd got virtually no sleep the previous night after my encounter with Isabella. I'd lain in bed, tossing and turning, jumping out of my skin at every tiny noise, convinced that she was coming for me. I finally drifted off to sleep at around three a.m, and then awoke twenty minutes later, drenched in sweat. That cycle then repeated itself until my alarm went off and I had to drag myself out of bed.

"Yeah, I, err, I didn't get much sleep last night."

"Celebrating, I'll bet?"

"Celebrating? Celebrating what?"

"Mate! Are you fakking kidding me? Celebrate what. Fakking 'ell. Pull the other one."

This was one of those occasions that I didn't know what he was talking about. "Huh? Pull what?"

95

"Last night! The bird in the straitjacket?"

My chest tightened, and I staggered backwards, steadying myself against a desk behind me. "*Isabella*?" I gasped. "You saw her too?"

Tom looked at me and blinked a few times. "Yeah, mate, I saw her. Didn't you?"

"Well, I, err… she… the straitjacket, it was…"

"Yeah! I know! It was what killed her! Fak me, that was a great episode, mate. The public loved it, your forums have gone mental, and you just managed to get the highest ratings of any show we've ever broadcast on the network. *Ever*!"

It suddenly dawned on me what he was talking about and I tried to steady my shaking limbs. "Oh! The show aired last night? That's where you saw her?"

"What the fak were you drinkin' last night, mate? Where the fak d'you think I'd have seen her? Waiting for me outside me' flat?"

He let out a huge guffaw as I tried to breathe deeply and calm the nausea that had been growing inside me. My whole body was covered in a cold sweat.

Tom looked at me for a few moments. "You sure you're okay? You look pale as fak. Like you've seen a ghost or somethin'!"

He burst out laughing again, before adding, "but there's no change there then, eh?"

My head was spinning and I felt like my heart was about to explode out of my chest. I crashed my way into the cubicle behind me and gratefully found a chair that I collapsed into, breathing heavily.

Tom continued, "the boss is chuffed to bits, and the fans are heaping praise on Kurt for surviving getting possessed. Some people are calling him a hero. How the fak did you get him to agree to being locked into that fakking freezer thing?"

"Huh? Oh, errr… you know. It was nothing, really."

He gave me a playful punch in the arm. "Hah! Modesty! Fakkin' modesty. You, me ol' China, are the fakkin' bollocks. You must be like that fakkin' hypnotist bloke, wassisname, to get Kurt to do all that!"

My heart rate was returning to normal. "Who?"

"You know. That tosser that bends all them spoons and hypnotizes people."

I thought for a moment. "Uri Gellar?"

"Yeah, that's him! You must be like Uri Gellar. I mean why else would the daft old sod agree to do all that crazy crap? 'Hey, Kurt, wanna sit in this tiny fakkin' metal box for an hour while we fak off and get lost?' 'Sure, dood, no problem'. Fakkin' genius, mate."

I had sweat pouring off my clammy face, and I wiped some off my forehead with the palm of my hand. "Errr, thanks. Did it air at the usual time? I'd just landed and forgot it was on."

"Yeah, mate, of course. Nine p.m."

I cast my mind back to when I'd put the episode together, and Isabella would have started talking to Kurt at roughly twenty-four minutes past the hour, taking into consideration the adverts. I thought back to the previous night and remembered looking at the clock on the DVR.

9:24p.m.

I let out a huge gasp of surprise and started breathing heavily. I put my head in my hands, and rested my elbows on my knees. I was shaking like a leaf.

"Mate?" asked Tom, putting his hand on my back to comfort me. Suddenly he took it away again with a start. "You're soaked! Are you okay? No, of course you're not! I'm gonna call the medics."

"No," I gasped. "I'm okay, I'm just… tired."

"I think you should go to the fakkin' 'ospital, mate. I'm not kiddin'; you really do look like you've seen a pillar an' post."

I removed my sweaty face from my hands and looked up. "A what?"

"A ghost, mate, a ghost."

I groaned and put my head back in my hands.

"Sod this," said Tom, a concerned note in his voice, "I'm getting you home, pal. You're uncle dick, no doubt about it, and you need some kip. We can do the edit of the next show tomorrow when you're feeling better. Cushtie?"

I hadn't understood anything he'd just said, but I knew he had my best interests at heart, and so I nodded. A few minutes later, I was in one of the network's plush limos used for ferrying celebs and execs to and fro, being whisked back to my apartment in Venice. My thoughts were darting about everywhere and, despite the fact that it was only 10:30a.m., I poured myself a glass of twenty-year old scotch from the bar in the limo. The warming glow sank down into my belly and gradually began to calm my nerves. As I started to relax a little, I tried to make sense of this final part of the massive coincidence; I'd been stirred by Isabella-with-the-straitjacket at exactly the same time that viewers at home had seen the other Isabella communicate with Kurt.

That thought made me pour another glass of scotch.

Coincidence.

Nothing more, nothing less. *There are no such thing as ghosts.*

Due to the comical LA traffic, it took me an hour to get to Venice despite it being less than twelve miles from the office. During that time, three generously-proportioned glasses of scotch had disappeared as I tried to calm my nerves. As I got to my front door, I looked further down the corridor at the apartment now rented by Isabella-with-the-straitjacket. I shuddered, and then opened my front door.

I was exhausted, I hadn't eaten, and the scotch was now compounding all of this; my limbs felt heavy and everything I did felt sluggish. I managed to make it to my bedroom, leaving a trail of clothes in my wake, and I climbed into my over-sized bed. Within seconds, I was deeply asleep.

I woke up at about seven p.m. that same day, and I felt refreshed. I showered and went for a walk along the beach, gazing out at the ocean while I watched the sun begin to set. It was absolutely beautiful, as always, and was a view I'd never get tired of. I thought back to the previous evening's incident, and slowly began to understand how stupid I'd been. Yes, of course, it was an incredible coincidence, but that's all it was; I was sure now, and I put my bizarre and erratic behavior down to exhaustion.

I had a beer in my usual little hole-in-the-wall bar that gave me a great view of what was left of the huge orange ball in the sky slipping down, seemingly into the ocean in the distance. As people on roller blades and skateboards trundled past, I felt calmer about what had happened, and although it had been the most bizarre coincidence of my life, that's exactly what it was and nothing more. I finally felt at peace about the whole thing.

As the evening darkened, I walked closer to home and had dinner in my favorite seafood restaurant, which also happened to overlook Venice beach. My fish was locally caught, simply grilled, served with steamed vegetables, and was absolutely delicious. I washed it down with a crisp Sauvignon Blanc from Sonoma, and watched the nearly-full moon reflect off the gentle ripples of the ocean. I could feel my body gradually returning to normal, the self-induced panic of the previous twenty-four hours melting away as I relaxed.

Back in my apartment building, I decided to walk past my front door and apologize to Isabella for appearing to have been slightly unhinged the previous evening. I stood outside her front door, and took a deep breath. I knocked twice and waited.

Nothing.

After a few minutes had passed, I knocked again.

Still nothing.

She was either asleep or out to dinner, so I went back to my apartment and suddenly realized that I was tired again, despite only having been awake for about four hours. For the second time that day, I crawled into my bed and drifted off into a deep sleep.

My alarm was set for eight o'clock, but by seven I was awake and feeling great. I did something that I hadn't been able to for weeks, and I went for a run. I wasn't a great runner, but I enjoyed it, and it allowed me to focus my thoughts as my feet rhythmically pounded along. Being able to live where I did meant that I was utterly spoilt for choices of running scenery; I could run along the beach path and watch the ocean, I could run through the marina and look at the boats, I could head inward slightly and run amongst the streets that were beginning to bustle in Marina del Rey, or I could simply get lost in the network of canals and enjoy the backs of everyone's multi-million dollar houses, smelling their rosemary hedges and mint topiaries.

That day I chose to run along the beach. My warm up fast-walk took me the two blocks to the ocean, and then I ran north up to Santa Monica pier, where I turned around and retraced my route back down the winding concrete path set into the man-made beaches of southern California. By the time I got home, I'd been gone for a little more than an hour, which was about right for the five miles I'd just run. I was sweating and out of breath, but I felt great, and bounded up the stairs instead of taking the elevator. As I let myself into my apartment, I glanced in the direction of Isabella's front door and immediately dismissed the idea of knocking again. There would be plenty of time to apologize for my behavior, and I didn't want to now appear that I was stalking her, on top of acting like a total lunatic.

I showered, ate a hearty breakfast, and then hopped into the company limo that was waiting for me so I could get back to work and where my car was parked. Tom was relieved to see me looking back to full health, and we spent the day cutting together what was turning out to be a far better episode than I'd been dared hope for. At the very least, it had plenty of comedic value.

At about four in the afternoon, I got an unexpected call from Mike Durkin, the head of the network, and nobody, as far as I knew, ever got a call directly from him. Evalina, his personal assistant was well known and loathed by everyone in the building, and had been christened Evil Eve by Tom; it was usually her you got the call from, not Mike. He was a loud, well-fed New Yorker, and face-to-face meetings with him were at best rare and, for most employees of the network, unheard of. He'd asked me to go to his office, so off I went.

"Mr. Durkin is waiting for you," said Evil Eve doing what I'm sure she considered to be a smile, but actually looked looked like she was bearing her over-whitened teeth at me, demonstrating that she could chew me up and spit me out if she so desired.

I walked up to the huge Mahogany door that led to his office and knocked firmly twice.

"Yeah," boomed a voice from behind the door. "Come in."

I opened the door and walked in to find the rotund figure of Mike with his back to me, staring out of one of the huge windows in his office, which took up a substantial portion of the entire top floor of the building. He turned around after I'd closed the door.

"Todd! Hey! How you doin'? Come in, have a seat."

His journey from the window to his desk took him via his impressive drinks cabinet, where he selected two crystal tumblers in one hand, and paused slightly over an array of crystal decanters, each containing a slightly different colored liquid, before choosing one and bringing it to his desk.

"I figure you're a scotch man, am I right?"

I was slightly taken aback. "Um, yes! Yes I am, as it happens. How did you know that?"

He guffawed at me. "Intuition. It's a knack I have; I can always tell a man's drink. I can also always tell when someone's bluffing, so don't ever lie to me Todd."

I felt like a kid sitting in front of the school principle. "You can count on that Mr. Durkin. I'm not a big believer in lying," I lied.

"That's good, Todd, I like that. And please, call me Mike."

He poured two healthy amounts of scotch and handed me one of the heavy crystal tumblers. He held his up in front of me and we chinked our glasses together, filling the room with a wonderfully sustained ringing note. We both took a sip; it was smooth and quite obviously very expensive.

"Forty year old," he said, almost to himself. "Very hard to find."

I still wasn't quite sure why he wanted to see me, but I figured that the vintage scotch meant I wasn't about to be fired. I took another sip, and waited.

Mike swirled his drink around in his glass and looked at it appreciatively. Then he looked at me and held me in his gaze. "Your show."

He gave me no hint in the way he said it as to whether it was good or bad in his eyes, and I didn't know what to say, so I kept quiet.

"Your fuckin' show," he said again with a half chuckle. "Over the years, this network has broadcast documentaries about Mandela, Iraq, Vietnam, and weapons of mass destruction. We've documented the space race, we analyzed JFK's assassination six ways from fuckin' Sunday, and the fall of the Berlin wall was made into a ten-part series. The end of the Cold War is still an ongoing subject, and our coverage of scientific breakthroughs is nonstop. We cover the truly important topics that the human race needs to know about. All very serious shit, I think you'll agree. Our viewing figures have always been decent, but a ways off the *Discovery Channel*." He took another sip of scotch before continuing. "And then what happens? I take a risk and air a show about you three running round chasin' ghosts, and guess what? You don't only get the highest number of viewers that our network has ever seen, but with that last one, the one in the psycho place, you eclipsed the fuckin' *Mythbusters*!"

That was news to me. "We what? We beat the *Mythbusters'* ratings?"

"You didn't just beat them, you whupped their asses! And, as I'm sure you know, that's unheard of. I wanted to have a drink with you and say thank you for what you've done."

I butted in, "well, to be fair, it's not just me, there's Brad and Kurt too."

He let out a loud snort. "Those two are fuckin' idiots. You have the magic, Todd. It's all you. I don't know how you do it, but it's fuckin' great. Don't stop."

I tried to keep the pretense of the show going, worried that he was testing me to try and see if I'd been faking it all along. "Like I said, it's Brad and Kurt. They just seem to have this affinity with the spirits and—"

Mike cut me off mid-sentence. "Horseshit! There's no such fuckin' thing as ghosts or ghouls or lost souls or whatever other crap you guys spout, and you know it. It's down to brilliant fuckin' editing, and something that the other copycat channels don't have."

I was a little taken aback at being called out on this, especially by the head of the network, and it made me nervous. Was he about to accuse me of falsifying the 'evidence' that we gathered?

I took another drink, and tried to sound as casual as possible. "And what's that?"

He guffawed a huge laugh at me. "*You*! That's what they don't have. They don't have *you*."

For some strange reason, I felt the need to confess everything. "Look, Mr D... Mike. It's not what it—"

In a sudden movement, he leaned forward, making the desk creak as his weight settled on it, and barked at me. "Shut *up*! Just shut up!"

I shut up.

Mike stared intently at me for a few seconds, and then settled back in his chair. He took a sip of his scotch. He said, much more calmly, "I don't want to hear what goes on. As far as I'm concerned, you guys are bumping fists with ghosts and shit. You know what I do want?"

I shook my head, slightly bemused.

"I want you to keep on doing it, whatever it is that *you* do. I don't give a crap about Laurel and fuckin' Hardy, you get me? Keep doing whatever it is that *you* do."

Once again I was shocked and didn't quite know how to react. He clearly knew that I was faking the whole thing, and he wanted me to know that he was behind my deceit one hundred percent, whilst at the same time not becoming a party to it. It was smart, sort of subtle, and one of the reasons that he was head of the network and I would never be.

Mike leaned over and refilled my glass of scotch. Not quite knowing what to do, I picked it up and had a big sip.

His face softened and he must have seen the confusion in my face; he opened his big palms towards me. "Look, Todd, here's how it is. You can tell me all you want that the noises people hear in the episodes is fuckin' ghouls and ghosts, but I know it 'ain't. I know that there's some funny business goin' on, and I'm pretty sure that you're behind it all. Those other two fuckin' morons couldn't find their way out of a paper bag with a hole at both ends, but, you know what? *I don't fuckin' care*. And do you know *why* I don't care? I don't care because I suddenly now have the biggest and richest companies in the world beating down my fuckin' door to advertise their shit during your show. I double the price of an ad slot, and they pay it without asking. After that last episode, I'm gonna up it tenfold. And they'll still fuckin' pay."

I sat there, still not knowing why he was telling me all this. To make me jealous of how much money he was going to make that year?

Mike continued. "And so here's the thing, Todd. You've done us proud. You really have. You're an asset to this network, and I don't want to lose you. And, more importantly, I don't want to lose you to another network."

The penny suddenly dropped, and I realized that I was the one in the position of power at that moment, so I just sat there and stared at him. We had two more episodes to do, and then my contract was up; I suddenly understood what the vintage scotch and cosy-cosy chat was all about. He knew that one of his other network-head buddies was about to try and snap us up with a big pile of cash.

I thought very carefully about what I said next. "Well, Mike, my contract is up in two episodes."

He eyed me carefully. "Yes, it is."

I took another sip of scotch. "I'll be honest, Mike. This network has been very good to me. To all three of us, in fact. I can't speak for Brad or Kurt, but—"

"They've already re-signed their contracts," he said, interrupting me.

That made sense. They didn't care about viewing figures or advertiser spending, they were as happy as clams that they could barrel around searching for ghosts; I also guessed that Durkin, worried about a pre-emptive counter offer from another network, would have at least doubled their money. Why wouldn't they re-sign?

"Oh," I said. "I didn't know. You must be happy about that."

He raised his eyebrow at me, and said nothing.

I continued. "As I was saying, this network has been good to me, so I have no burning desire to go anywhere else. I'm sure we'll be able to come to an arrangement, don't you think?"

He smiled and opened a drawer in his desk, from which he pulled a large envelope and slid it across the shiny mahogany surface to me. "I'm glad you see it that way, Todd. Here's my offer; take it home, think about it, and let me know on Monday."

He drained his scotch and stood up, letting me know this meeting was over. I stood, we shook, and I headed for the door.

"Oh, one more thing," said Mike. "Brad told me about *his* Spanish Inquisition idea. I think it's fuckin' great. I want the final two episodes of this season to be a two-part special, so pack your bags Todd, you're going to Spain."

I turned and looked at him. "I'm not sure our episode budget will cover—"

"Fuck the budget, Todd. Make it the best episode ever. You get me?"

I nodded and left with a huge smile on my face.

The *Mythbusters* weren't going to know what hit them.

XII

I sat in my Upper Class seat as the Virgin plane roared down the runway at LAX, and climbed into the sky. I was heading to London for a connecting flight to Spain, and I was in a state of utter disarray.

Even Brad trying to convince the airport security people that the X-Ray machine was haunted hadn't made me smile, or taken my mind off what was bothering me.

"Dude!" he'd blurted to the massively fat black woman sitting behind the X-Ray monitors, looking bored. "Did you see that?"

She looked up at him and tapped a key on the keyboard that stopped the conveyor belt, causing the line of waiting passengers to grow in size with every passing second. Her nails were about three feet long, and had rainbows and sparkles and all sorts of stuff on them. "Ecks-*cuse* me?"

"A spirit! I just saw a spirit inside your X-Ray machine. On the monitor, right there! There can be no other explanation!"

By this point, he was standing right next to her, peering and jabbing his finger at the screen, which she was clearly not happy about. "Sir, you can't be back here. This is off limits to passengers."

"But it's a lost soul! We need to try and communicate with it!"

The security lady rose from her seat and, it turned out, was about six foot six. She towered over Brad, her huge bulk blocking his view of the monitors. "Sir, you need to leave this area, *now*. I'm not gonna tell you again."

Brad was getting exasperated, so I left all of my things on the still-stationary conveyor belt and made my way barefoot to where he was. I put my hand on his shoulder.

"Come on, bro. You're not meant to be back here."

He turned to face me, the huge figure of the TSA lady glaring down at us both. "But, dude—"

"Not now Brad, let's go and have a beer. This spirit can wait."

He sighed and slouched past me. I looked up at the huge woman. "Sorry about that. He can get a little, err, excitable if he thinks he's spotted a ghost."

"I suggest, *sir*, that both of you become ghosts and vanish before I arrest the pair of you."

I didn't need telling twice, and I scurried back to get my things. The line of people waiting to get through the X-Ray machine was now enormous, and they were getting agitated, so I grabbed Brad and whisked him out of the view of the people who likely wanted to kill him for delaying them by a few minutes. We quickly made our way to the Virgin Upper Class lounge and found Kurt waiting there for us.

Scrappy bounded up to him. "Dude! There was a spirit trapped inside the X-Ray machine!"

"No way, bro!"

"Without a doubt. I saw it on the monitor. It couldn't have been anything else."

"How did a spirit get trapped in there?"

"I dunno, dude, but we should investigate airports in the next season."

"Definitely bro. That makes total sense." Kurt turned to me. "Are you in for next season, dude?"

"I wouldn't miss it for the world," I replied with as much enthusiasm as I could muster at that moment. The offer that Mike had given me was far more than I'd have dared ask for, but I also knew that it wouldn't be his highest offer, so after careful consideration I'd countered with one slightly higher. Mike had agreed without so much as a pause, and I immediately knew I'd undersold myself, but I was going to be earning some serious money and was happy. I even had a bonus for each episode based on viewing figures; I had a feeling the spirits were going to be very talkative next season.

"That is *awesome* bro! It just wouldn't be the same without you," gushed Kurt, not realizing just how right he was.

The rest of the wait for the flight was fairly uneventful, and we had a few drinks while I disinterestedly listened to Brad and Kurt babble on about what they thought they knew about Spain, how much Spanish they knew, which turned out to be not very much, and their musings about whether Spanish ghosts would communicate in Spanish or English.

"We probably need to learn the word for 'ghost' in Spanish," concluded Kurt.

"El ghosto?" suggested Brad.

Once on the plane I was, thankfully, secluded from Scooby and Scrappy by the layout of the Upper Class cabin; each person has a recessed area and a seat that turns into a bed. You can't see or hear the people either side of you, so I was finally able to reflect on what had happened earlier that day.

My weekend had been uneventful and restful. Monday, the day before our flight, had been my contract negotiations, and once Durkin had agreed to my new price, I'd been feeling jubilant about life in general. On my way home, I'd bought a bottle of expensive champagne and decided to share it with Isabella, who I still hadn't seen since that first meeting. I had the bottle of Perrier-Jouët Belle Epoque in my hand and knocked on her door once more. Again, I got no answer, so I headed into my apartment and drank it by myself. Later that evening, I knocked on her door again, but still got no reply; she must have been out of town.

The next morning I'd gone for a run and, on my way back into my building, noticed that there was still no name tag next Isabella's apartment buzzer. This struck me as slightly odd because our building manager was a bit of a Nazi when it came to proper protocols and, as he'd told me many times, a correct name tag is a very important protocol.

I showered, had some breakfast, and packed my suitcase. Our flight was just after five p.m., and I had a car coming to pick me up at two-thirty. That gave me time for a nice, relaxing lunch. On my way out, I knocked on Isabella's door again and still got no response. On my way back from lunch, I happened to bump into Frank Billings, our building manager.

"Hello, Todd," he said in his usual disapproving tone. I was never quite sure what he disapproved of, but he made it quite clear that he disapproved wholeheartedly of whatever it was.

"Hey Frank. I see you're getting a bit lax in your old age," I said with a chuckle.

"Lax? What do you mean lax? I take great pride in what I do!"

"I'm just bustin' your chops, dude! It's the name tag, that's all."

"What name tag?"

I pointed next to Isabella's buzzer. "Look, you haven't put Isabella's name here yet. You've normally done that within an hour of someone even thinking of moving in."

"Who's Isabella?"

"The woman who moved into the apartment across from me. She moved in last week."

"Have you been drinking, Todd? That apartment is still empty."

"Perhaps nobody told you? I bumped into her last week when she was moving in."

"Todd, I'm *always* informed when someone moves in. It's the proper protocol."

"Well, I'm telling you, dude, she's moved in. She scared me half to death with all her clattering around outside my front door the other evening."

"I don't think so, Todd. Do you see a name tag next to that buzzer?"

"No, which is what I'm giving you shit about, Frank! Your standards are dropping."

"My standards," he said, almost with steam coming out of his ears, "will never drop. Follow me."

I did so, and he led me up to my floor, stopping outside Isabella's apartment. "This apartment?"

I nodded.

"Nobody," he said, "is living here."

"Her name is Isabella."

In a flash he produced a bunch of keys, and rifled through them, quickly finding the one he wanted. "Let's see, shall we?"

"Is this legal?"

"I'm the building manager, and you've told me about a potential squatter. I need to check it out, so yes it's legal."

He knocked firmly and got no response. He knocked again, and still got no reply. He slid the key into the lock and marched into Isabella's apartment. I followed and, once in the living room, felt my chest tighten. I suddenly couldn't breathe, and I staggered sideways before slumping against a wall and sliding down in a heap. My brain was working at a million miles an hour, and yet my body felt like I was stuck in a vat of Maple syrup.

"*What the...?*" I gasped.

"Do you believe me n—" said Franking turning to me. "Todd? Are you okay?"

Frank rushed over and knelt down next to me. "Todd? Speak to me!"

I'm not sure what being in shock feels like, but I'm guessing that was it. I was utterly lost for words, I couldn't focus, I felt sick to my stomach, and I was trembling all over. The apartment was completely empty. Nobody had moved in, and the layer of dust on every flat surface suggested that no-one had even been in the apartment for several months.

I tried to control my breathing and get a grip, but I was very confused. I knew that my encounter with Isabella hadn't been a dream; my favorite dish to put my keys in had definitely been broken, and that had happened when I'd met Isabella and her straitjacket. She was moving in. I saw her doing so. But the apartment was completely and utterly empty.

"I—"

"Todd, do you need me to call a doctor?"

My eyes darted around some more, I had sweat pouring off me, and then I focused on Frank. "Um, no. I... err... I'm fine. I think my... allergies are playing up."

"Okay, well, I'm glad we cleared up this little misunderstanding. Aren't you?"

I hauled myself to my feet. "Um, yeah. Absolutely. Thanks Frank."

"And, just for the record, I'd never let someone move in to an apartment as dusty as this. Pre-move-in protocols are very important, you know. And I adhere to all of them."

I half walked, half staggered back into my apartment and sat down on a dining chair with a thump. What the hell was going on?

I'd seen Isabella. I'd spoken to her. I'd seen her straitjacket.

I ran to the bathroom and threw up into the toilet. My fish tacos weren't nearly as appealing on the way out as they had been on their way in. When I'd finally finished getting rid of my lunch, I slumped back against the wall and tried to make sense of at least some tiny part of it.

"Ghosts do not exist," I found myself saying out loud, over and over.

And then I had a thought. The people that actually owned the apartment might have had a friend that they'd let use it for a brief period but hadn't bothered to tell Billings, who would have had nothing but red tape for them. After all, it was the owners' apartment; they can do whatever they want with it, regardless of how much Frank likes his protocols.

I scrambled my way back into the living room and grabbed the apartment directory book. I flicked through the pages and finally found Joan and Tom Tucker, the owners of the apartment across from me. They were in their seventies and now lived in Florida, but the rent they were paid on the apartment was immense, so they kept it as a nice investment. I dialed the number.

After a few rings, a woman's voice answered. "Hello?"

"Hello. Mrs. Tucker?"

"Yes, this is she. Who is this?"

"Hello Mrs. Tucker, this is Todd Sykes. I live in the apartment across the way from yours in Venice, California."

"Oh my goodness! Of course! Hello Todd! How are you?"

"Oh, I'm fine, thank you, Mrs. Tucker. How are you and Tom?"

"Oh, you know. We're fine, but Tom's golf handicap isn't getting any better. My tennis serve, on the other hand, is going from strength to strength! We've been enjoying your show, by the way. All of our friends here are fans. They can't believe that we know you. We'll all gather round and watch an episode and the whole time they'll be asking me to call you to find out what happens. I keep telling them, 'just keep watching and you'll find out you silly old coot'!" she burst into a fit of laughter. "Did you know that the last one, the one in the prison thingy, was so hyped that there were even posters around our community making sure everyone gathered to watch it. That was pretty amazing, I've got to tell you. Your friend in that metal box? Wow, that was really close. You could actually *hear* the spirits talking to him, and they were *so* mean! You are so brave, Todd! I don't know how you got that spirit out of him; what do they call it? *Exorcising* it? Well, I hope you didn't get cursed or whatever when you did that to it. Oh, dear me! I've been rambling on, haven't I? I'm so sorry. That tends to happen at my age! What can I do for you, Todd?"

"Um, I was wondering about the apartment across the way from me."

"Oh, you know it's not for sale, dear."

"No, no. I don't want to buy it. I was wondering if a friend of yours had moved in?"

"Moved in? Oh no, Todd. Nobody has wanted to rent it for a few months. Well, that's not true. People have wanted to rent it, but just not been prepared to pay the going rate. Ha ha."

I took a deep breath. "So you've never heard of anybody called Isabella?"

"Isabel— oh! of course I have!"

I felt my whole body relax.

Joan continued. "Isabella is that poor woman in your last episode. What a tragic story."

Now I tensed up and had to fight off convulsions. "So, you don't actually know anybody called Isabella?"

"No, not that I know of."

"And you haven't given anyone permission to move into that apartment?"

"Oh no dear. Like I said, nobody is willing to pay."

"A favor to a friend?"

"No. Todd, what is this about? Do we have squatters?"

"No, no! It's all fine. I'm so sorry to have bothered you Joan. Give my regards to Tom! Bye!"

"But—"

I ended the call in a state of utter confusion. I sat there for a while until my front door buzzer went off and my driver let me know he was downstairs. A few minutes later I was in a company limo, being whisked to LAX. As usual, the bar was fully stocked. I grabbed a bottle of Heineken and pretty much downed it in one. My brain was desperately trying to make sense of what had happened, but I was having a really hard time. I'd reconciled the meeting with Isabella as me being a bit weird after a couple of freaky lock-ins, but it had now taken a huge turn in a direction that I couldn't quite comprehend.

And so there I was, sitting on the plane, a glass of nearly-empty champagne in my hand, staring blankly into space. I suddenly realized that having to baby-sit Kurt and Brad gave me something to take my mind off trying to figure it out. Now that I was all by myself, I could think of nothing else, and it was driving me nuts.

I was snapped out of my trance by a female voice. "Hello, sir."

I looked up and into the face of a beautiful and immaculately made-up air hostess, or whatever politically correct name they were referred to these days. "Um, hello! Sorry, I was a million miles away."

"That's not a problem, sir. Can I get a drink for yourself, at all?"

Her accent was crisp, English, and sounded what I considered to be posh, so I was surprised by her misuse of the reflexive pronoun. I chuckled, "sure, myself would like another glass of champagne. Ha ha."

She looked at me like I was a halfwit, and I wanted to point out that she started it, but decided to just keep quiet and watch as my glass was refilled. Even as the fizzy liquid was being poured, I started to zone out again.

Isabella.

I'd definitely met her that evening. It hadn't been a dream, and it couldn't have been an encounter with a ghost, because there is no such thing. There was a rational explanation for what had happened; there *had* to be, I just couldn't think of what it was. The apartment had definitely not been occupied. Frank hadn't been told, the owners weren't lending it to a friend, and the dust on the surfaces hadn't been disturbed for months. But Isabella had come out of the apartment; she must have done to have sprung up on me like that, so how did she have a key? And what happened to her after that night?

For some bizarre reason a Sherlock Holmes quote drifted through my mind: *when you have eliminated the impossible, whatever remains, however improbable, must be the truth.*

I downed my champagne in two gulps and signaled for more.

XIV

London Heathrow is the busiest airport in the world. It has won that dubious accolade many times over and, clearly, the day we landed there it was vying for that same award again. The place was absolute chaos, and I was dismayed that we had to collect our checked bags, despite this being merely a connecting flight. Even worse than this, of course, was that we all had to clear customs beforehand, which was something that Scooby and Scrappy had never done before.

I shepherded them off the plane, which was helped by us being let off first thanks to our Upper Class seats, and then we headed to the customs area. We walked and walked, and we walked some more.

"Fuck," said Kurt. "Are we going the right way?"

"Bro," gasped Brad as he ran alongside us on the other automated walkway going in the opposite direction to ours. "All the signs say so. You can't doubt the signs, dude."

"Don't worry," I mumbled, a little hungover, "we're going the right way, just be patient. Oh, and Brad, would it be possible for you to get on the walkway going in the correct direction when we get to the next one?"

"Huh? Oh, yeah, sure dude. Whatever you like. I was just kinda preoccupied, you know? I mean, dude, we're in *England*."

"Only for a little while."

"Yeah, but just think how many trapped spirits there are in this airport. I mean, bro, they—"

I cut him off. "None, Brad. There are *no* trapped spirits at Heathrow airport. Nobody has died here, and it's not even that old by British standards. There won't be any ghosts here, trust me."

"There are *always* ghosts, bro."

"Not here."

The opposing walkways ended, and I grabbed him by the arm and manhandled him in front of me so that when we reached the next perplexing choice of directions — forwards or backwards — I made sure that he was on the one going the right way. Eventually, we ended up at the area where you have to have your passport stamped.

Much as Brad liked to think of us as famous celebrities, our fame only extended to a reasonably niche group of American cable viewers. This 'niche group' still consisted of several million people, but it wasn't nearly enough to make us truly famous and, of course, the fact that the show was only broadcast in America further limited our audience. Perhaps our upcoming escapade would encourage a more international slant to the show? Either way, the downside of not being properly famous was that when we had to clear customs in London, we didn't get any special treatment other than our 'fast pass' lane, which merely gave us a slightly shorter line than everyone else.

"Dude," mumbled Kurt, "don't they know who we are?"

"No," I replied firmly, "and we're not about to tell them. Nobody knows who we are here, guys."

We shuffled forwards in silence for a few minutes and then Brad pointed to a lane a couple over from ours. It was completely empty and had a bored-looking customs dude sitting at his desk. "Whats wrong with that lane? I think we should use that one."

I looked around and saw a guard at the entrance to the lane and a small, discrete sign that said 'By Invitation Only'.

"That's for the VIPs, bro."

"We flew Upper Class. We're on TV. We're VIP, dude."

"Not here."

We continued to shuffle forwards and, about twenty minutes later, we were almost at the front of the line. Suddenly, there was a bit of commotion behind us as all the British people started turning around and straining their necks. Some camera flashes went off, and it seemed like everyone had their cell phones out and were taking pictures of something that I couldn't see.

"What's going on?" asked Brad excitedly.

"I've no idea and I don't care; it's almost our turn, so pay attention."

"*Look*!" hissed Kurt.

We all looked where he was pointing, which was at the VIP lane. Being escorted down it by two burly plainclothes guards was a man and woman. The woman had an artsy, bohemian look about her, dressed chic and casual, but the guy was wearing sunglasses and a baseball cap, as if that was going to make him look inconspicuous in a building full of people wearing the exact opposite.

"What a moron," I mumbled under my breath, a tiny bit jealous that he got to use the VIP lane and I didn't.

"But don't you recognize him, bro?" blurted Kurt, excited.

I looked again. "No. He looks like a douche."

Kurt was almost bursting with excitement. "It's the lead guitarist from *Arnage*! I'm sure it is! Remember them? The band was always fighting and doing crazy stuff? Great songs, but man they were fucked up."

I began to cast my mind back when I got waved on by a customs guy and forgot all about it. At almost exactly the same time, Brad and Kurt got waved on as well.

The man behind my desk had kindly eyes that he desperately wanted to look hard and mean. "'allo sir," he said, holding out his hand for my passport, which I dutifully passed to him. He looked at the photo, up at me, back at the photo, and back at me. He slid my passport under a scanner and looked intently at my face. I tried as best I could to not look guilty, which I wasn't, but felt like I was the world's most notorious criminal.

"Is Great Brittin' yer final destination today, sir?"

"No, we're just connecting. We're going to Spain."

"Oh, I see sir. And would this be for work or pleasure?"

"Work."

"And may I ask what it is that you do?"

"I'm part of a TV show in the US. We're filming an episode in Spain."

"A TV show, eh, sir?"

"Yes."

"Nice work if you can get it. What's it about?"

"Um," I said, suddenly feeling like an idiot. "Well, we sort of track down paranormal activity."

He frowned at me slightly. "I see, sir. Paranormal activity. So, ghosts, you mean?"

"Well, yes, I suppose so. Ghosts."

Suddenly there was a commotion from behind me. I heard Brad blurt over-loudly, "What do I *do*? I save lost souls, dude! We find trapped ghosts and we free them!" He turned and looked five booths away from him to Kurt and yelled, "Dude! Tell this guy! We save ghosts! Lost souls! Tell him!"

Like an idiot, Kurt yelled back, "Yeah, bro, that's right. That's what we do."

I put my hands over my face and rested my elbows on the kiosk ledge in front of me, letting out a huge sigh. "I'm so sorry," I mumbled through my hands.

"Friends of yours, are they sir?" asked my customs guy with a slight smirk.

I looked up slowly. "Friends, no. Colleagues, I guess so. They don't get out much. I really am sorry. You can deport them if you like."

I got a huge laugh in return as my passport and papers were stamped enthusiastically. "Deport them? Are you kidding me? I want to watch your show now! They're dynamite! What's it called?"

"*The Lost Souls*. But, like I said, it's only on in the US at the moment."

Another chuckle. "You should see the size of the satellite dish in me' back garden, sir. Enjoy yer stay, and I'll make sure your mad mates make it through okay."

"Um, thanks," I mumbled, and shuffled off to yet another set of escalators.

As I disappeared down them, I looked back and saw my customs dude persuading his colleagues to not have Brad and Kurt arrested and to allow them through and into the Queen's sovereign land.

Once at the bottom of what I hoped was the final escalator, I stood to one side and slightly out of sight. I knew full well that Scooby and Scrappy would go and stand by the first luggage belt they set their eyes on and expect that to be the one on which their bags would arrive, and so I watched them bumble down the escalator and do just that. I glanced up at one of the many TV monitors that make it quite clear where your luggage is going to come out, and then headed over to them.

"Hey guys," I said.

Brad spun around. "Dude! That crazy guy in the uniform almost didn't want to let me in! He thought I was drunk, or eating Chinese food, or something."

"Brad, you were babbling on about ghosts and— wait, Chinese food?"

"Yeah, he said I'd been eating Chicken Oriental, or something. Anyway, the dude was weird."

Thanks to Tom's Cockney rhyming slang, I knew exactly what the customs guy had thought Brad was, but I wasn't going to go there. "Brad, bro, he's a customs border agent."

"I know."

"Right, so raving on about ghosts and spirits might not be the quickest path to entry to a country."

"But, *dude*, we hunt ghosts, and—"

I held my hand up to silence him. "Think of it like this, Brad. A flight lands at LAX."

He nodded.

"And a guy gets to one of our all-American customs dudes."

"Oh, yeah! First line of defense, bro."

"And then this guy starts going on about coming to America to search for Allah in Santa Monica to talk to his spirit."

"Woah, the terrorist dude? No way, bro. That is *not* the same."

"Brad, Allah isn't a terrorist. He's the Muslim god. Sort of like a ghost or a spirit. Anyway, would you want that guy let in to *your* country? Babbling on like that about spirits?"

"Well, no, I guess, but we do this for *science*, man."

I took a deep breath and put my hand on Brad's shoulder. "Dude. Nobody knows who the fuck we are over here. Can you please understand that before you get us arrested?"

"I thought we were global, dude? Our network always calls us *International Ghost Hunters*. That means global, right?"

I sighed quietly. "Yeah, bro, they do. But that's mainly when we're schmoozing sponsors and advertisers. They want us to be a global force, so their brand is associated with that."

"So we're not?"

I cocked my head slightly. "Brad, when did you get your passport?"

"About three days ago, dude, and it was gnarly. I had to go and sit in some official office somewhere, and this guy grilled me about my background and why I needed a passport so quickly. I kept telling him: *ghosts*, and I tried to explain the importance of the paranormal and why we had to save all those souls, but he just didn't understand!"

"I take it he hadn't seen our show either?"

"I guess not, dude, because I'm pretty sure he cut the meeting short."

"Why do you say that?"

"I was only in there for three minutes, bro. But I got the passport, so I guess he understood."

I didn't have the heart to tell him that the only reason he ended up with a passport in the space of twenty-four hours was because our network's Chief Legal Officer had to intervene and make a few phone calls to various very highly placed officials in D.C. The person Brad had been talking to wanted to put him on the No Fly List.

"Yeah, maybe. But whatever, dude. You only got your passport a few days ago. So how could we have been global up to this point?"

Brad screwed his face up slightly sadly. "Have we been lied to, bro?"

I rolled my eyes. "No, Brad, we haven't been lied to. We've had the *potential* to be global, but no need to be so. Until now."

Brad's eyes lit up. "But our time has come! We've tracked down some souls in Europe that need saving. That is so awesome, dude. I can't wait." He looked around. "Where's our luggage? And why is nobody else waiting for theirs?"

I led them to the other end of the huge baggage hall, and we dutifully stood and waited for our suitcases to arrive with the rest of the people on our flight. By this time, I was pretty tired, and we dragged our bags towards the sign that pointed us towards the exit. Despite Brad's insistence to head through the red channel, the 'something to declare' option, I persuaded him that being able to communicate with ghosts wasn't something you had to declare to British customs, and so we made our way through the green exit, and finally into the arrivals hall. We shuffled our way through the mass of sunburned Brits heading back from whatever vacation they'd been on, and before we'd even had time to get clear of the crowd, a smartly-dressed man tapped me on the arm.

"Mr. Sykes?"

I spun around and looked at him. "Yes?"

"Welcome to Heathrow Airport, and welcome to England, sir. Your transportation is this way. My name is Lawrence, and I'll be your personal butler for the duration of your layover."

I corralled Scooby and Scrappy and we followed the tall, immaculately dressed, quintessentially English guy in the opposite direction to the rest of the bumbling crowd. Accompanying him were three equally well-dressed porters who took our luggage from us and vanished. He led us through a door festooned with signs that made it quite clear that pretty much nobody should be going through it, and to an elevator that required not only a keycard, but also an actual key to summon.

"Pleasant flight, gentlemen?" asked Lawrence as we stepped into the elevator and the doors closed.

"The flight was great, dude," said Brad, "but the guy in the uniform was intense."

Lawrence looked at him, slightly concerned. "Was everything okay, sir? We wanted to receive you directly off the plane, but what with customs being so strict and you being on an international flight, it made it difficult for us. I hope you understand."

I butted in. "No, no, it's fine. They've just never taken an international flight before, so the questions were a bit of a shock. That's all. Ha ha." I didn't add that he knew full well that if we'd been Robert DeNiro or Brad Pitt, there would have been no problem sneaking us off the plane privately.

The elevator doors opened, and Lawrence gestured us towards three large BMW sedans. All were black, and all had tinted windows.

"Would you gentlemen prefer one each?"

I could see that Brad was about to say we were a team and therefore only needed one, but I spoke first. "That would be great, thanks."

I settled back into the plush leather and had my door closed; silence and comfort engulfed me. My driver tilted his rear-view mirror so it faced the roof of the car, and said nothing at all to me, which suited me fine; I just wanted to be alone.

Less than two minutes later, we were driving through a hugely restricted area of Heathrow airport, across various small runways, well away from the terminal we'd landed at. We finally came to a stop at a distant building that had reflective windows and was pretty much as far away from the main throng as you could get in this massive, sprawling airport. Inside the building was nothing but pure luxury and comfort; Lawrence led us to our private suite that was like a large, spacious, and extremely comfortable trendy club-cum-living room, complete with its own fully-stocked bar. It was all very impressive.

"Thank you so much again for choosing Heathrow, gentlemen. I will be just down the hall if you need anything, and the phone there is a direct line to me. If you need anything at all, please don't hesitate to contact me. I will give you a ten minute warning before your flight is due to leave and will fetch you when the time is right. Enjoy your layover!"

He glided out of the room, and the door closed behind him with a secondary click after the usual one; we'd just been locked into our suite to ensure we didn't go bumbling off out and into someone else's. That was the whole point of this ultra-exclusive section of the airport: VIPs get to travel in total anonymity right up until the second they board the plane. Of course, you don't have to be famous to use this facility, you just need to pay Heathrow a couple of grand per passenger for the privilege, and this was something I'd insisted on prior to signing my new and very lucrative contract. I'd also insisted on having a private jet take us from Heathrow to our destination: Zaragoza in Spain.

It wasn't because my new contract had gone to my head that I'd insisted on these things, it was because I knew I'd be exhausted after an eleven hour flight to London, and wouldn't have the energy to keep control of Scooby and Scrappy for three hours as they charged around a foreign and huge airport during the layover. The other reason was that the nearest airport that any major carrier flew to, in any direction, to Zaragoza is roughly two hundred miles away, which means a four hour journey in a car or minivan once we landed in Spain, and that would have just about finished me off. Mike Durkin knew that this episode had the potential to catapult the show and his network into the major leagues and so, after a brave stab at hemming and hawing, he agreed to the relatively small extra cost of these little trappings; it was something I could very easily get used to.

"Dude," said Brad almost breathlessly, "I don't know why people complain about flying internationally. It's pretty sweet! Heathrow is awesome! Look at this place!"

"Yeah, err, Brad? This isn't the regular part of Heathrow airport. This is the ultra-exclusive part. We're only here for one reason."

"Because we're VIP, like I told you earlier, dude."

I resisted the urge to reply and instead poured myself a glass of Laurent Perrier champagne and tried to do a crossword in the Times newspaper. An hour and a half and several glasses of champagne later, I'd completed a total of two crossword clues and was ready to throw the newspaper out the window. Lawrence glided into the room and politely told us that we'd be heading for our plane in ten minutes. Sure enough, ten minutes later, we were back in our blacked-out BMWs and driving across various airport roads that led us to a gleaming Learjet.

We got out of our cars and climbed the short flight of steps into the plane. The engines weren't running yet, and other people were dealing with our luggage. Inside our Learjet 45, we found two plush, cream leather seats on either side of the aisle, with two more facing them. This pattern repeated itself one further time, allowing the plane to carry eight passengers in total luxury. Each seat had a large table that could unfold right over the lap of the passenger, which mine did and then had a glass of Dom Perignon placed on it by a very well put together flight attendant, if that's what they're called on private jets.

The flight was uneventful, and once we'd touched down at Zaragoza's tiny airport, we were whisked via a slightly clapped-out Mercedes to the Hotel Palafox in the center of Zaragoza. I wasn't expecting much after having been told the price of our suites, but I was impressed when I walked into the foyer of the hotel; the architecture was a blend of old-world Spanish, and modern styling, with lots of moody lighting thrown in for good measure.

By the time we'd checked in, it was just after six p.m., and I felt like this trip had taken about two weeks to complete. We were standing by the elevators, waiting to be whisked to the top floor where we had their three and only suites, all adjacent to each other.

Scrappy was, as usual, bouncing off the walls. "Dudes! We're in *Spain*, guys! How freakin' cool is that? We're gonna save some almas perdidas. Wanna take a walk around this place? I'll bet it's crawling with fantasmas!"

I looked at Kurt and screwed my face up slightly. Kurt said, "he's been trying to learn Spanish, bro."

"That's great, Brad, and I'm no expert or anything, but I don't think you can just repeat the words with an American inflection and claim you're speaking Spanish. Anyway, what did that mean?"

"Dude! Almas perdidas are lost souls, and fantasmas are ghosts! How cool is that?"

"We should probably check with a local tomorrow on how those should be pronounced, because the way you're saying it, 'lost souls' sounds like a pair of running shoes, and 'ghosts' sounds like a ride at Disneyland. And I'm fairly sure that's not right."

"Okay, bro, good thinking. So, are we gonna explore this city, or what?"

I'd been wearing the same clothes for two days, and was kicking myself for not taking advantage of the shower and sauna in the VIP suite at Heathrow. "I think I'm going to get an early night, dude. Have some room service, take a load off. It's been a long trip, and I want to be on top form for our lock-in."

"Me too," said Kurt, looking exhausted. "I'm done in, bro."

As usual, Brad looked crestfallen that he would actually have to spend some time asleep instead of careening around whatever city he was in looking for ghosts, but even he looked tired, and that was unusual.

"Look, Brad," I said as sympathetically as I could muster, "tomorrow's a down day, remember? We're getting acclimatized and recovering from our jet lag. We can explore the city then, okay?"

Scrappy's face lit up and he nodded enthusiastically. "Dude, that is an *awesome* idea! Let's meet down here for breakfast at six, and then we can—"

"Brad?" I interrupted.

"Yeah?"

"There is absolutely no way I'm doing anything before noon tomorrow. I'm going into hibernation for the next fifteen hours. Got it?"

He let out a sigh. "Yeah, bro. Sure."

"Let's meet for lunch instead," suggested Kurt.

The elevator arrived and we stepped in. Brad hit the button for the top floor.

"Sounds good," I said. "Let's meet in the restaurant at noon."

The elevator opened and we walked out. There were only three doors on this floor, one for each of us, and we quickly found our suites and said our farewells. Once inside my room, I discovered that my suitcase had been unpacked and everything hung up in the closet, which was a nice touch. I stripped off my clothes that felt caked-on to my body and put on a robe, before heading to the mini-bar and pouring myself a scotch. The moment the liquid slid inside me and warmed my body, I felt utterly and completely exhausted and headed for the bedroom.

The bed was big. Not as big as American-sized kings, but plenty big enough for me, so I lay down with the intention of watching a bit of Spanish TV.

The next time I opened my eyes it was the following day.

XV

"So where's our lock-in going to be?" asked Kurt, clearly excited beyond belief.

Our guide, Jose, smiled a huge smile, "Ah, seenyour, I take jou to the most especial church in the whole of Zaragoza. Not many people get to see thees."

Brad looked over at me. "Bravo team are ready, dude?"

"As far as I know, bro, yes. Duff's handling comms."

Jose was driving us in an SUV, with Duff and the rest of the support crew in a small truck behind us, and it wasn't long before we got to where we were going. As we pulled up to the massive and astonishingly beautiful structure, the sun was at about three-quarters in the sky and casting long shadows everywhere. I stepped out of the SUV and was rendered almost speechless by what I was seeing. In America, a building that was built seventy-five years ago is revered as something magical and other-worldly, but what I was looking at was clearly much older than that. It was a vast building that rose well over a hundred feet into the sky, a huge Belfry tower on each side of the facade we were facing, and the middle part of it was gilded with stunning gold embossings and carvings; it was absolutely spectacular.

You didn't need to be religious to appreciate the meticulous stonework and incredible attention to detail that had clearly been put into this breathtaking building. Quite how this gigantic and magnificent structure had been built without all of today's power tools and hydraulic equipment was part of why it was so special and, the more I looked at the astonishing detail in every carved piece of stone, the more I realized that we probably couldn't recreate what I was looking at without the use of computers and lasers, and a budget of several billion dollars. I quietly asked myself whether we'd moved forward or backward with the advance of technology, but that train of thought was broken by a voice.

"Seenyours! Welcome to the most famous church of Zaragoza: the church of Santa Isabel."

My chest immediately tightened and I found it hard to breathe. Isabel? My belief in coincidences only went so far, and this was close to pushing me over the edge. I felt nauseous, and I started to hyperventilate. My hands were shaking uncontrollably.

"Thees is famous for— Amigo, are you okay?"

I was having trouble breathing and I staggered backwards with a yelp. I collapsed and vomited profusely next to the front wheel of our SUV. I remained there on my hands and knees as Duff came running over, his training making him form a human shield between me and everybody else. Once he was satisfied nobody was trying to kill me, he knelt down beside me.

"Are you okay?"

I coughed, retched, and sniffed a few times before replying. "Err, yeah, sure. I guess my lunch didn't agree with me."

He produced some Kleenex from somewhere and gave them to me. I gratefully blew my nose and wiped my face clean. "Are you sure you're not sick, sir? Mr. Durkin has put me in charge of your personal safety above everything else. I wasn't supposed to tell you that, sir, but I think you ought to know. If there's a problem, you need to tell me so I can get you to safety."

I coughed a few times. "Sir? Duff, my name's Todd, you know that!"

"I do, sir, but you are now my personal charge and there are certain BG protocols I must follow."

"BG?"

"Bodyguard."

I let this sink in. "You're now my bodyguard?"

"That is my primary duty, sir, yes. My secondary duty is security for the rest of the team."

My head was still spinning, and now it had extra things to spin around. Durkin considered me important enough to assign a bodyguard to? That was insane. "Um, okay, Duff, thanks dude. I'm fine, honestly, and you can call me Todd again, okay?"

Duff nodded in a very military-type fashion. "Call you Todd. Roger that, sir."

I groaned and let him help me up.

"Are you okay, dude?" asked Kurt.

"Yeah, bro, I'm fine. Maybe it's just excitement about this lock-in?"

Scrappy bounded up. "Oh hell yeah, dudes! I'm *so* stoked about this, you have no idea."

Actually I had a pretty good idea of how excited he was because he hadn't shut up about it since we'd arrived. Yesterday had been a relatively relaxing lunch, followed by a walk around Zaragoza, which turned out to be beautiful. We'd gone on a totally random walk, with no destination in mind. On the way, we stumbled across all manner of amazing things: we walked across a bridge over the Ebro River that led us to the simply incredible Basilica del Pilar and La Seo Cathedral, and we ended up walking past the slightly pug-ugly but extremely historic Aljaferia Palace. Of course, on the way there were numerous stops in coffee shops and wonderful little bars for a snifter of something or other, which allowed Brad to demonstrate his amazing grasp of the Spanish language that, evidently, consisted of the words 'siete' and 'alfombra', neither of which being much use to us.

I dusted myself off, and gave Duff the nod to let him know I was okay and in no danger, and I followed Scooby and Scrappy as they bounded their way towards the front doors of the Santa Isabel church. I'd given myself a strict talking-to and made sure that I understood that the name of this church was nothing more than a coincidence. Again. I was having one of those weeks, where coincidences seemed abound, but that's all it was. I was *not*, I told myself firmly, about to bump into a woman called Isabel, or Isabella, clad in a straitjacket.

We left Duff and the rest of the crew to set up the slightly more complex comms equipment needed for this trip and headed for the huge church. As we approached the front door, I felt all of the hairs on my body stand on end. Not purely because of Isabella, but the awe-inspiring magnitude of the building itself had quite an effect on pretty much everyone.

Waiting to greet us at the large, double-arch doors was the resident expert on Zaragaoza and, in particular, the grisly history of Santa Isabel church.

"Hola," she said as we approached.

"Siete," replied Brad, as I got the camera rolling.

She flashed him a slightly odd look and then continued, "my name is Ana María Álvarez, but everyone calls me Ama. Welcome to Zaragoza, and welcome to Santa Isabel! It is a pleasure to have you here, gentlemen."

Her English was excellent, and her accent was non-existent. "Thank you, we're honored to be here," I said.

"So tell us about your ghosts," blurted Brad, almost giddy with excitement.

"Well," said Ama, "Santa Isabel has had a long and very interesting history. Possibly the most famous person known to visit each night is Pedro de Arbués; he was an official of the Spanish Inquisition. He took his religious duties of the Inquisition very seriously indeed and, some said, with much zeal. In his first month of office, he held two *autos da fé*."

"Some sort of car show?" asked Brad, like a bonehead.

"No, no. An auto da fé was, well, the literal translation at least, is 'act of faith'."

"Oh," said Brad, "you sounded like it was something bad. So he, like, prays and stuff?"

"Well," said Ama, patiently, "in a sense. He prayed for people's souls."

"That is so nice," said Brad, nodding like an idiot.

Ama continued. "While they burned to death."

"Woah! He was one of *those* Spanish Inquisition dudes? Gnarly."

Ama pressed on undeterred. "Yes. Once they were condemned and relaxed by the Inquisition, the auto da fé was the public celebration of the heretics' execution. And because he was so, how would you say, *hell bent* on pursuing the agenda of the Inquisition, he became a much hated figure in Zaragoza."

"Why was he so active in this area?" I asked, genuinely interested in what had gone on.

"Ah, well, Zaragoza was inhabited by *Marranos*. The literal translation today is pig, or dirty, but back then it was used to refer to Jews that had been forced to convert to Christianity, as it swept across the Iberian Peninsula. The nickname was originally simply because they didn't eat pork, but then took on a more racial undertone as time went on. The Spanish Inquisition was convinced that they all secretly practiced Judaism, and so their persecution was extensive."

"Dude," said Kurt, "why bother forcing a whole city of people to do something they don't want and then burn them alive for not doing what they didn't like or want to do in the first place? Seems a bit, well, stupid, bro."

Brad nodded solemnly. "Word," he said and fist bumped Kurt.

"Because," continued Ama, "the Spanish Inquisition wanted everybody in Spain to adhere to their strict version of Catholicism. And the message was clear: do this, or pay the ultimate price. Marranos that led exemplary lives, and were lucky enough not to be denounced by a neighbor trying to save his own skin, were eventually categorized as *conversos*, or converts. They were generally safe, but this could take years, and a lot of luck."

"And nice neighbors," I chuckled.

"That was what usually saved your life," said Ama, not smiling. "Pedro de Arbués started his brutal reign in 1474, and was responsible for countless deaths of people he considered heretics, some who were executed and others who died during their torture. In 1485, he was praying in the cathedral when he was assassinated."

"You'd think," said Brad, "that someone like him would be more careful when he was out in public. I mean, he can't have thought many people liked him if he went around burning everyone's parents and kids?"

"He was wearing a helmet and chain mail in the cathedral. He took precautions."

I only knew a few basic things about medieval armory, but I had a reasonable idea of what happened. "Let me guess, a knife in the armpit? The one area that chain mail didn't protect?"

Ama smiled at me. "That is the assumption, and there are no medical records to provide any evidence, but apparently it took him a little while to die from his wounds, so the armpit would make sense: loss of blood from the severed artery. After his death, he was quickly made a saint, and all hell reigned down on Zaragoza for having murdered him. It was not pretty. Many Marranos were executed within days, and many more followed over the coming months. The Spanish Inquisition assumed that it was a Jewish plot, aided by the conversos that they'd trusted, so the conversos suddenly became persecuted again, but worse than before. It was a terrible time in Spain's history."

"Sounds gnarly, dude," said Brad. "And this cat visits here every night?"

"Cat?"

"He means Pedro de Arbués," I said, slightly embarrassed on Brad's behalf.

"Ah, yes! He died in the cathedral, but legend has it that he roams between the cathedral and this church every night. He spent a lot of time in Santa Isabel, and some say he may even be buried here. Although that isn't confirmed."

Brad nodded thoughtfully. "That makes total sense. The dude's spirit travels between the two places he's most familiar with: where he died, and where he spent lots of time, and was buried. I'm feeling good about this, guys."

Ama tried to correct him, "we don't know for sure that he's buried here."

"Yeah, but it makes so much sense, right? I mean where else would they bury him? The dude dies in Zaragoza, the dude gets buried in Zaragoza."

Although he was sounding like a tacky advert for Las Vegas, he did have a reasonably valid point; they had no refrigeration back then, and the only transportation was with horses so it would take forever to get anywhere. The likelihood was that Pedro was buried in Zaragoza, so why not have him buried at Santa Isabel where they had a graveyard?

I butted in. "So what about all of the people burned alive? Were their ashes gathered and put somewhere?"

Ama looked at me like I was an idiot. "No, of course not. The people were burned on top of a huge fire. The amount of ash was immense, and often there wasn't just a single person on the fire."

"So the ashes were just scattered?"

"I suppose so. Probably when they had to clear the area to burn some more people."

Brad piped up, very excited, "Oh my *god*! So you mean you might have quasi-spirits free-roaming in this city?"

"Um," said Ama, "I'm not sure what you mean."

"Well, dude! When a person is killed by fire, it's scientifically proven that parts of them drift around the area that they died in the ashes. They're not a complete soul because they're in pieces, but they act like *partial souls*, and roam around the area where they died, looking to hook up with the rest of themselves."

"Brad, dude," I said, "it's a theory, it's not proven scientifically."

"I can send you the website link, bro. Proof."

I let it go. "So, Ama, are there any distinguishing things about the ghost of Pedro that would let us know it's him?"

"Well, apparently," she said in a tone that made it quite clear she thought all this was total nonsense, "he will accuse you of being guilty, he will tell you that you're going to burn, and also that you're going to hell."

"And how many people have come into contact with him?"

"Over the last few decades, about twenty or so people have said they've been subjected to what they call a ghostly inquisition. It always happens after dark, they're always alone, and always when the church is deserted."

Of course it did, I stopped myself from saying; a lone witness, in the dark, in a cold, echoey church. The perfect place for a hallucination or over-active imagination. I had no doubt that tonight wouldn't disappoint; in fact, I knew it wouldn't because I wanted to end this season on a massive high to build anticipation for the next one. I had a feeling that my little device would be quite active tonight.

"That makes total sense," said Brad, nodding, "this cat no longer has the power of the Spanish Inquisition behind him, so he has to work alone. That means he has to accuse people when they're alone. Well, he's got a shock coming tonight, guys."

"Yeah he has," said Kurt with the same naïve enthusiasm he has before each idiotic plan that Scrappy cooks up, "because we're gonna give him a taste of his own medicine."

Brad beamed at him, "you know it, dude!"

Fist bumps ensued all round, much to the bemusement of Ama.

"Okay, gentlemen," she said, "I am ready to do your, as you say, *lock-in*. Do you have any more questions?"

Scooby and Scrappy were, as usual, bouncing around with excitement at what was about to happen; they had no further questions.

"I think we're ready," I said.

XVI

It was cold inside the church and, as usual, the sun was beginning to set as our epic 'investigation' began. The rapidly fading light was having a hard time penetrating into the massive church we were in, and it wasn't long before we needed our flashlights to see. I got busy setting up the regular array of monitors that would come into play later on, and I also set up one more monitor that had a night-vision camera on top, pointing at us, and the whole thing was connected wirelessly to the truck outside with Duff and the crew in it. On top of that truck was a decent-sized satellite dish, and would feed us the signal to and from, as Brad christened them, Bravo team.

"Okay, I think we're ready," I said, plugging in the last cable.

"Awesome, bro! Let's fire it up and get this ghost-party started!"

Because this whole trip had happened so quickly, there'd been a lot of mad scrambling to make everything happen. Several assistants had been involved in booking the travel, contacting the various officials in Spain and in the US in order to get permission to do what we were doing, so I'd been unable to maintain my usual level of control over proceedings. In fact, it had been so last minute that most of the permits were still in process while we were in the air flying across the Atlantic, and the task of finding our ghost-busting counterparts had ended up in the hands of Brad.

"So," I asked him, "who is Bravo team? And where are they?"

"Dude, it's a couple in Tennessee. They love our show, and they conduct their own investigations around their town."

Inwardly, I groaned. This was either going to be an utter disaster, or hysterically funny. I hoped it was the latter. "Uh huh. And what are their names?"

"Amanda and Jim."

"Have they found any ghosts?"

"Oh, dude! They seem to be naturals. That's why I picked them. Their blog has so much evidence of the paranormal encounters they've had, it almost seems like they could be part of our show!"

"Wow," I said unconvincingly, "that sounds great. And where are they broadcasting from?"

"They were going to figure that out and let me know."

"And did they let you know?"

"No."

"So you don't know where they are right now?"

"Not exactly, no. But it'll be good, I'm sure."

I wasn't. "Well, let's fire up the comms and find out."

Kurt butted in. "Dude, this is so fucking cool! A sat-link to *another* ghost crew!"

Brad gave him a fist-bump. "Another TV first, dude."

I made sure that the output and input was being recorded, powered up the monitor, and switched on the wireless transmission kit. It took about thirty seconds to boot up, and then the screen switched from the wireless company's logo to live footage from, I hoped, Tennessee. The screen suddenly changed to what seemed to be a bedspread with flowers and autumnal leaves on it, all in green night-vision. We could hear some huffing and puffing, but not much else.

Brad made sure he had his face right in front of our camera. "Err, dudes? Is there anybody there?"

A high-pitched shriek blasted through our speakers, and the bedspread suddenly moved. As it got further away from the camera, I suddenly realized that I was looking at an ass of immense proportions, clad in white skin-tight leggings with flowers and leaves all over them. The ass jiggled and started to rotate, and then suddenly with a huge thump, it sat down in a chair in front of their camera, causing everything to shake for a few seconds. The monitor was now showing two people; the extremely wide Amanda with her huge, coiffed blonde hair, and her husband Jim who was as thin as a rake, bald, and sporting a goatee.

Amanda's large, round face beamed in full green-glory into the camera. "Howdy, y'awwwll! Ahhhm Ahhmayyyndahhh, ayynd theeyus eeys Jiiiyuum."

I was off camera and I put my head in my hands. Was this for real? For our grand finale to the most successful show ever to broadcast on our network we have some barely intelligible backwards hicks?

"Hey guys, glad you could join us," said Brad enthusiastically. "So where are you?"

Amanda replied in her *very* slow southern drawl, "Weyyyull suuun, wey're in the Geee-orge Jowenes Chuurch in Ooak Riyudge. Wheyer are y'all?"

This was going to be a disaster. The fact that I'm American and could barely understand them put paid to any hope of this going to non-English speaking countries.

Brad replied, "We're in Zaragoza in Spain."

"Wehll, oh maahh oh maahh! Y'all are iuun another *country*?"

"We sure are, ma'am. We're at one of the key locations during the Spanish Inquisition in the fourteen hundreds."

"The whut, honey?"

"The Spanish Inquisition."

"Huh. 'Ain't that a theeyang. Jeeyum, hayyve yeeewwww ever hearrrd of this Spaynish Eeeenkwisishun?"

Jim grunted in response. "Nah. Aah've not hurrrd 'boud it."

I whacked Brad on the arm and beckoned him over to me. He told Jim and Amanda to hold on and then disappeared from their view. I hit the mute button.

"Dude! Did you speak to these people before you selected them?"

"No, bro, but they've done investigations and got results. It's on their website. We communicated via e-mail."

I sighed and rubbed my face. "Brad, dude, they can barely speak English. How are they going to be a key part of our grand finale?"

Brad thought for a second. "Subtitles?"

"Dude, if we subtitle our own countryfolk, we'll have our show taken off the air. American audiences expect foreign people to be subtitled, but everyone we've spoken to in Spain speaks better English than we do!"

"Look, bro, let's just do the lock-in and see what happens."

I was incredibly unsure that this was a good idea, but we didn't have much choice at this point. I was kicking myself for not making sure I'd had time to vet Brad's choice of a second team, but I'd had so much to help Tom out with that it had been impossible.

I took the sat link off mute and said, "sorry about that guys; technical difficulties."

Amanda guffawed, causing her huge mass to vibrate and jiggle. "Huuuney, Aaahhhh knooowwww all ahbowt thayat. Me an' Jeeyum spent two whole dayyys gettin' this here theeyung up an' runnin'."

I dreaded to think of the state our sat-link kit would come back in after these two clowns had been fiddling with it, but I could worry about that later; the show must go on. The one consolation I gave myself was that at least the episode wasn't being broadcast live, which was something Brad had kept suggesting, so I'd be able to edit most of Amanda and Jim out.

"Okay Brad, want to do the intro monologue?"

"You got it, dude!"

I started recording and pointed the NV camera at Brad, signaling him to begin.

"Tonight's lock-in is something truly special, guys, and once again we're making TV history. Two things make tonight's show totally off the hook; one, we're in *Spain*, guys! As in Spain the country! A place called Zaragoza, to be precise, at one of the key locations of the *Spanish Inquisition*: Santa Isabel church."

A cold shiver ran down my spine at the mention of her name, and I forced myself to calm down and focus solely on what I was doing at that moment; holding a camera. I tried to take my mind off Isabella by thinking about how I'd edit this part of the episode, and I thought about everything that Ama had told us and how I'd weave it into this intro when I was back in the editing suite.

"And two, we're testing the well known theory that lost souls and spirits can actually use our real-world communication channels as a sort of spiritual freeway to move along back and forth as they see fit. So, we've set up a live satellite link from Spain all the way back to Tennessee in America, where we have an amateur ghost hunting team, Amanda and Jim, also in an old church."

I swung the camera round to show the monitor. Amanda waved frantically at us.

"Hey theyerrrr y'awwllll!"

Jim clearly didn't get to say much in this relationship.

I panned back to Brad. "Oh, man, this is so exciting! So, do you guys want to tell the folks at home about why you chose that church?"

"Shuuuweerrr aahhhh weeeyullll!"

I then had to endure a ten minute drawlathon as Amanda recounted the story, agonizingly slowly, of the church they were in: The George Jones church and cemetery in Oak Ridge, Tennessee. Built in the late 1800s, there have been numerous reported sightings of ghosts roaming around after dark, apparently the lost souls of some people that were murdered nearby. There was also a local preacher that apparently committed suicide by hanging himself in the bell tower, and people claim to have seen his ghostly form dangling from a noose, swinging back and forth, moaning and causing the beam he's hanging on to creak. Another key factor in their choice of location, I had no doubt, was that it was less than two miles from their house.

Finally she'd finished her tedious explanation that could have been done in about sixty seconds by most people, and I swung the camera gratefully back to Brad. "Guys, that is *awesome*! I think it's time for us to begin the investigation and set up our paranormal capturing devices. Stay safe, Bravo team; our lock-ins can get pretty scary!"

I pressed the button in my pocket a couple of times.

"Oohhhhkaayyyyy, Braaayyyyyuudddd, we weeeyulll."

I felt like someone had been pouring maple syrup in my ears for the last twenty minutes, so it was a relief to not have to talk to her for a while. For once the company of Scooby and Scrappy was quite appealing.

"Let's go, Alpha team," said Brad, as we made our way via NV cameras through the huge, ancient church. We'd set the monitors up, or 'base camp' as Brad now called it, inside the vast, stone entrance to the church, and now we were going to head deeper into the building. The exit from the vestibule was a huge pair of oak doors that curved towards each other at the top, with a good-sized wrought-iron circular handle on each door. Brad twisted one of the handles with some considerable effort, and finally the latch on the other side clicked and allowed the door to open, which in itself was no simple feat, bearing in mind the weight of the door. Once through the vast doorway, we entered the congregational seating area where row up row of pews stretched in front of us, and the utter majesty of the room we were in was nothing short of staggering, even when viewed through the small green screen of a night vision camera.

"*Fuck*," breathed Kurt.

"Dude, you can't swear. We're in church."

"Oh yeah, sorry, bro. This place just kind of takes my breath away, you know?"

"Oh yeah," said Brad, "I know. Feeling all the lost souls swarming around us right now, you mean?"

That wasn't what Kurt had meant at all, but I pressed the button in my pocket four times without any clear plan of what this episode would turn into. The way I figured it, the more options I had in the editing suite, the better it would be for the episode, the network, our show, and, most importantly, my bank balance.

Brad led us through the aisle between the rows of pews and before we knew it, we were in the area where the priest would stand to give the sermon.

"What's this bit called?" I asked.

"Church," said Brad.

"This is the chancel," said Kurt, ignoring him. "This is where the priest speaks from the lectern."

"Oh, then dude! We need to have a recorder set up right here. What if the spirit of an ancient priest wants to speak to us? This is the place he'd do it! Maybe the dead priest from Tennessee will come and visit and give a sermon."

"Mmmm, yeah, maybe," I said as I dutifully recorded Brad setting up an audio recorder on the lectern that would, undoubtedly, capture every single creak, groan, and clank from ancient wood and metal as it changed temperature.

Once that was set up, we bumbled our way past the chancel in darkness, our natural night vision ruined by the bright glow of the camera LCD screens, and stumbled across an altar.

"Woah, dude," blurted Brad in his exaggerated whisper as he panned his camera over the vast figure of, what I assumed was, the virgin Mary. "Look at this!"

Mary's statue was surrounded by stone pillars, more statues, and intricately bejeweled crosses that were about seven feet tall. It was hard to make out the exact details in the low-light conditions, but I could just tell it would be absolutely spectacular in proper light.

"We must be in the sanctuary," said Kurt, almost without thinking. "I'll bet there's a chapel behind this."

Brad looked at Kurt. "Have you been here before, dude?"

"No, bro, but I had pretty strict religious teachings growing up. I had to learn all the parts of a church."

Brad looked at me, his eyes glowing a demented green back at my camera viewer, and then looked back at Kurt. "Well, let's see if you're right, dude!"

We headed past the altar and, sure enough, found a fairly small door. Brad opened it and peered inside. "Does this look like a chapel?"

Kurt peered inside, panning his camera around. "Yep, dude, that looks like an apse."

"You said we'd find a chapel, bro."

"Apse is the official name for this room, dude. It's a chapel, but a small one behind the sanctuary and it's called an apse."

"So what happens in here?"

"Well, all sorts of things: prayers, confessions, repentance, forgiveness, accusations, denials, and who knows what else. But the whole point of the apse is that it's done in private with only the priest in attendance. It's meant to be just you and your conduit to God."

"Sort of like a therapist?" asked Brad.

"Err, sure. Yeah, bro, a therapist. Except that during the days of the Spanish Inquisition, the priest was about as confidential as a bull horn. The moment anybody confessed to anything, or accused anyone, the Inquisition was on their ass within hours. And then they ended up dead a few years later, after having been tortured for months at a time."

"Dude! That is *not* cool! I thought therapists had that doctor/ client privilege thing that stopped them talking to other people?"

I rolled my eyes, "Brad, back in those days there were no therapists or doctor privileges, or any of that. You simply told your problems to your priest, and he'd look after you. Well, that was how it was supposed to work."

"Except in the days of the Inquisition," said Kurt, "any priests not regularly reporting members of their flock to the gnarly dudes would come under scrutiny themselves for possibly being a secret Jew, and once that happened they were as good as dead."

"So," I said, genuinely shocked, "it was in their own best interests to sacrifice probably innocent members of their own congregations?"

"It sure was, dude. And they did. Lots of them. Scary, or what?"

"So," Brad blurted, and then remembered he was supposed to be whispering so the ghosts wouldn't know that all of the clattering around and people charging back and forth in the church were actually ghost hunters. His pantomime whisper returned. "So, this room was probably where lots of people confessed to that dude?"

"Pedro de Arbués?"

"Yeah, that cat."

"Quite possibly," whispered Kurt. "It's quite likely that, once poor old John Doe—"

"More like Jose Doe, dude. We're in Spain, remember?"

Kurt carried on undeterred. "Once the poor guy had come in here and spoken to his priest, a few days later he would be dragged back into here to be interrogated by Pedro and a few of his goons. In total private, so nobody would hear the screams. If Pedro wasn't convinced by the dude, or he didn't immediately confess to heresy, then he would have been arrested and, basically, fucked over."

"Dude, you can't swear."

"Sorry, bro, but that's how it went down."

Brad thought for a few moments as he looked around the dark room. "Guys, I think I've got an idea."

XVII

I was back at 'base camp', sitting in front of the array of monitors glowing brightly and greenly back at me. On one, I had a live feed from Brad's NV camera as he explored deeper into the church. On another, I had the two empty chairs that belonged to Amanda and Jim. On a third, I could see Kurt, dressed up as a priest, sitting in the apse all by himself.

Brad had declared that because the only sightings of Pedro had been by people by themselves and at night, the only way we'd draw him out and have him beckon fellow ghosts from Tennessee was to split up and be alone. I didn't bother to mention that all ghostly sightings happen at night and when the person is alone, because I knew this could provide some amazing footage.

The radio crackled. "Dudes?"

It was Kurt, so I waited for Brad to answer it. I looked at Kurt on the monitor and he was sitting on a chair that was beautiful and probably hundreds of years old. The robes and clerical clothing he was wearing were found in a closet by Brad and, I'm sure, when the principles in charge of Santa Isabel found out they'd go apoplectic. But by then it would be too late.

He was looking around nervously, and his radio crackled again. "Dudes? Guys? Is anybody there?"

Finally, Brad responded. "Yeah, hey bro. What's up?"

"Errr, I, errr, I'm just checking in. This room is a little creepy, guys."

"Of course it is, dude," said Brad unhelpfully, "you've probably got a bunch of ghosts in there with you."

I watched Kurt on the monitor as his head darted around, and the radio crackled again. "I think I feel them, dude. And I think one of them is pissed."

Brad responded. "Talk to them, dude. See if that Pedro cat is in there with you. That would be pretty gnarly. Perhaps you can interrogate *him*!"

"Uh, yeah, sure bro. I'll try that," replied Kurt like an idiot.

Suddenly there was a huge creak from a different set of speakers, and I looked at Bravo team's monitor. Amanda had just sat her planetary-sized body back onto the hopelessly mismatched chair that sounded like it was about to collapse; Jim dutifully took his place next to her.

"Weeeyyuulll, Brraaayyyyuudddd," she said, "Me an' Jeeeeyyyummm have set uhhhp theee eeekwwipppmeeyeennnt."

"It's not Brad, it's Todd."

The radio crackled into life. "Uhhh, Pedro de Arbués, are you in here with me?"

I was caught slightly off-guard because I wasn't used to having a live feed going on simultaneously, but I reached into my pocked and pressed the button on my device a few times, rapidly losing track of who was saying and doing what.

"Oooowwhhhh, Ahhhhh'mmmm soowwwreeyy Taaahhhhhddddd!"

I looked back at Bravo team. "Don't worry about it. And that's great, guys. Any unusual sightings so far?"

"Aaaahhh doohhhn't theeenk so, sweedie."

"Pedro de Arbués," said the walkie talkie, "are you here? I need to talk to you."

I looked at Brad's monitor and he'd managed to find some sort of garden area to wander around in. I had absolutely no idea where he was, and just knew instinctively that he was lost.

Kurt continued via the walkie talkie. "You think I'm afraid of your torture Pedro? Well, you're wrong. You and I need to talk, *now*. Face to face. Right now."

"Ohh!" said Jim from the monitor in front of me.

I spun my head back to their monitor. "Oh? Oh, what?"

The walkie talkie burst into life again. "Come on, you coward! Let's do this!"

"Uhh, beehhaaahhnnd you, Brayyuud."

"Taahhhdd," corrected Amanda.

"Behind me? What's behind me?"

"Weeyyulll, Ahh saw a ghowwwstly sumthin' beehahhhnd yuh."

It was driving me insane that these people couldn't speak at a normal speed. "A what?"

Amanda replied. "A theeyyung, huhhney. Eeyen the darrrk beeehaahhhnndd yuh."

Involuntarily I span around, using my NV camera's viewfinder to scan the room. I saw nothing, but felt a cold chill run down my entire body.

"There's nothing in here with me, Amanda. I just checked."

I looked at what Kurt was up to and he was out of shot. "Hold on, guys, I need to check in with Kurt."

I hit the radio. "Kurt, dude. Are you okay? Where are you?"

There was no response. I looked at Brad's camera and he appeared to be sitting in the middle of a bush.

"Kurt! Speak to me, bro!"

The audio feed from Tennessee was still active and suddenly I heard Jim say, "Theeyyerr it eeyyuz ahgayun. Raahhhht beehaahhhhhnd heeyum."

I span around again, but still couldn't see anything. I was starting to get a little freaked out.

"Kurt! For fuck's sake! Answer me!"

"Aaaahhhh theeeyyyuunnkkk aahhhh sawww eeeyyuutttt too!"

"What?" I span around again, and my breathing was quickening. "What did you see? Where? What was it?"

The walkie talkie crackled and I heard heavy breathing for a few seconds. "Dude. *Dude*! Fuck!"

I grabbed it and hit the button. "Bro! What? What's the matter?"

I got no reply. "Kurt! What's going on?"

Without warning, a huge clanking noise assaulted my eardrums from behind me, and I lurched forward, knocking over various monitors as I crashed my way to the floor.

"What the *fuck* was that?" I screamed to nobody, as bits of kit crashed and smashed around me.

It was too loud and too clear to be a metal joint cooling down, and it certainly wasn't wood creaking, so what the hell was it?

"Brraaayyyyuudddd? Are yeewwww oohhhhkaayyyy?"

I was on the floor and in pain from my landing, so it took a little while for me to get my breath back, which was now coming in small, short gasps. "Um, yeah, sure. I just slipped. And it's Todd, not Brad."

Where the hell had that noise come from?

"Aaarrrrrree yyeeewwww shuuuwwwerr yeewwweeeerrr oohhhkaaayy Taaahhhddd?"

I let out a groan as I moved and disentangled myself from everything that had fallen on top of me. As I looked at what was left on the table, I could see that the main thing I'd smashed was Kurt's monitor. I now had no feed to see what was going on in the apse.

The walkie talkie burst into life again. "*Fuck*! Help me! He's in here!"

I reached for the walkie talkie on my belt but it wasn't there, and I wasn't sure where my camera was. Both must have been knocked across the room during my fall, so I scrambled around in almost pitch dark trying to find either one of them. The dim glow from the LCD monitors wasn't helping much.

"*Guys!* I'm in big fucking trouble here! This dude is nuts!"

I could hear Kurt pounding on the door that we'd locked with a huge oak beam on the outside. I crashed my way through the bits of broken equipment on the floor, desperately searching for the walkie talkie. I felt a sharp pain on my left hand and knew I'd cut myself on something, but I didn't care; I needed to speak to Kurt. The walkie talkie had to be around me somewhere, but I just couldn't find it, and my flashlight was out of reach. I was getting really panicked.

"Jeeeyyuuummm, doo yeeww theeeunnk everrryyythheengzz ahhhhlllllrrraaahhhhttt?"

"Nuh, uhhh," said Jim. "Loook! Theeeyyeerrrr she eeyyusss aggaayyyunnn!"

I stopped what I was doing and sat up to look at their monitor. "She? She who?"

"Ahhh dohhhn't know hunneyy, buhht it looooks laahhhk aayyy layyydeyyy keeyyups staahhhndin' ohhverrr yuuww."

"Did you say a lady? There's nobody in here, Amanda. Are you sure you're actually seeing this? It's not a light spot or reflection?"

"Aahhh doohhhhwn't theeenk sow. Jeeyuum?"

"Sheee's theyyurr ahhhllrahhht."

My walkie talkie burst into life once more. "*Guys!* Fucking *fuck!* Get me the hell out of here *now!* Pedro has set the fucking room on *fire* and I'm trapped! *Help me!*"

"Eyyen her waaahhht dreyuss," Said Jim.

"Ahhh doohhhnnn theeyunk eeyuttt's a dreeyyuusss, Jeeyyyyuummm. Eeyut's suhhhm sortah waaahht coaaahht."

White coat? My heart rate suddenly went off the chart. I span around several times, looking at the room all around me. I couldn't see anything.

"Isabella?" I blurted without knowing it. "Are you here?"

"I think I'm lost," said the walkie talkie. It was Brad. "I'm in some sort of tool shed or something."

"Lost? Again? *Dude!* I'm not exaggerating here, this room you locked me in? It's on *fucking fire!*"

"Eeeyyyyyssaaahhhh-who?" said Amanda.

I still hadn't found the my walkie talkie, my flashlight, or my camera, and I needed to find at least the first two of them and then get to Kurt. He was clearly in trouble, so I decided to switch the cables from Kurt's broken monitor and plug them into Amanda and Jim's so I could see what was going on in the apse.

"Amanda, Jim, I'm gonna have to go offline for a while. Don't go anywhere."

"Buuhhtttt, weyyyuvvvve seyyutt uhhhpp—"

I yanked the cables from the back of their monitor and was suddenly attacked by a huge stab of pain that seemed to penetrate every inch of my body; it was instantaneous and unexpected agony, and I think I screamed.

When I opened my eyes, it took a little while to remember where I was and why I was there. Gradually it came back to me that I was unplugging cables, but I was now about six feet from them in a heap on the floor, and as the ringing in my ears slowly subsided, I could hear Kurt's terrified voice screaming for help. What had just had happened?

I felt like I'd been hit by a truck, I was tingling all over, and all of my limbs were shaking, but I pulled myself to my feet as quickly as I could. I knew I needed to find the walkie talkie, so I started to search for it again. Suddenly, out of nowhere, there was a huge bang on the door; I wasn't sure if it came from the inside or outside, but I knew it wasn't Kurt or Brad, because Kurt was still screaming about the room being on fire, and Brad was currently trying to find his way out of the shed he'd got stuck in. What was making these weird noises? Of course, the room being essentially pitch black wasn't helping my state of mind; I was becoming increasingly terrified.

The walkie talkie crackled, and it was Brad. "I think I'm locked into this shed thing."

Kurt exploded. "*Guys!!!* I'm gonna burn alive! Todd, where the fuck are you? *Help me!*"

Brad was now out of the equation, so rescuing Kurt was all down to me. There was no way he was going to be able to open that door from the inside, and there were no windows to escape through; I'm sure the Spanish Inquisition found that to be very handy.

"I haven't heard from Todd for a while," said Brad. "I hope he hasn't been possessed."

Another bang on the door made me let out a yelp, and then totally out of the blue, my flashlight switched itself on, the sudden bright light startling me and causing me to stumble backwards and trip over some object or other. I tumbled blindly in the dark, and banged my head hard on the stone floor as I landed; I suddenly had flashes of light sparking in front of my vision, and my head was swimming. I clawed my way onto my hands and knees and desperately crawled toward the bright flashlight. I grabbed it and quickly shone it round the room; I saw my walkie talkie and I lurched for it.

The moment it was in my hand, I heard a faint whisper that made my blood turn cold. It was distant, yet close at the same time. It was quiet, and could have just been a light breeze, had there been somewhere that a breeze could have come from.

"I'm out!" declared Brad triumphantly through the walkie-talkie.

"Thank christ for that, dude," screamed Kurt, coughing. "Now come and *get me out of here*! There's smoke everywhere!"

"Sure dude. Where are you again?"

"What? Fucking hell bro, the apse! You locked me in here! Behind the lectern. *Hurry!*"

I refused to believe what my brain was telling me I'd just heard, so I waited again to hear another breeze drift through the room, but after several seconds, it was clear there was none. No wind, no breeze, nothing.

And then I heard it again. It wasn't a breeze, or wind. It was a faint voice. A faint woman's voice, and it said the same thing as last time: "you're welcome".

I lurched to my feet, screaming. It couldn't be true! There are no such thing as ghosts, and Isabella had *not* just turned my flashlight on to help me rescue Kurt. None of that had happened. It was impossible; it had to be cross-talk from one of the speakers or something. It *had* to be, and the rational side of my brain was telling me that. The other part of my brain, however, the part that controls my fear and flight response, was screaming at me that it was a ghost and that I needed to get the hell out of there.

"Leave me alone Isabella!" I screamed around the room over and over, frantically spinning and shining the flashlight everywhere.

My flashlight beam caught the huge wooden doors and I ran to them, screaming, as fast as I could manage. My pulse was through the roof and I was finding it harder and harder to breathe; I was hyperventilating and needed to calm down, but the situation I was in didn't allow for that. I grabbed hold of one of the circular handles on the door and twisted it; nothing happened. I yanked on the door, and nothing happened. I pushed the door, and still nothing happened.

I pounded my fists onto the massive slab of oak, screaming for help, but of course no-one came. I kicked at the door desperately, and then I twisted the handle some more and charged at it with my shoulder, but still with no luck.

"Let me out!" I screamed. "Isabella, *let me out!*"

I was getting light headed, probably because of the hyperventilation, and I was gripped with pure terror. I twisted the other handle and charged at the door with my shoulder. Still nothing happened, and I could feel my chest tightening in a way I'd never experienced before. A shooting pain rocketed through me, seemingly from my stomach all the way up to my head and then back down again, and it almost completely debilitated me. Suddenly I knew I had just enough energy for one more attempt at the door, kind of like when you're in the gym and you know you have just enough strength left for one last rep and no more, but this felt more final, somehow. As if this was truly my last attempt. Ever.

My will was ebbing along with my strength, and so I tried to focus. The pain in my chest was getting worse, and breathing was becoming more and more difficult, but I fought against the pain and zeroed in on the door handle. I twisted it as much as I could, using both hands, and pulled myself as far back as I could manage before charging forward and slamming my entire body, shoulder first, against the door.

Whatever had been stopping it from opening gave way and I burst through and into the main part of the church. I'd been so convinced that it wouldn't open that I was shocked with the sudden freedom of movement my body had, and I didn't really know how to control my flight, so I ended up just sprawling through in a whirl of arms and legs. I hit the stone floor really, really hard, and any breath I had left was knocked right out of me by the impact. Various limbs hurt far more than expected, and my hyperventilation gave way to simply not being able to breathe.

The pain in my chest suddenly intensified and seemed to grip my whole body. I spasmed and tried to suck in air, but wasn't able to. As I lay there in a heap on the cold, stone floor of Santa Isabel church, I was just about able to clutch my chest, when my pain started to fade away as my consciousness did the same. I knew I needed to help Kurt, but there was nothing I could do; my body was utterly spent. My eyelids became heavy, and they began to close, the stabs of pain from my chest now felt like dull thuds, and I seemed not to care about them any more.

The last thing I heard before my eyes closed was either the breeze, or that faint, whispered, ghostly voice once more.

"You didn't say thank you."

XVIII

I died.

To be completely factual about this, I died twice, and that is no mean feat.

My first death happened on the floor of Santa Isabel church. After bursting out of the vestibule, I'd been so freaked out and panicked by everything that had been going on, that I'd gone into cardiac arrest, which had been the pain I'd felt growing in my chest as I scrambled to help Kurt.

Kurt had been correct: the room he was trapped in was indeed on fire, and Brad had managed to reach him in the nick of time. When he'd hauled the huge oak beam from off the door and opened it, smoke billowed out and Kurt stumbled to freedom, gasping for air and coughing his lungs out. In a surprisingly quick-witted move, he dragged Kurt near where the altar was and then ran back to base camp where he knew the external walkie-talkie was.

That was when he came across my body, slumped in the aisle between the pews. Once again, in an entirely un-Brad-like decision, he left me where I was, ran into the vestibule and quickly found the walkie-talkie, told Duff what was happening, and then ran back to me to find out what was wrong.

He'd called the cavalry first, and that had saved my life, and probably prevented the entire historic structure of Santa Isabel from burning to the ground. Duff burst into the church with two other members of the crew, both carrying fire extinguishers, and told them exactly what to do to put the fire out. He then turned his attention to me, and gave me CPR, which did nothing. My heart wasn't beating, I had no pulse, and I wasn't breathing. I was dead.

Out of what he called his 'immediate action' bag, he'd pulled a portable external defibrillator, or PED, and then proceeded to give my heart three increasingly large electric shocks in an attempt to get it beating again. The first two seemingly did nothing and, as a final last-ditch attempt, Duff ratcheted up the power to near maximum and gave me one final blast that got my heart going again. Apparently I regained consciousness briefly, but I have no recollection of that.

Thanks to Duff's training, the moment he'd got the panicked radio message from Brad, he'd speed-dialed the local fire and medical response teams, which he always had programmed into his phone wherever we were, and they'd arrived fast enough to stabilize me, and to make sure the entire church didn't burn to the ground. I was whisked in an ambulance to the local hospital, *Hospital Universitario Miguel Servet*, and immediately admitted. I was hooked up to various IVs, monitoring machines, and then sedated. Kurt had to be treated for smoke inhalation, but had no burns.

The following day, I recovered consciousness. I slowly blinked my eyes open and breathed a few times as I used my aching eyes to look around the room. My mouth felt like it was coated in fur, and that made me involuntarily try to swallow, which in turn made me gag and choke. I didn't seem to have a single molecule of moisture in my mouth anywhere. I closed my eyes again; I felt like I'd rather be dead.

Suddenly my head was lifted gently from the pillow, and a small cup was placed against my lips. It poured a small amount of water into my mouth and I gratefully swallowed it. A few more sips, and my head was rested back on the pillow.

"More," I croaked.

"Sorry sir," said Duff, "I need to give you liquid in controlled doses or you'll get nauseous. I promise there'll be more very soon."

"Duff?" I croaked. "Is that you?"

"Yes sir, it's me. I've been keeping watch since you were admitted."

I coughed again, and got some more water given to me in what seemed like a sort of Pavlovian Conditioning kind of way. I'd never had water taste so good in my life; the finest champagne money can buy couldn't taste as good as this did.

"Where am I?"

"Hospital, sir. Still in Zaragoza."

Another cough, more water.

"Why am I in hospital? God, I feel like crap."

Duff paused as he figured out how to tell me the news. "Um, you had an *incident*, sir."

"What sort of incident?"

He paused again. "May I ask what you remember?"

Cough. Water.

I cast my mind back. "I remember being back in base camp, and Kurt getting stuck in the room."

Suddenly I had a recollection of the previous night! The fire!

"Oh fuck!" I blurted. "Kurt! Is he okay?"

Duff nodded, "he's fine, sir. A bit of smoke inhalation, but nothing serious."

"So the room really was on fire?"

"Oh yes. The drapes were fully ablaze. He's under observation at the moment, but the Spanish authorities are waiting to speak to him about it."

"How did it happen?"

"I'm not sure yet, sir. I'll be debriefing Kurt shortly after I'm confident you're well enough to be left alone. Mr. Durkin says that is my second priority after your welfare."

I let out a long breath and closed my eyes. "Thank god for that."

"Well, it wasn't god. Brad acted with amazingly good instincts and basically saved both of your lives. To be honest, I wouldn't have expected it from him, but he did really well. What else do you remember, sir?"

I thought back to that evening. "I remember knocking over the monitor that had Kurt's feed on it. I think a noise surprised me and I fell, pushing it to the ground. Actually, I think that hurt. A lot. And then I couldn't find my walkie talkie, but could hear Kurt screaming for help. And so I decided to unplug Bravo team's monitors. That's when things went even more downhill."

"Ah, so *you* unplugged those cables?"

"Yes. Well, I tried to, but I think I got electrocuted or something."

"You certainly did, sir. The power cable to the monitor had a gash in it that was exposing the live wire. When you grabbed the plug, you must have touched it and had the voltage go through you. It's lucky you were in Europe and not Britain."

"Why?"

"Europe is like the US, and uses one hundred and ten volts, but Britain runs on two-twenty. You'd almost certainly have been killed, or seriously injured at the very least."

"Oh, terrific. Why did the cable have a hole in it? I don't think it did when I plugged it in. Well, I suppose it might have; I always connect the monitor end before the power end."

"That's one of the many things we're going to try and ascertain about that curious night, sir."

My throat was much more lubricated now. "Dude, can we stop with the 'sir' stuff? Just call me Todd like you used to. Please?"

"Yessir, Todd. What do you remember after that?"

I thought for a few seconds. "Um, I remember tripping over something and cracking my head on the floor. That hurt like hell.

Then my flashlight suddenly switched on and I was able to find the door, but it wouldn't open. I bashed against it a few times and finally it opened, and I fell to the floor. That's pretty much where I black out."

I suddenly remembered the voice that had said '*you didn't say thank you*', and my face gave an involuntary spasm.

"What?" asked Duff, clearly looking for any sign of something unusual. "What did you just remember?"

"Oh, errr, it was nothing. I think I was imagining it. Probably from the whack on the head."

"Sir, please? This is very important. What was that thing you just remembered after you opened the door?"

"Well, I, errr, I think I heard a voice, but I'm pretty sure it was just a breath of wind or something. It was very faint. I doubt it was a voice."

Duff paused for a while, looking at me. "And if it had been a voice, what would it have said?"

"I don't remember," I said too quickly.

Duff looked at me, and then smiled knowingly. "Well perhaps you'll remember later. Once you'd finally escaped from the vestibule, you suffered a massive heart attack, and only just clung on to life. It took me three goes with the defib to bring you back to life. You were dead for about sixty seconds, I reckon."

I opened my eyes. "I was dead?"

"No breathing, no pulse, no heartbeat. Clinically speaking, you were dead."

I closed my eyes. "*Fuck.*"

"It was a close one, sir, that's for sure."

I was bursting to tell Duff that I was convinced Isabella had been in there with me, and had even helped me, perhaps helped Brad too, and then I pissed her off by not acknowledging her help, but I just couldn't bring myself to. I'd sound like a babbling idiot still suffering the effects of the trauma I'd undergone. I also wasn't convinced that I believed it myself. Perhaps the voice had been the result of a concussion after hitting my head on the floor so hard? That was a far more believable reason for what I think I heard.

I asked for more water, and got it. Much more this time. Duff had clearly decided I was on the mend.

I turned my head slightly and looked at Duff. "Thanks, dude. For everything. You saved my life. I don't think I'll ever be able to repay you."

Duff smiled a tight smile. "Just doing my job, sir. But, you're welcome. I guess I should go and check on Kurt now that you're out of the woods."

Duff stood, and I suddenly had a burning question for him.

"Duff?" I blurted.

"Yes, sir?"

"Do you believe in ghosts?"

He gave a little chuckle. "Do I currently have my TV network hat on, or are you asking my personal opinion?"

"No, no. No TV network. Personally speaking, do you believe in ghosts?"

He opened the door to my room before looking back at me. "No, sir. Of course I don't. And I don't think you did either up until a few hours ago. But something very strange just happened, didn't it?"

Before I could answer, he'd slipped through the door, closing it behind him.

I lay my head back and closed my eyes again. Strange was an understatement. Had I just encountered a ghost, or had I been hallucinating and hearing voices because of the whole Isabella thing? Of course, the crack on the head in the vestibule wouldn't have helped my state of mind, especially when combined with the panic I was suffering while trying to save Kurt from burning to death. I supposed the huge electric shock wouldn't have done my brain too many favors either. The more I thought about everything my body had endured the previous night, the more I calmed down. Sure, there were some unexplained noises, and the two redneck halfwits claiming to see a woman behind me, but I could verify all that once I got out of the hospital.

I relaxed considerably, and actually started to feel quite calm about the whole thing. I knew that Mike Durkin was going to go up the wall at an expensive and ruined episode, but I could deal with him later. And anyway, who's to say we hadn't got enough freaky footage to at least put together an hour-long show? I mean, we had Brad sitting in a bush and then getting locked into a shed, Kurt somehow managed to set the room he was locked into on fire and come close to burning to death, and I ended up being dead. That could be quite an episode.

The door to my room opened, and I didn't bother opening my eyes. "Hey Duff, can I get some more water please?"

There was a metallic clanking noise and the door closed. Then there was a squeaking noise for a few seconds.

I spoke again, "Duff?"

"Ah, sorry señor! I didn't want to wake you! I am your doctor. How are you feeling?"

I opened my eyes and lifted my head. A man that looked to be in his mid-fifties was walking slowly towards my bed, pulling a metal cart of some sort. His hair was wispy and he'd attempted to comb it back over his head, but there wasn't really much left to comb. His face was gaunt, his cheeks hollow, and his eyes looked like they had huge bags under them. His white coat was grubby and had dark red stains in spots all over it. He looked utterly exhausted.

"Dude," I said, "are you okay?"

"Me, señor? Oh yes, I'm fine. It has just been a really long time since I slept. I'm sure you know what I mean."

"I sure do. It's been quite a night."

The doctor stood at the foot of my bed and looked down at the chart. "Cardiac arrest, eh?"

I nodded as best I could, thinking that his accent didn't seem in the least bit Spanish. "You're American, aren't you?" I asked him.

"I am, señor, yes. I moved here a very short while ago."

"So why do you keep calling me 'señor'?"

He chuckled, and then coughed. "Oh, it's a local tradition. Kind of fun, actually."

"Are you sure you're okay? You sound a bit sick."

"Don't you worry about me. How are you feeling?"

"I feel like utter crap. But better than I did, I guess. What's on that cart you're dragging with you?"

"Oh, this old thing? It's a force of habit. Ha ha. I never leave my tools unattended. You never know when there's a thief about! The safest place is by my side, so here they are. Look."

He wheeled his creaky cart into my view and it was an aging surgical trolley that contained some old-fashioned looking surgical implements on them. It was a little difficult for him to wheel it around in any direction but a straight line, and I wrenched my upper body further upright and looked down to see why.

It only had three wheels.

Panic flooded through me, but I tried to keep my breathing under control and I exhaled slowly through my mouth a few times before replying. As calmly as I could, which wasn't very, I said, "Uhh, are you a doctor or a surgeon?"

"Oh, in my time I've done all sorts. You know, jack of all trades."

More deep breaths, trying to control my utter terror. "Your cart only has three wheels."

"Oh, yes. I know. I keep meaning to get it fixed, but never seem to find the time. I'm sure you know what I mean."

"What do you mean, 'I know what you mean'?"

"Well, you and your pancreas. What have you done to get it fixed?"

I coughed a few times and sat up as best I could. "What are you talking about? My pancreas? Why do I need to have it fixed? I had a fucking heart attack! It's nothing to do with my pancreas. Are you sure you're a doctor? No, in fact tell me right now why the hell you're dragging a cart full of surgeon's tools around behind you. Who the fuck are you?"

"Oh, you mean nobody told you?"

I was beginning to get a little freaked out, and the bleeping from my heart rate monitor told me that it wasn't having a great time either. "Told me what?"

"Oh, dear oh dear. And this is supposed to be a hospital! You'd think they'd have the best interests of their patients at heart."

"Okay, dude. You need to stop all this waxing lyrical and get to the fucking point. What about my pancreas?"

"Nobody told you. I am deeply shocked that—"

"So *tell me*. Right now!"

The doctor looked me right in the eyes and I felt a chill run through me to my very core. In fact, the whole room seemed to drop a few degrees. He said calmly, "you have pancreatic cancer."

"I *what*?"

"It's in the very early stages, so it's barely noticeable, but it's there alright."

My pulse monitor was starting to increase, and the bleeps in the room were getting quicker and quicker. I had cancer? Why hadn't anybody told me?

I stuttered my reply. "So... so... is it curable? I mean, how serious is pancreatic cancer?"

"Well," said the doctor casually, "there's generally a five percent survival rate."

"A what?! *Five percent*?"

"But that's usually with people who wait until the cancer is easy to detect. By the time you get the abdominal pain and uncontrollable vomiting, it's too late and you're going to die within maybe six months. There's not much to be done when it's reached that stage, and before then it's almost undetectable. It's a nasty disease."

My breathing was coming in shorter gasps now, and a sense of panic was beginning to grip me. I tried to speak calmly, "so how do *you* know I have it this early?"

He chuckled. "I know lots of things about you, Todd."

I sat bolt upright in bed, feeling the IV needles in various places in my arms tug painfully at me. A few of the IV drip stands wheeled a few inches across the room.

"Just who the fuck are you?"

He chuckled again, in a way that was getting annoying, "oh, how remiss of me! I didn't ever introduce myself. Todd, I'm your doctor for the duration of your stay here. My name is Arthur."

My brain suddenly went into a whirl of confusion. Arthur? A surgical cart with a wheel missing and old implements on it? My mind then flew back to Saint Joseph's and the morgue. Surely it couldn't be?

My eyes went wide and I stared at Arthur. He looked back at me and smiled. "Remember me now, do you?"

"What? No! This is *not* possible! Get the fuck away from me! You don't exist!"

Arthur began to walk towards my bed. "I'm here to help you, Todd. Just let me treat you. I'll do a much better job than these people. And then I have your friend in the next room to treat."

"*What*?! Kurt? What are you going to do to him?"

Arthur smiled mockingly. "*Help* him, of course. I'm a doctor."

My chest suddenly had stabbing pains running through it, and I recognized the feeling all too well. Breathing was almost impossible, and my whole body felt like it was shutting down.

Arthur was on the left side of my bed, and the door to the hallway was on the right, so I lurched with all my strength to my right and a break for freedom. As I left the general area of my hospital bed, various IV needles were yanked out of me, causing all sorts of metal stands behind my bed to fall over and clatter about all over the place, and the needles stung as they were ripped from my skin, but they didn't even come close to the pain in my chest and heart. I finally broke free from my IV cables, but then collapsed on the floor, gasping for air, which was becoming increasingly difficult to take in. I crawled as best I could and tried to reach the door when three wheels creaked and wobbled into view. A pair of legs was next to them. I was gasping and choking.

Multiple alarms were going off from the machines I'd torn myself away from.

"Goodbye, Todd," said the voice that belonged to the legs as the door opened and he wheeled his crippled cart out of the room. The door closed behind him.

I suddenly spasmed and wasn't able to breathe. I was in agony for what seemed like forever, but was probably about thirty seconds, before my body finally decided enough was enough.

That was the second time I died.

XIX

"Kurt!" I screamed, suddenly resuming consciousness. "Kurt!"

Out of nowhere, Duff was by my side. "Sir? It's Duff. What's the matter?"

"Kurt! Is he okay?"

"Yes, sir. He was rescued from the flames in time, and—"

"No, no! The doctor that went to check on him and treat him. Did Kurt survive?"

"No doctor needed to treat him, sir. He just had mild smoke inhalation. He was only brought here as a precaution. The nurses kept an eye on him."

I gripped Duff's arm. "*Please*, Duff, go and check on Kurt. Please?"

"Well, sir, I'm not leaving you alone for another second, but I'll have a nurse check on him. I need you to relax."

I breathed out slowly. "Thanks, Duff."

He partially opened the door and asked a nurse to check on Kurt. A few minutes later, the door to my room opened and in he walked, the man himself.

"Hey bro," he said, slightly congested. "I guess that was a close one!"

For once I was genuinely happy to see him. "You're not kidding, dude. What a gnarly night! Are you okay?"

"Oh yeah, I'm fine. The big question is how are you? You died, dude! Twice, from the sound of it!"

"Yeah, I noticed. My insides feel like each organ has been thrown from a fifty story building and then run over with a truck, but I'm sure I'll be fine. What the hell happened in the apse?"

Kurt dragged a chair over to the side of my bed and sat down next to me. "Dude. Oh my god. That Pedro guy is an absolute maniac. I was getting a bit creeped out by the whole room being so dark, but accidentally I somehow found this huge candle. Next to it was a box of matches, so I lit one and used the flame's light to make sure it was actually a candle and not some priceless artifact. It was a candle, dude, so I struck another match and lit it. I've got to say, though, the flickering light didn't really make things any less scary." He thought for a second, and then said. "In fact, I think it made things worse."

Ordinarily I would have immediately jumped to the obvious conclusion of how the very dark room with the huge lit candle got set on fire, but I was looking at this through a slightly different lens at that moment. "And then what happened?"

"Well, I began to challenge Pedro to appear and be interrogated by me, and at first nothing happened, but then there was this freakin' *huge* crashing noise somewhere near me, and the next thing I know, one end of the room is totally on fire. I try to get out, and of course I can't because there's a fucking great oak beam across the door. It was him, dude, no question."

My heart rate had begun to increase, and Duff could see that on the monitor. He gave a polite cough. "Kurt? I think it's time Todd was left to rest. He can't have any stress right now."

Kurt spun around. "Oh crap! Of course not! I'm *so* sorry dude! Look, rest up and we'll see you back at the hotel soon. I'm so glad you're on the mend, bro."

He left and Duff closed the door behind him, before sitting back in his armchair in the corner of the room.

"Thanks," I said. "I was getting a bit freaked out thinking back to that night."

"I could tell, sir."

"I hope I don't have a visit from Brad, or that might be my third strike! And then I might be out. For good."

Duff chuckled. "Oh, don't worry, sir. You won't have a visit from him."

"You haven't tied him up, have you?"

"Oh no, sir. That nice Mrs Álvarez agreed to show Brad round Santa Isabel in the daylight. He's going to be busy all day filming lots of great stuff in case you didn't get enough footage. I thought that might be for the best."

I smiled and rested my head back. "Thanks Duff, you're awesome."

I began to think how lucky Kurt had been that crazy Arthur hadn't gone and done something horrible, and then I suddenly realized where my train of thought was going and immediately chastised myself. There are no such thing as ghosts. The whole Arthur thing must have been a dream, unless there is some grubby, half dead looking doctor wandering around this hospital with a three-wheeled cart carrying old surgical implements on it.

I must have spasmed or had some sort of facial tic at the thought, because Duff suddenly piped up. "Care to talk about it, sir?"

I paused before answering. Did I want to open this potential can of Todd-has-gone-nuts worms? Did I really want to be viewed in the same light as Scooby and Scrappy by people at the network? The answer was no; of course I didn't.

"Talk about what?" I asked as innocently as I could.

"Oh, nothing, sir. It just looked like you had something on your mind."

"No, no, I'm just still a bit shaken, you know."

"I understand, sir. If you decide there's anything you need to talk about, you know where I'll be."

"Thanks, dude."

I drifted off to sleep for a little while, and about an hour later, I was woken by a doctor in a gleaming white coat.

A voice behind him said, "it's okay, sir, I've frisked him and checked his creds. He's the real deal."

The doctor smiled tightly, clearly not enjoying Duff's mega-security. When he spoke, his accent was impossible to place. "Mr. Sykes, how are you feeling?"

"Um," I said wiping the crust from my eyes, "much better, I think."

"That's good, really good. Your EKG output is normal, which suggests you haven't done any damage to the tissue or muscle wall of your heart." He smiled down at me, "but all that being said, I'd really like you to not have another heart attack for a while."

"Um, sure, okay. That sounds like a good idea. Why did I have a heart attack in the first place? Do I have high blood pressure or something?"

"That's hard for me to tell due to the circumstances that you were admitted under, but when you get back to America, you should immediately go and have a full physical with your doctor, and ask to have your blood pressure checked every week for a few months. To have two heart attacks in one day is very unusual and, obviously, not very good for your health. When you're discharged, I'll give you a folder full of readouts and information that you should give to your doctor to give him an insight into what happened over the last twenty-four hours."

I felt a knot in my stomach. "Wow, this was serious, wasn't it?"

He paused for a few moments. "Extremely serious." Another pause while he thought about whether to say the next part of not. "Being completely honest, you are lucky to be alive. In fact, not just alive but alive without any obvious brain damage or lingering organ problems. It's quite remarkable."

"Woah, dude! Brain damage?"

"Mr. Sykes, your heart shut down twice, for over a minute each time, in the space of about twelve hours. Once your heart stops, the rest of your vital organs stop receiving the vital blood and oxygen that they need. To have that happen once is bad, but survivable, but to have it happen again so quickly, and for as long as happened to you is, well, it's usually bad for the patient. But not you, Mr. Sykes. You seem to have an angel looking over you."

I swallowed hard and must have gone pale. The heart rate monitor kicked it up a notch.

"Mr. Sykes? Are you okay?"

Duff was up and at my side immediately. "What's the matter?"

I swallowed again, despite the fact that my mouth was completely dry. "I'm fine," I croaked. "I just need some water."

Once I'd drunk two cups of water and had time to calm down, the doctor spoke again. "So, I strongly urge you to undergo serious evaluation when you get back home. If there are lasting effects from this incident, they may not show up right away." He turned and looked at Duff, "and I'm saying this as much to you as to Mr. Sykes. If you really want to guard his body, he needs a full medical evaluation."

Duff nodded. "You got it, doc. Leave it with me."

The doctor nodded and looked back down at me. "Well, Mr. Sykes, unless you have another *incident*, I think you can be discharged in the morning. We'll keep you under observation tonight, just as a precaution. Any questions?"

I looked at him for a few seconds. "Um, yes actually. Several, in fact."

"Oh, yes?"

"How long have you worked here?"

He blew air through his lips as he thought. "Hmmm, let's see. Roughly fourteen years."

"So you know all the other doctors here?"

"All of them. Very well. Why?"

"What's your take on Arthur?"

"Who?"

"Arthur. I was told he worked here?"

I could feel Duff eyeing me suspiciously.

The doctor rolled his eyes to the top of his head in thought. "Hmmm. Arthur? No, I don't believe anybody by that name works here. Well, there's an Arador; could you have misheard the name?"

"Very probably," I said, more confused than ever. "Is he working today?"

"I believe he was earlier, but his shift has finished now."

Could I have misheard? About the only thing I could remember from high school Spanish lessons was that the letter 'd', when between two vowels, was pronounced much more softly, and ended up being more like a 'th' sound. Arador... Arathor... Arthor... Arthur? I was under quite severe sedation at the time, after all. It was a possibility that was worth holding on to, for the sake of my sanity if nothing else.

"Oh, okay. One final question. Do I have pancreatic cancer?"

The doctor suddenly screwed his face up and jerked his head backwards slightly. "Pancreatic cancer? Where did that questi— No, not that I'm aware of. Not that I was looking, of course. You had a heart attack. We'd need to do a full imaging scan of your torso to establish that, and even then it's highly unlikely that any cancer would be detected. The pancreas is in a very awkward place deep in the abdomen, buried beneath the liver and behind the stomach. As doctors, we sometimes refer to it as the *hidden organ*, and because of its location, most imaging techniques can't see the pancreas clearly enough to spot early signs of cancer. Why do you ask? Do you have abdominal pain?"

"Yes, sir," said Duff, concerned, "why *do* you ask?"

I grinned like an idiot. "Oh, no no. I'm just, err, a bit of a hypochondriac sometimes. Thanks doc. You've been fantastic."

He looked at me a little strangely. "Thank you, Mr. Sykes. Well, here's hoping to us not meeting ever again, no offense intended. Stay healthy."

"Thanks doc, I'll sure try!"

He turned, nodded at Duff, and headed for the door. He opened it and looked back at me. "And anyway, you're in good hands with this guy."

The door closed and Duff looked down at me with slightly narrowed eyes. "Pancreatic cancer?"

I shrugged. "Err, yeah. I was just asking. I read about it, and thought one of the tests they'd done might check for that."

Duff looked unconvinced and resumed his seat in the corner of the room.

What was left of the day passed uneventfully, and I drifted off to sleep with the help of some sedatives to make sure I didn't dream about anything that might raise my heart rate. The following morning the nurses and, more importantly, Duff, seemed happy with all of my charts and readings, and I was allowed to leave the hospital. Duff drove me back to the hotel, and instructed me to rest for the remainder of the day; a Learjet would be waiting at Zaragoza airport to pick us up the following lunchtime to whisk us back to London, and then Virgin America would take over for the remainder of the trip back to Los Angeles.

A knock on my suite door at about two p.m. rescued me from flicking through the endless number of satellite TV channels that the hotel had in all manner of languages. I'd spent the previous hour ad-libbing my own lines over a Japanese soap opera that I'd muted, but the novelty had long since worn off.

"Come in," I said.

The door opened slowly, and Brad stuck his head around it. "Dude! Dude! You're alive!"

I stood up. "What do you mean, 'I'm alive'? Didn't Kurt tell you?"

"Yeah, dude, but never trust anything connected with the paranormal until you see it with your own eyes."

I sat back down again. "Oh yeah, right. Okay."

Brad headed immediately for my mini-bar and grabbed a Sprite from it. He poured the can into a glass and then downed the whole thing in one, kind of negating the glass-aspect of it. He screwed his face up for a few seconds, then looked victorious about something, then looked like he needed to go to the bathroom, and then finally let out an enormous burp.

"Dude," I said, pissed off. "What was that?"

"What?"

"What do you mean, 'what'?"

"I needed a drink, bro."

"You do understand that if you only take a sip, the rest of your drink isn't going to disappear, right?"

"Dude, we're like Special Forces: eat and drink fast whenever there's a lull in battle, because you never know what's coming next or when you'll get to do so again. What if I suddenly got trapped in a haunted elevator on the way down to the pool? I'd be thankful that I was hydrated."

"With Sprite."

"Yeah, dude. Hydration and sugar for energy. The perfect combination. Anyway, bro, how're you feeling? What a night! That was some crazy paranormal activity we had there. I hope that Pedro cat didn't mess with our recorders and spoil our evidence. And speaking of evidence, I wonder what Bravo team found? I haven't spoken to them since you had to be medevac'd to hospital."

I'd actually forgotten all about them, too, what with nearly dying a couple of times and all. I wondered what they *had* seen on their monitor; this 'woman in a white coat' that was standing behind me that they were so sure they'd seen several times. This was troubling me considerably, because most 'paranormal activity' that we recorded on video was usually a tiny flash of light that lasted less than a tenth of a second and was almost impossible to see until you've watched the footage played back in slow motion about twenty times. For the final edit of the show, these 'ghostly apparitions' that we'd capture on video had to be clearly marked with a circle so that viewers at home at least had a sporting chance of spotting the thing. Most of the time, even that doesn't help, so we play the clip over and over, at a slower and slower speed to allow the viewer to at least think they saw something.

The apparition we capture is never, ever recognizable as anything even vaguely human, so for these two redneck nitwits to have identified whatever it was behind me as a woman *and* wearing a coat-type thing, which I just knew was going to be a straitjacket if I could see what they were seeing, was disturbing to say the least.

"Hey Brad, I'm so bored cooped up in here. Do you have the footage from Bravo team?"

"Sure dude, I downloaded it from HQ this morning. I haven't looked at it yet, but do you want to see it? I'm supposed to be meeting Kurt in a few minutes to go to a strip club."

"You're going to do *what*? It's the middle of the day!"

"Yeah, but Kurt kept saying he wanted to tap some ass, or something, so I figure he wanted to see some Spanish chicks in action.

I rolled my eyes. "*Tapas*, Brad. Tapas."

"Exactly."

"No, no, it's not…" I paused and then changed my mind, not wanting to get into a protracted conversation with a halfwit. "Never mind. Well, have fun, and don't forget to bring me that footage before you go."

"You got it, dude," said Scrappy before bounding out of the room.

XX

There was a commotion of voices outside my room, and I could hear Brad complaining as he left the elevator. "Dude, that wasn't ass. That was food. There was no ass involved."

Kurt replied, sounding a little perplexed. "Ass? What are you talking about? Who said anything about ass?"

"You did, bro."

"No, I didn't. I said we were going to have lunch."

"No, you said we were going to tap some ass. Ass, dude! Not food!"

"Oh, fucking hell, Brad! I said *Tapas!*"

"That's exactly my point, bro. And there was no ass. But the food was good, I'll give you that. The portions were a bit small, though."

I groaned, and resumed my fetal position on the bed where I'd been for the past hour after viewing the footage that Brad had brought to my room. I didn't really know what to think and felt sick, cold, and haunted right to my very core. My mind kept replaying the feed that Amanda and Jim were receiving from me, and it was troubling beyond belief. A very faint, but visible figure appeared behind me in the grainy, green footage exactly when

Bravo team said they could see something. The figure was clearly a woman and, as I'd feared, she was wearing what appeared to be a straitjacket. It was really, really faint, but at the same time wasn't impossible to spot if you were paying attention.

The moment I'd seen her appear behind me the first time, while Kurt was trying to interrogate Pedro, I immediately ran to the bathroom and vomited in the sink. I sank down onto the floor and suddenly realized that I was trembling uncontrollably. I took long, deep breaths, and tried to calm down, but there was no denying what I'd seen: there appeared to be a ghostly figure standing behind me while I was sitting in the vestibule.

After about twenty minutes of trying to compose myself, I returned to the desk in the living area of the suite, and watched the next bit of footage. Once again, there she was, just as Bravo team had said. I felt immediately nauseous again, but fought to control my urge to vomit so I could watch the final sighting, which was when I was scrabbling around on the floor looking for my flashlight as Kurt screamed that he was going to burn to death. I was trembling as the moment approached and, sure enough, she shimmered into faint view, but this time it seemed that she was laughing.

Laughing?

Could this be possible? She was laughing at my attempts to find the flashlight?

I lurched as fast as I could toward the bathroom, and nearly made it before projectile-vomiting at the doorway, all over the decorative rug that was welcoming me into the bathroom, and collapsing in a heap on the floor.

"No!" I'd screamed out loud. "No! It is *not* possible!"

I crawled my way back into the bedroom, my thoughts an utter scrambled mess, and dragged myself onto the bed, where I curled up in a ball and rocked from side to side. Everything I knew to be true about ghosts, in other words that they didn't and couldn't possibly exist, seemed to be unravelling around me, and I didn't quite know what to think about anything any more. *Had* there been ghosts tripping waiters over in Virginia? Could it be possible that the dumb waiter had been tampered with by something paranormal while Kurt was inside it? And what about Isabella? And Arthur? Could they have been trying to get at Kurt as he lay in the ice box?

"*NO!*" I screamed out. "*No, no, no, no, no!*"

I rocked back and forth faster, and stayed doing exactly that until I'd heard Brad and Kurt emerge from the elevators. Before long, there was a knock on my door; I called out in a raspy voice to whoever it was that they could come in. I heard the main door to the suite open, and I heard Kurt's voice.

"Dude? Dude, where are you?"

"Bedroom," I croaked, as I sat up and tried to act normal.

When he'd reached what I assumed was the door to the bathroom he let out a yelp. "Ugghh! Dude! Fuck! That is *gross*."

I heard him make his way through the suite and into the bedroom. He poked his head around the door. "Are you oka— Fuck! You look terrible! Are you alright?"

I coughed up some phlegm and had to swallow it, which almost made me vomit again. "Err, no, man, not that great. I think I must have eaten something that didn't agree with me."

He looked at me. "Someone puked on your fucking rug, dude."

"Yeah, I know, Kurt," I said, pissed off. "Who do you think that was?"

"Oh yeah, sorry bro. Do you want me to leave?"

I suddenly felt really bad. He had, after all, almost burned alive in a small room in a church many thousands of miles away from his home. I shook my head. "No, dude. I'm sorry. Sit down, I want to ask you something."

He perched himself on the edge of my bed. "Ask away, bro."

I sighed, and then paused for a few seconds as I considered whether this was a good idea or not. I quickly decided it wasn't, but I asked anyway. "Do you truly believe in ghosts?"

He looked at me like I was an idiot. "Of course, dude. Doesn't everyone?"

"Well, actually, Kurt, no. Everyone doesn't."

"Really? Maybe they haven't seen our show. I mean, the evidence we gather is irrefutable. Right, bro?"

"Well, that's sort of what I wanted to talk to you about."

"Sure, dude. What about it?"

I fiddled with my hands, and looked down at the bed I was sitting on, before I answered. "The evidence we gather, man. Do you think *all* of it's true?"

Kurt gave a little huff of derision. "Of course not, bro! Not *all* of it. I mean, sometimes, Brad is convinced that a noise is a word or a flash of light is a ghost, but occasionally I'm not so sure. But here's the thing, dude, *I'm not the expert*! Brad is. He has such a talent for this that whatever I think is right or wrong, bro, I have to defer to him. He's a true natural with the paranormal. Did you know he's thinking about having his DNA tested to see if he's part Vampire, or something?"

"No, I didn't know that, and that's fascinating. But, look, what I'm trying to get at is that sometimes you disagree with some of the conclusions that Brad comes to with the footage we record?"

Kurt thought for a few moments, and nodded a few times, and then said, "yeah, I guess so. But, like I said, dude, he has a true connection to the paranormal, so what I think doesn't count."

"It does, dude."

"No, it doesn't. He has a gift that I don't."

I sighed again. "Kurt, man, listen to me. You are just as qualified to have an opinion as Brad."

"No, dude, he—"

"*No*, Kurt. He doesn't have a connection to the paranormal. He's just like you and me. He's just louder in his conviction that he knows what's being said or what we've seen. And here's the thing, Kurt, I'm not asking you what you think *Brad* thinks, I'm asking for *your* opinion. So can we forget Brad for a few minutes?"

Kurt looked a little shocked. "Err, sure dude. Whatever you want. Are you feeling okay?"

"Yes and no, Kurt. Yes and no. I need you to tell me whether *you* think that every ghostly sighting that we document is true."

"Most of them, sure, I mean, remember some of the gnarly things the ghosts have done to me?"

"I remember all too clearly, Kurt. But are there any less scary things that we've documented as paranormal activity that perhaps you didn't think were?"

"You mean, did I lie?"

"No, dude! This isn't about lying, it's about how much personal conviction you had in the conclusions that some of our shows came to in their final edit. Remember, the show is all about entertaining the public. It's TV, dude, not science."

Kurt stood up and looked down at me. "Look, man, I'm not sure where this is heading, but it kinda freaking me out, you know? We conduct scientific investigations."

I realized I'd gone a little too far, too quickly. "Yes. Yes, we do Kurt. We do scientific investigations, but the final edit of the show is all about entertainment."

"Based on science."

"Yeah, mostly. But, do you remember a few months ago? When we were in that abandoned elementary school that was allegedly haunted?"

"It was haunted, dude. No question."

"Do you remember what happened during the intro monologue that Brad was recording while we were standing outside the school?"

"Of course I do, bro. A huge branch fell off the tree in the parking lot. Someone could have been killed, dude!"

"Right, and did it fall off the tree because of paranormal activity?"

"No. It was an old tree, and one of our crew accidentally reversed a truck into it. The impact knocked the old branch loose."

"Did you watch that episode?"

"No, dude, I never do. Why would I? I was there. I don't need to go through it all a second time."

"Okay, well I'll give you a recap of how the the teaser for the show opened: a short snippet of Brad giving his monologue is shown before him suddenly lurching forward and ducking."

"That was when the truck hit the tree, bro."

"Right. Except, we don't show that. The next shot we see is a huge tree branch on the floor of the parking lot — the same parking lot that Brad is in — and a voice-over explains that the spirits are mad that we're there and so they try to scare us away by dropping a branch from a tree nearby."

Kurt thought for a few seconds. "But that branch fell across the other side of the parking lot. It had nothing to do with us."

"I know. But we still used the footage in the teaser to suggest that the ghosts were trying to scare us."

"That's lying, bro."

"It's not lying, Kurt, it's called 'reality television'. We take the 'reality' that we record, and we edit it to make it into more interesting 'television'."

"Oh. I didn't know that. Where are you going with this, dude?"

I looked down at my bed and took a few deep breaths as I continued to debate myself on whether what I was about to do next was a good idea or not. In the end, it just happened.

"Kurt, I want to show you something," I said quietly.

"What, dude?"

"Remember when you were trapped in the apse?"

"Of course I do, bro. I nearly burned alive!"

"And you couldn't understand why I didn't help you?"

"That was a bit weird, dude, but when I found out what happened to you, it all made sense."

"Yeah, but there's a little bit more to it than just me having a heart attack."

Kurt narrowed his eyes slightly. "Did Pedro fuck with you, too?"

"No, bro. It seems that he was too busy with you in the apse. Something else happened to me, and I want you to watch the footage that Bravo team were seeing so you can see it for yourself."

"Uhh, okay, dude, sure."

I stood up a little shakily, and led Kurt over to the desk. I rewound the footage to the appropriate place and hit play. We watched a green, grainy me staring slightly below the camera, my head darting left and right as I listened to Kurt on one side, and Amanda and Jim on the other.

"Woah, dude. They really speak slowly, don't they?"

"Yeah, tell me about it, bro. They were one of the reasons I couldn't focus on your predicament."

Through the speakers, we heard Kurt begin to try and interrogate Pedro, and I looked away from the screen. I didn't want to see it again, just the very thought of what I knew I'd see caused the hairs on the back of my neck to stand on end.

"Holy fucking *hell*, dude!" yelled Kurt. "It's Isabella! Oh shit, this is bad."

I snapped my head around to look at him. "How do you know that? How do you know who it is?"

Kurt hit pause and turned to me. He screwed his face up slightly. "How do I *know*, dude? I was locked in her fucking cell wearing a straitjacket. I saw her, dude. That's Isabella. No question."

"Wait, you *saw her* in that cell?"

Kurt suddenly looked uncomfortable. "Yeah, I did. Well, I think I did. Only briefly, and very faint, but I'm pretty sure that's what she looked like. It's burned into my brain, man."

"So that flash of light behind you in the footage was definitely her?"

Kurt shook his head. "Oh no, dude. I have no idea what that was. Maybe another spirit? Who knows. I saw Isabella in front of me in the corner of the cell, and out of view of the camera. She appeared for maybe a second, perhaps two, in her straitjacket, pretty much like how she was behind you in this footage."

I was almost speechless. "But... but... why didn't you say anything?"

Kurt shrugged. "Brad knew more than I did about what was going on. I trusted his judgement. And anyway, I was pretty freaked out, so maybe I forgot to mention it."

My head span, and I sank to the floor putting my face in my hands. Involuntarily, I said quietly, "Oh my god. What the *hell* is going on?"

Kurt crouched next to me. "Bro? Are you okay?"

I took some more deep breaths, desperately hoping that I wasn't about to have another heart attack, and tried to calm down. "Uhh, yeah, I'm fine. Let's just watch the rest of the feed."

Kurt looked a little concerned, but did as I asked and continued to play the footage. He watched, while I kept my head in my hands trying to figure out whether I was going insane or not. I heard everything that was happening, and winced at the moment I was sent tumbling to the floor, sending things crashing all around me.

Kurt turned to me. "Fuck, dude! What happened?"

"Just keep watching," I said, my face still buried in my hands.

I knew that in the footage I'd be bumbling around in the dark, looking for my flashlight or camera, and from the speakers I heard Kurt's radio message screaming for help because he was about to burn to death. Suddenly the real Kurt in my room leapt to his feet, sending his chair crashing to the floor behind him.

"Oh holy *fuck*! No! *No!* That isn't possible!"

I snapped to attention. "What, dude? What isn't possible?"

Kurt took a few breaths. "Isabella, dude. She's laughing at your attempts to save me."

What was left of the contents of my stomach ended up all over Kurt's sneakers.

XXI

On the one hand, it was nice to be home, but on the other I was a total and utter wreck. Viewing the footage of what was going on behind me in the vestibule had completely freaked me out. I was distressed to the point of not being able to sleep, and my every waking moment was spent thinking about the fact that I seemed to suddenly have fairly conclusive evidence that ghosts did, in fact, exist.

But that couldn't be right. There was absolutely no way that a ghost could exist, my brain kept yelling at me. A person dies, their heart stops beating, blood stops circulating, and everything switches off. That's it. There is no soul that gets lost for Brad to go and find; what people bleat on about as someone's 'soul' is simply their personality and traits. Once the brain is switched off, there is no personality, and the person is dead. There is no 'soul' to float off up into the sky; it's as simple as that.

So what had I seen behind me in the vestibule?

I couldn't stop thinking about it, and my thoughts kept alternating between being convinced that somehow ghosts did actually exist, and then worrying that I was turning into Brad and making things up out of flashes of light and creaking wooden beams. It would have been far easier to lean towards the latter thought had it not been for the fact that Kurt had, unprompted, seen Isabella as clearly as I had. He'd even spotted her laughing.

And what about Arthur? Once again, I tried to convince myself that I'd misheard his name and he'd said Arador in a Spanish accent, but I knew that wasn't the case; his accent was American. I'd heard perfectly well; his name was Arthur. And he was dragging a battered old cart with ancient surgical implements on it that, when I'd described it to one of the nurses before I was released, had earned me the *don't-be-an-idiot* look.

"Our doctors," the Spanish nurse had said, almost offended, "do not 'drag' trrrolleys of esurgical eemplements around the 'ospital with them! What about esterilization, eh? And it 'ad thrrree wheels? Dangerous, señor! Dangerous! No, no, no. At thees 'ospital, we take esafety and cleanliness very eseriously indeed. All esurgical implements are kept locked away until needed, and they are then esterilized."

So, clearly, the guy who visited my in my room didn't work at the hospital, but who was he? He looked like a doctor, sort of. A slightly grubby doctor, admittedly, but he had the white coat and all that. And what about the pancreatic cancer? Was that true? It couldn't possibly be; my 'proper' doctor that arrived afterwards said it was extremely hard to detect and special tests were required; tests that I hadn't had.

I must have dreamt him up. That was the only logical explanation. Perhaps I'd fallen into a half-sleep, had a nightmare, and then woke up in a panic, causing my heart to stop again. That made sense, although I couldn't shake the feeling of how real he'd seemed.

But Isabella?

She was there alright. Or *something* was, and Kurt had seen it too. So if she was there, why couldn't Arthur have been? If I gave in and convinced myself that one ghost existed, then it stood to reason that others did too, which would mean that Arthur had paid me a visit, and I very probably had early-stage Pancreatic cancer. I mean, if I was going to believe in ghosts, then I might as well believe that they can see inside us and know things that we don't. In for a penny, in for a pound, as Tom would say.

Back in Spain, once Kurt had cleaned my vomit from his sneakers, I'd let him mull it all over, and suddenly he had an epiphany.

"Dude! Oh my god! It's all falling into place!"

I was shaking by that point, and was sitting in an armchair across the other side of the room, trying to act as normal as possible. "What is?"

"We were in the Santa Isabel church, dude! *Isabel*! Isabella! Oh, fuck, this is big. Conclusive proof that spirits can piggyback on our comms frequencies. She came all the way from America to Spain, and not just to Spain but to a church with *her name*! It's almost like we sent out a calling card to her! Brad's gonna freak when he hears this!"

"Yeah, I'm sure he will. Look, Kurt, I think I need a lie down. Tell Brad I'll show him the footage later."

"Oh yeah, sure bro! Sorry! What with all this amazing evidence, I forgot you were sick! I'll let Brad know."

Kurt left, and I lay down on the bed, my head spinning and my limbs trembling as I tried to process what I'd just seen. A few minutes later, the door to my suite crashed open and a few seconds after that, Brad burst into the bedroom, clearly unable to contain his enthusiasm and let me get some rest.

"Someone puked on your rug, dude," were his first words to me.

"Yeah, I'm feeling a bit better, bro, thanks for asking."

"What? Oh yeah, sorry man. How are you? That was a close call with the heart attack and everything."

His bedside manner needed some work. "I'm assuming you've spoken to Kurt?"

"Yeah, bro! He says we got some pretty amazing evidence."

I took a deep breath and let it out slowly. "We did, man. We sure did."

I showed him the footage, and he nearly went into orbit. "*Dude*! Oh my god, dude! Kurt said it was good, but it's way better than that! This is the best visual evidence we've ever gathered! Man, I should have thought about the Spain connection sooner; this is totally *epic*! There's no way even the biggest non-believer can refute this right here."

In a tornado of excitement, he vanished as quickly as he'd appeared and then went to the bar with Kurt to celebrate. By contrast, I'd spent the rest of the evening in my room, desperately trying to hold on to at least a shred of my sanity. The trip home was a blur to me, the luxury and decadence of my modes of transportation going almost unnoticed by my pre-occupied and deeply troubled brain. As soon as I'd landed, a limo had whisked me home and I crawled straight into bed and did my best to sleep.

It was now lunchtime the following day, and I still hadn't figured out what was going on. Suddenly, my buzzer sounded, scaring me out of a troubled trance that I'd ended up in. I dragged myself to my feet and shuffled over to the entry phone by my front door. To say my progress was slow would be an understatement; whoever was down there had been able to buzz three times with a good pause in between each one before I reached the door.

I picked up the handset. "Hello?"

"Oh, fak! I thought you weren't in! Thank fak for that. It's Tom. Let me up, mate."

"Tom? What are you...? Never mind, come on up."

I buzzed him in, and when he walked into my front door, he looked troubled as well. He sat down with a heavy thump on my couch.

"A fakkin' 'art attack, eh?"

"Two heart attacks."

"Fak me. How're you feeling? You look like shite."

I groaned. "Thanks for your support and kind words. I feel like crap."

"I could murder a beer, mate."

"Help yourself. You know where the fridge is."

"Wicked, mate. Thanks," he said as he got up and headed to the kitchen. "You want one too?"

"No, no, I'm fine. I'm on all sorts of meds, so I probably shouldn't."

"Oh yeah, good thinkin' mate. We don't want yer jam tart havin' another funny turn, do we?"

He came back to the sofa and sat down, a bottle of Sam Adams in his hand. It was refreshing to see him. Utterly manic as he was, Tom always had a very grounding effect on me; it was one of the many reasons I enjoyed working with him so much.

"It's good to see you, dude," I said.

"You too, mate. I can't believe what went on over there! It sounds like you were in a right old fakkin' two-an'-eight."

My brain scrolled through the list of Cockney Rhyming Slang that I'd built up over the years of working with him, and equated 'two-and-eight' with 'state'. 'Right old state'.

"Yeah, man. I was. I nearly died, dude. Well, actually, if you want to get technical, I did die. Twice."

"And Kurt nearly burned to death. How the fakkin' 'ell did he set that room on fire?"

I breathed out loudly and shook my head. "He's convinced one of the inquisitors from the Spanish Inquisition was in there with him and used a candle to set fire to the drapes."

"A candle? I thought you lot were always in total darkness?"

"He got freaked out because of the dark, dude. Then he stumbled across a huge candle in the dark, then somehow also stumbled across some matches, and lit it."

"So he knocked it over?"

"That's what I thought, bro, but now I'm not so sure. I have some gnarly shit to tell you, and it's been driving me absolutely crazy, dude."

Tom looked a bit sheepish, and was about to speak when my buzzer suddenly went off again. Tom leaped to his feet, walked over to it, and pressed the door release button.

"Dude! What are you doing? You don't even know who that is!"

He turned and looked at me. "Yeah, I do mate. I invited them."

"Them? Them who?"

I suddenly realized that he must have invited Brad and Kurt to join in our little chat. It made sense; we needed to figure out what to do with the footage that we'd gathered and how to make two shows out of it. The build-up with all the fascinating information about the Spanish Inquisition was great, but the actual time during the lock-in was over extremely quickly, and probably lasted just over an hour if we were lucky. In the few minutes that I hadn't been panicking about ghosts, my thoughts had been consumed with what we were going to do for our finale episodes. I just hoped that the grainy footage we'd captured would be dramatic enough to fill the second hour of the show.

There was a gentle tap on my front door, and Tom opened it. "Alright, guys? Come in."

A clean-shaven skinny guy walked in, and he looked familiar to me. I couldn't quite place him, but I knew I'd seen him before. Behind him appeared a huge woman with a close-cut brown-hair bob, and she squeezed herself sideways through my front door frame. She also looked familiar, but my brain was ticking over trying to place her. They followed Tom into my living room, and he gestured to them to sit. The skinny guy sat in an armchair at the end of the sofa, and the enormous woman chose to sit on the sofa. She filled most of it, and it made all sorts of creaking and groaning sounds as her weight settled in.

And then it suddenly hit me. "Oh my god! Amanda! Jim! It's you! You look a bit different! What are you doing in LA?"

Amanda was about to speak, but Tom beat her to it. "Mate," he said a little awkwardly, "I need to tell you something."

I was confused by why Jim and Amanda had flown all the way from Tennessee. "Uhh, okay, bro. What?"

He pulled out a dining chair from the table nearby, and sat down hard. "Oh, fak, mate. I'm so sorry."

I glanced around from Jim, to Amanda, and then to Tom to try and figure out what he was going on about. "Sorry about what?"

He put his head in his hands and let out a huge sigh. "It was all a fakkin' wind-up, mate. All of it."

I swallowed hard, and blinked a few times. As calmly as I could, I said, "Tom, tell me that in plain English that I'll understand."

He took another deep breath. "It was all made up, mate. Isabella. She wasn't really there."

My stomach felt like it turned upside down, and then rotated around its vertical axis a few times. "Wh... what? No, you're wrong. She was there alright! Ask Jim and Amanda!"

There was a slight pause and then Amanda spoke for the first time since walking into my apartment. "No, Todd, she wasn't."

Her articulation was perfect, and her accent was neutral west-coast. I snapped my head around and looked at her. "What the fuck? Your accent...?"

"They're actors, mate," said Tom. "I thought it'd be funny. A nice end of the season surprise, you know?"

I lurched to my feet and yelled, "funny? Fucking funny, dude? I nearly fucking *died*!"

Tom shuffled uncomfortably in his seat. "Yeah, I know, mate. I didn't know it was going to go that far. I'm so sorry. And that's why I've been fired."

"You should have— wait, you've *what*?"

"I've been fakkin' fired, mate. You're currently the network's biggest asset, and anything that interferes with that gets removed immediately. Durkin went fakkin' mental when he found out the gag I'd played on you, and I was dragged into his office, yelled at for half a fakkin' hour, and then escorted out of the building by armed fakkin' guards. I didn't know your jam tart was going to have a soddin' seizure, mate. You've got to understand that."

I was now utterly confused. "But I saw Isabella behind me. So did Jim and Amanda, or whoever they are."

Jim spoke quietly, and his accent was perfectly neutral as well. "No, Todd, we didn't see anything. We pretended that we did, and we kept egging you on. But we didn't really see anything."

I paced up and down. "But I *saw* her dude! She was right behind me!"

"How did you see her?" asked Tom.

"The footage from the feed they had of us!"

Tom lowered his head. "Where did that footage come from, mate?"

I thought about it for a few moments. "I dunno, but Brad downloaded it from our server."

"Right, so who do you think put it there?"

I suddenly felt sick, as a realization crashed down upon me. "You doctored it, you motherfucker! You doctored it, didn't you?"

Tom paused for a few seconds. "Yeah, I did. I added a faint image to the footage in a couple of places. But after I found out what happened to you, you were never supposed to see it! I sent an e-mail to Brad telling him not to show it to you, and I thought I'd deleted it off the server. I guess there was a backup, or something, and by some miracle Brad found it. I'm so sorry, mate."

I was suddenly furious. "*Mate*? Mate? I'm not your fucking mate. Not anymore! You nearly killed me, you asshole. In fact, you *did* fucking kill me! Twice!"

Tom suddenly got defensive. "Woah, take it easy pal! I didn't know you were going to have a fakkin' coronary! It was meant to be a joke."

I thought about everything that had gone on that day. My hands suddenly clenched into fists. "A joke? A fucking joke? You bastard. You really think it's funny that once I've had a heart attack you send some guy to visit me in hospital, pretending to be Arthur with his old surgical tools and shit? You think that's funny? That's the reason I almost died a *second* time, dude! No, I *did* die a second time! I could have ended up with fucking *brain damage*, man!"

Tom screwed his eyes up slightly and looked at me. "Who the fak is Arthur?"

"Oh, don't give me that shit. Just end this crap right now. I want the truth."

"No, seriously, mate, who's Arthur?"

"The guy from a few weeks ago in Saint Joseph's. The dude who died on the operating table. Wait, what do you mean, 'who's Arthur'? You sent someone to pretend to be him."

Tom rubbed the back of his head and let out a sigh. "Mate, I didn't have some super-huge budget to pull a prank on you. Brad told me he had to find a second team for you to communicate with, and I thought it'd be funny if I helped out. I offered to take the job off Brad's hands, and hired Amanda and Jim to be a ghost-chasing couple in 'Tennessee'. They were actually in a sound stage in Studio City. But that's it, mate. I didn't have budget for any type of extravagant in-person acting stuff. Especially when it's six thousand miles away. You must have been hallucinating."

My head was now spinning. "But... but... how did you make those noises?"

"Mate, how many times do I have to fakkin' tell you? I had no budget. I didn't make any noises. I spent a couple of hundred bucks to hire some pretend ghost-hunters, a bloke I know let me borrow a sound stage for a few hours, and that's it! It was all a blag, mate."

I took a few deep breaths as my anger bubbled inside me. "Get out. All of you, right now. *Get out!*"

Tom opened his palms toward me and was about to speak, but I cut him off. "Get the *fuck* out of my apartment. *Now!*"

"But, mate, I—"

"I am *not* your fucking *mate*! Just get out, you sonofabitch!"

All three of them shuffled out, offering the odd word of protestation, and I slammed my front door in Tom's face just as he was about to try and appease me one final time. Whatever he had to say, I didn't want to hear it.

I sank to the floor, more confused than ever. The images of Isabella were fake, I now knew, but what about everything else? Arthur, and the voice in the vestibule that seemingly switched on my flashlight? They'd happened, and hadn't been down to Tom. Or *had* they happened? Could it be possible that I'd imagined the whole thing? And if I'd imagined them with such realism, what did that say about my state of mind? Was I going mad?

I'd been sitting on the floor for several minutes, when suddenly a enormously loud crashing noise from outside made me quickly look up; it was so loud and jarring, I half wondered whether the building was about to collapse. Were we having an earthquake? The noise seemed to echo through the walls of my whole apartment, and the glass in the windows rattled. What the hell could have caused that?

I scrambled to my feet and ran to the window.

XXII

Larry was our FedEx guy. He was in his seventies, and the nicest guy you could ever hope to meet. In typical accountant fashion, he'd retired from being a corporate accountant at the exact year he was supposed to, got paid the exact amount of pension and retirement fund he was supposed to, which was exactly the correct amount he needed to live very comfortably, and was finally able to spend quality time with the love of his life: his wife of forty-eight years, Annie. They absolutely cherished each other, and he longed to be with her every hour that he was away in the office, often working late into the night, crunching numbers, checking receipts, making sure that every tax break available was taken advantage of for the huge company that he worked for, knowing that his hard work would pay off when they retired.

And it had; through his shrewd accounting skills, safe investment choices, and diligent work ethic, they'd amassed a very nice retirement fund, on top of what he would get from social security, and his pension from his long-standing job. To say that Annie and Larry were happy was an understatement, and they had a wonderful year of relaxing, taking lavish cruises, and just enjoying themselves for pretty much the first time in their entire lives. They had nothing to worry about, a healthy income, and the rest of their lives to have fun.

A little over twelve months after he retired, Annie was abruptly diagnosed with stage four breast cancer, and died a few months later. Larry was by her side the entire time, of course, and her passing devastated him. Once she was buried, his grave site reserved right next to hers, he sank into a deep depression, trying to will himself to death. He believed in the afterlife, and he wanted to be with his one and only true love; he didn't want to be all alone any more, and he almost succeeded.

And then one day, a concerned neighbor paid Larry a visit and asked him if he fancied a day out. Larry objected, of course, because all he wanted to do was stay at home with the drapes closed, and pine for his lost love. The neighbor persisted, and he took Larry with him on his daily FedEx delivery run, which turned out to be a revelation to Larry. They drove around the local neighborhood, stopping frequently, and giving people packages. Absolutely everybody that answered the door was happy to see them, and delighted with what they'd brought. To make people happy made Larry happy and, after that day, had spent his first night since Annie's death cooking a healthy meal for himself, and he felt less despondent. He missed her, of course, and he chatted with her while he cooked, and he told her all about his fascinating day being a FedEx assistant.

A week later, he had a full-time job delivering packages for FedEx, and suddenly he had a purpose in life. Of course he didn't and wouldn't ever forget Annie, and in fact he talked to her more every day during his deliveries than he'd ever been able to while he was an accountant, and he knew that he'd be with her one day. But until then, he had a new job to do; a new mission. He had to bring happiness to people, and what better way to do that than deliver parcels and packages to them? He knew that Annie was with him on every delivery, and although he missed her terribly, sometimes crying himself to sleep with her memories, he knew that she was proud of what he was doing, and she didn't want him to be doing anything else. She was waiting for him, and that was what counted.

Purely because of where I lived, I was quite often his final drop off of the day, and I'd lost count of the number of times that Larry had come in and had a coffee or a beer after delivering something to me. He truly was the nicest man on the planet, and would often talk of his wife with heavy tears in his eyes, telling me stories of their cruises and vacations.

"Todd," he would say to me, deadly serious, "I worked all of my life to enjoy the time when I could retire and spend it with Annie. The world doesn't work like that, son, and I found it out the hard way. Annie's waiting for me, I know that, but you have to make the most of every moment that you have *right now*. Enjoy yourself. Today. You might die in a car accident tomorrow. And then where would you be?"

His FedEx truck was always identifiable because, despite corporate protocols, he had various stickers on the back of it that all basically had the same theme: *why can't we just be nice to everyone*? There was a gay rights sticker, a women's right's sticker, a racial equality sticker, a pro-choice sticker, and so on. It had become fashionable over the years to find cool stickers to give to Larry to add to the collection on his truck, and I'd supplied a large 'Human Rights' sticker that had fallen out of a magazine, which he happily added to the back of his truck.

It was this sticker that I was focusing on as I sprinted towards the FedEx truck that had impaled itself into the side of my apartment building.

Once I'd heard and felt the impact, my front-facing windows had offered no help in seeing what had gone on, so I'd run into the corridor, bashed the elevator button a few times and then given up because it had been taking so long. I lurched my way down the escape stairs, just knowing something terrible had happened. I burst out into the lobby by the mailboxes and ran out onto the street. There were screams, sirens were blaring far off in the distance, and I looked to my right and saw the FedEx truck parked at an odd angle, across the sidewalk, when I suddenly realized with a sinking feeling in my stomach that the truck wasn't parked at all.

I ran as fast as my legs would carry me, which didn't feel like it was fast enough, and my lungs began to burn while my chest heaved, but my adrenaline made me ignore any pain or discomfort I was feeling; I had to make sure Larry was alright. As I got closer to the truck, I noticed some sort of flash or flicker by the front of the truck, and my brain took a second or two to figure out that a small fire had suddenly begun burning somewhere near there. I'd thought it was only in Hollywood that vehicles caught fire when they crashed, but that seemed to not be the case.

I was really close now, and I called out to him. "Larry," I gasped as best I could. "Larry! Can you hear me?"

It was because I was shouting and panting for breath that I almost missed the hissing sound, and it struck me as odd when I finally heard it. Suddenly my nostrils were filled with a sort of putrid, rotten egg smell, and I realized what the hissing actually was. I tried to stop as fast as I could, and I began to turn left to hightail it away from the truck, when suddenly a huge blast of heat engulfed me, and I was deafened by a thunderous roar. My body was thrown away from the truck as a huge fireball erupted from the part of the building that the truck had hit, and I landed hard on the ground, rolling a few times.

I lay on the cold blacktop for a few seconds, my ears ringing deafeningly, and I was dazed and winded; I began to smell singed hair. Fearing that my head was on fire, I reached up as best I could and patted the top of my head, only to find some crispy clumps where previously hair had been. My whole body felt hot and in pain.

As my senses slowly began to return to me, and the ringing in my ears started to subside, I became more aware of my surroundings. My hearing became clearer, and I suddenly heard sirens blasting away much louder from close by; then I detected the smell of what seemed like burning pork. I slowly pulled myself up into a sitting position, and saw a steady stream of flame blasting its way from inside the wall of the building. The truck looked in remarkably good condition, bearing in mind it had just taken the full brunt of an explosion.

Two fire trucks, and a paramedic ambulance pulled up and parked about a hundred feet away from the FedEx truck. The fire crew were clearly concerned about the size and intensity of the blaze, and I heard one of them yell to another to find the gas cut-off. They knew just from looking at the damage to the building what had gone on and didn't want to risk their lives going anywhere near it until the gas had been stopped. Fire hoses were hooked up to the truck, and two guys in full protective gear ran as fast as they could carrying the big two-man hose closer to the truck and began spraying the area all around the blaze, but not seeming to worry about the jet of flame blasting out from the building. In fact, if anything, they seemed to be avoiding spraying the fire from the gas line.

Immediately, the temperature around me dropped and the residual flames that had been burning away on the truck were put out. I sat there just watching what was going on, as the paramedics hovered nearby wanting to get to either me or the truck once it was safe to do so. About twenty seconds later, the fireball from the building vanished almost as quickly as it had appeared.

"Clear!" came a shout from somewhere and immediately the firefighters ran closer to the truck. The two person hose was still blasting away, keeping the building cool so it didn't burst into flames, and the firefighters moving closer had single-person hoses that they were running with. A third fire truck showed up from the opposite direction and was able to park much closer to the fire now that the gas had been shut off; more people with hoses emerged and doused what was left of the flames. Now that the gas fueling the main fire had gone, the rest of the smaller blazes were extinguished pretty quickly, and the ambulance could also move closer. Two paramedics then ran to the truck, and a third came to check on me.

"Are you okay? Sir? Sir, are you okay?"

I was dazed and a little confused, and I looked up to see a bald guy bending over me. "Err, yeah, sure. Yeah, I'm fine. Just a little shocked, that's all."

"Well, you're safe now, sir. My name's Chad, what's yours?"

"Err, Todd."

"Well, Todd, come with me, and I'll take a look at you over by our truck. Do you think you can move?"

I nodded and, just to prove it, hauled myself to my feet; I suddenly realized that I ached all over, so Chad helped me over to the paramedic truck, and gave me the once over, checking my pupil dilation and all the other stuff that trained medical people do.

"Did you bang your head?" he asked.

"No."

"Are you sure?"

"Yes."

"How many fingers am I holding up, Todd?"

"Three."

"Okay, very good."

"Would you like to have a full check-up in the hospital?"

"No, I'm fine, thanks. I was just shocked by what happened, that's all. How's Larry?"

"Who?"

"The guy driving the FedEx truck."

"I don't know, Todd. I came and assisted you immediately."

"Any chance you can find out for me? He's a friend of mine."

I'd been sitting on the back step of the ambulance, facing the FedEx truck, and I saw a paramedic leave the cab, shaking his head and looking down. I stood up and intently tried to gauge body language, but it was tough from so far away. The moment Chad had been tasked with something else, I made my way over to the FedEx truck, and peered in from the passenger's side. My heart went into my mouth, and I felt sick. Sitting behind the wheel, calm as could be and looking like he was asleep, was Larry. I let out a gasp, and my eyes began to well up.

A voice from behind me suddenly piped up "Sir? Sir? I need to get you away from here."

Tears were now tumbling down my face as I turned around and looked at the policeman talking to me. "He's dead, isn't he? Larry's dead."

"Sir, I really must ask—"

"He's my *friend*, goddammit! Tell me if he's dead! I need to know."

The cop let out a controlled sigh. "Yes, sir. He's dead. And I'm sorry for your loss."

"How did he die? The fire? He doesn't looked burned."

The policeman gently led me away from the truck. "Our initial estimation of what happened, based on what limited evidence we've gathered so far, is that he — Larry, you say?"

"Yes. Larry."

"Well it seems that Larry had a cardiac arrest as he was driving down this street. He died, and his foot rested heavily on the gas pedal, which made him accelerate to quite a speed before he crashed into the building and damaged the service line that carries gas into the building. Eventually, the gas leaked out, and some sort of spark ignited the cloud of gas. As for why he's not burned, well that's a mystery to me, sir, to be honest. Bearing in mind where his truck was positioned during that gas fire, it's nothing short of a miracle."

We were now well away from the truck and almost back to the ambulance. "Fuck," I breathed.

"Live near here, do you, sir?"

I nodded. "I live in the building he hit. My name's Todd Sykes, if you need to check."

"Oh, no, sir. You've been through quite enough today." He suddenly consulted his notebook. "Wait, Sykes you say? That is quite the coincidence."

I sat down on the rear step of the ambulance once again and looked up at him. "What is?"

"If I'm not mistaken, you're who Larry was coming to deliver a package to. We contacted FedEx to make sure their truck hadn't been stolen and they told us where his next drop-off was to be. Turns out it was you."

I closed my aching eyes and put my head in my hands. "Oh my god. He died just because he was bringing me a pair of shoes. *Fuck.*"

"Is that what the delivery was? Well, if it's any consolation, sir, it's fairly safe to say that whoever he was delivering a package to, his heart attack would still have happened. You mustn't blame yourself."

As the reality of what had happened sank in, I let out a long breath and a tear formed at the corner of my eye. It quickly became large enough to spill onto my cheek and dribble down. I was too upset to do anything about it.

After a few seconds of silence, the cop spoke again. "Look, I hate to ask this, but did you see the accident happen?"

I shook my head. "No. I heard the impact and felt the building shake, and then ran down here to see what had happened."

"So you didn't see the other three involved?"

I looked up at him again and screwed up my face slightly. "What other three?"

"Look, sir, I don't want to distress you. If you didn't see anything, let's just leave it at that."

I didn't want to leave it at that. I needed to know who these other three people were. "Please, officer, my friend has just died. I need to know what else happened. Who were the other three people?"

He shifted slightly uncomfortably from foot to foot a few times. "Well, to be honest, sir, we don't know. An eye-witness apparently saw them leave the front door of your apartment building roughly a minute before the FedEx truck crashed."

I sensed that he wasn't telling me everything. "Uh huh. And?"

Once again, the officer took a few breaths, clearly deciding whether to continue with this information or not. "Did you have any people visit with you today, sir?"

I swallowed hard. "Yes, officer, I did. Three people. They left just before the accident."

"Hmm," he said. "And would they have been two men and a woman?"

"Yes."

"Two slim men, and a larger woman?"

"Yes."

"Friends of yours?"

I narrowed my eyes slightly. "One of them was, yes. Where are you heading with this?"

The officer took a deep breath before replying. "They all died in the accident too."

XXIII

I staggered back into my apartment, partly from the pain I was in, but more from the shock of the pieces of information I was connecting in my head. I closed my front door and slumped back against it, breathing heavily, desperately trying to figure out if I was going stark raving mad, or whether the conclusions I was coming to might actually be true.

I paused for a few moments with an idea lodged firmly and stubbornly in the forefront of my mind. It was stupid and irrational, but I acted on it anyway. I turned and yanked open my door, marching furiously down the corridor to the other apartment on my floor that, in the back of my head, I knew to be empty. In psychiatrist-speak, I was undergoing *cognitive dissonance*, or in other words I had two completely contradictory thoughts in my head and, for whatever reason, had convinced myself that both were true.

I hammered on the door. "Isabella! Isabella, open up! We need to talk!"

Nothing happened.

I continued to bang and yell for a few minutes, but the door never opened. I rested my head against it and let out a long sigh with my eyes closed, almost feeling detached from my body; I had no idea what was going on any more, and couldn't believe that my life had become so confused so quickly. I trudged back to my apartment, closed the door, and then headed towards the living room when I noticed my drinks cabinet in the corner of the room. The beautiful, gleaming bottle of Johnny Walker Blue Label was beckoning to me and, although I'd been told not to drink whilst taking these meds, I also needed something to calm my nerves. The doctor's advice lost out to Johnny's persuasion, and I poured myself a glass of scotch, downing it in one.

I let out a gasp as the warmth of the liquid almost seared the back of my throat. I poured another glass and took it with me to the sofa to try and figure out quite what was going on. It seemed like I'd been trying to do just that for days now, and things had only got more complicated each time I came to some sort of conclusion or other. I was seriously concerned about my sanity, and losing it wasn't something I'd be able to handle. When I was a kid, my much loved Grandma ended up with Alzheimer's, and every week I'd visit her with my Mom and have to suffer an hour of witnessing how quickly and tragically her previously excellent brain was decaying in such a short space of time.

It began with her forgetting a few things, and quickly turned into her not remembering the last time we'd visited. Before long, she couldn't remember what she'd eaten for lunch, and then one day when Mom and I walked in, she didn't know who we were and freaked out because she thought we were strangers trying to hurt her. To know that someone capable of completing three or four crosswords each day, in-between other chores, could suddenly not know her own daughter and grandson truly showed me the fragility of the human brain, and it absolutely broke my heart. Could I be suffering from early-onset of Alzheimer's? I knew it was uncommon, but it wasn't unheard of. The thought made me shudder and take a sip of scotch; to me, there is no crueler disease than one that takes your brain power away.

I sat down heavily and recalled everything I'd learned in the last hour of craziness: Larry had undergone a massive heart attack and died pretty much instantaneously. A medic I spoke with told me he doubted Larry would have even felt anything at all; here one second, gone the next. No pain, no gasping, just... gone. That, at the very least, was one consolation I could take away from his death; he didn't suffer or even know anything about it. Even though I didn't believe in any of that stuff, I now hoped he was where he'd wanted to be for so many years: with Annie.

What the cop had told me was more troubling, however. The three people who had been seen leaving my apartment building, two slim men and a significantly overweight woman, had also perished in the accident. They'd had the misfortune to be walking along the sidewalk at the exact location that the FedEx truck had mounted it and crashed into the building. All three had almost certainly been crushed to death by the impact, but if by some miracle they'd survived, the explosion from the gas line and subsequent stream of flamethrower-like fire from the building had burned their bodies so badly that nothing remained from the knees up other than their badly charred skeletons. Ironically, all of their shoes were in perfect condition, which was what enabled me to give a positive identification to the police officer when he'd asked me whether I knew what shoes they were wearing.

"What *shoes*?" I'd asked a little incredulously.

"Err, yes sir. If you happen to know the shoes they were wearing it might help us out."

"Don't they have IDs on them?"

"Well, sir, I'm sure they probably did, but we're not able to, err, gain access to them."

"Why not?"

"They've been burned, sir. But their shoes are still intact."

My head span again. "Fuck! Shoes? Christ! Well, err, Tom always wore Adidas sneakers. And I think he was wearing light blue ones with three white diagonal stripes running down each side, and bright white soles. The other two, I don't quite—"

211

The cop had interrupted me. "That's okay, sir. That's all the information we need. Thank you so much for your help."

"It was them, wasn't it?"

"Very probably, sir. The shoes you described matched one of the victims exactly."

Without warning I'd then projectile vomited all over the street, some of it splashing onto the officer's neatly pressed pants.

I shook myself back to the present and took a sip of my scotch. What was I supposed to make of this? I'd had, or at least I *think* I'd had a visit from Isabella and Arthur, both of whom seemed to be toying with me and having a good old laugh at my expense, but then seemed to help me out; Isabella helped me find the flashlight, and Arthur diagnosed me with pancreatic cancer. That suddenly reminded me of something and I lurched for a note pad and pen on the table. I wrote a reminder to make an urgent appointment with my doctor for next week.

With that done, I sat back and had another sip. I couldn't believe Tom was dead. I couldn't say that we were best friends or anything like that, but we'd worked together for several years now and I'd become very fond of him. His endless enthusiasm was infectious and, to be honest, if it hadn't been for him, the show wouldn't have become nearly as popular as it had. I thought back to a staff meeting about *The Lost Souls* after episode three. I didn't know Tom very well at that point, and his accent was even harder to understand than it had been up till now. Our ratings were not good, and the network was demanding we improve them or the show would be cancelled.

"Wot a fakkin' two and eight," said Tom as the meeting concluded. The production staff shuffled out, as did Brad and Kurt, and it was just Tom and me left in the room.

"A what?"

"A two and eight mate, a two and eight. A state. Wot a fakkin' state."

"Oh, right. What is?"

"The show! I reckon this thing could be fakkin' *huge*! But we're just not gettin' any juicy footage. Or noises. Or fakkin' anythin', to be honest. You lot're setting up all them recording devices and gettin' jack shit!"

Brad was the star of the show. It had been mainly his idea, and somehow he'd known someone who'd known someone that had been able to arrange an audience with Mike Durkin. Mike had seen something in Brad's persona and thought that it could be good TV, so he'd agreed to create our show, but they needed a third member; someone who would be able to handle the technical angle of the lock-ins, and a friend of a friend of Tom's had suggested me. Tom called me one day, and we met for coffee; the rest is history.

I got the feeling that Tom knew I wasn't completely sold on the whole ghosts-being-real thing, but obviously I never came out and said as much. Nor did anybody involved with the show, because that would be an efficient way of not being involved with it any longer. I looked at him. "Yeah, well, Brad says that the ghosts and spirits are worried or scared because of the cameras filming them, or something."

He let out a snort. "Yeah, 'course they are. You know what we need to do, Todd? We need to fakkin' well make 'em not worried, and we need to figure out a way of making these ghosts come out to fakkin'-well play. Do you think you can do that?"

I remember looking at him with a slightly screwed-up face. "What do you mean?"

He chuckled back at me. "I dunno, mate. It can mean whatever you fakkin' want it to mean. We just need to hear some ghosts, or we're gonna get the fakkin' heave-ho."

That had been a Thursday, and Tom's words rattled around inside my head for the next day or so. Was he really suggesting what I thought he was suggesting? He wanted us to have some artificial help when we communicated with the afterlife? Wasn't that lying to our viewers? But then again I thought, the editing of every reality show in the world lies to their audience, because if they didn't they wouldn't have an audience. Reality TV is not interesting unless someone edits it to make it interesting, so why couldn't that same theory apply to our show? If there were some ghostly noises that appeared in our recordings, nobody would have any idea where they came from, and they would add some weight to Brad and Kurt's desperate attempts to make something out of static noise.

I spent Saturday morning deliberating how I could add ghostly noises in post production without anybody noticing, and then had a revelation. A quick trip to Radio Shack reignited all of my unused electronics degree passion and knowledge, and the rest of the weekend had been spent in a happy blur of soldering-iron smoke, circuit boards, and wires. After a few designs had failed to do what I needed, I'd refined them and built a little device that did exactly what I wanted. I set some digital recorders around my apartment and tested my new device. The result was exactly what I was after: a hiss of inaudible random-frequency static with each button press of the device, and I just knew that Scooby and Scrappy would be able to turn these meaningless bursts of white noise on the recordings into words from the netherworld.

And, of course, they did just that in the very next episode, but it was far better than adding the noises in post production because Brad and Kurt got to hear the ghostly noises played back during the lock-ins, and in pitch darkness. This all added to the tension and their conviction that what they were hearing was, in fact, ghosts speaking to us. The ratings for that fourth show were low at first, but then it went viral thanks to the internet forums, and suddenly we had a massive following of people who were convinced they'd either seen or heard ghosts, and the staff of the show were getting inundated with suggestions for locations that we should visit. All of a sudden, and seemingly overnight, our show had become a huge hit with a newfound following of millions and millions of people. The next show was even more popular, and the next followed the same trend, and on it went until we quickly became the network's most popular show.

I couldn't believe that by building a ten dollar white noise generator, I had just given the network a smash hit, and enabled millions of 'believers' to reaffirm their conviction that ghosts existed.

After the sixth episode had aired, and our viewing figures continued to go through the roof, I got a call from Tom. "Mate, fakkin' 'ell! We're a smash hit!"

"Err, yeah," I said, "I guess we are."

"I need to buy you a pint, mate. To celebrate."

"Um, okay. When?"

"When?" He guffawed down the phone. "When? Now, you daft old sod. Fakkin' when? Pull the other one!"

Tom pulled up outside my apartment twenty minutes later and I squeezed myself into his tiny Lotus Exige, and off we sped. Each time he changed gear, my whole body lurched forward before being thrown back against the bucket seat as he floored the throttle.

"Christ, don't they have automatic gearboxes in Britain?"

Tom looked at me briefly as he dropped it down a cog, as he liked to say, and was suddenly doing about ninety miles per hour, weaving through ponderously slow Cadillacs and SUVs.

"Yeah, in the fakkin' family car bollocks. A proppa driver uses a fakkin' manual gearbox. Automatic? That's for fakkin' poofs."

"Oh, okay, well, I quite li— *aaaaaahhhhhhhhhhhhhhh*!"

The tiny, light Lotus was as nimble as it was quick, and Tom lurched to the left to avoid someone in a a huge pickup truck pulling out of a side road without looking. "Fakkin' twat!"

I'd had no idea where we were going, but a few minutes later, we pulled into a small parking lot with potholes all over it that belonged to what looked like an abandoned one-story building. Tom climbed out and I sat still. He leaned down and stuck his head back in the car. "Come on, mate. We're here."

"Where is 'here'?"

"The Cock 'n Bull, mate. A proppa English nuclear sub in America."

"Nuclear what?"

"A pub, mate. A pub. And authentic, too. The food is bang on."

"Is this place even open?"

He let out a huge laugh. "Yeah, mate, of course it's open. Follow me."

I reluctantly got out and followed Tom, suddenly noticing an old, dilapidated British red phone box by the corner of the building. All of the panes of glass had been smashed, and it didn't make the place look any more appealing, but I followed him nevertheless.

We walked in and it took my eyes a few seconds to adjust to the lower light inside due to the fact that there were only two small windows for the entire place. I could make out two pool tables in the far corner, two dart boards in front of me, and a long bar on my right. The place was pretty much empty, and the only seats that were occupied were a couple of clumps of people around the bar.

"Awlreet Tom?" asked someone in the group nearest the door.

"'Allo, mate! How's it goin'?"

"Aye, pretty good, ta."

Tom turned to me and gestured. "This is Todd, a good mate of mine."

There were murmurings of acknowledgement that they'd been introduced, but I got none of the slightly false American-style 'heeyyyyyy, it's *so* great to meet you' that I was used to. Although slightly unnerving at first, it was a refreshing change, but I quickly realized that I had no idea what to say, mainly due to the fact that nobody had asked how I was, and that was the traditional American greeting: Hi. *Hi.* How are you? *Great, how are you?* Great.

It was abundantly clear that nobody gave a shit how I was, so I just nodded and said hello. We walked the length of the bar, and Tom put his hand on the shoulder of a smallish guy in his sixties or seventies; he had two laptops open, both streaming different soccer matches from Europe, and he was intensely focusing on a crossword in the paper in front of him.

"Sergio," said Tom, "always a pleasure."

"Tom! My good friend, Tom!" Sergio gripped his hand and gave a hearty handshake. "How are you, señor?"

His English was perfect with a hint of an accent, and he looked like a poster child for the ideal grandfather.

"This is Todd," said Tom. "Todd, this is Sergio. Football addict and crossword nut."

Sergio chuckled. "No, no, señor. Crossword trainee. Still learning, my friend; still learning!"

A voice boomed from behind us. "Fochin' 'ell! Alright Tom? Where the foch have yew been?"

Tom turned around. "'Ere and there, mate, 'ere and there. How's tricks?"

His name turned out to be Dave, and we watched him walk behind the bar and stop in front of us. "Well, the fochin' missus is givin' me a fochin' 'eadache, but other than tha', I can't complain. 'Ow 'bout you?"

"Yeah," said Tom, "I'm hangin' in there, mate. This is a friend and bloke I work with, Todd."

Dave was short, stocky, and bald, and he beamed at me. "Alright mate? As yer a friend of Tom's, the first round's on me. Whatchyew 'avin?"

Suddenly I felt the entire bar looking at me, except Sergio who was busy cheering at some Italian team having scored a goal on one of his laptops. He suddenly erupted, "goooaaaaallll Itaaaaaaaaalia! Ha ha haaaahhh!"

A friendly voice came from the other end of the bar. "Oh shut it, Serge. The Italians are a bunch of poofs. I dunno why you watch that shit!"

"And yer not even a fochin' eyetiye, ye' daft old bollock," added Dave, "You're from fochin' Chilly."

The bar burst into laughter, and Sergio chuckled away. "It is the beautiful game, amigos! Who cares what country it's in? And besides, I have ten bucks on this one!"

More guffaws from the end of the bar.

Dave looked back at me expecting an answer on what beer I would have, so I quickly glanced at the taps across the bar, and said, "I'll have a Stella, please Dave."

The whole place seemed to relax, happy that the token American wasn't about to order a Bud Light. As the hours went on, and the pints were sunk, I was slowly accepted as one of them, and I even helped Sergio with a crossword clue. Tom and I had celebrated the success of the show far harder than certainly I'd been expecting, and we both ended up needing to take a taxi home. The next morning had not been pleasant for me.

I was just recalling how horrible the hangover had been when I was suddenly dragged from my thoughts by a strange gargling sound.

It took me a few seconds to figure out what it was, but then I realized that it was my front door buzzer. It sounded like a buzzer would if the batteries were nearly dead, a sort of gurgling, whining noise. The buzzer system in this building didn't work on batteries and was connected to the main power, so it was odd that it would sound like this, but I hauled myself to my feet and headed to the front door.

I lifted the handset and put it to my ear. "Hello?"

All I heard was static. "Hello?" I said again.

Still nothing but mush.

I put the handset back and began to walk back to the living room when the buzzer made its strange half-strangled noise again. I quickly turned and picked it up.

"Hello?" I said. "Is there anybody there?"

The hissing noise of static was still there, but something else was faintly audible, and I tried to hear what it was. It was tough because it was a sort of hissing noise against the background of white noise, but then I heard something that definitely wasn't white noise.

It was a crackly and somewhat distant voice.

"You're welcome," it said.

XXIV

I'd run screaming from my front door intercom into my bedroom and thrown myself onto the bed, quickly crawling underneath the duvet. My heart rate was going at a million miles-per-hour and I was having trouble catching my breath.

I had *not* just heard what I'd thought I heard.

"It's impossible!" I yelled from under my bedding. "Isabella, you don't exist! You *can't* exist! It's just not possible!"

The buzzer let out its strangled squeak again, and I screamed as loudly as I could, "*fuck off*! Isabella! Just leave me alone! *Please*!"

I took long, deep breaths, and began to calm down. I was imagining things, that was what it was. Trauma because of Tom's sudden death on top of my heart attacks had caused my mind to play tricks on me. That was the logical explanation; there was no other one.

The buzzer stopped making its horrible sound, and I slowly crawled out from my bed. As I reached the doorway from the bedroom, it squawked again causing me to shriek and run into the living room, where I downed my scotch in one go. I staggered around the room, gasping and clutching my throat, my head suddenly spinning and beginning to pound. I sat down with a thump on my couch, my head resting in my hands and the buzzer now thankfully silent.

A sudden and totally unexpected thump on my front door made me jump out of my skin. I stood and hurled my crystal glass at my front door, smashing it to pieces. *"Just leave me the fuck alone*! I can't take this any more! Leave me *alone*!"

The was silence for a second or two, and then a woman's voice said, a little unnerved, "Err, Mr. Sykes?"

"Isabella? Is that you?"

"No, sir, this is officer Smith with the LAPD. Are you okay, sir? Sir?"

I let out a few quick and deep breaths and tried to calm down. She banged on the door again. "Sir?"

"Yes! Yes! Hold on, I'm on my way. Sorry. I, err…" I stopped because I didn't quite know how to finish the sentence.

I got to the door and pieces of broken crystal were everywhere. "Hold on, I just need to clean something up. Sorry!"

"Please take your time, sir. I know you've been through a lot today."

You have no idea, I thought to myself, as I grabbed a broom from the closet and swept up as much of the broken glass as I could see. A little sheepishly, I opened the door and saw a tall brunette in police uniform just about smiling at me as she re-holstered her Glock. Her smile was disarming and friendly, and I felt myself relax a little, despite the fact that I'd clearly just freaked her out.

"Um, hello," I said.

"Drop something, did you, Mr. Sykes?"

"Um, sort of. Well, no, actually. No. I threw a glass at the door because I thought… Oh, god, I don't know what I thought. Today has been really hard. I'm so sorry. You must think I'm a lunatic or something."

Her expression relaxed somewhat. "Of course not, sir, and I understand. Losing someone close is never easy. Is it okay if I come in? I just need to ask you a few questions to complete our endless paperwork. I hate to do this so soon, but we need to get answers to these questions while it's still fresh in your mind."

"Oh, of course, officer Smith, please come in. It's no problem."

"I tried buzzing from downstairs to give you fair warning, but I guess the intercom must be playing up because nothing happened."

I spun around and stared at her; my mouth opened and closed a few times. "It... err... You? You were pressing the buzzer? A very short while ago?"

She frowned slightly. "Yes, sir. Several times in fact. So you heard it buzz?"

I let out a huge sigh of relief and wanted to hug her, but figured that I'd probably get shot after the way the officer had seen me acting. "Ah, yes. Well, sort of. It sounded weird and when I picked it up I just got white noise. Anyway, please come in, officer."

"Thank you, sir. And please, call me Jane."

I screwed my face up slightly. "Jane Smith? Your parents weren't big on originality, I take it?"

She smiled and gave a little giggle. "Well, you can blame my parents for my first name, but my husband's the reason for my last name. You're not the first to mention it, and in fact voting is generally a nightmare; I might as well have put down 'Mickey Mouse' considering the amount of scrutiny my ID comes under!"

I showed her in, relieved that it had been a real person buzzing, and not a ghost. We sat on my sofa and she asked me a bunch of questions about what had happened after Tom and the other people had left, and did I know who they were. The truthful answer was that I had absolutely no idea, but she kept pressing me on why they were in my apartment if I didn't even know their names.

"Amanda and Jim are the names I knew them by."

"But you believe that to not be their real names?"

"Well, I don't know. I'm assuming it is."

"Something is making you think otherwise though. Why is that?"

"I didn't say that."

"You said 'the names you knew them by'. That suggests to me you think they were aliases. Why were they here?"

"Tom invited them."

"For what purpose?"

I then had to quickly decide in my head which would be the fastest route of getting officer Smith out of my apartment: saying I didn't know, or telling her that I'd have to talk to my network's legal department before answering. I couldn't have the story of a hoax being played on us getting out into the public domain; that would be the death of the show. That's if there was still a show after all this crap had gone down.

"To be honest, officer, I have no idea."

"You don't know why these two other people were in your apartment?"

I paused. "Well, I think Tom wanted them to be something to do with the show, but more than anything he just wanted me to meet them."

"And why would that be, sir?"

I sighed and my head slumped forward. "Officer, I've had a really shitty day. Two good friends of mine have just died in the same freak accident. I've told you everything I know. There is nothing more sinister going on here, and I really just want to be alone with my thoughts. I'm sorry if this comes across as rude, but would you mind leaving please?"

She smiled tightly and closed her notebook. "Of course not, sir. But please, if you think of anything else that we should know, give me a call. Here's my card."

I took it from her and felt like the most terrible human being on the planet for being so abrupt. "Thank you officer, err, Jane. In fact, I'm sorry; I really am. That was very rude of me. Would you like a cup of coffee or something?"

She smiled a little more warmly at me and said, "Look, Mr. Sykes, I'm really sorry to have pushed and pushed; it's just our training. We have to think that everything is suspicious!"

I smiled back at her. "I'll try and figure out why those two were here with Tom, and I'll give you a call and let you know what I find out. And please, call me Todd."

"I really appreciate that, Todd. I'm looking forward to your call. I'm truly sorry for your loss. Next time, the coffee's on me as my way of saying sorry."

I nodded. "Deal. I'll call you in a few days with an update."

We shook hands and I showed her out, closing the door behind her. I examined the dent in the wood where the heavy crystal glass had hit it, and decided not to have it repaired as a reminder to myself to be more rational in future. What had happened to the good old cynical ghosts-cannot-possibly-exist Todd? That whole trip to Spain had messed me up big time, followed by the tragic death of a friend and colleague, not to mention Larry, and I needed to get over it away from where it happened. Perhaps I should go on a vacation? Hawai'i seemed tempting, but a little too obvious. I wondered if the Travel Channel could help me out; wherever the current show was being filmed was where I'd go, I told myself.

I walked back into my living room, feeling calmer, and poured myself another scotch into a fresh glass before sitting down on the sofa. I turned the TV on and was immediately confronted with a grainy, green image of Kurt in a straitjacket, locked in a cell, and calling out Isabella's name. Involuntarily, my entire body shuddered violently and I spilled most of my drink over my leg and the sofa; I frantically bashed at the buttons on the remote and, after what seemed like an agonizingly long period of time, the channel changed to a random Mexican one, and I took a few deep breaths trying to calm my racing heartbeat. I'd inadvertently stumbled across a re-run of an episode of our show, and it just happened to be *that* episode, at *that* moment.

"Coincidence," I said out loud, almost without realizing it.

I drained what was left of my scotch and went and poured myself another small one that went down the hatch immediately. I was beginning to feel quite buzzed from the amount of liquor I'd poured down my neck so quickly and, no doubt, the meds.

Nevertheless, my nerves needed further calming, so a larger scotch was poured and I took it back to the sofa.

I hit a few buttons on the remote and the babbling mustachioed, overweight, short latin alpha-one dude trying to chastise a heavily made-up woman about a foot taller than him was silenced, and the TV switched to the Travel Channel that seemed to be about to wrap up a commercial break. Wondering where I'd be heading in a few days time, I took a sip of my scotch; the break finished, and I ended up watching a show about Idaho and what great potatoes they have.

I rolled my eyes. "There's no way I'm taking a vacation in Idaho," I grumbled quietly to myself as I scanned the channel list for something that might help me choose a slightly more exotic vacation destination.

Suddenly the buzzer squawked out it's horrible half-dead-sounding wail. I let out a sigh because I'd got comfy on the sofa, but at least I didn't have to be scared of it any more; Jane must have forgotten to ask me another question that I'd do my best to avoid answering, so I had another sip of scotch and reluctantly hauled myself to my feet, only to discover that I was a little light headed. I put my glass down, realizing that perhaps I'd had enough for now, and made my slightly wobbly way to the front door. I picked up the intercom phone.

"Officer Smith?" I asked.

The hissing was as loud as ever, and I tried to hear something resembling words, but it was impossible.

"Jane?" I asked again, louder.

This time I got a reply. Again, it was a very faint whisper just slightly more audible than the white noise, but it was definitely a word.

"Isabella," it said.

I immediately froze. I'd definitely heard it.

"Officer Jane Smith? Is that you?"

I got another meaningless hiss in return.

"Jane Smith?" I asked extremely loudly.

A louder hiss came back. "Isabella."

Totally panicked, I hurled the handset to one side and yanked my front door open. I ran as fast as I could down the corridor and down the emergency steps. Once again, I burst through the mail area and sprinted to the front of the building. I yanked open the tinted glass door and found that Frank Billings, our building superintendent, was busy fussing over some poor guy who had his head in a bundle of wires.

"Are you sure you're qualified for this level of advanced electronics," whined Frank in a patronizing manner, "because I've read online that there are certain calibrations of wires that—"

The guy that was buried in cables, with a huge belt kit full of clever looking electrical tools replied as patiently as he could muster. "Listen, bud, I know what I'm doing. Okay? I installed this fucking thing."

I could see that Frank was about to unwisely chastise him for foul language when I became the focus of his attention. "Oh, Todd. Hello," he said in an even more disapproving tone than normal.

I was panting and gasping from the speed I'd made it down here. "Oh, hi Frank. Testing the buzzers, are you?"

"The buzzers? You meant the sophisticated intercom system we have?"

"Yes, I suppose I do."

"Then no. All power to that entire system was knocked out because of your friend."

I suddenly saw a red mist, and before I realized what was going on, I had Frank pinned against the wall with my hand gripped tightly around his neck. "Because *what*? You stuck up, officious little prick! You mean my *two* friends who *died* today? *Those* friends?"

"Hey," said the man in the wires, "chill out, bud. Don't let this asshole wind you up and do something stupid. Let him go. He's not worth it."

I suddenly realized what I was doing and released Frank. He immediately doubled over and began theatrically coughing and spluttering. "You'll be hearing from the housing committee about this, Sykes," gasped Frank as he hobbled away from me, clutching his neck.

The repair man got back to work with a chuckle. "What a douche."

"Thanks dude," I said, "I've had a rough day."

"It sounds like it. I'm sorry, man."

"Are you sure none of the buzzers are working in the apartments?"

"Oh yeah, absolutely. The fire took out a loom of wiring that provided electricity to the main system for the intercoms. They haven't been working since the accident."

"So there's no battery or anything in the handsets that could allow one to make a noise since then?"

"Nope. Absolutely not. No way in hell. Why do you ask?"

"Um, I, err... I thought I heard my intercom make a sort of squawking noise."

"No way, man, it must have been something else in your apartment. This whole system has been dead for hours and will be for a while longer."

"Oh," I said, suddenly beginning to tremble again, "thanks, dude."

I ran back inside, my head spinning again. If there was no power to the intercom, then how had someone managed to communicate through it to me?

Twice.

I staggered through my apartment front door, lifted the handset from where it was dangling, and put it to my ear.

Nothing.

Not a hiss, not a crackle, absolutely nothing at all. Just like the repair guy had said it would be. My head span and I felt dizzy, lurching slightly to one side and putting my arm out to steady myself. I was completely and utterly panicked, and now convinced that Isabella *was* following me around. What other explanation could there be? My brain now refused to accept the whole

226

coincidence idea, because there were just too many of them for that to be a plausible option.

I made my way unsteadily back to my living room, and downed the rest of my scotch in one go. I felt sick to my stomach and my head began to swim even more.

I felt utterly wretched and just wanted this whole ghost thing to be done with. I suddenly regretted mucking around with the afterlife and mocking them all the time. It seemed like I'd finally pissed off some spirit or other, and Isabella was out to settle a score. What other explanation could there be?

Ghosts absolutely do not exist! I tried telling myself that over and over, but it suddenly seemed clear that they did exist. And, therefore, if ghosts existed, then had my assumptions about god been wrong all this time? *Could* a god exist? It stood to reason that if spirits and ghosts existed, then a god is as equally feasible, however unlikely I'd thought it before, because all of my previous assumptions now had to be considered wrong. Isabella was stalking me, of that I had no doubt.

The thought of how helpless I was generated a wave of nausea inside me that seemed really keen to see the light of day. How do you go about stopping a ghost intent on following you round and, seemingly, protecting you? Because that's what it appeared she was doing, whilst having her own fun of course. Tom and the two actors made me have a heart attack, they all die in a freak and horrific accident by a kindly old guy who died peacefully and wanted more than anything to be with his deceased wife.

"*NO!*" I screamed out loud! "Isabella! Please stop this! I can't take it any more!"

The buzzer squawked again, and I jumped out of my skin. I was utterly terrified, my brain completely confused, and my entire body was trembling.

I looked up and called out, "if there is a god up there, please help me! Help me stop Isabella and I'll become a believer! Please help me!"

The buzzer gave a weak whine and I completely lost it. I ran to my front door, yanked it open and charged to the stairwell. If there *was* a god, then he would need to stop me from doing what I was about to, and then I'd believe, because he clearly wasn't helping with the Isabella situation.

This time I sprinted *up* the stairs, taking them two at a time, arriving at the very top, finding a padlocked door leading out on to the roof. The nearby fire extinguisher made short work of the flimsy padlock and I emerged onto the roof, squinting into the sunlight. My apartment building was four floors high, the maximum allowed by the local building codes and, although not particularly high in the world of committing suicide, I figured it would be high enough to get the job done. I really couldn't take any more torture from Isabella, and had decided to put an end to it all. My nerves were frayed, my brain was a scrambled mess, and there's no way to get rid of a murderous stalker ghost; I was done with life.

I scrambled over the air conditioning ducts and made my way to the edge of the building. There was a small wall about two feet high that was intended, I supposed, to let people know that the edge of the roof was the other side, but it looked more like something to be accidentally tripped over. I climbed onto it, looked down, and regretted it; a building with four floors doesn't sound like much, but when you're standing on the edge of it knowing you're about to jump, it suddenly looks like you're perched on the edge of the Empire State Building. I wobbled slightly and took a deep breath.

I closed my eyes and looked up at the heavens. "If you exist, god, now's your chance to give me a bit of faith and save me."

Nothing happened, except for me getting a bit dizzy. The next thing I knew I was falling.

I had to assume, as I fell, that god didn't exist after all.

XXV

It was a little surprising to me that I felt the landing. I'd been kind of hoping that I wouldn't feel a thing and that would be the end of it, but as I lay there, my back hurt a bit, as did the rear of my head. Would this be the moment that I'd float up to the afterlife and meet Isabella? I hoped so, because I wanted to punch her in the face.

"Todd? Todd?"

That seemed strange, I thought to myself. I didn't seem to be hearing the voice as a disembodied soul, but through my actual ears, and I was fairly sure that I should be seeing things from about ten feet above my sprawled body, watching horrified bystanders come rushing to my aid.

The voice spoke again, "Todd! Sir! It's me, Duff. Can you hear me?"

I slowly opened my eyes to find myself looking up at the concerned face of Duff and beyond him was clear blue sky. "Am I dead?"

"No, but it was damn close. What the hell were you doing?"

"Trying to commit suicide."

"You were *what*? Durkin's gonna freak out. Thank Christ I got here in time."

I thought for a moment. "Where's here?"

"The rooftop."

I looked each side of me and saw the labyrinth of air ducts and piping. "I'm supposed to be down on the street."

"Yeah, well, just as you were losing your balance, I was able to get a hand to you and pull you back. Sorry if the landing was a bit hard; I didn't have time to be graceful about it, but it was a hell of a lot softer than if you'd fallen the other way."

I groaned; it seemed Duff was my guardian angel. Lying there on the roof, I felt a little foolish. Committing suicide? What was I thinking?

Duff helped me to my feet and escorted me back downstairs. It turned out that he'd seen my altercation with Frank, and as he got closer he'd seen me freak out and run back into the apartment. Duff chatted with the repair guy about what had happened and had then taken the elevator up to my floor. Just as he was stepping out, the door to the stairwell had slammed shut; he found my apartment empty with the door open, put two-and-two together, and headed for the staircase. He was just about to head down when he heard me battering the crap out of the padlock with the fire extinguisher and realized which way I'd gone; he'd got to me just in time.

Back in my apartment, Duff closed the front door and peered at the dent in it. He looked around, and noticed a piece of the broken crystal that I hadn't managed to sweep up. He picked it off the floor and sniffed it before continuing into my living room; he looked at the glass on the coffee table.

I sighed. "Yes, Duff, I had a glass of scotch. Or two."

"You're not supposed to drink on your meds, sir."

"Yeah, I know, but I was having a rough day, dude."

Duff gave me a disapproving look. "The doctor was quite clear that—"

"Look, dude, it didn't hurt. I didn't keel over and collapse or anything."

Duff screwed his face up slightly. "With all due respect, you tried to jump off a four storey building a few moments ago. I'd say it didn't interact well with your medication. Were you hallucinating?"

Now there was an interesting thought. Could the 'voice' that I'd heard have been a hallucination because of the combination of medication and alcohol? It was certainly a possibility. Tom and Larry had definitely died in a freak accident, but perhaps that was exactly what it was and nothing more?

I looked at the floor and put my head in my hands. "I think I must have been, dude. I was hearing a voice through an intercom that had no power. That can't happen. I must have imagined the whole thing."

"Those meds you're on are pretty strong, sir. When they tell you not to drink while taking them, they mean it for precisely this reason. Who's voice was it?"

"I'm not sure," I lied unconvincingly. "But I assumed it was some ghost or other."

"Male or female," pressed Duff.

"Err, it was hard to tell. The voice, if that's what it was, was a hissing, static-type sound. I'm pretty sure I imagined it. And in fact," I said, trying to get off this topic, "I've suddenly become really tired. I guess this going nuts and trying to commit suicide business is tiring! Ha ha."

"I think some rest is an excellent idea, sir. You've been through a lot the past few days."

"Thanks Duff. And I'm sorry I disobeyed doctor's orders and ended up trying to kill myself. Thanks for saving my life, dude."

Duff nodded in a typical military-style, self-effacing fashion.

I wobbled my way to the bedroom door. As I reached it, Duff said, "I'm going to spend the night here, if that's okay, sir? I just need to make sure there are no incidents until the alcohol and medication mix has worn off. I'm sure you understand?"

The way he'd said it made it very clear that I didn't actually have a choice in the matter.

"That'd be awesome. Thanks, dude. Help yourself to whatever you like and make yourself at home."

He nodded and I closed the door. The drapes in my bedroom were still closed, and the whole room sank into a welcoming blackness. I fumbled my way to the bed and climbed onto it, not bothering to take off my clothes. My entire body suddenly felt extremely heavy, and my eyelids wanted to do nothing other than slide shut, which is exactly what they did.

The next time they opened it was thanks to a gentle insistence from Duff, who was softly shaking me awake. "Sir?"

I prized my eyelids apart and slowly came to, realizing that I was in exactly the same position as I'd been in when I'd fallen asleep, and it was still light outside, judging from the glare that was seeping in from the cracks in the drapes. I tried to ask Duff why he'd woken me up so soon, but all that came from my mouth was a croak and it felt like someone had been pouring sand into it for the last hour. I smacked my lips together and worked my tongue, desperately trying to generate some moisture but it wasn't happening.

"Here's some water, sir."

When I tried to roll over and have some, I was surprised by how stiff I felt all over, but I finally had a stretch, causing lots of vertebrae to crack, and I was able to accept the glass of water that tasted magnificent as it rehydrated my mouth and insides. And then I noticed the tray of food that Duff had put on the bedside table; bacon, French toast, orange juice, and coffee.

"Dude, you didn't need to—"

"It was no trouble, sir. And I thought you'd need some sustenance after yesterday."

I thought for a few seconds. "Yesterday? You mean I slept through the night?"

"Oh yes. I checked on you several times, but I don't think you actually moved all night. I did wonder at one point whether you were dead, but your snoring assured me you weren't."

I ran my hand through my hair, which felt greasy, and I let out a sigh. "Thanks, man. I don't know how I'll ever repay you."

Duff then told me that he didn't need repaying because this was his job, and he left me to eat. I showered, feeling extremely clear headed, and as the hot water washed over me, I thought about things; I thought about ghosts and I thought about god, and then I realized that I didn't know what to think any more. As I was drying off, I suddenly realized what I needed: I needed some help to figure it out.

It turned out that Duff wasn't about to leave his bone-headed charge to do something stupid, so he became my chauffeur as well as my bodyguard and, basically, refused to leave my side. Once it became clear that this wasn't a subject up for debate, I told him where I wanted to go, and he drove me there in a bodyguard-cliché black SUV with tinted windows. He even insisted I sit in the back.

The building we pulled up outside was one I'd driven past many times before without paying much attention to, but the name had sunk in and was the reason I was here: it was the only church that I could think of to go to. It wasn't particularly historic, having been built in the 1920s and, compared to Santa Isabel, looked a bit industrial. It looked like it had been designed by a German: all the architectural boxes were ticked of what a church needed, but it lacked soul.

I pushed open one of the the double doors of Saint Monica's church in, not surprisingly, Santa Monica, and made my way inside. Not having ever been religious, I didn't really know my way around churches, so I was playing things by ear. This place was famous in gossip circles, being the church of The Terminator, Brooke Shields, Kelsey Grammer, and Martin Sheen, to name but a few. Even Xena the Warrior Princess was married here, apparently.

Once through the vestibule, I entered the main part of the church with huge, high ceilings and archways, and row after row of pews. It didn't feel quite as church-like or imposing as Santa Isabel, and that was probably because it was so new. There were even trendy-looking colored spotlights blazing their beams over the inner arch of the roof, and inside wasn't bone-chillingly cold, as European churches seemed to be.

The place was fairly empty, but I guessed they didn't get that much traffic when sermons weren't going on. There were a few people sitting in pews, heads down, some mumbling quiet somethings to themselves and their god. I made my way slowly and, I hoped, respectfully down the aisle to the front where there was a fairly subtle religious altar-type thing, above which in a huge arched alcove was a painting of Jesus and, what I assumed was Mary on his right, and Joseph on his left. For a change, Jesus wasn't nailed to anything and actually looked quite cheerful; for some reason, knowing that this church was built less than a hundred years ago, made it less daunting and serious, and the accoutrements dotted around the place were less grim than I'd seen in Spain.

I headed to my right for no other reason than every single movie I'd seen where a character has to do what I wanted to do turned right at the front of the aisle when the pews ended. My hunch, perhaps thanks to being in Hollywood's shadow, was correct and there it was: the confessional box. I'd never even seen one in person before, let alone been into one but, thanks to the movies, I knew what it looked like; this one had a sign hanging on it.

Confessional hours 5:30p.m. to 6p.m.

I blinked a few times and made sure I was seeing the times correctly. Really? Half an hour per day is all the time allotted for the faithful in Santa Monica to confess? Perhaps they led such vegetable-fueled, hybrid-driven lives that they didn't need to confess very often? Whatever the reason, I was there at just after one p.m., and therefore had quite a few hours to hang around; my frustration must have shown because there was a quiet cough next to me.

"May I help you, my son?"

The voice wasn't American; it had a faint Irish lilt to it.

I spun around to find a guy in full black robes complete with white clergy collar. I guessed he was in his sixties, he wore glasses that were too big for him and came from the seventies, had white hair that was receding around his forehead, a large nose, and slightly droopy jowls.

He gave me a friendly smile and continued. "You've not been here before, have you?"

I shook my head. "Err, no. I, err, I sort of wanted to confess. But it seems you're closed."

He nodded. "We have limited funds, my son, so confessional has a short window. Is there something bothering you?"

"Um, no. Well, yes. But don't worry. I'll come back later, I suppose."

"Are you sure, my son? Just because the confessional isn't open doesn't mean I don't have time to listen."

I was starting to get panicked now. I was expecting it to be like in the movies: I slip into the box, a few minutes later a priest arrives and we communicate through a shrouded window that prevents either of us from seeing the other's face, I confess my terrible sins, and I leave with total anonymity. But here we were having a chat in the middle of the church, and it didn't seem right.

"I guess I'll come back later," I blurted, and spun on my heel to leave.

"My son," said the priest softly, "please wait. You clearly have something on your mind, and I get the feeling that you're not of this faith. Are you looking to find God? To find the path that only He can offer?"

I froze. How had he known that? This priest had just summed up in one sentence the very thing that I'd been grappling with for hours: I needed a path of some sort, and perhaps some god or other would help me find it.

"Come," he said in a soft voice, "let's go and have a cup of tea. I have all the time in the world for you, my son. You seem troubled."

I nodded and followed him to the vestry where he fiddled about with a small electric kettle for a while trying to make the red light come on. Finally a good thump with his palm did the trick.

"It looks like you need a new one of those, ha ha," I said, like a bonehead.

He let out a chuckle. "This has been my faithful kettle for nearly ten years. There's still some life in her yet!"

His vestry was small, but homely. There were many books strewn around the place, piles of papers, and on the wall were little notes with ideas for sermons alongside reminders to pick up his dry cleaning. A bookcase on one wall contained lots of books about religion, bibles, and even literary classics like Poe, Shakespeare, and Tolstoy. The kettle coughed and burped noisily in the background, and the priest sat down behind his desk. He took his glasses off and gave them a wipe on his robes before putting them back on and fixing me in his kindly gaze.

"I'm father O'Reilly," he said softly, "and who might you be?"

"Err, I'm Todd."

"What what seems to be troubling you, my son? Because troubled is definitely what y'are."

The sentences he was using were ones that only an Irishman can pull off, in a Yoda-kind of way. I suddenly felt incredibly stupid. "Um, well, it's nothing, really. It's silly. Never mind, let's forget all about it."

He shut me up and completely disarmed me with a friendly and wise smile. "Not so fast with the rushin' off, because I don't for one second think it was nothin' or silly. Whatever it is, it's enough for a non-religious young man to come and want to confess to me."

I blinked a few times. "How do you know I'm not religious?"

He chuckled. "Your hairstyle, son. Your hairstyle."

The kettle came to a hissing and popping crescendo and the red light went out with a somewhat anti-climactic dull ping. Father O'Reilly got to his feet and poured the boiling water into a china teapot, before bringing the whole tray and putting it on his desk.

"My hairstyle?"

He guffawed. "I'm just pullin' your leg, Todd. I watched you walking around the church and you looked like a fish out of water! But I'm right though, aren't I?"

I nodded. "Yeah, I never really got the whole religion thing."

"It's not for everyone, my son. So what brought you to see me on this fine day?"

I was desperately trying to figure out if I should just get up and leave or not, and then I remembered my day of utter torment yesterday and decided to go through with what I'd come to do. It couldn't hurt.

"Father," I said tentatively, "what's your take on ghosts?"

His eyes widened with slight surprise; I'm not sure what he'd been expecting me to be troubled about, but this wasn't it. "Ghosts, eh? Well, well, well. Do you want *my* take, or the Catholic church's take?"

"Either. Both, I suppose. I mean, you're a man of the cloth, and there's a certain leap of faith required to believe in the whole god thing. Do you feel the same way about ghosts as you do your god?"

He poured two cups of tea and added some milk, then he sat back, pressed his fingertips together and pondered in silence for a few moments.

"Well," he said, "as far as the Catholic church goes, ghosts do not exist. God put you on this earth and, when you die, you either go to the Kingdom of Heaven, or you end up in Hell. There is the concept of trapped spirits, but the church considers those to be demons sent by the devil, and they aren't the same as ghosts. So, basically, you're either alive, in Heaven with the almighty Father watching over you, or in the hands of the Devil. A ghost would have to be none of those things, and the Heavenly Father wouldn't let that happen."

I nodded. "Oh. So no ghosts."

"No ghosts."

"And what do *you* think about ghosts?"

He took a sip of tea, and I did the same. "Ah, well there's a thing. You see, my son, in my sermons I take the view of the Catholic church, obviously, but we're all capable of independent thought. The way I see it is this: by believing in God in the first place, I'm already acknowledging that there are all manner of otherworldly things that us mere mortals can't begin to comprehend or understand, so who's to say there aren't some lost souls that haven't made it to their final destination? Sort of like my suitcase that ended up in Murmansk."

"Murmansk?"

"Mmmm. I was only flying to San Francisco. Anyway, the point is, things get lost. So why not souls too?"

"But you just said that god wouldn't let that happen."

"He works in mysterious ways, my son. Mysterious ways. Sort of like baggage handlers."

"But... but... saying that whichever god works in *mysterious ways* is just the go-to phrase that religious people roll out whenever there's been a tsunami or earthquake and thousands of innocent people die for seemingly no reason. Or why he won't give us a cure for cancer. No, in fact, why he invented cancer at all!"

"Ah yes, my son, but that's the key word, isn't it? *Seemingly*. God has his Grand Plan, and we don't understand it. Therefore, sometimes it seems that He works in mysterious ways. If there was no cancer, what would all those scientists toil over and win awards for, eh?"

I was getting frustrated. "But, that doesn't make any—"

He chucked again and smiled at me. "My son, we could sit here all day and go round and round in circles, with me using that same defense over and over. *Grand Plan, mysterious ways*, and so on. It's a simple way for people to retain belief in their faith when real-world events contradict what they've been told about their compassionate God. Every religion employs the same tactic."

"So you don't believe it either!" I blurted.

Another sip of tea. "Do I believe that our Heavenly Father is infallible? No. Do I believe that he controls every single action of every single molecule on this planet, all day every day? No. Just because I believe He created us, doesn't mean I can't believe that things evolve too, and for that reason, my son, I can be open to the possibility that ghosts exist."

I was slightly taken aback. Perhaps this religion thing wasn't as bat-shit crazy as I'd alway thought. Father O'Reilly seemed to be fairly balanced in his take on things. "Oh. Okay then. That's refreshing to know."

"So why are you so interested in my view of ghosts?"

"Well, it's just that yesterday I had a sort of epiphany. Well, more of a realization actually. I figured that, just like you said, if ghosts exist, then why couldn't, theoretically, a god exist too?"

"And what got you thinking about that, my son?"

"Oh, nothing really. It's just that a ghost made me try to commit suicide yesterday."

XXVI

Apparently, it's a sin in the eyes of the Lord to try and commit suicide. Father O'Reilly's jovial manner was replaced with a more serious one after he found out what I'd tried the day before.

"Suicide? Why in the name of Mary and Jesus, and all that's holy, would you do that, my son? Whatever for?"

"Um. I was being haunted by a ghost. I think she might be in love with me, or out to get me, or something." I felt as ridiculous as it sounded out loud.

The priest got up, locked his hands behind his back, and began pacing up and down. "So tell me, Todd, did this ghost instruct you to take your own life?"

"Well, no, but I was driven to my wits end over the course of several days. And as far as I can figure out, she'd just killed four people, two of which were my friends, because they'd played a prank on me that had inadvertently put me in hospital."

O'Reilly sat down again with a thump. "I think you'd better tell me the whole story, my son. From the beginning."

I began with that fateful night when we'd locked Scooby Doo in Isabella's cell, and I took him all the way through to when I almost jumped to my death before being rescued by Duff.

241

He didn't say a word for the entire time, and sat there processing the huge amount of information I'd just unloaded onto him; then he let it all sink in for about twenty seconds after I'd finished.

Finally, he spoke. "You asked God for help. You asked Him to save your life and stop you from committing suicide."

"Yes."

"And what happened?"

"Duff got to me just in time."

"And was Duff supposed to be coming to visit you yesterday?"

"I didn't ask him. I just assumed that he'd decided to pay me a —"

My voice trailed off as the realization of where the priest was taking this conversation sank in.

Father O'Reilly said quietly, "God did exactly as you asked. He saved your life."

I shook my head. "No! No, it was a coincidence! And if he was going to save my damn life, couldn't he have done it a bit sooner? Like before I'd left my apartment? Or, at the very least, before I was standing inches from death? And please don't give me the *mysterious ways* line."

The priest smiled. "If God had saved you before you'd even left your apartment, would you be here right now?"

I thought for a few moments, and suddenly wasn't sure. I'd made the promise to someone up there that if they saved my life, I'd become religious. If I'd have bumped into Duff on my way out of my apartment, would I be sitting here right now? The honest answer was, I suddenly realized, no. The only reason I was sitting here, in a church and explaining my troubles to a priest, was because I'd come so close to death and the fact that I'd gone as far as I had, had freaked me out.

"No," I said quietly.

"His ways could be seen as less mysterious this time around, then."

I let out a huge sigh. "Yeah, I guess they could."

"You asked for help. You got help. You asked to be saved. He saved you."

"It still could be a coincidence," I said feebly.

Father O'Reilly chuckled again. "How were you expecting to be saved? A giant Monty Python hand arrives and plucks you off the roof? No, he sent Duff as your guardian angel to rescue you, and timed it to perfection, as only He can. He made sure you showed up here."

I sighed and let that sink in. "But why?"

Father O'Reilly chuckled quietly and sat back down. "In what ways does He move?"

"Yeah, yeah, mysterious ones. There's a plan, etcetera, etcetera."

"Have you had suicidal thoughts since? Or had you before?"

"No! Never! I've never once even entertained the idea. I always saw it as the coward's way out, and I'll never try it again because it's absolutely terrifying once you realize that you're unstoppably committed and in free fall on the way to your death. What do I do, Father?"

He thought for a few moments. "What do you think you should do?"

I'd been hoping for some sage advice, rather than soul-searching psycho-babble. "I'm not sure. I'm out of my element, to be honest."

"I cannot advise you on matters that are between you and the Heavenly Father, my son. But, tell me: do you usually honor your promises?"

"I do. It pis— annoys me when people promise something and then don't go through with it."

Father O'Reilly sat back in his chair, beamed at me, and then pressed his fingers together again. "Then, my son, I think you have your answer."

I thought about this for a few moments. "I guess I did promise."

"In return for His help, yes."

"And it would seem that he, whoever 'he' is, came through for me." I paused. "So how do I go about becoming religious? Do I have to drink wine and eat crackers and stuff?"

The priest let out a laugh. "I think, my son, it'll be best to take this in baby steps. Like I said earlier, religion isn't for everyone. Why not come to the Sunday sermon that will be given by my good self tomorrow? I'll make sure it's not too heavy for you, break you in nice and gentle, as it were."

As I lay in bed that night, Duff still keeping watch in my living room, I felt more confused than ever. I'd gone to church for answers, and come away with more questions than ever. By the Father's logic, I'd been saved by god in the guise of sending Duff at exactly the correct time. But what had happened could just as easily be explained away with a good old coincidence. Either option was equally as likely and, depending on which side of the 'god exists' debate you were on, either one was conclusive and the other ridiculous.

Even trying to get to the bottom of ghosts through the church hadn't illuminated anything; the church itself says they don't and can't exist, yet the priest said that he couldn't rule it out. None of it was helping, and I felt like I was going crazy trying to make sense of it all.

After another half-hour of tossing and turning, I had a sudden epiphany, and leapt out of bed. I put my robe on and then yanked open the bedroom door; Duff shot to attention.

"What's wrong, sir?"

"Wrong? Nothing. I need to talk to you about something."

He rubbed his eyes, and then stood up. "I'm listening, sir."

I really wished he'd stop with the 'sir' thing, but he seemed incapable when he was in BG mode. I walked to the fridge and poured myself a glass of orange juice while I tried to organize my thoughts. Back in the living room, I took a sip and looked at Duff.

"Did god send you to save me yesterday?"

He screwed his face up a little. "I'm sorry, sir? God?"

"Yeah, were you, like, heading to the mall or something and suddenly had a flash of inspiration to come and visit me?"

He shook his head. "No, I'd been planning to pay you a visit and had scheduled it into my day. The timing was, how shall I put it, *fortuitous*, but I don't think God had anything to do with it. Unless He knew a day ahead of time that you were going to try and jump at that exact moment."

"What do you mean?"

"Well, you tried to jump on Friday, but on Thursday, Mr. Durkin asked me to pay you a visit; make sure you were still in once piece. So, I planned my Friday — I always try to plan my days out to maximize efficiency — and I visited you right on schedule. Why do you ask? Is this related to the church visit today?"

"Yeah, kind of. I'm just trying to make sense of everything. Or something, at least." I paused and looked at the floor. "Look, Duff, there's some back-story leading up to why I ended up on the roof."

"I suspected there might be, sir. May I enquire as to what that back-story is?"

I sat down into one of my armchairs with a thump. "Yes, you may. Have a seat, Duff, this takes a while. Oh, and you'll probably think I'm bat-shit crazy at the end of it."

"Try me."

For the second time that day, I regaled the entire story, beginning with Kurt being in the straitjacket. Either my story was captivating, or I bored everybody into some sort of zoned-out trance because, just like Father O'Reilly, Duff didn't say a word until I'd finished.

After about thirty seconds of silence, Duff finally said, "hmmmmm."

I blinked a few times. "Hmmm? Is that it? Hmmm?"

Duff stood and paced around the room. "Are you going to church tomorrow?"

"I don't know. Should I? I did promise."

"Why not give it a try? It might make you feel calmer about everything."

I thought for a few moments. "Yeah, okay. I will. What's your take on the ghosts thing I just spent the last twenty minutes telling you about? That was the part I wanted advice on, not so much the church thing."

There was silence for a few seconds, and then Duff spoke in a quiet voice. "You really want to know what I think?"

"Yes! Of course I do!"

"Tell me: have you seen or heard from Isabella since you tried to jump?"

"No, not a peep. It's been great."

"So the only times you've heard from her have been either when you were hopped up on mega-meds in hospital, or when you were drinking on meds that you absolutely shouldn't be drinking on?"

"Yeah, I guess—" I stopped speaking. Suddenly reality crashed down around me, and I realized where Duff's clinical and logical mind had ended up. "Oh, shit. I've been hallucinating, haven't I?"

"I'm no expert, sir, but that's certainly what the evidence currently points to. Why not see what the next few days bring, without any booze inside you, and perhaps we'll know more then?"

I bade Duff goodnight and crawled back into bed, feeling simultaneously confused and idiotic. Of course it was the meds; that made so much sense. Why couldn't I have figured that out? I was on serious meds, hospital-prescribed-only meds, expressly warned not to have any alcohol whilst taking them, and then I drank three quarters of a bottle of scotch in the space of about two hours. Of course I was going to end up hallucinating. I suddenly felt tired all over again.

I pulled the duvet up to my chin. As I felt myself sink into the lush mattress and the bed begin to love me, I suddenly remembered the whole thing about god. Where did that dude fit into all this? If my brain had been making it all up, then there was no need for me to go to church tomorrow and follow through with my promise.

Was there?

The fact remained that, Isabella haunting me or not, I'd asked a god to save me and, whatever your take on what happened, I hadn't gone splat on the sidewalk. And I'd come really, really close to doing so. So close, in fact, that Duff told me I'd actually begun to fall forwards when he'd managed to grab hold of me and yank me back onto the roof.

The two arguments were simple, and totally opposing.

You believe in a god: Duff was sent at the last moment to save me, and also to give me a solid reason to go to church and become a believer. God has an important job for you, and he's watching over you because you're special.

You don't believe in any type of god: It was a fortunate coincidence that saved my life, and nothing more. People ask god for help all day every day and never get it. This was just a coincidence, and you should be happy you're still alive, you fucking idiot.

As I lay back and tried to figure it out, it suddenly occurred to me that I'd been so wrapped up in my own confusion that I hadn't really thought much about Tom or Larry. They were both dead; one having died peacefully, causing the other to die in an horrifically violent and dramatic fashion, along with Tom's two co-conspirators. *Could* this have been Isabella exacting revenge, or was that a ludicrous notion?

I suddenly realized the problem with trying to figure out or analyze the afterlife, spirits, or the gods: the lack of physical evidence for any of it means that you can interpret events whichever way your brain is feeling that day, and how desperately you want to believe in that stuff. Of course, the lack of evidence is the reason I'd never believed in all this stuff before: I'm not the sort of person to just accept things on blind faith. If you tell me there's a dude with a beard sitting on a cloud creating everything and running our lives, then you'd better be able to come up with some way of showing me that he's there, or I'm going to call bullshit. Of course, this is the exact argument that the 'mysterious ways' defense was invented to counter, and it's nonsense.

I suddenly had a moment of clarity, and the old 'me' returned in earnest; perhaps the cocktail of alcohol and meds inside me had finally been metabolized, and my rational thinking had returned.

Of course this whole ghost thing was a load of old nonsense! Isabella was a figment of my heavily medicated and scotch-sozzled brain, and Arthur had been a hallucination that had manifested itself in my brain after my terrible experience in Santa Isabel church. It was all mental; there was no physical evidence of the existence of ghosts, including the horrible accident that happened today. That didn't prove anything about ghosts, it merely proved that poor Larry's ticker had given out, and Tom and the two actors were in the wrong place at the wrong time.

I felt a calm descend over me. My rationality was returning, and I knew that ghosts did not exist, and neither did any type of god. Regardless, I decided I'd show up for Mass tomorrow because I'd made a promise and, I figured, what harm could it do? I wanted Father O'Reilly to know that I stuck to my word, just so he'd know I was a decent human being and not a total mental-case, as he must currently be thinking.

As I drifted off into a peaceful sleep, I said quietly with a smile on my face, "Isabella, I know you don't exist. If you want to change my mind about that, which you're not about to do, give me a sign tomorrow that you, Isabella the ghost that was with me in Spain, is real and actually does exist."

I chuckled to myself and felt my body drift off to sleep. I whispered one final sentence before entering a deep, deep sleep.

"And please make it non-violent."

XXVII

I burst through the doors of Saint Monica's into blinding sunlight and ran, screaming, down the sidewalk. I didn't quite know where I was going, but I was utterly terrified and so I turned right. Briefly, in my peripheral vision, I saw Duff's black SUV, but that barely registered; I needed to get away from the church. From everything and everyone, particularly Isabella.

I ran and ran and ran, sweat beginning to pour from my face. I wasn't jogging or walking fast, I was sprinting as fast as my legs could carry me, lurching here and there as the sidewalk dipped or roots poked through the concrete. I was gasping and trying to swear and scream all at the same time, the result of which was me making sort of throaty yodeling noises, and made me look and sound like a total lunatic.

I vaguely remember crossing one street at full speed, maybe two. Or was it three? At some point I'd clearly run into the path of a vehicle because I got honked at as I heard the squeal of tires. There was then secondary honking sound from the car behind, clearly annoyed that the first car had bothered to stop for a pedestrian in the first place.

I ignored it all and ran on. I ran and ran and ran, and my lungs burned, my legs beginning to feel like jell-o made from lead. I'd been trying to scream for the entire way, but I'd quickly become out of breath, which made the screaming difficult and each gasp for air increasingly sounded like a yelp. I didn't care; I just needed to get the hell away from that place, because I knew Isabella was there. Somewhere, deep in the back of my brain, some nerve impulse or other was telling me what an idiot I was because she's a ghost. You can't run away from ghosts, the connection of synapses tried to tell me, but I wasn't having any of it and so I ran and ran; Forrest Gump would have been proud.

After what seemed simultaneously forever and the blink of an eye, I could see the glittering ocean and gorgeous blue sky. Beautiful palm trees stretched in a line perpendicular to the way I was moving, and across the road in front of me, also running perpendicular to my direction, was a sandy path with beautifully manicured grass borders. The entire supply of Baby Joggers that had ever been produced seemed to be traversing this path at a multitude of different speeds; trying to cross it would be like a real-life version of Frogger.

I didn't care, and I pressed on. I got closer and closer to the light at Ocean Avenue and I knew that, once I crossed to the other side to brave the Baby Joggers, I'd have to turn either left or right, because straight-on was a dead end. Everyone assumes that Santa Monica residents open their back doors and wander onto the beach, but they don't; there's an enormous cliff that you have to walk down a lot of stairs to reach the bottom of, and then enjoy the process of crossing Pacific Coast Highway, or PCH, which is like the Baby Jogger Frogger on steroids, and *then* you're on the beach. There's only one set of stairs down to PCH, and my panicked brain was desperately trying to remember whether they were to the left or right of me.

As I approached the light at Ocean Avenue, the crossing sign thankfully changed to the illuminated walking figure and, for the first time since I'd left the church, it was my right of way, so I continued my mad dash across the street. My clothes were drenched in sweat and I was trying to gulp down air as I ran; I knew I'd have to stop soon, but not yet.

I made it across the street and then had some tough choices to make. There were Baby Joggers moving left and right all over the place, and all were different sizes being pushed at different speeds. Some were single and some were double wide, and this all had to be factored in as I made my moves, but there was no way I was going to slow down. I leaped to the left of a slow-moving Baby Jogger and then immediately had to lurch to the right in a single large bound to avoid the next one that was coming fast from the opposite direction. Then I found that my escape from the next line of moving mayhem was blocked. I had no choice but to leap back behind the Jogger I'd just avoided to let some of the heavier traffic pass.

Of course, my respite only lasted a few seconds as I saw another bleached-blonde, slightly chubby mom huff and puff her way at full steam directly at me. Clearly this was her way of losing the baby weight, and she wasn't going to let something as insignificant as another human being get in her way. She was moving fast, so I evaluated my options and made a bound forward again; I'd gained ground, I was feeling good. And then I heard the dreaded shout that anyone who has walked or run on Ocean Avenue in Santa Monica has heard. It sent a chill down my spine.

"Left! Left!" The woman's voice screeched. "Left! *Left!*"

The first point of confusion is, obviously, who is she shouting at? The simplest way to resolve that quandary is to just assume that it's directed at me.

The second confusing part is, basically, what the hell is she talking about? Who's left? And left of what? Does she want *me* to move left and her pass on the right, or is *she* going to come past on the left of me, which would involve me moving to the right?

I looked in the direction of the squawking noise and saw a double-wide Baby Jogger being propelled by a stick-thin woman, her breasts clearly massively enhanced to match her bizarre, surgical trout-pout lips, and wearing what was, at the time, a trendy military olive-green cap sort of thing. Her running shoes were so clean that it looked like she bought a new pair at the end of each day.

Left? Where did she expect me to go? She was taking up the entire space, left *and* right. I had a sudden flash of inspiration and turned and ran in the direction that she was going in, but sprinting again as fast as I could manage. I now had her on my tail, and I'm convinced she sped up.

"Left," she kept barking unhelpfully at me, "*Left!*"

I was hemmed in on either side by a train of Baby Joggers moving in opposite directions, and up ahead I could see I had a ponderous and very large backside clad in frighteningly tight lycra shorts, ambling along at a snail's pace; she may well have been pushing a Baby Jogger too, but she was so wide that most of my view in front of her was blocked. I frantically looked around for a break in the Frogger Jogger traffic either side of me, knowing that I had about ten seconds to get out of the lane I was trapped in or I'd be mown down by the two zeppelins closing in on me fast from behind.

"*Leeffffffffffttttttttt!*"

My pace was slowing, my lungs were on fire, and I was getting panicked. I wished I could stop her and ask her precisely why she was screaming 'left' at me when I quite obviously couldn't go left or right, but I had no strength and no breath left to do so. As I approached the enormous rear of the woman up ahead and I thought all my options were used up, a sudden break appeared in the Baby Jogger traffic to my right. It wasn't much, but I went for it and leapt through as fast as I could.

The plastically enhanced woman behind me sprinted past bellowing, "I *said* left!"

Whatever that meant.

But things were looking up; I'd managed to escape the Jogger Frogger level, and was heading for the safety of the sidewalk, mere feet away from me. I was just about to slow down when stars suddenly burst in front of my eyes, all the breath was knocked from me, and I tumbled to the ground, an intense pain suddenly developing in my head that resulted in a full-bore throbbing agony.

Once my tumbling body had come to a halt, I curled up and clutched my head in my arms, gasping for air. My vision was swimming, and the stars and sparks were still blasting away as I tried to focus. The impact had been significant, and whoever it was I'd collided with had clearly been running too, but in a direction at odds with the way I was traveling. I hurt all over and must have looked like a bag of shit, drenched in sweat and sand, gasping and choking for air.

"Argle doogle ohdaaay," said a voice that swam around my head, bouncing off every bit of the inside and making my brain hurt more.

My body started shaking and I worried that I was having some sort of seizure, but as my nerve responses slowly regained some sort of normality, I realized that my body was being shaken by someone.

"Derrr! Argh doo kay?"

The syllable sounds were kind of similar, but still made no sense. My body was rocked and shaken some more, and my head pounded.

"Serrrr!"

It was getting closer to English now, and then suddenly my brain snapped back into action and understood.

The voice spoke again and sounded concerned, "Sir! Are you okay?"

It was Duff.

I opened my eyes blearily, and saw he had blood pouring from his nose; that explained the pain in my head. I was still gasping for breath, but I tried to speak. "Dude... Isabella... fuck!"

"Just lie still, sir, get your breath back. You can debrief me when you've calmed down. It doesn't appear that you're injured."

I didn't feel uninjured, but I stayed quiet and focused on trying to get some oxygen back inside me, and also to calm down. My head was spinning, and my limbs were trembling. I felt like a total wreck.

There was a *whoop* sound from close by and a car stopped; two doors opened and closed and I heard footsteps coming our way. I prized an eye open and tried to focus my swimming vision, but all I could see was a dark blue shape.

"Santa Monica PD! Both of you, stay where you are!"

I had no idea what Duff was doing, but I was in no position to go anywhere so I happily complied with the officer's request.

"Sir, did this man hit you?" asked the police officer to Duff.

"No," snuffled Duff, "but do you have a Kleenex I can use?"

A door opened and closed again and apparently a box of Kleenex appeared. I could hear Duff cleaning himself up, letting out great big snorts as he tried to clear a nostril of gunk and blood. I, on the other hand, contentedly lay still and didn't move or say anything.

"Feeling better, sir?" asked the cop to Duff.

Another, final cough, and some phlegm was coughed up and spat out. "Yeah."

"Did this homeless man assault you, sir? We had reports of a drunken homeless man charging down California Avenue, bumping people out of the way and running in front of traffic. I'm gonna guess it's this guy."

Duff chuckled.

"I'm not a fucking homeless person!" I blurted through a sand-filled mouth. "And I'm not drunk!"

"Sir, please mind your language."

"It's true, officer," said Duff, "he really isn't drunk."

"You *know* him?"

"Yes sir. I'm actually tasked with being his BG."

There was a pause, and then the officer said, "he has a bodyguard?"

"He does, and I'm it."

"What the hell are you guarding him from?"

"Well, to be honest, officer, himself."

"Yeah, no kidding."

"In the last ten days, he's undergone some very traumatic events, not least of which have been two cardiac arrests, and the death of two good friends. He's, how shall I put it, in a fragile state of mind right now."

"I can see that. And your bleeding nose? How did that happen?"

"He'd run off, scared, and I was trying to find him. He was running one way, me the other, he leaps out from behind a Baby Jogger, and whammo! The principle on the floor, and the BG with a bloody nose."

I heard the officer say, "I'm going to have to confirm this with your charge, you understand that?"

"I understand, and I'll go and sit on that bench. It's far enough away from your partner so I can't ambush him, but close enough so he can happily shoot me if I try anything. He can point his gun at me the whole time if you like? I'm used to it."

The cop laughed. "You're a pro. Let me guess, ex-Special Forces?"

Duff laughed but didn't say anything, and I heard him trudge off and, presumably, sit down on said bench.

The cop knelt down next to me. "Sir?"

I coughed and spluttered and spat sand out of my mouth, before croaking my response. "Yeah?"

"Is all that true? He's your bodyguard, you had some heart attacks, and so on?"

I nodded and coughed some more, my breathing finally back to normal. "Yes, officer, it's all true. Can I get up now?"

The cop helped me to my feet and I tried to clear sand from my eyes. Once I'd done that I discovered that the entire rest of my body was caked with sand and dust, glued to me courtesy of my sweat; no wonder they assumed I was homeless. Just to add to the overall effect, I suddenly had to cough up a huge ball of sandy-horribleness from deep in my lungs and spit it onto the grass. An 'ewww, gross' from a Baby Jogger pusher could be heard as she steamed past.

The officer led me over to one of the many water fountains scattered along the sandy trail and I greedily gulped water down, before using it to rise my face and hair as best I could. Luckily, I still had my ID on me, and so the police were finally satisfied, and they told Duff to take me home and keep an eye on me. He nodded and promised he would.

"Come on, sir," said Duff, "let's get you home."

He began to make his way back towards California Avenue, but I stood where I was. He looked back at me when he realized that I wasn't following, and I said, "there's no fucking way I'm going back near that place."

"The church?"

"The church. Isabella has cursed it, or haunted it, or something. I'm not going back there."

Duff thought for a few moments. "To be honest, sir, I don't really feel comfortable leaving you—"

I butted in and said resolutely, "I'm staying put, Duff."

He nodded, realizing that I meant it, and instructed me to sit on a bench and not move, even if there was an earthquake. I had to sit still, so I happily did just that while I tried to make sense of my scramble of thoughts as I watched Duff head back in the direction of the SUV. Judging by the speed that he arrived with the wagon back at the curb, I'm guessing he sprinted the whole way back to the church.

I climbed in, closed the door, and let out a huge breath of air.

"Feeling better, sir?"

"Yes, and no. Physically yes, mentally no."

"Care to talk about it?"

For once, I did. "Yes. I do. Last night, after talking to you, I'd kind of got my head back in shape. I knew that ghosts didn't exist, and that it had been the meds and my stupidity that had caused me to hallucinate and imagine crazy stuff."

"Okay, this all sounds good," said Duff as he pulled away from the curb. "Where did it all go wrong?"

"Well, I was so confident that ghosts couldn't and didn't exist that as I was drifting off to sleep, I became a bit of a smug dick. I baited her."

"Mmm-hmmmm," said Duff warily.

"I told her that I didn't believe she existed and I knew that now. No more funny business with me hallucinating; she didn't exist. Simple as that. But then I decided to give her one last chance."

"Last chance to do what?"

"To prove to me that she exists. I told her that if she showed me a sign then I'd believe."

"What sort of sign?"

"I didn't say, I just told her to prove to me that the ghost that was with me in Spain existed."

"Did she show up?"

"No, not exactly. But she certainly gave me a sign. A great big flashing neon fucking sign."

I saw Duff's eyes screw up slightly in the rear-view mirror. "And this was what made you run from the church?"

"It was."

"What was the sign?"

I sighed before replying. "She made everyone in the church speak in Spanish, dude."

XXVIII

"You ain't goin' fuckin' anywhere until you've seen a goddamn shrink!"

Durkin was not impressed. I was sitting in his office, getting both barrels for what had been going on.

"I really don't think that—"

"Horseshit! You've spent the last few days runnin' around Santa Monica screaming about ghosts and shit, and you tried to jump off a roof, for crying out fuckin' loud! That ain't normal behavior, Todd; you need some fuckin' help."

I lowered my head. "I've just been a bit, erm, confused after what happened to Tom and all..."

His voice softened slightly. "Yeah, that was a terrible thing. Talk about wrong place, wrong fuckin' time. Poor guy. One of the best producers I've ever worked with too. When's his funeral?"

"Tomorrow," I said quietly.

He snatched his phone off his desk and seemingly tried to punch a button through and out the other side of it. "Eve? *Eve!* There you are. Make sure there's room in my schedule to go to Tom's funeral tomorrow."

259

He paused as he drummed his fingers on his desk. "How the fuck should I know where it's being held? Find out! What the fuck do I pay you for?"

The phone was slammed down. I now understood why Evil Eve was continuously pissed off.

"Look, Mr. Durkin," I'd said, figuring that it would be back to Mr. Durkin after what I'd been getting up to, "I'm sorry that the Spain show got all screwed up, and we ended up with no footage that was usable—"

Durkin waved his hand to shut me up. "Todd, we got two solid hours out of what you guys were doing. Tom, rest his soul, told me he could have made a three-hour special out of it, no problem."

I blinked a few times. "You mean he edited it himself?"

"Yeah, while you were all fucked up in Spain, I stuck him in a room with the best editor I could find, and they came up with what you promised: a fuckin' top notch two-hour special. And, man, that footage of Laurel and fuckin' Hardy locking themselves in closets and burning rooms, I gotta tell you, it's compelling stuff. It even looks like *you* actually believe in ghosts too from the way you reacted in that little room!"

He threw his head back slightly and guffawed. I guess that meant that Duff had kept quiet about the reason behind my recent meltdowns, and that was a good thing. If Mike Durkin knew that I'd suddenly started believing in ghosts, which I still wasn't one hundred percent certain I did, he'd probably fire me. I would no longer be the anti-clown that I appeared to be in his eyes.

This was Monday, the day after the Santa Monica debacle, and inside I felt more than a little stupid. After I'd told Duff what Isabella had done, he'd brought the SUV to a screeching halt by the side of the road and whipped out his iPhone. After less than thirty seconds of investigation he'd uncovered the true reason behind why everyone was speaking Spanish in the Mass at Saint Monica's, and it wasn't because Isabella had taken control of them all to send me a message. Every Sunday at Saint Monica's, to cater to the not inconsiderable population of the area that doesn't speak

English very well, they hold a Mass in Spanish. It's the same time every week, and we'd just happened to arrive for that one because I'd insisted on having another hour in bed when the alarm had gone off, missing the Mass I'd planned to attend.

I tried my best to laugh convincingly. "Well, I don't. But I was pretty freaked out in the dark, listening to Kurt about to burn alive."

"Fuckin' clown."

"So the episode is done?"

"Yep, both parts. Lots of juicy ghostly stuff for our batshit crazy viewers to get their teeth into and debate forever on the forums. You gotta love those folk!"

"But we missed our air date."

Durkin chuckled. "Yeah, we did. But the public loves a good sob story, so we delayed it out of concern for you and wishing you a speedy recovery. The trailers for the non-show ran every half hour for days and went on and on about how ghost-chaser Todd had been stricken down by the lost souls he was hunting and trying to help, and he's in critical condition in hospital, and so therefore out of respect for you, we're running a repeat this week. Of course, we also told the viewers that they'd never believe their eyes when they saw what the ghosts had done to you, and they'd be able to see all of that very soon. The forums went fuckin' nuts. So many people were posting and hypothesizing about what had happened to you that the fuckin' servers crashed."

"They did?"

"They did. And then we had to delay again out of respect for Tom's death, and that lit the forums up a second time. Another fuckin' crash. I'm gonna fire the IT department if they let it happen again. Fuckin' idiots. Oh, and you won't believe how many people think that a ghost killed Tom in revenge for uncovering their secret. Morons!"

Involuntarily, I gripped the armrests of the chair incredibly tightly but kept my demeanor as calm as I could. "They do?"

"Yeah, they do. You should have a read, it's fuckin' hilarious. Anyway, I've booked you an appointment with a shrink for noon today. She's fuckin' brilliant. My wife and daughter visit her regularly and come back with tubs of fuckin' pills that seem to make them happy all the time, so that's all-fuckin'-right with me, if you know what I mean?"

I nodded, not knowing what he meant. "So, is the show going to get another season, or are we done?"

He screwed his eyes up slightly. "Done? Fuckin' done? Are you fuckin' kidding me? Of course we're not fuckin' done! This is the most popular show our network has ever had! We have so many people wanting to talk about it that it blows our fuckin' computers up!"

He sat back and chuckled. "Look, Todd, go and see this quack, get some pills or whatever you need. Have a massage or somethin', on me. Just chill the fuck out. You've had a shitty couple of weeks, and you need to relax for a few days. And then give Mork and fuckin' Mindy a call; they've got a new adventure they're all excited about."

This troubled me slightly; I wasn't sure I wanted to go and start messing around with ghosts again, and I wasn't sure things would be the same without Tom. Who would we get as our new producer?

Mike stood up. The meeting was over.

"And don't," he said with a chuckle, "set fire to any historic landmarks this time! Our insurers are not happy with us."

He reached out his hand and I shook it. "Thanks, Mr. Durkin."

"Mike! It's Mike, Todd, I already told you that. Oh shit! I nearly forgot! We need a new producer for the show, and I'd like it to be you."

I blinked a few times. "Err, instead of me being out there with Brad and Kurt?"

"No, no, no. I want you to star in the show, *and* be the producer. You'll be great at it, and I'll have a bunch of assistant producers back here running 'round doin' shit for you. Whaddaya say?"

"Um, I…"

"Obviously, you'll be compensated well for your new additional position. If you're game, I'll have a new contract for you to look at couriered over this afternoon."

I thought about it briefly, agreed that I'd take on the new role, and left. Duff drove me to the psychiatrist's office, which turned out to be in Santa Monica of all places. Most of the beach cities in Los Angeles county have different colored and styled street signs, presumably to give each city its own character and feel. When the signs turned what a paint company christened as 'Santa Monica Blue', I involuntarily shuddered. I wasn't happy being back here so soon, but I tried to be rational about the whole thing; once again, what I thought had been Isabella haunting me had easily been explained away as something else.

Duff pulled the SUV up outside a nondescript building at the corner of Wilshire and Yale and I hopped out. I took the elevator to the fourth floor and knocked on a plain, wooden door with a slightly cheesy brass plaque next to it.

Dr I. Wazowski, Ph.D, Psy.D, it said.

I knocked and waited. A short, slightly overweight, brown-haired woman wearing glasses answered the door.

"Todd?"

"Um, yes."

"Welcome! I'm Dr. Wazowski, please come in."

She was easy-going and affable, and she led me into a waiting room that was perfectly nice, and utterly devoid of character at the same time. Through the next door was her office, which was also plain but comfortable with a desk in one corner, a couple of armchairs around a small coffee table, and the obligatory sofa. I was disappointed to see that it wasn't one of those dark leather ones that all shrink offices in movies have.

"Please, take a seat," she said. "Anywhere you like."

I'd never been to see a psychiatrist before, and didn't think I ever would. To be honest, I was a little underwhelmed by the whole experience, expecting some beach-front, low-lit, plush-leather extravaganza like the TV always depicts it: walls festooned with bookcases containing leather-bound first editions of all sorts of huge and smart-looking books, glass and chrome minimalist furniture everywhere you looked, floor-to-ceiling windows overlooking a sunset over the ocean, and exotic plants tastefully dotted around the room.

Dr Wazowski's office was nothing like that.

"Would you like a drink?" she asked. "Cup of coffee, perhaps, or a nice green tea?"

"Err, coffee would be great, thanks. Milk, one sugar, please."

She disappeared into an adjacent room and clattered around for a few minutes, returning with a mug of coffee. The mug had a cartoon picture of Casper the Friendly Ghost on it, which was more than a little disconcerting, but I dismissed it as nothing more than a coincidence. I'm sure that the doc had amassed all manner of 'hilarious' cartoon mugs over the years to put her clients at ease. If she'd have been a dude shrink, I had no doubt that she'd be wearing a Looney Tunes tie.

She sat down with her own cup of something hot; her mug had Yosemite Sam on it.

She smiled at me. "So, Todd, what brings you here today?"

"Err, well, to be honest, my boss told me to come."

She scribbled on her notepad. "I see, and why is that?"

"He thought I should come and see you."

Another smile. "And do *you* think you should have come to see me?"

I didn't want to be rude, but I decided honesty was the best policy. "To be perfectly frank, no I don't. I'm here to make him happy. He's also a difficult man to change the mind of."

I was surprised that Durkin hadn't briefed her on exactly what had gone on.

"Ah, I see. So let me rephrase the question. Why did your boss make you come here today?"

I sighed slightly. "Well, various reasons, I suppose. I've had a rough few days, beginning with a couple of heart attacks. I lost a couple of friends of mine in a horrible accident that I witnessed.

264

Oh, and I very nearly succeeded in jumping off the roof of my apartment building."

She nodded and scribbled some more notes, as if what I'd just told her was the most normal thing in the world. Inwardly I was a little annoyed that I hadn't received a more dramatic response from her. "First time, was it?"

I wasn't too sure what she meant. "Um, first time doing what? Coming to see a psychiatrist?"

"No. First time trying to jump off a roof."

"Oh, I see! Yes. I've never had suicidal thoughts before, and I want to make that clear. It was all down to the traumatic week or so I had; have you ever had two heart attacks in the space of twenty-four hours? It's really unpleasant."

"I can imagine."

I laughed. "Actually, I doubt it. Anyway, after that I had a few rough days and then watched two friends of mine die in an horrific auto accident and utterly fail to save their lives or even pull their bodies from the burning wreckage."

Dr Wazowski smiled sympathetically. "That generally only happens in movies, Todd. We have firefighters for a good reason."

I sighed again. "Yeah, I guess. I still feel like I failed, though. I was right frickin' there for crying out loud. I should have been able to get to them and—"

"And what, Todd?"

I suddenly realized that I had tears tumbling down my cheeks. "And... and... I don't know. Saved them somehow?"

"I read the report of the accident, Todd. The driver of the truck was dead before the impact, and your friend Tom was pinned against a wall by several tons of truck. There was nothing you could have done, Todd. You need to come to terms with that, hard as it may be."

I threw myself back onto the sofa and lay looking up at the ceiling with my arm dangling onto the floor. "Agh! That is *much* easier said than done. I feel responsible for their deaths. I mean, if only they hadn't visited me on that day. Or if I'd been more hospitable and they'd left a little later, then they'd still be alive."

Tears were tumbling down my face now and I grabbed a Kleenex from a box on the coffee table; I wiped away what I could and then blew my nose. "Sorry. It's just that, well, Tom was a good friend and colleague of mine. And I'd become fond of Larry too; he was the guy driving the truck."

"It's okay, Todd," she said soothingly, "it's completely natural to grieve. What you mustn't do, though, is blame yourself or think that you were, in any way, responsible for their deaths, because you weren't."

I suddenly realized that I had to get a grip. She'd disarmed me and I was beginning to open up to her, which was something I promised myself I wouldn't do. I had to assume that she was a Durkin spy that would report everything back to him the moment I left, and there was no way I could leave any hint of me thinking I'd had a ghost chasing me around; that would, without question, be the end of my career with the network. I decided to change the subject, and see where that took me.

"You're right, Dr. Wazowski. Oh, by the way, I didn't catch your first name."

"Oh, I'm sorry Todd, how remiss of me. I usually introduce myself to get rid of all the Mr this and Dr that formalities; I find it makes things so much more easy-going. I can see that you feel the same way."

I smiled. "I certainly do. So what should I call you, doc?"

"Please," she said fixing me firmly in her gaze, "call me Isabella."

XXIX

"Québec?" I said.

"Québec," replied Brad.

"Why are we going to Québec?"

"Ghosts, dude! Why else?"

"Yes, Brad, I understand the purpose of our visit, I'm just wondering what's so great about Québec when it comes to ghosts."

He paused while he thought. "Well, it's got ghosts there, bro! What more is there to know? We're gonna go, and we're gonna find them! I've missed this so much! I'm super psyched to be back in the saddle, just like you dude, right?"

"Err, yeah, sure," I replied as convincingly as I could, even though that was the second last thing in the world that I wanted to be doing. The absolute last thing in the world that I wanted to be doing was standing near the ticket counter of United Airlines at Los Angeles airport at seven o'clock in the morning, waiting for Kurt to show up.

"Kurt's late," said Brad unhelpfully.

"Yes, he is." I was tired and felt like crap, but I continued to insist that we wait for him before tackling security so I could chaperone both of these clowns through their favorite playground. "But we have time to spare; we can wait."

I'd reinforced several times to our travel planner the importance of having time to spare at every airport we visited, because getting through one with Scooby and Scrappy was never a fast or efficient process, so I wasn't concerned about missing the flight. What I was concerned about was whether I wanted to be traveling three thousand miles to dick around with some ghosts that I wasn't sure if I believed in or not.

The psychiatrist hadn't been much help, especially after she'd dropped the carefully planned bombshell that her first name was Isabella. That had completely freaked me out and I'd scrambled my way off the couch, lurched for the door, and then slammed my shin into the annoyingly low wooden coffee table that I'd forgotten about. I crashed to the floor in agony, rolling around and rubbing my shin like a man possessed. Before I knew what was going on, she'd been looming over me with what I think was a smile on her face.

"Get the fuck away from me!" I'd yelled as a state of panic began to engulf me, and I rolled idiotically around on the floor again.

"It's okay," she said in, what I had no doubt was, a reassuring psychologist's calming voice. It wasn't working.

"No it isn't," I half-screamed, as I scrambled to my knees and made a painfully slow escape attempt toward the door. "Leave me alone!"

She said something else, but I wasn't listening, and as I scrambled to my feet, she said it again. It was just as I was almost at the door that the words had sunk in.

"I'm joking, Todd."

I stopped and breathed heavily a few times, my hand resting on the doorknob. I calmed my breathing as best I could and replied quietly, "what did you just say?"

"I said I'm joking. My name is not Isabella, it's Ivana."

I dropped my head and let out a long breath as my pulse began to slow. "Then why the fuck did you say your name was Isabella?"

"I wanted to see if it got a reaction out of you, Todd. After reviewing your recent history from all angles — medical, actions, reactions, personal, professional — I realized that something had changed in you, and that change had come recently. I needed to figure out what might have triggered such a change, and it was by total luck that I stumbled upon what I thought it might be; I think I turned out to be right."

I twisted the handle on the door and pulled it open slightly. "Great. You get to tell Durkin how smart you are, he thinks I'm a fucking lunatic, and my career is finished. Thanks a bunch. I think I'll leave now."

"I'm not going to tell anybody, Todd. Patient/doctor confidentiality, remember?"

I pulled the door further open. "That doesn't apply with Durkin. He gets what he wants. Why do you think he's the head of a TV network?"

She chuckled slightly. "Oh, Todd, I know Mike extremely well, and I know he'll expect me to tell him confidential things about our session, and I will. Except that they'll be made-up confidential things. I'll use some big psychiatrist words, and tell him you're on all sorts of pills with long and fancy names, and not once will I use the word 'ghost'."

I sighed and closed the door before turning around to look at her. "So you really do know."

"Let's say I had a hunch. A sort of elephant-man sized hunch, in fact. It was fortunate that my first initial is an I, which allowed me to get right to it, and I'm glad I did. You need to talk about this to a professional, Todd. Please, come and sit down and we'll start again."

With a mixture of relief and reluctance I did as she asked and went and lay on the couch. "So what tipped you off about the connection to Isabella?"

She made herself comfy in an armchair, a notepad resting casually on her lap. "Well, I must confess I don't watch your show but, yesterday in preparation for today, Mike sent me the final unaired episode when you had your troubles. He was convinced this held the key to what happened; you did end up in hospital after all."

I nodded. "Yes I did. And you very nearly put me back there."

She smiled. "Sorry about that. Perhaps it was a little thoughtless of me after what you've been through."

"Yeah, you can say that again."

"Anyway, I watched the part where you get extremely scared, and I watched it a few times more, and I suddenly noticed something in the audio that isn't particularly clear when you casually listen to it. There's lots of crashing and banging going on, as well as other people shouting and saying things all at the same time. So, to the joy of my husband and neighbors, I turned the volume up on our very big TV and sound system to nearly full and listened to it over and over again, before I finally understood what you were saying. You asked if someone called Isabella was in the room with you. Who's Isabella, I thought to myself, and I wrote that down as a question I'd be casually asking you during our session."

"But you didn't casually ask it. You knew when you used her name. How?"

She smiled. "One of those fate things, I suppose. After dinner that night, I decided to see what was else Mike put on his network, and so for the first time ever I tuned to your channel; what do you think was on?"

I snorted slightly and shook my head. "You've got to be kidding me. *The Lost Souls*? And the episode where we discover Isabella?"

She nodded, still smiling. "That very episode. It was rather good, by the way, and I was hooked after the first thirty seconds or so; I ended up watching the rest of it with a lovely glass of Merlot. And then I learned about Isabella, and how she was trying to sneak up on Kurt before you rescued him, so you prevented her from achieving her aim. Perhaps she'd followed you to Spain to reap some sort of revenge on you? After all, wasn't that the point of the episode? To prove that ghosts could piggyback on our communications channels and fly all over the world?"

"It's all bullshit," I said firmly. "All of it."

"What is?"

"Ghosts. The whole Kurt being sneaked up on and being possessed crap. It's total and utter bullshit. It's not real, and what you think you're seeing and hearing is all down to me."

"Are you sure about that?"

"Of course I am! I'm the one with the gadget that nobody knows about, I'm the one that edits the episodes, I have *total* control over what you see and hear, and how you see and hear it."

"What gadget is that, Todd?"

Shit. I realized I'd let my mouth run away with me; she was good. I'd walked right into her trap and given away one of my secrets. "Oh, nothing, it's just a thing we use in AV production."

Her smile tightened. "Oh, so other people *do* know about this gadget? Give it to me straight, Todd. Mike isn't going to know any of this, I give you my word. Who else knows about the existence of this gadget?"

I was getting fed up of sighing, but I did so again. "Nobody. Just me; I know because I built it."

"Okay, so if Mike finds out about this without you telling another soul, it'll be me who spilled the beans, in which case you can sue me and have me struck off."

"It's your word against mine."

"And my reputation on the line. I handle exclusive clients: celebrities, rich oil-Sheikhs and their many wives, TV execs, the Hollywood elite, and so on. If a single sniff of me being indiscrete became public, I'd be ruined in a heartbeat. You may not have noticed in your panic, but the door you were going to leave from was a different one from the one you entered by. You can't get back to the waiting room unless you have my magic keycard; you come in one way, you go out another. That way there's no chance of celebrity guy A bumping into celebrity guy B, who's wife he was known to be sleeping with, on his way out. You even exit the building on a different street, hence the corner location." She looked very pleased with herself. "So tell me: what gadget?"

For some inexplicable reason, I immediately decided to open the protective gates of my memory and unloaded everything on her: how I made the episodes so interesting, what my gadget did, how it came to be in existence, what had happened in the previous few episodes, and my terror in Saint Isabel's Church. I talked non-stop for well over an hour and she didn't say a single word for the entire time. Once again, this was either due to me boring my victims to sleep, or my story being a compelling one.

"And so," I said finally, "that's why I ended up in your office."

Ivana had been scribbling furiously in her notebook for so long that I half wondered if her pen was about to catch on fire. She scribbled for about twenty seconds more and carefully and slowly screwed the cap of her expensive-looking fountain pen back on.

There was silence for another thirty seconds, and I was more than happy to lie still and say nothing during that time. I felt emotionally spent after having told the most traumatic emotional events of my life to a total and utter stranger. It had felt good, though, in the same way that a really huge sneeze feels good once you've felt it building up for a while.

I wasn't sure where this left me or my career, so, good as it felt at the time to spill the beans, what that meant for me was anybody's guess. But it was too late to worry about that now.

"Wow," was Ivana's final assessment of what I'd told her.

I screwed my eyes up slightly. "Wow? Is that all you have to say? Wow?"

"It's a professional psychiatrist's wow, which makes it more meaningful. That is quite a sequence of events. So where is your head at now? Ghosts or no ghosts?"

I thought for a little while. "Honestly? I have no idea. That's why I'm so freaked out. Every time I convince myself that Isabella's spirit is real, a perfectly ordinary explanation comes along that proves it was nothing to do with ghosts. And then, once I've convinced myself that ghosts don't exist, something weird happens that makes me switch opinions again. All this flipping back and forth is driving me crazy. Literally, it seems."

"Hmmm," she said. "Generally, when somebody constantly changes their opinion from one to another and back again, although they can be confused they do generally see one point of view as having more weight than the other. It may only be slight, but both perspectives are never one hundred percent equal. At this precise moment, Todd, which do you favor over the other?"

She was right; one notion did feel slightly truer than the other, even though it went against all my instincts and logic. "Isabella is haunting me."

"Even though you don't believe in ghosts?"

"Yes. It goes against every grain of my being, and I don't want to believe that, it's just that there have been too many incidents, even though they've been explained away as non-paranormal, and too many coincidences that I can't help but feel Isabella, or some spirit or other, is pulling strings, or whatever they do, and is screwing around with me."

"But part of you won't accept that?"

"No, of course not. It's ludicrous! There's no such thing as a soul; we're made up of molecules, including our brain, and when we die that's it! There's no little part of us that floats up into the sky and hovers around for a while. We're dead and gone. It's as simple as that."

"So why are you favoring the ghosts theory?"

I let out a huge sigh. "Because I can't explain the sequence of bizarre coincidences any other way. I mean, a few things, like me having a 'visit'," I used air-quotes at this point, which I wanted to punch myself for, "from Arthur can be explained away by the meds I was on, and I suppose the intercom working when it shouldn't might be down to me drinking too much on some other meds, but what about poor Tom? Everyone keeps saying 'wrong time, wrong place', but come on, doc! Tom and the other two pull a prank on me and then wind up dead, all at the same time, and in the most unlikely fashion you could think of. And what about the woman outside my apartment that night? The one with the straitjacket? How do you explain that? The church, too; I know they always have a Spanish Mass at that time, but the fact that I ended up at it after baiting Isabella like that? Yes, you could say coincidence, and one of those incidents on their own could be easily explained away, but it's been a non-stop stream of so-called coincidences. I just can't buy that."

My thoughts of what happened in the shrink's office were shattered by a thump on the shoulder.

"Dudes!" gasped Kurt, breathing heavily. "Sorry I'm late."

"Bro! There you are!"

"Yeah, man. I got almost to the airport and then remembered that I'd forgotten my passport. I kinda figured that Canada was close enough to America to not need a passport, y'know? I checked my itinerary and it told me I needed a passport, so I went back home to get it. Then I parked in the wrong terminal and had to run over here. Man, this airport's big!"

"Where did you park, dude?" asked Brad.

"At the international terminal."

"Why?"

"I needed my passport. The international terminal seemed logical, bro."

"But we're flying to Chicago, dude. That's where we change planes."

I couldn't listen to any more of their drivel, and cut in. "Well, we're all here now, and we have plenty of time before our flight, so let's make our way to security, yeah?"

"Let's do it, dude," chirped Brad enthusiastically.

I made both of them locate their boarding passes and passports and give them to me. "I'm going to hold onto these until we get to the checkpoint, okay?"

They both nodded eagerly in return. I continued, "and let's go over a few ground rules. One: the x-ray machine absolutely is not haunted. Are we clear on that?"

"That one a few weeks ago was, dude."

"No, Brad, it wasn't. It's an x-ray machine, so the images you see look a little ghostly and may show up some unusual shapes, but the machine was not haunted, and nor will the one we use today be. Clear?"

Brad nodded.

"Two: the metal detector you will walk through does *not* beep if you have a connection to the paranormal. The reason it beeps is because you're carrying something metal on your person."

"No way, dude. That last one, it beeped and I didn't have anything metal on me. I'm telling you, bro, it picks up on spiritual vibrations."

I sighed. "Brad, you had your cell phone ear-piece clipped to your ear."

"That's not metal, dude."

"Once you'd removed it and put it in the tray, did the machine beep?"

"No, and that was spooky, man. It's almost as if the spirit realized he'd been busted and left me just in time."

"You probably felt him leave, bro," added Kurt, still slightly out of breath.

"I think I did, dude. It was just as I was—"

I cut him off. "So we're going to remove everything from our persons before we go through, okay?"

Brad and Kurt nodded.

"Three: do not, under any circumstances, speak to any members of the TSA about ghosts. If you're asked a question, keep the answers to one word. Do not, for any reason, mention ghosts. Understood?"

They both nodded again, and I could sense their almost childlike excitement about our upcoming mission. We were all set.

"Okay," I said, "let's go."

XXX

The following morning, we met for breakfast in our hotel.

"Is there some sort of French convention in town?" asked Brad as he sat down.

"What do you mean, French convention?"

"Bro, everyone is insisting on speaking French. I said 'hello' to some dude that was getting out of the elevator when I was getting in, and he replied 'Bon Jovi', which I thought was a bit weird. There was a woman in the elevator and I asked her why he'd said that. She told me it was French for 'hello', and that I'd be hearing it a lot today. Sure enough, bro, the next person I said hello to said the same thing. Everywhere I turn, man, someone's jabbering away in French, so I'm thinking: French convention!"

I screwed my eyes up slightly. "We're in Québec, dude."

"I know, bro. We just spent, like, fifty hours on planes to get here."

"They speak French in Québec."

"They do?"

"They do."

"But Canada is just like America, bro, and they speak English, not French."

Kurt butted in. "We're in a different part of Canada, dude. They speak French here."

I knew this conversation had the potential to go on for several hours, so I changed the subject. "So where are we having our lock-in?"

I was uncomfortable with this whole trip, not having been involved with any of the arrangements, but I was working on the assumption that if I didn't know where we were going, nor would Isabella, who I still wasn't sure existed. If she did, surely she hadn't followed me to Québec?

Brad was beside himself with excitement, and threw his arm out to the side in a sweeping motion, catching a waiter firmly in the stomach and sending him and his tray of plates crashing to the ground. "Oh, crap! Sorry, dude!"

There was a lot of mutterings in French, none of which sounded complimentary, and finally Brad continued. "Right here, dude! In this very hotel!"

I looked at Kurt, feeling a little uneasy at the prospect of having my lodgings in the place that was supposed to be haunted.

A very grumpy French Canadian appeared, bent down, and slowly and deliberately began picking up bits of plate and food in a manner that made it quite clear he wasn't enjoying it one bit, and he'd be extremely happy when we left.

Kurt said, "it's awesome, dude! Québec is the oldest city in North America, and this building that we're in right now, is the most haunted building in Québec: Le Château Frontenac!"

My stomach churned and I felt queasy. "Is it."

"Yeah, bro! This place was built in the late eighteen hundreds and, to this day, it remains the Governor of New France's residence! How awesome is that?"

Brad was silent for a few seconds as he studied his napkin. "So why does this say 'Fairmont' on it? And why does the Governor have so many guests in his house? I mean just look around us, dude. There must be a hundred people all having breakfast in here."

"No, no, bro, the Fairmont hotel group bought this place a while back, but it is still technically known as the Governor's residence."

Brad screwed his face up as he thought some more. "Well, isn't the guy pissed? I mean, his house gets bought by a hotel and all these people pour in to have breakfast? Come on, dude, that is pretty gnarly for the guy."

"He's dead, Brad," said Kurt patiently. "He *was* the Governor here, but back in the seventeenth century. His name was Louis de Buade; he's the dude who haunts this place!"

Brad's eyes went wide and he looked from Kurt to me, back to Kurt, and then back to me. "Dude! Are you serious? This place still *belongs* to the spirit that's trapped inside here and haunting it?"

Kurt nodded solemnly. "That's the deal, bro. That's why we're here; to help this poor guy."

"This is gonna be the most amazing lock-in ever," gushed Brad. "Why's he still here?"

"I'm not sure, dude, but legend has it that he's looking for his fiancé."

Brad suddenly lurched forward and said, conspiratorially, "she died in one of the rooms in this hotel. I can feel it, bro. I can feel it." He turned to look at the ceiling. "Don't worry, Lou, we're here to help you. We'll reunite you with your love; this is what we do, so don't be scared, okay?"

Kurt tried to say something, but was ignored by Brad, who was slowly lowering his head, finally allowing his forehead to rest on the table. Placing an outstretched hand to each temple he started to moan in a continuous hum that began to get louder and louder. I kicked him in the shin and he sat up with a yelp.

"Bro," he said, "what was that for?"

"To shut you up, dude! They were about to call the paramedics!"

"I was trying to connect with the spiritual vibes that must be pouring off this area of the house — the place where they all would have eaten. The communal eating room. And I'll bet that

279

Lou and his fiancé had a special table somewhere in here that set him apart from everyone else. I mean, this is *his* house, and all."

Brad slowly rolled his eyes to the top of his head in an almost theatrical attempt at pretending he wasn't looking up at the ceiling. Suddenly his eyes snapped back down and his expression became serious. "Oh my God! I just felt Lou's loss. I think he noticed that I'm the only person that's remembered it's actually *his* house, and he's opened up to me. Or I think he *wants* to open up to me if we can find a channel! This is almost freaking me out, dude. I think we need to find out which room his fiancé was staying in when she died."

There was a silence of a few seconds before Kurt filled it. "She died in Europe, dude."

How I wished that had been caught on camera.

For about five seconds, Brad's face went through a fair number of emotions, before finding the one his brain had been looking for, which was disappointment. Then it contorted to a slightly-strangled victory smile, and he said, "I knew it! It's just as I feared, guys; Lou's fiancé was in Europe and he had a *mistress*! That's who he's looking for, not his fiancé; I'll bet the mistress was staying here and probably died here too. We might bump into her as she walks around the hotel tonight."

Kurt put his coffee cup down with a loud chinking of china-on-china. "What makes you think that, dude?"

Brad shrugged. "I just sort of, like, had a sudden flash of inspiration or something, bro. I dunno where it came from. Perhaps Lou made his connection?"

Kurt let out a long breath. "That's the only explanation dude. You absolutely nailed it, and yet you've never even heard of this place have you?"

"Never, bro. But I definitely felt a connection to a spirit just then."

Ordinarily I would have rolled my eyes as Brad's made up story got more and more bold and confident with every new piece of information he learned, desperately trying to squirm his way out of some misguided assertion about something that proved to be completely wrong. This time, though, I was curious to know how Kurt would respond.

"You did, dude, and it must have been Louis de Buade, because there's a *woman* that roams the hallways at night too. She's only wearing a nightdress—"

"Just like a mistress would," butted in Brad.

"Exactly, bro, just like a mistress would be wearing, so he's probably looking for her. She spends the nights sleeping in the guest beds, and sometimes people wake up in the night and see her lying next to them."

"In bed?"

Kurt nodded. "Gnarly, huh?"

"Super gnarly, dude. Well, tonight's their lucky night; let's reunite these two lovers! What's her name?"

"Nobody's sure, bro. There's no positive link to her and Louis de Buade either."

"There is now, dude. I've just proved the link, and it's strong. Really strong. Man, this is gonna be good."

I wasn't quite sure what to think. Brad hadn't exactly *nailed* the description of the woman, in fact he'd been quite vague about it, but Kurt had filled in the details and the two sort of matched up. Of course, it could easily have been a coincidence.

Another one.

I tried to shake myself out of that line of thinking and get back to work-mode. "What time are we shooting the externals?"

"The what, dude?"

"The externals, you know. The shots we take of us wandering around the outside of the place in daylight, looking quizzically at things and appearing to see things that other people don't. They get interwoven into the final edit. You've planned out the filming schedule for the day, right?"

Kurt looked at me blankly and, after questioning him for a few minutes, it seemed that the preparation for the trip was this:

1. Kurt reads about Le Château Frontenac on the internet.

2. He tells our travel people where to send us and the crew.

3. The crew are informed where they're going.

4. We turn up at the airport.

And that was about it.

Nobody had asked permission from the hotel about blundering around their building in the middle of the night. The authorities hadn't been consulted and, more importantly, no booking had been made with a local expert on the particular building or area we were interested in.

I let out a sigh. "Dude, there's a lot of behind-the-scenes preparation and planning that go into our adventures. Didn't you know that?"

He looked a little crestfallen. "No, bro. I just thought we went places and looked for ghosts."

I felt bad for him because he'd been so proud of arranging this episode. "Look, man, leave it with me and I'll try and get everything sorted to shoot tomorrow. I've got some calls to make, but I'll see you guys for dinner tonight. I'll meet you in the bar at seven-thirty, okay?"

They nodded, looking a little dumbfounded, and I headed to the business center to get to work.

In some respects it was quite nice to be so incredibly busy for the day, as it took my mind off Isabella and how haunted this place was supposed to be. I mean, if it's *that* famously haunted, then don't all the ghosts know about it too? My head was still going back and forth on the ghosts/no-ghosts issue, but I now figured that this trip would be kill or cure: I was going to be spending several nights sleeping in an allegedly haunted place that apparently has a high level of paranormal activity. If Isabella was real, I'd know about it in this place, surely? Perhaps a visit from the nightdress lady? A glimpse of Louis de Buade at the end of a corridor, maybe? If, however, I saw no paranormal activity at all, then I was comfortable with drawing a line under everything that had happened and file it away under the 'unfortunate coincidence' category.

By six-thirty, after a non-stop stream of web searches, e-mails, and phone calls, I'd somehow managed to arrange everything and was in need of a beer, so I headed to the hotel bar. I was feeling pretty pleased with myself; aside from getting sign-off from the local police to film the episode, I'd eventually found a local expert who was willing to turn up tomorrow and be filmed with Scooby and Scrappy, but those had been relatively easy. Naturally, the hotel manager was less than enthusiastic about turning off all the lights in the corridors of the hotel and allowing three clowns to charge around in the dark while the place was full of guests. At the same time, our TV network wasn't going to be impressed if I asked them to spend a couple of hundred grand and book every single one of the six hundred and eighteen guest rooms for a night. While the manager was politely telling me that there was no way in hell we were going to be able to do what we wanted, my brain started charging off in all manner of directions, trying to figure out where we could film in the dark and in close proximity to the main part of the hotel. The bar immediately sprang to mind, and perhaps some of the business meeting rooms? They wouldn't be occupied at night.

I was just starting to worry about how terrible this episode was going to be when the manager saved the day without knowing it. "The cellar would be nice and dark, of course."

I looked at him and almost wanted to hug him. "The cellar?"

His English accent was crisp and precise. "Oh yes, we have quite an extensive wine collection, and therefore need an extensive cellar. There's also the grand ballroom that will be unoccupied and dark. It's on the second floor."

I beamed at him. "Those sound ideal! We'll compensate you for using them, of course."

He smiled back at me. "No need, *monsieur*. As long as you promise the name-drop the hotel as often as you can, that will be fine. Our seventh floor renovation is almost complete, and we want as much advertising as we can get. Does that sound agreeable?"

I blinked a few times. "Did you say a floor was being renovated? The whole floor?"

"Yes. It's been a bit of a, err, *ennui*, to be honest. An *annoyance*, as you would say, to lose so many rooms for several months, but it had to be done. The wooden panelling needed some treatment, and we've tried to do some, err, how do you say, *modernization* of the rooms whilst retaining the original old-world charm of the building."

I couldn't believe my luck, and felt like all my Christmases had come at once. "So nobody's on that floor during the night?"

"No, nobody at—" He suddenly realized which station my train of thought was heading for at full speed. "Ah, *non monsieur*. That will not be possible, for sure."

"Why not? The floor is empty, our insurance is beyond astonishing, we'll only need a few hours to film, and you won't even know we're there. We'll be super-quiet; we always are so we don't scare off the ghosts."

I somehow managed to say that final sentence without bursting out laughing. Our recent track-record for level of quietness was far from impeccable, but he didn't need to know that.

A slight pause ensued, and I could tell he was at least considering it, so I pressed on. "And just think of the publicity you'll get! It won't be just rumors any more, because we'll prove that you have a ghost or two in your building. You'll have ghost-cred, dude! People will come and stay here just to see the ghosts, believe me. The paranormal community is absolutely huge, and are very enthusiastic; you'll have people traveling from LA, Seattle, and who knows where, *just because of this episode*. And, of course, we'll compensate you personally for helping us."

He thought about it for a few moments, and I wasn't sure if this was because my spiel had been so good, or whether he was wondering what to do with the fact that I'd basically told him I'd happily bribe him to make it happen.

"So, *monsieur*, the cellar and the ballroom are not sufficient for your needs?"

"Well, dude, here's the thing: all of the sightings are quite clear about where these ghosts are seen. There's never been a report of anybody seeing any paranormal activity in the cellar or the ballroom, it's always in the hallways and guest rooms. We'll check the cellar and ballroom, of course, but the likelihood of finding any spirits is low. We always operate where the action is, you know? The sharp end."

"The...?"

"Sharp end. Where the action's at. Ghost central! Come on, bro, we need to use that floor."

It had taken a tiny bit more persuasion and an agreement on a sum of money that he'd get as a backhander, but the manager had gone away happy. The hotel would get some extra revenue in a time when an entire floor was out of use, he'd got a nice little bundle of cash in his back pocket, and we got to film on a whole floor of the hotel in the dark without other guests to worry about: everyone was a winner.

As I finished my beer in the dark paneled bar, seven o'clock was rolling around, and I suddenly realized that I was tired and had no desire to have dinner with anyone. I sent a text to Brad and Kurt letting them know I was going to have a quiet evening in my room, and then I wrapped up in my scarf, hat, heavy coat, and gloves, and headed out of the hotel into the freezing cold and snow.

I didn't really have any idea where I was going, so I turned right out of the doors to the hotel, and through the grand, stone entrance arch. Right in front of me, across the street, was a sort of park area with a big statue in the middle. Beyond it, I could see small and quaint-looking store fronts, some with lights on and what looked like logos that could only be French bars or restaurants, so I made my way across the road to the left of the park area, and down a slope that was steeper than it looked. It was at this point that I discovered how much grip Converse have in snowy conditions: none.

Picking myself up, I slowly and carefully made my way the final twenty feet to the gently cobbled street with the restaurants. The majority of the lights were coming from my left, so that was the direction I headed once the slope leveled out. The first place I saw, almost immediately in front of me, was called *Cool-as-a-Moose* and was a Canadian souvenir store selling lots of things with maple leafs and moose antlers on them. I walked on, avoiding the huge mounds of snow here and there, and wandered past some small alleyways and a couple of restaurants, before one place caught my eye: *Restaurant la Crémaillère*.

From the moment I walked in, I knew it was a good choice. The staff all spoke in hushed tones and were incredibly attentive without being annoying. The atmosphere was refined, but relaxed too. As I munched on my perfectly cooked lamb, my wine calmed me and I began to feel better about life. Today had been a great day. A productive day.

Three glasses of wine later, I paid my bill and had my coat deftly put on for me. Just as I was about to walk down the stone steps to leave the restaurant, I noticed a guestbook. Never having bothered with the things before, I suddenly felt an impulse to leave my mark somewhere. I picked up the pen next to the large, black, leather-bound book and wrote:

Amazing food! Great service! Highly recommended!

And now I'm off to look for some ghosts!

- Todd Sykes

I felt quite happy with myself and pushed open one side of the double doors to head out into the freezing cold. The chill hit me straight away and I pulled my coat and scarf up around my neck and ears. I turned right and headed back towards the hotel, taking extra care with my footing to compensate for both the ice that was beginning to form, and the red wine inside me. I could see the

Moose store about fifty feet ahead of me and knew that after it was a steep slope I'd have to somehow climb without repeatedly face-planting.

A slightly scary slip on one uneven cobblestone made me reach out for the wall nearest to me. The place I'd slipped was fortunate because I hadn't quite reached the alleyway yet. If I had, then there would have been no wall to lean against, resulting in another tumble onto the ice. I grappled with the brickwork as my feet slipped and slid in random directions, each one seemingly wanting to take its own route back to the hotel, as I tried to regain my balance. Once stable, I stood there for a few moments to regain my composure and my breath, and then set off, extra carefully, across the entrance to alleyway.

Completely without warning, a ghost appeared in front of me out of the gloom of the alley, a strange eerie white glow around her entire body. Her face was pale, and gaunt, with dark, seemingly hollow eyes boring into me. I wasn't sure if this was what I'd actually expected a ghost to look like or not, but that wasn't forefront in my mind at that moment, and I leapt back with a startled yelp. I lost my footing on a cobblestone, probably the same one that had made me stop here in the first place, and crashed to the floor; my head took a good whack on the icy stones, and I was suddenly seeing stars and flashes of light. I saw a blurry, pale apparition loom over me as I tried as hard as I could to focus and regain control of my panicked body.

Isabella had found me.

XXXI

"Monsieur! Monsieur! Êtes-vous blessé?"

My eyes rolled around my head as I tried to focus and do something useful to help my current predicament. The ghostly apparition kept lurching down toward me, babbling nonsense, so I lashed out with my arm as best I could.

"Get the fuck away from me!" I screamed, my body slipping on the ice beneath me.

The ghost took a step back and said, in a slightly surprised voice, "Anglais? Err, English? You speak English?"

I tried to roll over onto my front so I could crawl to my feet and make a break for it, but all I did was slither around like an eel for a while, before finally flipping over and winding myself upon landing. The ghost was getting worried, which seemed strange.

"Monsieur! Arrête! Please, stop! You will hurt yourself!"

I lay there on my stomach, gasping and panting, not quite knowing what to think, when suddenly the ghost proffered a hand to help me to my feet. Slowly and carefully, I accepted and became vertical again, enabling me to finally focus on the white, glowing apparition in front of me.

"Bonsoir," she said cheerfully.

"Errr, hi," I said looking at her with clearer vision now, and it was quite obvious that she wasn't a ghost at all. She was a woman in her late teens who had painted her face white with an iridescent paint, and had then darkened the area around her eyes with eyeliner, and added some little touches of makeup to give her face a gaunt and dead appearance. The grubby, white-ish, slightly tattered nightdress she was wearing would have guaranteed her hypothermia after a couple of minutes in temperatures like this, but then I noticed the thick white thermals poking out from underneath. The eerie glow all around her was probably provided by a can of fluorescent something-or-other from a local costume store.

"Are you okay, monsieur?"

I blinked a few times to make sure I had a grip on reality now. "Uh, yeah, sure. Why the hell are you dressed like that? You nearly gave me a heart attack!"

She giggled. "Je suis désolé, monsieur! For sure, I didn't mean to scare you. I am a student, and we have to make some money on the side or we cannot drink properly! This job may be a little étrange or, how you say, err, strange, but it is fun! Just watch!"

My head was spinning again, but not from the bang to the head. Job? Fun? Huh?

I was about to ask her a question when she moved almost effortlessly across the icy cobblestones and disappeared from view behind an ornate wall; clearly her footwear was not the same as mine.

I cautiously slipped and slid my way across the icy patch and onto the firmer ground of the path that had been extensively salted for much of the day. Finally, I felt safe again, and I felt comfortable with the fact that Isabella had *not* found me, and I'd stumbled across some strange student dressing-up thing, and nothing more. I was just beginning to wonder why exactly she would be dressed like that, when another ghost appeared from the other side of the cobblestoned street. He was moaning and waving his arms around, and then babbled away in French in a very dramatic fashion. One of his hands was holding an old-fashioned gas lamp that was flickering away just a little too perfectly and a lot too brightly; the brilliant white of an LED bulb was unmistakable in this darkness.

As he came into full view, I saw he was wearing some sort of formal nineteenth century outfit, and was also sprayed in the fluorescent paint of the female ghost. A group of about thirty people spilled out after him, all bundled up in arctic clothing and flashing away wildly with cameras. The group laughed as the ghostly apparition made an extremely dramatic gesture and said something that must have been funny. I watched, speechless, as the white-painted ghost, no doubt the Governor of New France, led the group up the cobblestone street in the direction of the Château Frontenac. The Governor finished a dramatic sounding monologue, his arms cartwheeling around him, and brought the group to a halt.

Bang on cue, the lady in the nightdress sprang into view behind them, screeching her lines in what, she hoped, was a ghostly-sounding wail. The tourist group, no doubt many glasses of wine to the wiser each, all leapt around with a delighted shriek and soaked up the over dramatic delivery of whatever it was she was telling them. The Governor then had his reaction to act out while he was busy being shocked at her presence, and the crowd all turned back to the front with a gasp. He yelled something and lurched off toward the hotel, stopping only a few feet away from the crowd, at the bottom end of the small park. The huge, beautifully lit château loomed over the entire area and was quite a sight to behold. By the time the group had finished moving to follow the Governor, the female ghost sprang into view once again, but this time in front of them and right next to him. He looked even more shocked for a moment, and then threw his arms open and they embraced in another babble of French.

Perhaps Brad's theory had been right all along.

I smiled, shook my head slightly, and trudged past them to the road that led up to the hotel. I gave the icy sidewalk a wide berth and walked up the middle of the road instead, taking advantage of the snow ploughs and grit that visited frequently. Once safely back inside the hotel, I headed for the bar, had a nightcap and fully relaxed myself before heading to bed.

The next morning, we met for a thankfully uneventful breakfast at nine a.m. and I said nothing of last night's encounter. At ten, we waited in the lobby for the local area expert to arrive, a guy named François Morel. The lobby of the Frontenac, as the locals seemed to refer to it, was vast and was spread out in a large T shape. Along the leg of the T were a few touristy boutiques that basically sold the same crap as *Cool-as-a-Moose*, but at three times the price. The main doors to the hotel were along the top of the T and beautifully crafted from a dark wood: three sets of revolving doors side-by-side, each set with two regular push-to-open doors either side.

Of course, revolving doors are a total and utter pain in the ass, especially if you're dragging a suitcase behind you, but at least in the US the revolving doors are American-sized: extra wide. The revolving doors in the Frontenac must have been the original ones from the late eighteen-hundreds, because if you weighed more than a hundred pounds they were a bit of a squeeze. While waiting for *monsieur Morel*, we sat on one of the leather couches in the lobby area and watched people considerably heavier than one hundred pounds attempt to drag their enormous wheelie suitcases, that were also over one hundred pounds, through a revolving door and get stuck.

Hotels in America have revolving doors as well, in an attempt to look classy, but at least they have the decency to leave the regular swing doors unlocked either side, allowing sane people to be able to just walk into the hotel. Not the Frontenac; the doors either side of the revolving ones remained locked, and the almost-polite sign informing you to use the revolving doors, instead of the perfectly good one you're standing in front of, actually meant what it said. Try that in the US, and you'd have a class-action lawsuit accusing you of repressing civil liberties.

Just as one revolving door got stuck again, another began to spin and I glanced at it. This had to be François, without question;

he was a little short, a little chubby, had John Lennon glasses on and, to top it all off, a small black beret. All he was missing was a string of onions round his neck.

Evidently, I looked like a Californian cliché too, because the moment he burst through the spinning door, he cast his gaze around and immediately zeroed in on me. I wasn't quite sure what to make of that.

"Monsieur Sykes?"

"Errr... Oui, dude."

"Tres bien, monsieur! Magnifique!"

I smiled and nodded back at him, hopefully letting him know that I didn't speak a single word of French other than *oui*.

His voice was slightly gravelly, as if he'd been smoking two packs a day since he was twelve, and that probably wasn't far from the truth judging by the smell of cigarettes wafting off him. He was well into his sixties at least, and looked like he'd seen a few things in his time, but he seemed friendly enough.

François let out a huge guffaw, "Of course, *mon ami*! You are American! You have no need of French! Only Spanish! Ha ha!"

I glanced uncertainly at Brad and Kurt, relieved that there were no cameras rolling at this point; I was sure that, if captured and immortalized, his comment would be considered politically incorrect and at some point in my life would be unearthed and get me fired or sued, despite the fact that I hadn't said it.

I needed to take charge, so I looked down, what with him being a good four or five inches shorter than me. "It's great to meet you François."

"And you *aussi*, Todd."

We shook hands and then I introduced him to an over-excited Scooby and Scrappy who seemed to be almost bursting with questions for him. He looked at them both with polite distaste and turned back to me, smiling enthusiastically again. "Are you ready to begin? I have so much to show you about Le Château Frontenac!"

I smiled back. "You got it, boss! Let's go!"

He led us around the outside of the hotel for a while, pointing out where bits had been repaired, and new parts had been added over the decades, all the while giving us the history of Québec. This whole guided-tour got recorded by a fourth, never spoken of cameraman who now always joined us for the external shots so all three of us ended up in a majority of the footage.

François finally got round to what we had hired him for. "So, *messieurs*, let me tell you a little something about Le Château Frontenac. It was buil—"

"It used to be the residence of the Governor of New France!" blurted Brad, unable to contain himself any longer. "In fact, it still is, and that's why the dude is so restless. I mean, this place is still *his*, but others have taken it over. Man, that would make anyone mad. Even me!"

François looked at him for a few seconds. "Non, *monsieur*. This is not the residence of the Governor of New France."

"It is, bro," said Kurt extra-knowledgeably.

"No," François said patiently, "it is not."

"It is," said Brad.

François sighed, probably wishing he'd asked for more money. "Louis de Buade, the Governor of New France, died in 1698. The Frontenac was not completed until 1893!"

Brad shrugged. "That's not so long in ghost years. Maybe it just took a really long time to build?"

Our guide smiled tightly. "*Deux oreilles et une bouche*, yes?"

Brad nodded enthusiastically. "Totally, dude."

François glanced at me and I shrugged an apology. He smiled and continued. "*Bon*. The residence of the Governor of New France is a few miles away and used to be the Château Saint-Louis before it burnt to the ground in 1834. But it had been in the hands of," his nose turned up slightly in distaste, "the *British* since 1759, after the famous *Battle of Québec*."

He took his glasses off, rubbed them on the bottom of his cardigan, put them back on, and continued. "We lost."

"So is that why they moved the Governor's residence to the Fonfronfrack?" blurted Brad.

Another sigh from our small French-Canadian friend. "No, *monsieur*, as I have told you, the hotel is not the Governor's residence. It was built in 1893 by the Canadian Pacific Railway to attract wealthy travelers that were using the railroads. The building, when complete, was named after Louis de Buade, who was the Count of Frontenac, and the Governor of New France. That is the only connection it has to the late Governor, *monsieur*. What actually used to be his residence is now a street of houses in a suburb of Québec."

"Oh," said Brad, a little deflated. "So why do people say old Lou is wandering the halls of the Frontifrick?"

François smiled. "There have been several sightings of Louis de Buade roaming the halls of Le Château Frontenac, but I very much doubt it's him."

I made a mental note that finally he'd said something we could edit to our use. Simply cut off everything from "but" onwards, and we'd have a useful quote that backed up why we were here, because there didn't seem to be any other reason now. Where the hell had Kurt done his research?

"So," I said scrabbling for some historical event that I could use to our advantage for the show, "I'll bet this place has seen some interesting things! Can you tell us about any of them?"

François beamed at me. "But of course! Le Château Frontenac was used as the meeting place of none other than Franklin D. Roosevelt and Winston Churchill in 1944 to discuss their strategy for World War Two!"

"Holy crap, dude," gasped Kurt. "No way!"

"Indeed it was. And it became what was known at the time as an *action center*, where they met regularly throughout all of 1944. Both men had grand rooms looking over the large river you see over there, the Saint Lawrence River. The rest of their staff had to stay in a less grand hotel, naturally." François chuckled. "Oh, and in 1953, Alfred Hitchcock filmed his movie *I Confess* here. In

2001, the hotel was sold to the Fairmont Group for the princely sum of nearly two hundred million dollars."

There was a slight pause as all this sank in, before Brad broke the silence. "So where does the nightgown chick fit in to all this?"

Another tight smile. "Ah, well, *monsieur*, once again, there have apparently been sightings of a woman wearing a nightgown sleeping in people's beds in the hotel, but there's no definitive connection to any particular historical figure."

"So it's not the dude's mistress?"

"Errm, no, I don't believe so. In fact, I'm not even sure he had a mistress. He had a fiancé that died in Europe."

"Spirits travel, dude. We have conclusive proof of that from a few weeks ago, don't we, guys? Todd and Kurt both nearly died, it was awesome. Well, not awesome because they nearly died, you know, just, err, awesome that we proved that ghosts can use a, like, modem or something to travel between countries."

François glowered ever so slightly at Brad. "*N'importe quei, mec. Avez-vous finis?*"

Detecting that it was a question from the upward inflection at the end of the sentence, Brad's head made a strange movement which was a combination of a nod and a shake to hedge his bets.

"*Bon.* As I said, there is no connection other than speculation that the one ghost is Louis de Buade, and there has never, *ever*, even been the suggestion of the lady ghost being his mistress. For sure, I think it would be best for this to remain unspoken of, don't you?"

"Absolutely," I said, butting in, "we won't mention anything about a mistress."

"Unless we get conclusive proof, bro. Remember, this is scientific research we're doing. We gotta document everything, dude."

I could feel François' eyes boring into me. Clearly Louis de Buade was someone admired by the people of Québec, so for our show to suddenly announce a completely unsubstantiated slur on his character that Brad had made up over breakfast probably wouldn't go down so well.

"Brad," I said calmly, "we'll see what evidence we get and decide if it's conclusive or not. There hasn't been a link for this long, so I doubt they're connected. Okay?"

Brad nodded. "Okay, dude. Good plan. Oh man, this is gonna be amazing!"

François turned his head slightly towards me, and said quietly, "*merci*, Todd."

That made me remember that I knew two words of French, and I nodded back to our extremely patient guide and spoke quietly to him. "Don't worry, François, I control the edit. I'll make sure none of this nonsense makes it to air."

François smiled gratefully at me as Duff appeared behind us. "Guys, everything is set up and ready to roll. Just say the word and we'll get started."

I looked over at the trucks in the courtyard, with mile after mile of cable snaking everywhere. "Thanks, dude. For everything."

He nodded solemnly, and headed back to the trucks.

The moment I'd been dreading had very nearly arrived.

XXXII

François gave us plenty of interesting facts about the history of the hotel and the surrounding area that I was confident we could create a compelling introduction to this episode. Although the fundamental reason for being here had essentially been shot down in flames, I knew that some careful editing and, more importantly, the omission of parts of his sentences would create just about what we needed as the premise for ghost-hunting in Le Château Frontenac.

"I've got a new amazing piece of paranormal tech, dude," said Brad as we huddled around packing our bags and backpacks.

Kurt looked up at him. "Oh yeah, bro? What is it?"

Scrappy was almost beside himself with excitement. "Dude! Oh, man. It's, like, just awesome, bro! It channels paranormal activity into a central matrix of something insanely clever, and then figures out the true meaning of the signal it received. I can't wait to show you guys!"

I was excited too: after the disastrous start to this episode, any bit of ghost-hunting technology that Brad brought along would add to the drama that I could take full advantage of, and get my credibility back with Durkin and the network.

"Sounds totally awesome, man," said Scooby as he fastened up his backpack. "Are we ready to do this, guys?"

Brad nodded solemnly and he made it clear he wanted us to all link hands in a trio, so we did. He closed his eyes and lowered his head. "Spirits. Ghosts. Partial souls. This is Brad speaking to you. We have a show in America called *The Lost Souls*, and we're here to help you. It's what we do, guys. So don't be afraid, we're here to solve your problems. Work with us, guys, *please*. You won't regret it."

He gave a grim squeeze of his hands that let Kurt and me know his little prayer, or speech, or whatever it was, was over. "They'll show themselves to us tonight. I could feel their excitement just then."

We walked over to the bank of three elevators in the main section of the lobby and were greeted by the manager. He explained that we had one elevator designated exclusively for our use. It had been locked to only service the basement, floor two, and floor seven, and nobody else could use or summon it without a special key that we each were given. We got our cameras out and switched them on, the LCD screens glowing vivid green as the night-vision lenses struggled with the huge amount of regular light in the lobby.

"*Au revoir, messieurs, et bonne chance!*"

The moment that the elevator doors closed, we were plunged into total and utter pitch darkness. There wasn't even the slightest bit of ambient light for the night-vision lenses to use, so all three of us stood in complete darkness as we descended to the basement. When the doors opened, there was some very faint light from somewhere because suddenly I could make out some shapes in the viewfinder of my camera. The further we moved away from the total enclosure of the elevator shaft, the more ambient light our cameras picked up, and the more we could see, sort of.

The wine cellar in the basement was absolutely huge, but not particularly interesting. There were racks and racks of wine against the walls, and in the central space of the basement were huge, thick, square supporting pillars that, I assumed, were holding the hotel up. We bumbled our way around for a little while to allow our cameras to get their dose of green, wobbly footage.

"I'm not getting anything, dudes," said Brad, eventually.

"Me either," confirmed Kurt.

I was relieved that they'd both come to this conclusion so quickly, because there was absolutely nothing of interest to film down here. "From what François was hinting at, it seems that all the paranormal activity takes place higher up the hotel. Why don't we set up base camp here, and then go check out the Ballroom?"

Scooby and Scrappy agreed this was a good idea, and went and examined some wine bottles while I set up our bank of monitors and prepared all of our recording devices. We then had another totally dark and silent ride in the elevator, this time stopping at the second floor. The doors opened and our camera screens suddenly burst into life as we stepped out into a room that, at least, had some windows. The moonlight spilled in, as well as the ambient glow from every other illuminated thing nearby; lamp posts, neon signs, the moon, the moon reflecting off the snow, and so on. Although the frosted-glass windows were plentiful, they were also half covered in snow, and grimy, so the level of light was just about perfect for us.

I scanned around with my camera's viewfinder. The room seemed to be vast, with high ceilings and what appeared to be stone arches on each side. Huge chandeliers were dangling at fifteen-feet intervals from the top of the roof. The main part of the room was full of large circular tables surrounded by ten chairs each, and a large stage area at what I assumed was the front of the room.

"Woah, dude," said Brad. "Do you think there's some sort of, like, ghost convention going on tonight?"

"Could be, bro," said Kurt.

"Ghost convention? What are you talking about?"

"Well, it's just that there was a rumor of a ghost congregation in Québec during this very week."

"We found it out from the internet forums, dude," added Brad, "so we know it's true."

I screwed my face up slightly. "What does that have to do with this room?"

"Look at the tables and chairs, dude! What do you need, a step-by-step guide? They're *here*, bro. Having some sort of ghostly get-together. There's no other explanation."

I bit my tongue and said nothing. I suddenly realized why I used to have such a total conviction in the fact that ghosts didn't exist: Brad.

Kurt suddenly said, "I'm feeling something, bro. I think we need to see if the PDD can help us out."

"The what, dude?"

"PDD, man. You know?"

"No. What does P. Diddy have to do with anything? Is he staying here too?"

Kurt sighed. "Pee. Dee. Dee, dude. Your Paranormal Detection Device. The new gadget!"

Brad thought for a second or two. "Oh yeah! Man, you're right! Let's see what we've got going on in here."

Brad rummaged around in his backpack and triumphantly extracted something that was roughly the same dimensions as a shoebox. "This is it, guys. The absolute bleeding edge in paranormal detection."

He handed it to me and I immediately saw that I'd been right about the dimensions. "Brad, it's a painted shoebox."

"Yeah, dude, that's just a THU — a Temporary Housing Unit. Like I said, this is totally state-of-the-art and is still in prototype form. The dude that invented it loaned me the only one in existence, and I'm helping fund the completion of the project. You know, get a proper casing for it so it can go into mainstream production."

I rolled my eyes. Whichever clown had come up with this, whatever it was, must have thought all his Christmases had come at once; not only was he getting a bunch of cash, and I was sure that Brad would have invested heavily in this idea, but he also got free promotion on the most popular ghost-hunting show on TV. The rest of the paranormal community were going to go nuts for this if it ever made it to market.

I pointed to an LCD display that had been partly glued, and partly taped to the outside of the shoebox. "What's this for?"

"That shows a copy of what the LCD screen inside the device is showing. I had the guy add this to his design last minute so that it won't be just the word of the person wearing the device; we'll have conclusive proof to record on camera, too."

I looked at the shoebox again, and then back at Brad. "You *wear* this?"

"Yeah! Watch, I'll try it out right now."

He took the lid off the box, and inside was a mass of wires, some connected to things, others just dangling with their exposed metal ends glinting back at me. At one of the narrower ends of the box was, as promised, another LCD display, but less hastily attached. To the side of it was a small circuit board, which was where some of the tangle of wires ended up. Quite how this thing had made it through airport security was a mystery to me; it looked like something straight out of Wile E. Coyote's *ACME* catalogue.

"Those wires there," said Brad excitedly, pointing at the wires in the main part of the box that didn't seem to be connected to anything, "that's the genius part, dude. Well, that and what the device does with the signals. That's pretty genius, too."

"What signals, bro? The wires aren't connected to anything."

"One end is, dude. All of these wires are connected at one end to a highly sophisticated, and very sensitive computer chip that processes paranormal signals. The other end of the wires extract those paranormal waves from the areas of the brain that most people aren't able to access, which has been proven to be where the paranormal processing, that experts like us are able to detect, happens. This device will enable your average Joe Schmoe to unlock his paranormal potential. Is that cool, or what?"

I desperately wanted to ask Scrappy Doo if he actually believed the crock of shit he'd just spouted, but the cameras were rolling, and this was yet more footage that would, if nothing else, pad out what could become a slightly dull episode. "Yeah, that's awesome bro. Let's try it out."

I somehow managed to stifle my desire to burst out laughing as I watched Brad place the shoebox over his head and secure a chinstrap, which was simply a piece of elastic tied to both sides of the box, under his chin. He shoved his hand up inside the box near the back of his head and fiddled around until he located the on/off switch and flicked it. The LCD display on the outside of the box lit up, and I could only assume the one inside had done the same.

"OK," it read, and then went blank.

"Are you ready to make some TV history, dudes?" Whispered Brad in his over-the-top theatrical whisper.

"Let's do it, bro," said Kurt solemnly.

Brad bumbled off with the box on his head, and immediately collided with the edge of one of the backs of the chairs. The LCD screen lit up and Kurt leapt over to see what it said.

"Bro! Did you feel a ghost just then?"

"Yeah, dude. I think one of them had some fun and hit me. Did you see the readout?"

"Oh man, this is wild," gasped Kurt, making sure his camera got a close up of the screen. "It says 'HIT', dude! They must have been planning to attack you, and we got it captured."

"That, right there, folks," said Brad looking in totally the wrong direction, and actually facing away from my camera, "is rock solid proof. The spirits plan to have their fun and punch me, we pick up their signal with this amazing device, and just seconds later, I get an impact from them probably pushing or guiding me into a physical object. That was wild, dude."

Once again, not wanting to spoil this great moment, I neglected to mention that fact that when Brad had walked into the table, he'd hissed 'shit' quietly to himself. The device, that I was pretty sure I now understood, picked up on this and interpreted it as 'hit', which was then displayed. Kurt saw that, and the rest of the wonderful moment was captured nicely. The shoebox, I realized, was not as primitive as it looked, but was still a load of nonsense. The unconnected-looking wires were, I suspected, just that, and somewhere on that circuit board was a microphone, with its frequency response set to be sensitive to very high, and very low sound waves, ignoring everything in-between. This fitted with the commonly held belief of the paranormal community that all spiritual voices and communication happens at extreme ranges of frequency. I assumed that any input in the correct frequency ranges from the mic was sent to some sort of crude single-word voice recognition chip and, if it got a match from its dictionary, would display the word. I guessed that the word 'shit' was not in its dictionary, and the closest match it got was 'hit'.

Brad took the device off his head and switched it off. "I think we should set up some devices in here to record anything that goes down."

Kurt nodded enthusiastically. "I was thinking the same thing, dude. A camera in the corner over there, and an audio recorder on some of the tables?"

"Perfect, bro. Let's get to work."

Brad was in charge of positioning the audio recorders, one of which went on the table next to the chair he'd walked into, and Kurt was setting up an NV camera on a tripod. He suddenly made a dramatic discovery.

"Guys," he hissed, "guys, you gotta see this! We are definitely surrounded by spirits, and powerful ones too."

"What've you got, bro?"

"It's my camera, dude. The battery is *totally flat.*"

"Oh man! You mean the spirits sucked the juice right out of it to stop us from recording in here?"

"There's no other explanation, dude."

I interjected. "Kurt, is that a camera from my collection?"

"No, bro, this is one I kept with me last night, just in case, you know?"

I didn't. "And you're sure you charged it fully all night?"

"Positive, dude. I didn't have a wall charger, but I had the USB cable plugged into my laptop all night."

That little mystery was now cleared up. Kurt had obviously closed his laptop, shutting off the power, meaning the camera didn't get charged. "I've got a spare, let's use this one."

"That's if the ghosts haven't sapped that one, too, bro."

"Let's find out," I said patiently.

Lo and behold, my properly charged camera worked fine, and I rigged it up with a good view of the room.

Brad came over. "That is *so* freaky, dude. I guess the spirits only had the strength to suck one battery pack dry. Good thinking on the spare, Todd."

We explored some more and discovered a sort of backstage area, hidden from the view of the ballroom. There were piles and piles of chairs, tables that were stacked, and all manner of boxes with everything you'd need to cater to a large number of people. There also seemed to be some sort of dressing room area with some old dresses and coats hanging from a portable rail on wheels. At the far end of the dressing room area was a large mirror, a wooden table with a random assortment of used make-up things, and a wooden chair.

"Man," whispered Brad, "I wonder if this is where Lou's mistress gets ready before roaming the halls?"

"Dude, we don't know she's his mistress, we can't say that, remember?"

"I've got all the proof I need, bro, but okay, okay. Until we get more *mainstream* proof, I'll keep that fact to myself."

I suppressed a sigh, happy with just one aspect of this: making lawsuits go away wasn't my department.

"Let's try your box again," I suggested, trying to get this episode going.

"Great idea, dude!"

Brad whipped out his shoebox and placed it on his head again, before fiddling around up inside the shoebox once more.

"Brad," I whispered, "why don't you just turn the thing on before you put it on your head?"

"Oh, I can't do that, bro. When the device boots up, it needs to process the brainwave pattern of the wearer to calibrate itself. I need to have it on my head when I switch it on."

Kurt nodded knowledgeably from the side of us. "Makes sense, dude."

Brad finally found the switch and turned the shoebox on again. "Ready, guys?"

"Go for it, bro."

Brad set off and within five seconds had found the leg of an upturned table to crack his chin on. He collapsed to the ground, and Kurt rushed to his aid while I recorded everything.

"Oh my *God*! Todd, come here, quick! Record this! It's *wild*, dude!"

I moved as fast as I could, camera rolling, and recorded what Kurt was pointing at, which was the LCD panel. It read "DUCK".

Kurt was almost beyond himself with excitement. "Brad! Brad, can you see the screen? They were messing with you again, man!"

"Yeah," groaned Brad, rubbing his chin, "I guess so. They could have told me to duck before I'd walked into whatever it was."

"They wouldn't have had any fun doing that, dude."

It didn't take too much brainpower to figure out the word that Brad had actually hissed when he'd walked into the table leg; the dictionary in the shoebox clearly didn't have profanity in it.

Brad sat up and took the shoebox off his head. "I've had an idea, guys. We need to do a scientific experiment."

XXXIII

My radio crackled in the darkness. "Guys, it's Kurt. I'm in position."

"Good work, dude. What room are you in?" asked Brad.

"Seventy-five fifty-nine. I'm not sure why I picked this one, it just felt right, bro."

"That's awesome, man. I totally trust your psychic senses. Especially after that mad chick tried to get you and then crazy Arthur possessed you. I reckon that really increased your paranormal detection ability."

"Yeah, Isabella really heightened my senses, that's for sure."

Just hearing her name made me shiver all the way down my spine and then back up again. Just as that sensation finished, I noticed the shoebox LCD flash briefly out of the corner of my eye. I looked over at the bizarre contraption just as the screen went blank again. I thought I'd seen Brad switch it off, but perhaps there was some half-assed wiring connecting the batteries to the switch and it still had some juice going through it.

Brad was downstairs in the basement, monitoring the feeds, I was still in the backstage area, and Kurt had been sent up to the half-finished seventh floor to go and lie in a bed and wait for the woman to show up.

"Kurt," whispered Brad through the walkie-talkie, "what if Isabella is *here*, dude? You know, she's, like, totally attending the ghost convention, or something?"

My pulse was already beginning to rise, and I hit my walkie-talkie button quickly. "Isabella is not here, Brad. We left her locked up in the mental hospital, remember?"

There was a pause, and I looked around me, suddenly feeling very uneasy about things. The radio crackled and Brad spoke again. "You never know, dude. Her and Kurt seemed to have quite the connection, so maybe she found out he was going to be here or something?"

"Dude, it is *not* Isabella, okay?"

"Woah, okay, bro! It was just a thought. Chill, dude!"

The LCD screen flashed again, but this time I was looking right at it. I stared, slightly dumbfounded, and the writing suddenly vanished as quickly as it had appeared. Had I really seen what I thought I'd just seen? My eyes were now out on stalks, and I could feel my heart pounding in my chest, its rate of beating suggesting that I was running a marathon.

The LCD screen had clearly been displaying the word 'IS'.

I tried to process this from a rational standpoint; I'd concluded that the device had some sort of crude speech recognition chip. I'd said the words 'is' and 'Isabella' loudly into the radio, and it was unlikely to have her name in its dictionary, so the closest match it got was simply 'is'. That made total and utter logical sense, but I couldn't help thinking about my previous sentence. I'd said that it "is *not*" Isabella, and then the alleged paranormal scanner picks up the word "is"; could that, in fact, be a message from her letting me know that it actually *is* her? No, surely not. That was beyond the realms of possibility, especially from a shoebox. I gave myself a mental slapping: that had been a coincidence, and nothing more.

"Okay, Kurt, dude, lie down, close your eyes, and try to go to sleep just like we discussed," came Brad's voice from my radio.

"Roger that, bro."

"All stations, all stations," whispered Brad.

I pressed the button. "You mean me, dude?"

"Yeah. Kurt is going to go to sleep. We need to be ready to detect the slightest hint of activity from the ghost chick, okay? She might make her way up there at any moment."

"I'm ready, bro."

I walked over to the shoebox and, using my camera's view finder, I looked inside. I found the on/off switch; it was glued to the rear of the box, and had the words 'active' and 'off' written in Sharpie on the cardboard above it. I could quite clearly see that the switch was in the 'off' position, which made this even stranger. I hissed a few words towards the front of the box, assuming that was where the mic was, but nothing happened on the screen. I tried again, and still got nothing. I said the word 'Isabella', but the LCD screens remained blank.

I was more than a little freaked out at this point, and the darkness all around me suddenly seemed oppressive and far scarier than it had ten minutes ago. I made my way back into the ballroom area where there was a little bit more light, and I sat at one of the tables, placing my NV camera on the table, facing me.

"I hope I'm not interrupting dinner," I said, trying to lighten my mood a little. "And I hope I'm not sitting on anybody's lap! Ha ha."

A sudden, massive crashing noise scared the wits out of me, and I lurched from my chair, colliding painfully with the table next to me. I collapsed in a heap on the floor, all of the wind knocked out of me, and my ribs burning from where they'd made contact with the wooden table edge. If nothing else, at least I now had some good footage for the trailer.

I was out of breath and panting, and, I suddenly realized, trembling slightly. I grabbed my walkie-talkie and hit the button. "Brad! Brad! Did you hear anything just then?"

Nothing.

I waited about twenty seconds and then hit the button again. "Brad! For fuck's sake! Are you there?"

Still nothing.

I looked around me in the gloom and couldn't see much at all, which simply freaked me out even more. Had I damaged my walkie-talkie in the fall? Or was it something else? I wasn't quite sure what the 'something else' was, but I hoped that wasn't the reason.

I tried again. "Brad! Brad! Speak to me, man! Kurt! Respond if you're getting this! Someone! Anyone! Respond, please!"

I released the button, and the finger I'd used to press it was now trembling. Seconds went by, and there was no response from either of them. This was not looking good at all. I tried to think of what my next move was going to be; should I head upstairs to a floor I'd never been to, or back down to the basement, where I was at least a little bit familiar with the layout?

The radio crackled into life. "Yo! Dude, Brad is here."

I let out a huge sigh of relief and hit the button. "Brad! Where the fuck have you been?"

"Sorry, dude, I was checking out some of the wine they have down here and I left my radio on the base camp table. They have some wine that dates back to the fifties, dude! How insane is that? Wouldn't it have gone off by now though?"

"Fucking hell, Brad! You were supposed to be keeping watch on the monitors, dude!"

"Oh yeah, sorry, bro. I just got a bit bored, you know? It's dark down here."

"Did you hear anything just then?"

"Like what?"

"Like a big crashing noise."

"Nuh-uh, bro. I didn't hear anything. Why do you ask?"

"Err, no reason. And why isn't Kurt answering?"

"Ah, I told him to switch off his radio when he went to sleep so he wouldn't be disturbed."

I let this sink in for a few moments. "You did *what*? How are we supposed to stay in touch with him, dude? What if he has another, err, encounter?"

"Todd, dude, you seem really strung out. I've never seen you like this before, are you okay?"

I tried to control my breathing. "I'm just concerned about Kurt. Isabella, Arthur, remember?"

"You said she wasn't here, bro."

"Yeah, well, what if she is?"

"Then he'll turn his radio back on and let us know, dude; we're professionals, remember? If the spirits detect radio waves, they'll know he's not alone and maybe the mistress won't lie down with him. We have to take risks in our line of work, you know that, bro."

I took some more deep breaths. "Yeah, okay dude. Good thinking. I need to go and check on something. Make sure you keep your radio with you at all times, okay?"

"You got it, bro. Over and out."

I pulled myself to my feet, my ribs letting me know they'd be nice and bruised tomorrow, and picked up my camera from the table. I knew the loud noise had come from the backstage area, and I knew that I had to go and check it out. Before I did that, I decided to see if the static NV camera in the corner had seen anything, so, using the viewfinder on my camera to guide me, I threaded my way through the tables as I tried to calm myself down. I got to the camera, pulled open the viewfinder, and then very nearly lost the plot completely.

The camera was stone dead; the battery must be flat.

"*No!*" I yelled, almost without realizing, and frantically looked around me in the darkness. This could not be happening. That camera was fully charged, I knew it was, and it had been recording just fine when we'd first set it up. Although it's theoretically possible for a rechargeable battery pack to catastrophically fail, it is extremely unlikely.

Now I was really scared.

Trying to be professional, just like Kurt apparently was, I fished around in my pocket, took out a spare camera battery with my trembling hand, and replaced the dud. I checked what had been recorded, and the answer was: not much. It seemed that the moment we'd walked away from it, the battery had died. I hit record, and made sure that it was working properly before embarking on the next part of what I knew I had to do: check out where the crashing noise had come from. I slowly and carefully made my way around the back of the stage and through the hidden doorway, and immediately saw what had caused all the noise; for some incomprehensible reason, the stack of tables that Brad had smacked his chin on had collapsed. Three tables were now sprawled across the floor at strange angles, but nothing else seemed to have moved, as far as I could tell. After scanning the room with the NV viewfinder, I tried to re-stack the tables, but it was impossible; they were too big and much heavier than they looked. Instead, I dragged them out of the way as best I could, and went and sat down at the dressing table.

I pointed my camera at the mirror and looked at myself in the viewfinder. My huge, green eyes reflected back at me. "Something weird is going on," I said, my voice sounding shaky; this wasn't an act to make the show interesting, I was genuinely freaked out beyond belief. "I can't help thinking this has something to do with Isabella. But whatever it is, it's really screwed up, guys. I'm getting worried, especially for Kurt. He's up there all alone and without comms. Who knows what's going on?"

That gave me a sudden thought, and I grabbed the shoebox. Feeling utterly ridiculous, I put the stupid contraption on my head, secured the chin strap, and fumbled around for the 'on' switch. The LCD monitor inside the box was insanely bright and flashed "OK" at me before going blank again. The backlight from the small screen was glowing faintly in front of me. I coughed to clear my throat, partly because I needed to, and partly to see if that would generate some random words on the screen. Nothing appeared.

"Isabella," I hissed.

Nothing.

"Goddamn you! If you're here, show yourself! I'm sick of this bullshit!"

I heard a noise from the ballroom. Nothing too loud, but it was definitely a noise. I tore the box off my head and scrambled for my radio. "Brad! Brad!"

"Yeah, bro?"

"Did you come up to the ballroom?"

"No, dude. I'm still sitting here in the dark."

"Has Kurt moved? Is he in the ballroom?"

"I don't think so dude. I haven't heard from him, and he'd have switched his radio on if he was mobile."

I let out a long breath. "Okay, bro. Over and out."

I slowly got up from my chair and headed into the main ballroom, scanning everywhere with my NV camera. All of the tables and chairs seemed to be in the right positions, and no chandeliers had fallen from the roof. I was making my way methodically around the room looking for something that could have made a noise, and was about to give up when I saw what it was. I'd reached the back of the room and suddenly noticed the tripod that Kurt had set up; it had collapsed, and the camera that I'd just replaced the battery of was now face-down on the wooden floor. Could that have been yet another coincidence? An accident? Had Kurt not tightened the wing-nuts properly on the stand? Had I pushed down too hard when connecting the new battery? Or had his camera actually been fully charged, too, and the power had been sucked from both batteries by some mysterious force, and this was a less subtle method of letting us know to not film in the ballroom?

I was now in a state of utter panic. I bolted back to the backstage area, crashing painfully into tables and chairs as I went. I dropped back down onto the chair in front of the mirror, my thighs screaming out from the battering they'd just taken, and shoved the shoebox back onto my head. It was still on, so I didn't need to faff around trying to find the 'on' switch.

315

"Isabella!" I blurted. "Are you here? Or some other spirit? Just fucking show yourselves! Stop playing games with me! I can't take it any more, and I'm hurt, okay?!"

Without warning the LCD screen lit up and my eyes focused to the intensity in the darkness of the shoebox.

"KURT"

It went blank again. I blinked a few times. "Kurt? What about Kurt? You won't show yourself to my eyes, but you want to play these games in my head? Well I'm sick of it!"

The LCD screen lit up once more.

"DIES"

Almost darkness engulfed my head once more. "Dies? What the fuck do you mean? Dies? You must be near to me to be doing this, am I right?"

The screen lit up one more time.

"HERE"

It went blank again and I thought about what it had just said. "Kurt... dies... here."

Could that have been a coincidence from words that had been picked out from what I'd just said? I couldn't take the risk. I ripped the box from my head, tossing it aside, and grabbed my radio.

"Brad! Brad! This is fucking urgent!"

A crackle. "Yeah, dude, I'm here."

"We need to rescue Kurt now. The ghosts are going to kill him tonight! Your box just told me so!"

"They wha... it did?"

"It did! Call the elevator right now, and bring it up to floor two. I'll be waiting. And *hurry* dude, Kurt's life is in serious danger, I'm convinced of it."

"I'm on my way, bro."

I took a few breaths to try and calm myself down, and then made my way as fast as I could back to the elevators.

We had to find Kurt, and get the hell out of this place.

XXXIV

The elevator took forever to go from floor two to floor seven, and when it finally did arrive, the doors took their sweet old time with some warm-up creaks and groans before finally sliding apart at a snail's pace.

"Which way, bro?" I asked Brad as soon as we were out in the corridor.

"No idea, dude. Kurt's the only one that's been up here."

Our rooms were on a much higher floor, and the layout seemed to be totally different down here; the corridors weren't straight, as you'd expect from a modern hotel, they twisted and turned at strange angles at seemingly random places, and sometimes the corridor would split off in two different directions. I looked left and right into the gloom, natural moonlight trying its best to penetrate the grime and snow piled up against the windows. I suddenly realized I'd left my NV camera downstairs.

"Don't worry, bro, we can share mine," said Brad, and we set off in a random direction.

The remodeling work seemed to be nearing completion although a few room doors were missing, and from what I could tell from the eerie green glow of the viewfinder, some of the painting still needed to be finished. The whole floor smelled of never-used wooden furniture, brand new carpets, and paint.

"What room did he say he was in?"

"Seventy something," said Brad unhelpfully.

"Dude, every room on this floor is seventy something. What were the other numbers?"

There was a pause as we huffed and puffed our way down the dark corridor. "I think there was a five in it too, bro."

"Do you remember where in the number the five was?"

"No."

I stopped and grabbed Brad's arm. "Okay, look. In that case we need to check every room to try and find him, okay? Ideally we'd split up and work as a team, but I don't have my camera. Are you ready?"

"Let's do it, bro."

I tried the walkie-talkie once more, just in case Kurt had finally turned it on, but got no response, so we burst into the nearest room, scanned around with the NV viewfinder, and found nothing. The next room was the same. And the next. And the next. I was starting to panic; I didn't know how many rooms this floor had, but from the size of the place, I knew it would be a lot. Scanning each one with the NV camera was taking forever, and my fear was increasing with every minute that passed. I just knew, deep down, that Kurt was in big trouble, and we needed to find him and wake him as quickly as possible; I just hoped it wasn't too late.

I'd finally come to a definitive decision on the whole ghosts or no ghosts debate: ghosts existed, and they were in this building.

We kept trying room after room with no luck, and Brad kept changing his mind about what possible room number Kurt had told us. We must have been on that floor for a good twenty minutes, and I decided that it was time to stop messing about.

"*Kurt!*" I yelled, and my voice echoed its way down the corridor. "Kurt! Dude! If you can hear me, come out into the corridor right now! We've had some... err... developments, bro!"

318

I caught faint echoes of my own voice as they bounced their way in and out of unfurnished rooms and uncarpeted corridor sections, but heard no reply. I tried the radio once more, but got nothing. I could feel my heart trying to beat its way out of my chest, and the pulse in my neck was pounding away like a jackhammer; I'd felt sensations similar to this very recently in Spain and it hadn't ended well for me, but I just couldn't calm myself down. I needed to find Kurt and make sure he was safe; Isabella wasn't about to take another of my friends away from me.

"Okay," I gasped to Brad, "screw the NV now. You take the doors on the right with your camera, and I'll use my hands to check the beds in the rooms on the left. Okay?"

"You got it, bro."

I burst into the room nearest to me and promptly tripped over a thick roll of carpet that had yet to be laid. I hit the concrete floor hard, cracking my head and sending starbursts all over what vision I had in the gloom. Clambering desperately to my feet, my head was spinning and my vision was blurry, but I lurched forward to the area where the bed was and tumbled onto it; it was empty. My head was killing me, but I had to push through the pain and keep on searching, so I crawled my way off the bed and staggered back to the hallway door, using the wall to support myself as I went.

I made sure there was nothing to trip over in the next room, and found the bed to be empty again. This continued for about ten more rooms and then, as I came back into the corridor, I noticed Brad leaving a room door closed, not having gone in it.

"Dude! You missed one."

"Huh? One what, bro?"

"A room! *That* room. You didn't check it."

"Oh! Yeah, dude. The door's locked, so I didn't want to disturb whoever was in there. You know, be considerate, and all?"

I blinked at him in the darkness. "*Locked*? Brad, this floor is deserted. In fact, it isn't even finished! And you've found a locked door and don't think it's significant?"

"Maybe that's where they keep their tools, bro."

"Fucking hell, Brad! That's the room Kurt's in! He locked the door behind him, like everyone does in a hotel! What's the room number?"

"Seven five five nine. I told you there was a five in it."

He'd also told me there had been every single other digit in it, but I let it go. "Okay, bro, let's get that door open."

"You got it, dude. Pass me the key."

"What key?"

"The key to open the door."

"We don't have one, Brad. Kurt is inside, and he's locked himself in. We need to break it down!"

"Are you *sure* you're okay, dude? You're normally against ideas like this because it damages the historic property we're in, and—"

"Okay, well fucking bang on it then!"

Brad looked shocked, and tapped on the door with his knuckles. I shoved him out of the way and banged on it with my fists as hard as I could. "*Kurt! Kurt!* Dude! Are you in there? Open up, man, or talk to us, or something!"

We waited a few seconds and got nothing. I hammered on the door again, and yelled at the top of my voice, but still got no reply. One more huge pounding session, and my hands were stinging in pain, but with no result.

"Okay, screw it. We're kicking it in. You ready?"

"Are you sure this is a good idea, bro?"

"No, Brad, I'm not. But I think Kurt's life is in danger. Are you with me, or what?"

"Let's do it, dude."

"Okay, stand back," I said, and copied what everyone does in the movies. I stood in front of the lock, lifted my foot and slammed it against the wooden door.

A massive tremor of pain shot up through my leg, and I collapsed to the floor with a yelp.

"That didn't work, dude," whispered Brad.

"Agghh! Shit! Shit, shit, shit!" I rolled around in agony for a few seconds, and then stopped. "Brad, why are you whispering?"

"I thought we might want to be stealthy, bro."

"Brad," I said, between gasps of air to calm the pain, "I just tried to kick a door down. What's stealthy about that?"

"Yeah, good point, dude. Let me try."

He stepped back and charged at the door, slamming his shoulder into it, before bouncing off and ending up in a heap next to me.

"What the hell is this door made of?"

We both got to our feet and were about to try again when I spotted something that might help us. I'd already looked around for spare tools left by the crew working on this floor, but it seemed that they were all put away somewhere secure, which was a shame; a sledgehammer would have come in handy at that moment. I ran towards the fire extinguisher I'd seen and grabbed it. I took it back to the door and, using the flat end, smashed it into the door just below the keycard lock. The door gave a satisfying crunching noise and it shifted nearly an inch into its frame. I pulled the canister back again and slammed it into the door, splinters of wood flew everywhere as the door was pushed away from the lock, and the door itself began to cave in where the base of the fire extinguisher had hit it.

One more solid whack was all it took to open the door, but at the same moment, the fire extinguisher, clearly not designed for this sort of punishment, ruptured, and sprayed white foam everywhere. It blasted against the door, ricochetted off the walls, and streamed directly up and into my face. I screamed as the foam retardant splattered into my eyes, and I threw the canister in a random direction down the corridor, where it kept on spewing out its contents. The remodelers were not going to be happy bunnies, but that was the least of my worries at that moment.

Trying to wipe the foam from my eyes, which now felt like they were, ironically, on fire, I blundered into the room in even more of a panic.

"Kurt? *Kurt?*"

My vision was now badly blurred, and I made my way as best I could to the bed. I felt around and the bed was empty, but the covers had been pulled back and the pillow had a dent in it. Kurt *had* been in here, was my guess. I stumbled my way back around the bed and accidentally kicked something on the floor. Bending down, I felt around for a few seconds before I found it; it was his walkie-talkie, confirming that he'd been here.

"Shit! Brad, look," I said, still rubbing frantically at my stinging eyes. "It's Kurt's radio!"

"Oh, fuck, bro. What happened to him? Where is he?"

"Dude, I can barely see. Will you do a sweep of the room? He might be in the bathroom or something."

I heard Brad charge off and crash his way into the bathroom. He yelled back to me. "Empty, bro! There's no sign of him."

My eyes were really hurting now, so I scrambled to my feet and stumbled my way, with Brad's assistance, into the bathroom. I splashed water onto my face and tried to rinse my eyes out as best I could, which hurt more than I could ever have imagined. The burning sensation decreased a little, and my vision improved somewhat, but it was still as blurry as if I had a film of oil over my eyeballs. I coughed up lumps of phlegm and foam that had been sprayed into my mouth and nearly vomited.

"We've gotta find him," I croaked.

For the first time since I'd known him, Brad actually looked concerned or perhaps scared; it was hard to tell with gel-o-vision. "We will, dude. We will."

I thought for a few moments, trying to formulate a plan. "Okay, look. He's on this floor somewhere. We need to split up and find him, but I'm virtually useless without my NV camera, especially now my eyes are screwed up. Here's what we're gonna do: You keep watch in this room, in case Kurt returns. Perhaps he went for a walk to look for the nightgown chick or something. I'm going to go back to the ballroom, get my camera, and come back and join you for a proper search of this floor. Okay?"

Brad thought about it for a few seconds. "Sounds good, dude."

I staggered my way out of the room and headed back towards the elevators. It seemed to take forever to reach them, but that wasn't helped by both the darkness and my severely impeded vision. Eventually I got there and spent what seemed like hours trying to insert my special key, before I took the now terrifyingly dark ride down to the second floor, my heart pounding so loud I thought I could hear it echoing around me.

The elevator doors opened and I made my way back into the ballroom, very grateful for at least a dim glow of light. The tables and chairs all seemed to be in the same place, as far as I could make out in the gloom, which I had to take as a good sign. I moved as fast as I could to thread my way through them and headed for the backstage area; I was confident that was where I'd stupidly left my camera.

Just as I was approaching the hidden door, I heard a faint noise that sounded like a click. I froze where I was and strained my ears to try and learn more about what might have caused the sound. I heard nothing for a few seconds and then there was a faint rustle. I took several very slow and very deep breaths to try and calm myself down, and then inched my way forward and into the backstage area. As far as I was concerned, the noise of my heart beating at about three thousand beats-per-minute was loud enough for everyone in Québec to hear, but I tried to keep my movements as quiet as possible.

I slowly inched my head into the backstage area, and heard a humming noise; not a humming from a generator, but someone faintly humming a tune.

I took another silent, slow step and paused, straining my right ear towards the noise, just to confirm that I was hearing what I thought I was. The humming continued, and some subconscious part of my brain told me that I recognized the tune, but the rest of my brain was too busy being scared out of its wits to process this and come up with the name of it. I looked at the corner of the wall that would allow me to see into the dressing room once I peered round it; it was two paces away.

I held my breath and took another gentle step forward. I let it out as slowly and silently as possible and tried to calm myself as much as I could. My heart rate was still hammering away, and my fear and apprehension were at an all-time maximum. I slowly took a deep breath and held it, and then took another agonizing step forward. Once I was still, I turned my head away from the edge of the wall and slowly released my breath, hoping this would minimize the sound from whatever was round the corner, which was now right next to me. All I had to do was lean forward and I'd be able to see round it.

My hands were shaking, and my legs were trembling, but I knew I had to see what had decided to show itself. I took another deep breath and ever so slowly poked my head around the corner; once my screwed-up eyes had time to focus, I nearly collapsed in terror, or shock, or surprise, or something. The dressing room was exactly the same as before, with the same mirror and wooden chair in front of the wooden table, and there were still an assortment of make-up paraphernalia scattered around. The one difference was that someone was sitting on the chair, and my eyes went wide with surprise. This made my still-blurry eyes sting with a vengeance, and I let out a small yelp of pain before jerking my head back into cover.

The humming suddenly stopped, the chair made a scraping noise, and I began to seriously panic.

What had been making the humming noise was a woman, dressed in a slightly tattered white nightgown, her brown hair tumbling down her back. It wasn't just the fact that it was a woman in a nightgown, but she was giving off a glare so bright that it made me screw my eyes up, and she appeared to be semi-transparent. The fake ghosts doing the scary tour were iridescent, but this woman was completely glowing; it seemed that the Scooby Doo cartoons had been right all this time.

Did the scraping noise of the chair mean the ghost had stood up? I didn't dare look around the corner again in case she saw me, and I needed to get this on film and documented. I could prove, once and for all, that ghosts did actually exist, and this would be coming from a categorical non-believer; you can't get much better marketing than that. Perhaps now I'd come to a definitive decision on their existence, this allowed them to be truly visible to me?

I heard a faint rustle of what I assumed was the nightgown, and then an eerie voice began to whisper something that was hard to make out, but sounded like, "I... am... Isabella..." There was a pause. "I... am... looking... for... you..."

The voice was a high-pitched whisper, but very faint. Perhaps the ghosts had a hard time projecting their voices back into the real world? I had no idea, but what I did know was that the voice was moving towards me, probably having heard me make that noise. I wasn't sure what to do, so I pinned my body against the wall, and tried to will myself invisible. If she discovered me then I'd cross that bridge when I came to it, but for now staying silent and still was my only option.

A bright glow came into view out of the corner of my eye, and I tried to control my breathing again. Not moving my head, I swiveled my eyes in the direction of the glow, and watched the blurry, semi-translucent figure of what I was now confident was Isabella making her way slowly out of the dressing room. She turned away from me and continued to move slowly towards the door that led to the ballroom on the other side of the backstage area.

The ghostly figure continued to whisper things in broken sentences, but I couldn't make them out any more. My eyes were still stinging from the fire retardant, but I tried to focus as best I could, and suddenly the realization of what I was seeing set in: this was Isabella! The ghost that had pretty much ruined my life and murdered several of my friends, as well as making me try to commit suicide, was now right in front of me without having any idea, it seemed, that I was there.

I suddenly became extremely angry, and my blood began to boil. How dare she do this to me? Killing my friends and the two actors who were just doing their job, she thought that was okay, too? I'd stood on a fucking rooftop and tried to jump because of her! That was *not* okay, and the more I tried to process what was unfolding in front of me, I realized that I'd probably never, ever have this opportunity again. I slowly rubbed my eyes to try and improve my vision, but all it did was smear the remainder of the retardant over my eyeballs and make them hurt more.

I was in pain because of her. She had ruined my life, killed people I cared about, and made me go almost insane. What a fucking *bitch*!

Without realizing what I was doing, I lurched away from my corner in a blind rage and headed for Isabella's back. Just before I reached her, I let out a banshee-type wail and launched myself at her glowing form. I had no idea if ghosts, when they're projecting themselves down into the real world, had a physical form or not, but I was determined to find out.

It turned out that they did, and I collided with her otherworldly figure, tackling her to the floor in a tumbling heap of arms and legs. I landed on top of her, and immediately slammed my fist into the first part of her face I could see.

"*Fuck you!*" I screamed, almost like a madman. "*Fuck* you!"

I punched her again in the side of her head, which really hurt my fist, so I gripped her head with both hands, lifted it up, and smashed it down onto the floor. I heard a crunching noise as her ghostly nose got the good news from the wood beneath us.

A yelp came from the front of her glowing face, but I wasn't about to let her get away with this. She'd killed three people, and she needed to pay. She'd ruined my entire life, and turned me into a nervous wreck. This was payback time.

I continued to scream as I lifted her head once more, and thrust it down again, this time using as much bodyweight as I could to help it on its way; Another crunch against the floorboards, and I heard a soft moan. "You fucking *bitch*! You killed my friends! How *dare* you? Just leave me *alone*!"

I scrambled around with my hands, whilst still pinning Isabella to the floor with my body, trying to find something I'd noticed earlier, after the tables had fallen. I was breathing heavily, I could barely see properly, and I was scared beyond belief, but I knew I had to finish this, and I grabbed hold of what seemed to be a solid-silver candlestick.

Her long hair was sprawled across her nightdress, and she was still giving off that otherworldly glow. I raised the candlestick above my head and smashed it down onto her ghostly skull. The horrific crunching sound wasn't what I was expecting, but I raised it above my head once more and slammed it down. Another terrible and almost sickening crunching noise echoed around the backstage area, and I was splattered in some warm liquid. I was amazed that ghosts could take such physical forms, but it was feeling good to get some revenge.

I raised the candlestick again and slammed it down onto Isabella's skull, resulting in another crunching noise; there were no more moans from her, and she stayed completely still. I remained sprawled on her once-again-lifeless body for a few minutes, and she didn't move or make a sound; a sudden euphoria washed over me.

I'd done it!

I'd finally got rid of my nemesis! Maybe she'd now been freed and sent up to wherever it is that spirits go. And, what's more, I'd done it in the ballroom, with the candlestick; *Clue* would have been proud.

I rolled off her ghostly body and lay on my back, immediately feeling a warm liquid soak into the clothes underneath me. I was gasping and panting, and desperately trying to calm down so I could regain some composure; I'd completely and utterly lost it just then, and that was frightening in itself, but I'd done what I had to. I took several very deep breaths and allowed a smile to creep across my face; I'd done it! I'd faced my tormentor and had finally defeated her. I just knew that my ghostly troubles were over and I could get back to my normal life. I also knew a thing or two more about ghosts than before, which would come in handy for our future shows.

Suddenly the whole room was bathed in light, and I screwed my eyes up to try and block out the sudden brightness after having been in the dark for so long. Someone had turned on all of the lights in the room and was now crashing their way through the ballroom, from the sound of it.

I lay where I was, breathing heavily, still physically and mentally exhausted from everything that had happened, but I felt a pleasant calmness all over me.

The crashing of chairs and tables stopped, and an out-of-breath voice gasped in disbelief.

"Dude, what the fuck have you done?"

EPILOGUE

That all happened a few years ago, and my life changed quite dramatically afterwards, and I'm talking immediately afterwards.

The first thing that happened after Brad had found me sprawled next to the body, covered in blood, was that I was arrested by the Québec police, or the Sûreté du Québec as they call them. I spent a couple of nights in the local jail, which allowed my brain to finally recognize what tune the ghost had been humming: the theme tune to *The Lost Souls*. I was extradited back to the US and locked up again. During that entire time, the network's army of lawyers, along with Mike Durkin, tried to figure out what the hell had gone on that night, and why I'd beaten Kurt to death in a fit of blind rage.

It took a while to piece together the events of that night, but it turned out that Kurt had got bored trying to go to sleep, and so got up to have a wander around the halls. Completely forgetting his walkie-talkie and then accidentally locking himself out of the room, he'd blundered off down the hallway in the opposite direction to the elevator, but that was fine because, like many hotels, the hallways on each floor do a complete loop. He must have reached the elevators shortly after we'd disappeared from view around one of the many kinks and corners of the floor layout.

He went down to the ballroom, looking for me, but of course I'd already left. This next part is speculation, but I suspect he was trying to bait the nightgown lady by deciding to dress up like her. Perhaps this was where the ghostly-tour actors got dressed each night, because the tattered nightgown was hanging on the coat-rail-on-wheels, and Kurt had found a drawer full of wigs and put one on. The next drawer had revealed the ghostly glow-spray, and he'd given himself a massive dousing. That, combined with my ruined and blurry vision, had been why he'd appeared so ghostly and seemingly semi-translucent, and had freaked me out so much. Then, of course, he'd decided to mumble things that made it sound like the ghostly apparition was claiming to be Isabella, and the perfect storm had arrived. Me: terrified, half-blind, and scared for my well-being, is confronted with what had seemingly been screwing up my entire life for weeks, not to mention murdering people in the process. I'll never know exactly what he was mumbling that terrible night, but at the time, and taking into account the state I was in, I was convinced I'd heard those fateful words, and that had probably been what had sealed his fate.

Maybe, who knows?

Once back in the US, I was grilled by the police as well as our lawyers, while the rest of my time was spent in my cell. Durkin went absolutely ballistic when he came to visit me the one and only time. He barely let me get a word in edgeways as he screamed and shouted, and called me all sorts of unpleasant things. At the time I just sat there and took it; I was numb with shock at what I'd done, and I now had the guilt of Kurt's death on my already fragile state of mind. I barely ate, hardly drank, and simply couldn't sleep at night. This wasn't helped by prisons not having the most comfortable beds in the world, but that wasn't the main reason. Any short periods of sleep I did have were fitful and full of horrible nightmares, the sort that people are always happy to wake up from and realize it was all a dream; when I woke up, however, it was all very, very real.

I'd killed a friend with my bare hands, and my life was now completely ruined. That's all it takes: a momentary lapse of judgement for whatever reason, and your life can be turned on its ass. There wasn't much in the way of a defense, or any way that I could argue it wasn't my fault: I'd smashed the poor guy's skull in with a candlestick for absolutely no reason that anybody except me could possibly understand.

Once this had become clear to the network's lawyers, they dropped me like a hot potato, no doubt on Durkin's orders. The network immediately issued press releases distancing themselves from me, and in short order washed their hands of me entirely. The show was cancelled, obviously, and Brad just never could find another niche to slot into, so his career was done as well. Durkin got it in the neck from the top brass, and had been enthusiastically encouraged to resign, which is what had prompted his visit to me, just to let me know that I'd ruined his life. The network publicly thanked him for his time running the place, and then immediately distanced itself from him, too. I doubt he'll ever get another job like that one, and I seriously doubt the network will ever green light any ghost hunting shows ever again.

All in all, I'd managed to completely fuck up the lives of lots of people including my own, and I'd actually, physically killed someone in the most up-close-and-personal way possible.

LA County threw the book at me, and the network got in on the act by suing me for tens of millions of dollars in lost revenue. Brad did the same when he figured out that, without the three of us together with our bizarre chemistry to temper the fact that he was a total buffoon, no TV show in the world wanted anything to do with him. Finally, Kurt's parents, once they'd finished grieving for the loss of their son, sued me too, but I can't quite remember what for.

I hired my own lawyer, who immediately told me I was screwed. The fact that this was such a high-profile and widely-reported story meant that the public had basically declared me guilty before I'd even gone near a courtroom. But, of course, I *was* guilty, so it was hard to argue with that. I explained about Isabella and everything that had gone on to lead me to attack what turned out to be Kurt. She clearly was not a believer in ghosts, and I tried to explain to her that I hadn't been either, and perhaps one day she might change her mind on the subject.

She wasn't having any of it, and immediately told me that the only option was to plead guilty due to diminished capacity. The evidence was irrefutable: I *had* committed the horrific act that I was being accused of, so she decided to try and have my sentence reduced because I was, basically, insane. If successful, this would also make all of the lawsuits go away.

My bail had been set at a ridiculous amount of money: five million dollars. I could probably have scraped it together at a pinch if I'd sold most of my belongings, but I didn't feel like being anywhere other than jail. It fitted my mood, and meant I was safe from any attempts at retribution. My lawyer kept an eye on our show's forums, and apparently there were some pretty angry people out there, pissed off that I'd ruined their favorite show.

Finally, months and months later, I ended up in court and took the witness stand. I acknowledged that I'd done it, and that I felt terrible about the whole thing, and then must have been incredibly convincing about the whole Isabella, ghosts, and paranormal thing, because it ended up being a twelve to zero vote from the jury that I was, in fact, a total lunatic and needed to be locked up. After that verdict, the gossip magazines began to dissect my life prior to that moment, trying to find some scrap of evidence that I'd been a dangerous psycho all my life and 'the system', whatever that was, had failed to spot it.

According to my lawyer, the prosecution had been thankfully stupid and tried to make an example out of me by going for a conviction of first degree murder, which meant they had to prove some sort of pre-meditation on my part. In the end, I got a conviction of voluntary manslaughter due to diminished capacity. The judge was fairly sympathetic towards me, partly because I was a nervous wreck in court and didn't once protest my innocence. I was, and still am, deeply sorry for what I did, and it seemed that the judge understood that.

As he was delivering his verdict, he declared this to be one of the most bizarre and tragic cases of his career, and he felt extremely sorry for Kurt's relatives, but also for me. He mused as to whether my multiple heart attacks and heavy medication, combined with too much alcohol had been a contributing factor in my decreased mental state, but then confessed that he wasn't a doctor and therefore had no idea what he was talking about. The gossip mags, which had ignored all three of us for years, suddenly elevated our celebrity status from C to a definite A+ for a short period, and we had our pictures splashed across their covers for weeks as some of their fearless reporters went "beyond the feds" to uncover the "true story of jealousy and drama" that apparently was rife behind the scenes of *The Lost Souls*. They unearthed nothing more than wild speculation that enabled their circulation ratings to soar, and I quickly became depicted as some sort of egotistical, maniacal, stop-at-nothing, back-stabber, who despised Kurt because he got more time in front of the camera than me.

My sentence ended up being ten years in a mental institution in Norwalk, California. The judge told me that he'd done his best to be sympathetic, and had taken into account all of the extraordinary circumstances surrounding this case; the facility I would be in was a low security one, designed to help me through my mental problems instead of punishing me for them.

As prisons go, this one isn't bad at all; it's sort of like a farm with guards around the perimeter. We have cattle, pigs, chickens, and a huge vegetable garden that I've actually come to quite enjoy working in. It's peaceful, I'm left alone, and I'm well away from the truly crazy inmates who spend their days screaming at walls, or jumping up and down yelling gibberish at the tops of their voices. By the time my garden duties are over, the crazies are usually sedated for the rest of the evening and night, and I can have my dinner in peace. The food isn't that bad, and the staff are extremely pleasant and understanding, so life could be a lot worse, bearing in mind what I did.

I'm not crazy, but there aren't many other explanations that people could possibly grasp to explain what I'd done or why I'd done it. Any other plea would have almost certainly seen me now sitting in some hardcore hellhole like San Quentin jail, having an unpleasant time in the showers. So, aside from the fact that I'd brutally murdered a friend of mine, ruined my entire life, destroyed quite a few people's careers, and put an end to one of the most popular reality shows on TV, I had to look on the bright side.

I have the possibility of parole in a little over three years from now, so maybe I'll get out earlier than the full ten stretch, who knows? I sometimes wonder if the nurses and orderlies in here know that I'm perfectly sane or not, because I'm probably their lowest-maintenance customer. My tomatoes have come out nicely, too.

Well, it's almost time for bed, so I need to head back to my room to be locked in until morning; Isabella will be visiting me later, as she does every night. I never see her, of course, I've learned that much about ghosts, but she's there, and she talks to me. Sometimes she might knock things off my desk just for fun, and other times I feel her lying next to me while I'm drifting off to sleep. It seems that she has mood swings, because some nights are calm and pleasant, and I thoroughly enjoy her company, but other nights we get into fights and I end up screaming and trying to throw things at her. Then my door bursts open and before I know what's going on, I'm strapped down and sedated to make sure I go to to sleep.

I don't know why she does that now and then, and I sometimes wonder if she's annoyed that I'm not a ghost. She certainly seems to plant the odd suggestion that perhaps I should be a ghost because of how much fun we'd have together, and I've seriously considered doing something about that, but it's difficult because of my one and only recorded attempt at jumping off a roof: I'm on round-the-clock suicide watch. I'm not allowed anything sharp without supervision, nothing remotely rope-like, and even the tools that I use in the garden have been carefully selected to be as non-dangerous to a suicidal maniac as possible. Maybe I'll be able to make Isabella's wish come true one day, who knows?

The nurses, a few months ago, noticed some jaundicing of my skin around various extremities, but they assured me it was nothing to worry about and they'd modify my diet to fix it. When I began complaining about abdominal pain two weeks ago, my jaundiced areas getting yellower with each day, I think the real doctors who monitor us took notice because I'm now scheduled for an MRI, a CT, and a PET scan that will focus on my abdominal area to check for the spread of Pancreatic cancer. If they detect it, apparently my chance of survival is not good.

Now where have I heard that before?

Isabella may get her wish sooner rather than later.

My one consolation for her, when she visits me each night, is that at least this mental institution is nicer than the one I rescued her from.

I think she likes that.

ACKNOWLEDGEMENTS

Carissa: as always, you are my muse, my rock, and the person that comes up with the names of my characters that I don't just borrow from people we know. I will always love you for all of that, but most of all just for being there for me. Thank you.

Ninja: our beloved cat who was taken from us just a year into his life by a reckless driver who couldn't wait to rush off and stop at the red light fifty feet away from where they hit him. You are missed every day, and I especially miss you lying on my lap, fast asleep and purring loudly as I write.

Sophia and Nick: I've watched and helped you both grow up, and you bring joy to my life every day, even when I have to ground you for something. Don't ever stop being yourselves; you are amazing and I love you both dearly.

Chad: thanks for your firefighting expertise that came in handy for part of this book, and also for randomly turning up with armfuls of beer and food when I least expect it. Oh yeah, I borrowed your name and your wife's too for this book. You're welcome.

ABOUT THE AUTHOR

Matthew Wilkinson was born in England and now lives in southern California with his family. Having taught himself to program assembly language, or 'machine code', at the age of nine, he spent the following thirty-plus years making video games for every game console that came into existence.

Despite his love of programming, he always had a passion for writing fiction and telling a good story. The first book he wrote was before he'd reached double digits, and was the (then) fourth book in the Hitchhiker's Guide to the Galaxy series. He was frustrated that Douglas Adams hadn't written it yet, so he did it himself. Douglas Adams still remains one of the most influential and inspirational authors for Matthew to this current day.

This is his second book, and he hopes you enjoy it. If you don't, feel free to berate him on Twitter (@AuthorWilkinson) or e-mail him (Matthew@Matt-Wilkinson.com) and give him a good old verbal kicking. He likes that.